Pas de de Don't

Pas de Don't

Chloe Angyal

AMBERJACK
PUBLISHING

CHICAGO

Copyright © 2023 by Chloe Angyal
All rights reserved
Published by Chicago Review Press Incorporated
814 North Franklin Street
Chicago, Illinois 60610
ISBN 978-1-64160-908-1

Library of Congress Control Number: 2023931786

Cover design: Jonathan Hahn
Cover illustration: Sarah Gavagan
Typesetting: Nord Compo
Author photo: Vivian Le

Printed in the United States of America
5 4 3 2 1

For Brittney, Cécile, and Vanessa,
who showed me how to love romance novels.

Author's Note

This book features on-page depictions of coercive control and its aftermath, as well as the off-page death of a parent. I've done my best to treat these topics with the care that they, and you the reader, deserve.

If you're experiencing coercive control, or need help supporting someone who is, there are free and confidential resources available to you.

In the United States:
The National Domestic Violence Hotline
https://www.thehotline.org/
800-799-SAFE (800-799-7233)

In Australia:
The National Sexual Assault, Family & Domestic Violence Counselling Line
www.1800respect.org.au
1800-RESPECT (1800-737-732)

Prologue

New York City, June

Heather's chest heaved as the heavy gold curtain thudded gently onto the stage and the orchestra played the final, plaintive notes of the score. For a beat, a sublime empty moment, the theater was silent, and Heather could hear nothing but her own ragged breaths. She stood in the wings, mentally replaying her second-act solo, spotting a handful of mistakes and tucking them away to correct before next season—but as far as she could tell, it had been her best performance yet. Panting, she waited for the audience to hand down its judgment.

A second later, the theater erupted into applause. Out in the dark, beyond the velvet curtain, people cheered, whooping and roaring in a way that stuffier ballet-goers would frown upon. Heather exited the wings to center stage, where Jack waited, his forehead glistening with sweat under his sleek golden-brown hair. She smiled up at him, relieved and delighted that the final performance of the spring season had gone so well.

"You were amazing," she said, pulling the damp fabric of her white tutu away from her ribs, a hopeless attempt to get air onto her skin. She brushed the back of her neck, where a few sweaty strands of her long brown hair clung to her. She'd started act two with every hair lacquered in place, her skin powdered to a ghostly white—but now her bun had loosened, and her cheeks felt flushed, sparkling with sweat.

"You too," Jack panted, sounding unenthused. He tugged on the bottom of his royal blue velvet jacket, straightening the line of shining silver buttons at the front. "Your arabesque was low just now. We'll work on it." Her smile faltered a little, but then he flashed her a dazzling grin, and she hiked it back up. Jack always picked the wrong time to give her feedback, but Heather knew he meant well.

She glanced over his shoulder and saw the stage manager holding up his fingers, counting down from five. She hastily arranged her feet in first position and stood up straight as the curtain rose to reveal the source of all that gratifying sound.

No matter how many times she'd done it, taking a solo bow at the front of the stage was thrilling. Jack had told her that the awe had worn off for him years ago, because he'd been promoted to principal just two years after he joined the company. But even though Heather had been doing it more lately, especially since she'd been made a soloist, it still felt like the first time every time. To stand before the audience and know that they were cheering for her specifically—not for the corps de ballet as a unit, but for her alone? It was what she and Carly had been dreaming about since they were eleven-year-olds at the company school: the kind of shining, surreal moment that all ballet dancers imagined but so few got to experience.

As she swept one arm in front of her, pliéd into a deep curtsy, and bowed her head, Heather's legs trembled, and it wasn't only because the second act of *Giselle* was an exhausting marathon of dancing.

From the corner of her eye, Heather saw someone walk onto the stage with a large bouquet of flowers in their arms. She stood and turned. It wasn't the orchestra conductor, as was customary for curtain calls, but Mr. Koenig, the company's longtime artistic director. He strode toward her, his suit jacket unbuttoned and flapping around his middle, his pale face split by a wide smile. Then she noticed the microphone in his hand. Heather's stomach dropped in shock, and she willed herself to keep the smile fixed on her face. Since she'd joined the company a decade ago, she had seen Mr. K, as the dancers called him, do this enough times to know what that microphone meant. And if she was right, her life was about to change forever.

Heather glanced over at Jack, raising her eyebrows as the question passed between them, and he cocked one eyebrow mysteriously.

"Ladies and gentlemen," Mr. K said, stopping at Heather's side and looking out into the packed theater like a duke surveying his lands, the bright stage lights bouncing off his polished bald head. The applause ended as audience members settled back into their seats.

"I'm delighted that you enjoyed tonight's performance of *Giselle*," Mr. K went on, his usually icy voice warm for the crowd, "and that you so clearly admire the artistry and talent of our dancers, Jack Andersen and Heather Hays." Another outbreak of applause, and at Jack's name, some whoops that sounded like they'd come from women in the audience. Mr. K waited for the noise to peter out, and Heather resisted the urge to fidget, willing her hands to be still. She flicked her eyes toward the wings, looking for Carly, but her best friend must have gone straight to the dressing room as soon as the corps left the stage.

"It has been a pleasure and a privilege to watch Miss Hays grow into the artist she is today, and I look forward to many more years of watching her dance . . ." He paused for dramatic effect, and Heather was sure they could hear her heart pounding up in the family circle. "Which, from now on, she will be doing at the rank of principal dancer."

The house exploded in applause, both Heather's hands flew to her mouth, and Mr. K thrust the huge bouquet of red and pink roses toward her. She pried one shaking arm out to accept it, tears of gratitude, relief, and pride in her eyes.

"Congratulations, Heather," Mr. K said, smiling down at her.

"Thank you," Heather gasped. She tried to meet his gaze, to tell him over the roar of the audience how much this promotion meant to her, how honored she was to accept this responsibility. But he was looking at something else. He lifted the microphone to his mouth again.

"It seems, ladies and gentlemen," Mr. K addressed the crowd, his tone sly, "that this isn't the only happy surprise in store for Ms. Hays tonight." He smiled again, and the audience gasped as one.

Heather looked slowly over her shoulder and nearly dropped the flowers in shock. There was Jack, his sweat sparkling under the lights and his eyes as bright as his sumptuous blue costume, his smile huge and boyish and just for her.

Kneeling in front of her, presenting a small velvet box.

Sydney, June

Marcus had never been one of those ballet boys who had to be coaxed and bribed into wearing tights. He knew there were dance schools that put off the transition from bike shorts into full-on tights as long as possible, for fear of scaring off the few precious boys they'd managed to convince to take ballet.

But the first time he'd tried on a pair, his costume for an end-of-year concert when he was ten or eleven, they'd made him feel strangely powerful. Suddenly, he could feel every muscle in his legs, feel his calves straining against the snug, stretchy fabric, ready to contract and spring back into the jumps his teacher had choreographed into the routine for him. He'd looked down and realised that his legs looked longer now, like one continuous line of strength extending from his waist all the way to his toes. He'd felt ready to dance, invincible—like a superhero whose power was pirouettes.

Tights still made him feel that way, even twenty years and hundreds of costumes later. Standing in the wings of the Opera House as the sound of the orchestra swelled out of the pit, Marcus felt warm and alive and ready, a welcome counterweight to the nerves fluttering in his stomach. The nerves would vanish the moment he stepped on stage, though, along with all thoughts about the outside world. He wouldn't have time to think about his father's grim prognosis, or about his mother's slow-motion grieving. There would be no room for anything but the music, his partner, and the choreography.

Moments later, Marcus swept onto the stage, greeted Alice with a courtly bow, and the pas de deux began. Dancing with his best friend was easy; he knew she always needed extra support in her pirouettes, and she knew that performance adrenaline made him throw her higher in the second lift than he did in rehearsal. Dancing with her was fun, too; as he held her waist in an arabesque, she looked over her shoulder and made eye contact. That part was choreographed, but the wink she gave him was not. Marcus resisted the urge to roll his eyes.

After the opening section of the pas de deux, Alice exited stage right, and Marcus took his place in the upstage corner to begin his jump- and pirouette-heavy solo. In the quiet, heavy moment before the music began, he let his eyes flick down his legs and carried out the superstitious ritual that had begun the very first time he'd pulled on a pair of ballet tights: he pictured himself with a cape and a mask, too. He knew it was silly and childish—he'd once made the mistake of telling his brother about it, and Davo had mocked him relentlessly for weeks—but he couldn't remember the last time he'd started a performance without it.

The first few jetés felt good, and they carried him downstage to where, out of the corner of his eye, he saw Alice watching from the wings as he set up for a difficult series of fouettés and turns à la seconde. After a few rotations, the audience, unseen beyond the stage lights, began to applaud, and the sound vibrated in his chest. He could have sworn he saw Alice cheering him on from the wings, undulating in a goofy full-body wave that made her look like one of those inflatable men outside a car dealership. He set his free leg down, gave the audience a confident smile and stepped forward into a deep plié, ready to jump.

He felt something was off the moment his feet left the floor. The tour jump required him to spin twice in the air, keeping his body entirely straight and his legs crossed at the ankles, and land back in the same plié position where he'd started. But his legs felt out of line with his hips—or out of line with his ankles, he couldn't tell, and he didn't have time to figure it out. He came down hard in a messy fifth position and immediately felt a jagged, white-hot pain shoot up the back of his left ankle before both legs gave out.

A horrified collective gasp rose from the audience, but Marcus barely heard it. He fell onto all fours in the middle of the stage, squeezing his eyes shut against the pain so hard that he saw black spots pop and dissolve. He felt rather than saw the stage manager frantically signaling the curtains shut, and a few seconds later the orchestra faltered into silence. Then Alice was kneeling at his side, gripping his shoulder and telling him over and over again that he was going to be okay.

Panting in pain, Marcus collapsed onto his side, then onto his back. He looked up, past Alice's face and high into the rafters of the theatre. At his feet, but also a million disconnected miles away, someone cut into his tights to get at his throbbing, searing ankle. And then the outside world flooded in: his father weak and emaciated in bed, his mother brushing away tears as she stood over the kitchen sink.

He had never felt so powerless.

Chapter 1

New York City, one year later

"When did you take these?" Heather asked. Her index finger shook as she swiped through the grainy photos on Carly's phone.

"Last night," Carly glowered. Her cheeks were pale under her freckles, as if she'd barely slept, and her red curls seemed to vibrate with rage. "He's lucky I didn't march over there and tear him a new asshole."

Heather tried to swallow the dread in her throat as she leaned closer, squinting at the images. The lighting was dim, and the angle wasn't ideal, but even so, there was no mistaking it: That was Jack. And nestled in next to him in the plump restaurant booth, gazing adoringly up at him as his hand gripped her waist, was—

"Melissa?" Heather's mouth stumbled over the other woman's name, like her tongue and lips had gone slightly numb. A mild spring breeze wafted through the open windows, but the living room felt airless, and Heather felt her toes starting to tingle with panic, as if the pale blue walls were closing in.

"Melissa," Carly confirmed. "He isn't just cheating; he's cheating with a fetus. She's a decade younger than us."

Heather shook her head, trying to make sense of what she saw. Jack loved her, had loved her for years. He had proposed to her in front of a packed house at Lincoln Center, for God's sake. What the hell was going on?

"Maybe it's not what it looks like?" Heather said, raising her eyes to Carly's scowling face. "I mean . . . this is just dinner, and it's just one photo, it's . . . ," she trailed off helplessly. Tears swam in her eyes, and through the blur, she saw Carly's scowl tighten, then instantly soften.

"Heather," Carly said in a quiet, determined voice, "I was there. I hid behind a planter and watched them for half an hour. It wasn't just dinner. They're definitely . . . there's definitely something going on."

Heather squeezed her eyes shut, and tears skipped down her cheeks. "I don't understand," she practically pleaded. She hated the desperation in her own voice. "He said he was ready to commit."

Sure, it had taken him a few extra years to propose, but she'd wanted him to be sure when he popped the question. And when he finally did it, he really *did it*. Yes, she had seen him flirt with other women, had watched the way he charmed the wealthy socialites who lined up to meet him at the company's donor events. But as he always reminded her, that was just part of the job. It wasn't real. What was real was *them*. Jack and Heather. What was real was this apartment they shared and their lazy Sunday mornings strolling through the flea market on West Seventy-Seventh Street. The way he looked at her during a curtain call, like he hadn't even noticed the fifteen hundred applauding ballet fans in front of them.

Heather glanced around the spacious living room, looking anywhere but at Carly and her phone. Across the room, a framed black-and-white photo of a shirtless Jack loomed on the wall, the deep-cut grid of his six-pack thrown into sharp relief as he hit the peak of a picture-perfect cabriole jump. It had been part of a shoot they'd done together a few years ago, a glossy profile for *Vogue*. The headline had proclaimed them "America's Ballet Sweethearts."

Panicked questions chased each other around her head. How long had he been sneaking around with Melissa? Who else in the company knew? Heather forced herself to look at the photo of the gorgeous corps member pressed against her fiancé, and at the expression on Jack's handsome, angular face. With a stab of anguish, she realized he was giving Melissa his curtain-call look. Heather thought she might faint.

"What did I do wrong?" she whispered to herself.

"You didn't do anything wrong!" Carly exclaimed, dropping the phone and handing her a box of tissues. "If anything . . . ," she trailed off, but Heather didn't need to hear the end of her sentence.

If anything, Carly had been about to say, Heather's only mistake was saying yes to going home with Jack all those years ago. Carly had never been Jack's biggest fan, and the feeling was mutual. But then, Heather thought, Carly had unreasonably high standards for men, which was probably why she hadn't settled down with anyone yet.

"I can't believe he'd really do this," Heather said, wiping the tissue over her exhausted face. Flirting with donors was one thing, but actually cheating? With a member of the company? "He promised we'd set a date soon."

Heather's whole body still ached from last night's performance and from the accumulated fatigue of the eight-week spring season. She had come home from the theater and fallen into bed, while Jack had gone out with some of the guys from the company—or so he'd told her. When she'd woken up this morning his side of the bed had been empty, and a brief text message, sent at 1:07 AM, informed her he was going to crash with one of his friends.

Misery twisted her stomach as she pictured the blissful look on Melissa's round face, so young and smitten, so delighted to be at the center of Jack's attention. Heather knew that feeling well. At the beginning, she had basked in it, had almost felt herself grow more beautiful and more captivating in the light of his piercing blue gaze. Jack Andersen, international ballet royalty, the son of a Danish ballet star and his statuesque American ballerina wife. . . . When he looked at you, when he smiled at you, it was like you were caught in a glowing spotlight. Blinded to everything but his sleek golden-brown hair and the charming, boyish way he cocked his head.

"Maybe I didn't give him enough time? Maybe the thought of wedding planning has been freaking him out? Maybe I wasn't patient enough?" *Maybe*, a cold-as-steel voice whispered in the back of her head, *you always knew he would do this. Maybe you always knew you weren't enough.*

"What are you talking about?" Carly demanded, rolling her eyes. "*He* asked *you* to marry him. And on the night you got promoted to principal. You have been plenty patient. Way more patient than he deserves."

"What's that supposed to mean?" Heather asked, rising off the couch, her pulse quickening. Her knees cracked as she stood, and she felt last night's pas de deux throb in her lower back.

"He kept you waiting for that ring for *ages*." Carly gestured emphatically at Heather's left hand, sounding exasperated.

"I know, but he wanted to be sure. We both did. Marriage is a massive commitment."

"Yeah, one he's clearly not serious about," Carly retorted.

"That's not true." Heather ran her fingers through her hair in frustration.

"Heather, come on. He's dragged his feet for years, first on proposing and now on setting a date, and he's been using the time to mess around with someone we work with!" Carly stood too, knocking one of Jack's white cashmere throw pillows to the floor. "Do you honestly think you can ever trust him now?"

"I don't know," Heather shot back. Her heart was pounding, and spiky tendrils of anger crawled from her stomach into her chest. "I know he's not perfect, but he loves me. And I know he's not your favorite person—" Carly snorted. Heather ignored her. "—but it's not like I'm perfect, either."

As Jack frequently reminded her.

"Perfect or not, you deserve someone who's kind to you, Heather," Carly said, repeating the words she'd said dozens of times in the seven years since Heather and Jack got together. "Kind to you in public *and* in private."

"Jack is kind to me! He just wants me to be the best version of myself, okay? Which is what I want, too. And the best version of myself would at least try to see his point of view. Maybe there's another explanation." She gestured at Carly's phone. Knowing Jack, there would be an explanation. *And knowing you*, that icy voice whispered again, *you'll let yourself believe it.*

"Another explanation for why he's putting his hands all over a nineteen-year-old when he's engaged to you?" Carly's eyes were wide, her forehead creased in disbelief.

"I—maybe—I don't know, okay, but I love him, and when you love someone, you forgive their mistakes."

"Heather, he didn't, like, dent your car—he cheated! I know you love him, and I know you're scared—"

"I'm not scared!" Heather shot back. "Relationships are complicated! Not everything is black and white!"

"Yeah, you're right," Carly said with a grim laugh, her red curls bobbing at the movement. "That picture is in color! God, I can't believe you're making excuses for him again."

"I'm not making excuses!" Heather shouted back. "You're just looking for the worst in him, like you always do. You're *glad* he cheated, because you've never liked us together."

For a moment, Carly looked speechless, something Heather had never witnessed in their two decades of friendship. She stared at Heather, her mouth slightly open, apparently too shocked to yell back.

Heather glanced away so she wouldn't have to see Carly's face, her eyes landing back on the *Vogue* photo. They'd posed for some gorgeous shots that day, and Heather still thought longingly of how her delicate gown had clung to her skin and swirled around her ankles. Somehow only Jack's photo had ended up framed and hung on their wall.

Carly exhaled slowly, and when she spoke again, her voice was low and steady. But it sounded almost pleading. "Of course I'm not glad. I don't want him to have cheated, but he did. And you deserve someone who's going to be kind and faithful to you, always."

When Heather didn't reply, Carly took a step toward her and reached for her hand. "Please, just listen to me. You can't stay with him. You can't *marry* him. Please, don't make excuses for him this time. You deserve better than this. You have always deserved better than this."

She doesn't understand, she's never understood, that ice-cold voice whispered. *She doesn't know what it feels like to be chosen by someone as dazzling as Jack. She just stands on the sidelines and snipes, throwing bombs and leaving the rest of us to pick up the pieces.*

"I know what I deserve, and I know what I want," Heather said, looking her best friend square in the face. "I want to have a mature, adult relationship—one that actually lasts. I wouldn't expect you to understand."

At Carly's sharp intake of breath, Heather instantly regretted her words. She looked to the coffee table, fixing her eyes on the two cups of iced coffee Carly had brought with her. They were pale and watery with melted ice now and sweating in a pool of condensation.

Carly shook her head, looking defeated.

"Fine," she said dully. She yanked her bag off the floor and tossed her phone inside. "Enjoy your mature, adult relationship with the man who's fucking a teenager."

Carly turned sharply and strode to the apartment door, shaking her head. A moment later, the door snapped shut, and Heather was alone.

* *

Heather stared at the door, her heart hammering under her pajama shirt. A hot wave of shame crept up the back of her neck as the seconds ticked by.

She and Carly almost never fought, except about Jack: Jack asking her to move in so quickly after they started dating, Jack being jealous of the time she spent with her best friend. But despite Carly's repeated criticisms of him, they'd been soul sisters since they were tweens, when Heather had been new to the company's school.

Carly had taken a spot next to her at the barre on that first, nerve-racking day in the imposing gray building that towered over Sixty-Sixth Street. During one of the very first exercises, Heather had looked anxiously at her reflection in the mirror and caught a glimpse of Carly, standing behind her, doing tendus with her eyes crossed and her tongue sticking out the side of her mouth. Heather had giggled, and the knot in her stomach started to loosen. *Maybe this place isn't so scary after all*, she remembered thinking. They had been best friends ever since.

They made for an odd pair sometimes, the rebel and the rule-follower, and she sometimes wished Carly would grow up a little. But Heather had always wanted a little sister, and Carly was like a little sister and a cool aunt, all in a best friend's body.

Like all the other girls in their class, she and Carly had both had crushes on Jack. Boys in ballet were generally treated like golden children, because there were so few of them and it was so hard to keep them enrolled. But Jack really was a golden child. In his youth he'd been blond and freckled, with big blue eyes, an impish smile, and obvious natural talent. He had grown up surrounded by ballet, and even as a boy he'd carried himself with the easy assurance of someone who had never questioned that he belonged in this world. Not just in it, but at the top of it. Teachers praised him constantly. He was always surrounded by admiring boys, and the whispers of smitten girls chased him wherever he went.

Carly's crush had faded—once, when they were fifteen, she'd told Jack he had his head so far up his own ass it was a miracle he could dance at all—but Heather's had persisted. By the time they both graduated from the school and were made apprentices in the company together, he was already a standout in the corps de ballet. The year he spent as a soloist felt like a mere formality, a short stop on the way to stardom. Everyone knew Jack Andersen was born and bred to be a principal dancer at New York Ballet, just like his parents before him.

Heather had spent those first few years in the company trying to stay afloat, spending almost every night on stage with the corps before trudging home to the Chinatown apartment she shared with Carly. Usually Carly would nod off on the subway and Heather would pinch herself to stay awake, watching over her friend and rousing her just in time to stagger off the 1 train at Canal Street. Once home, they'd take turns showering in the tiny, dingy bathroom and then spend an hour breaking in and sewing their pointe shoes for the next day's class, rehearsals, and show.

When Heather thought about those years now, most of it was a blur of exhaustion, but one night was preserved in her mind in ultra-high-def clarity: the night of the fall gala, her third year in the corps. Jack had found her on the edge of the dance floor and asked her to dance with him. She'd ignored the jealous whispers of the other young dancers around her—and Carly's raised, skeptical eyebrows—and said yes.

She still got goosebumps thinking about that night. Jack had looked so handsome in his designer tux. He had held her with such firm assurance, his arm wrapped securely around her back and his cold cufflinks pressing thrillingly into the flesh revealed by the backless dress she'd bought at TJ Maxx on a break between rehearsals. She remembered thinking it was like something out of a teenage fantasy. But they weren't teenagers anymore, and it was real: he really wanted to kiss her at the end of the night, really wanted to keep kissing her the following morning, really wanted to sling his chiseled arm possessively over her shoulder as they walked the shaded green streets around his apartment on West Seventy-Fourth

Street. Heather had never had a boyfriend before, had never really had the time or the energy, but she threw herself into being Jack's girlfriend, knowing that even on his moody, mean days, he loved her just as much as she loved him.

And once it was clear they were an item, Jack and the company had been eager to capitalize on their story: The superstar and the scholarship kid, the son of ballet royalty and the daughter of a single mom. The principal dancer and the girl who, the coverage always seemed to imply, he plucked from corps de ballet obscurity and transformed into a rising star. Even if it wasn't strictly true—as Carly always reminded her, Heather worked her butt off to get into the company and to keep her place there—the coverage still made her feel like she'd won the lottery when Jack chose her. He could have had anyone in the world, but he loved *her*.

The first time a member of the marketing department had suggested she and Jack sit for a magazine interview about their partnership, she'd been flattered. No, she'd been *delighted*. It was thrilling to proclaim their love for each other in the pages of a national publication, pose for photos perched on the fountain just outside NYB's theater. The caption for the photo had read "partners on stage and off," and a few weeks later, that was the truth: Mr. K cast Heather in her first featured role, partnered by Jack.

But the more she and Jack told the press-friendly version of their story, the less true it felt. Carly told her repeatedly she was selling herself short. But everyone else in her life—even her own mother—thought Jack was a catch, that his unexpected interest in Heather was a good thing. She was so lucky, her mom had told her the day after the *Times* ran a profile of them, that she'd found someone stable, someone who could take care of her. Heather knew that was true, but after a while she came to both crave and dread the interviews and the photo shoots. Now she almost never felt the sparkling golden charm Jack had shone so extravagantly on her at the beginning unless a reporter was in the room.

Heather looked out the open window, wondering if Carly was already on the subway back to the Chinatown apartment. Carly had held on to the lease after Heather moved in with Jack, and another corps member now lived in what had once been Heather's room. Up on Seventy-Fourth Street, in walking distance from the theater, she felt so far from Carly and from that time in their lives. She loved Jack's apartment—it was bright and airy; it had a dishwasher, the holy grail of New York City real estate—but sometimes she missed that cramped little place, with its leaky kitchen faucet and hissing radiator pipes.

Or maybe she just missed the person she'd been when she'd lived there.

Heather picked up her phone and dialed Jack's number, pacing the living room as it rang. Three times. Four times. Finally, on the fifth ring, he picked up.

"Hey, babe," he said breezily.

"Hi," she said, hoping her voice sounded normal, despite her throat feeling tight with anxiety. "Did you have a good night?"

"Yeah."

She stopped and waited, hoping for more, but Jack offered nothing else. He sounded like he had the phone pinned between his shoulder and his jaw, as if his hands were otherwise occupied, and Heather had a sudden, unwelcome vision of him standing at the end of an unmade bed, yanking his jeans up and zipping his fly as he answered the phone. She gave her head a little shake. There was an explanation, she told herself as she took a deep, steadying breath. There had to be, and she had to know what it was.

"Was it just you and the guys?"

"Yeah, of course," he replied. Well, that was a lie.

"No one else from the company showed up?"

"No, babe, it was just a boys' night." Another lie. There was an edge in his voice now, the way there sometimes was when she challenged him. "It felt really good to blow off some steam."

"I bet it did," she replied, unable to keep a hint of sarcasm out of her voice. She could feel her fingertips starting to tingle with rage as she gripped the phone tighter. He was lying straight to her—well, not to her face, but he was lying to her so easily, so seamlessly. How long had he been doing that?

She willed herself to keep going, though a part of her wanted to nod and smile, hang up the phone and go on with her day—with her life—like she'd never seen the photo on Carly's phone. *I know you're scared*, Carly had said, and she'd been right. Heather had done so many things, forgiven and explained away so many things, out of fear of what would happen if she didn't. But she couldn't explain away that photo.

"I just saw a photo of you and Melissa at the restaurant last night," she said, amazed by how calm she sounded even as her heart hammered against her ribs. "So it doesn't seem like it was just a boys' night."

She heard it, the precise moment when he froze in the middle of whatever he'd been doing and slowly picked up the phone in his hand. When he spoke again, it was in a familiar honeyed tone, warm and inviting. The way he'd spoken to her at the start. She'd seen him turn it on for a reporter or a cocktail party full of donors, and now he was turning it on for her.

"Babe," he said in a confident, confiding tone, "she showed up, and we hung out for a bit, and that was it."

Oh, bullshit! a new voice roared in her head. This time, it was hot and indignant, and it sounded like Carly.

"How long?" Heather gritted out.

"I don't know, an hour, maybe a little more," he said smoothly, and she could picture his small, elegant shrug and the charming smirk curving his mouth.

"No, how long have you been sleeping with her?"

"Heather, come on, that's crazy." She could almost see his eye roll, the dismissive little shake of his head. His smile would be more brittle now, but even his thinnest smile was dazzling and hard to resist.

It's not crazy, that new voice said. *You're not crazy. Don't let him do this.*

"Just answer the question, Jack. Tell me how long you've been sleeping with our colleague while planning to marry me." When was the last time she'd challenged him like this? Had it been years? She barely remembered. She stared at the throw pillow on the floor as she spoke, suddenly relieved she didn't have to say this to his face, didn't have to watch the frustration gathering in his eyes as he prepared to explain to her that this was how relationships worked: sometimes you screwed up, but you were always forgiven. Which somehow always meant him screwing up—hurting her, disappointing her—and her always forgiving him.

"I can't believe you're accusing me of cheating when you're the one who hasn't been giving this relationship your full attention," he said, sounding wounded.

Heather felt a twinge of guilt and then pushed it away, willing herself not to apologize out of habit.

"You've been so busy since Mr. K promoted you," he went on, "it's like all you have time to think about now is you." She could hear movement in the background, as if he were pacing around, working himself into a petulant rage.

But that isn't true, she thought. She thought about Jack constantly. About whether they had enough of his favorite vodka in the freezer, or whether he'd think she was frivolous for buying flowers at the farmers market, or whether something she was about to say would set him off.

In her silence, he kept talking. "So I'm sorry if your feelings are hurt. I'm sorry if I haven't been the perfect boyfriend or the perfect fiancé, but you've been so wrapped up in *yourself*," he drawled derisively, all the honey and warmth gone from his voice, the self-pity, too.

Heather's mouth fell open in disbelief. She'd endured his rants before, but this time Carly's voice was fresh in her mind. "I never asked you to be perfect," she interrupted him, faintly. "I just asked you to love me."

"I do love you," he shot back, "which is why you can't blame me for feeling neglected when you've been so self-absorbed lately. *You* got promoted and *you* suddenly became too busy and important for *us*." *For me*, he meant. For Jack, the shining, sparkling center of the universe, whose needs and moods took up so much space in her brain, and in their lives, that she sometimes felt like there was no room left for her. That's what love meant to him, and somehow, in the last few years, she'd come to believe that was what it meant, too.

"Which is a bit rich," he continued, "since we both know Mr. K never would have promoted you if you hadn't been with me. You shouldn't be accusing me, babe, you should be thanking me. If it weren't for me, you'd still be in the corps with Carly." As usual, there was extra disdain in his voice as he said her best friend's name. Then, "If it weren't for me, no one would even know who the fuck you are."

She gasped, rage flaring in her chest. Her eyes, which had remained miraculously dry during his rant, suddenly swam with hot, humiliated tears. It was like hearing her worst fears, her cruelest inner thoughts about herself, repeated back to her from a giant loudspeaker. But worse, because they came from the man she loved, who she believed loved her the same way. From a mouth she'd kissed and let kiss her thousands of times. She wanted to throw the phone and retch, but before she could do either, her mind snagged on something he'd said: *"I'm sorry if I haven't been the perfect boyfriend. . . ."* The perfect *boyfriend*.

Oh, God.

"Were you doing this before we got engaged? Were there others, before the night I was promoted?" Even as she asked, Heather knew the answer, and she knew he wouldn't give it to her.

"Listen to me," Jack started, his condescension and anger crackling through the phone.

"No." She'd listened long enough. Let him make and explain and enforce the rules long enough. She didn't know what she would do now, but she knew she couldn't do this anymore. Couldn't be this person anymore. Heather squeezed the phone tight and willed her voice, and her stomach, into stillness for one more moment.

"This is over," she choked out. "We're done. I'm done."

Heather hung up the phone and dropped it onto the coffee table, hand shaking. Unable to stay motionless, she paced again, chewing on her bottom lip. She had spent years imagining her future with Jack, even when he was just a crush. Ever since he'd asked her to move in, she'd had it all planned out: They'd spend the rest of their careers dancing together, traveling the world and performing for audiences in far-off places she'd never get to visit otherwise. When they retired, he'd be asked to run a company somewhere, like all the big NYB stars did. She'd go with him and teach, or they'd stay here in the city and spend their long weekends at his family's house in the Hamptons. She'd even started a short mental list of names that might suit a tiny, golden-skinned child one day.

When she'd woken up this morning, the plan had been so clear. Now, she stopped and stood in the middle of their living room. She closed her eyes against the bright June sunlight, trying to picture a life with Jack. Or a life without him. Any kind of future at all. All she could conjure was a fuzzy cell phone photo of him with his arm snaking around Melissa.

The room spun as she sank onto the couch. She looked around the living room, searching for something to fix her eyes on, the way she did when she got dizzy from doing too many fouettés, and her gaze landed on her phone.

The home screen photo was one she'd taken of him a few days after they'd gotten engaged. His handsome face was cracked into a huge, open-mouthed grin, his straight white teeth gleaming and a few stray hairs burning gold in the sunlight. She looked at it closely, noticing for the first time that his gaze wasn't quite directed at the lens. He was looking past the camera. Past her.

Heather moved almost without thinking, marching into the bedroom and pulling her suitcase from under the unmade bed, then wrenched open the closet and threw everything she'd need into the small carry-on.

Over years of touring with the company, she'd developed a routine for packing that began with a thorough list and ended with all her clothes neatly folded into a series of color-coded packing cubes. No time for that now. She stripped off her pajamas, threw them in, and pulled on a roomy black T-shirt dress. She shoved her feet hastily into a pair of sneakers, then tossed her worn denim jacket into her big leather shoulder bag.

Her suitcase packed and zipped, Heather opened the drawer of her bedside table and reached in to unplug her phone charger. She was about to shove the drawer shut when something caught her eye: a royal-blue velvet jewelry box.

The one Jack had used to propose to her the night she'd been made a principal.

Heather pulled it out and ran her thumb over the soft fabric, straining to remember the mingled joy and relief she had felt that night. They had danced *Giselle* to close the spring season, and though they were utterly exhausted, running on nothing but fumes and adrenaline, it was the best they had danced together all year. Heather had felt a kind of magic buzzing through Jack's hands in their final pas de deux, and in the last moments of the ballet, the way he looked at her as she slipped back into the darkness of Giselle's grave made her feel like the most precious and beautiful prize he'd ever laid eyes on.

Heather closed her eyes, conjuring up the intoxicating applause that thundered in her ears after Jack rose from his knee and slipped the ring onto her hand. The audience was clapping for her promotion and her engagement, but they couldn't know what each of those accomplishments represented to her. Security, stability, a place to feel settled and safe after so many years of work and doubt. She had finally proven herself to the company, and to Jack. After years of holding her breath, she could exhale at last.

She opened the box and stared into its plush, empty interior. With numb, clumsy fingers, Heather pulled the sparkling ring off her left hand and placed it inside, then snapped the box shut and dropped it onto her pillow. She pulled up the handle of her suitcase and seized her keys from the entryway table.

A moment later, she was gone.

At the top of the stairs at Seventy-Ninth Street, Heather hoisted her suitcase up against her side. The heat of the subway swam around her as she picked her way down, and by the time she'd swiped her MetroCard and struggled through the turnstiles, sweat had gathered at her temples. She straightened up, looked around, and let out a stuttering sigh of relief, grateful for the first time ever for weekend track work. Carly was still waiting at the far end of the platform.

Even from here, Heather could see Carly was dejected: Her chin was tucked into her chest, her upper back curved in a slump. Even her ponytail looked droopy. Another wave of shame swept over Heather, and she made her way along the grimy platform as quickly as she could with her suitcase in tow.

"Carly," she called when she was ten feet away, and she could hear the watery wobble in her own voice. "I'm sorry."

Carly looked up, her eyes bloodshot and her cheeks flushed. Heather opened her mouth to speak, but Carly had spotted her suitcase, and her tear-streaked face lit up with a smile.

"Sorry," Carly said, fixing her face before stepping closer and pulling Heather into a tight hug. "I know this sucks, and fuck him. But I'm so relieved. We're going to go home and drink wine and eat dumplings and watch *First Wives Club*, okay? You can stay as long as you need to, but you're going to be okay. And fuck him," she squeezed even harder, "forever."

For a moment, Heather was surprised by how quickly Carly had accepted her apology, but she shouldn't have been. If anyone knew about losing your temper and saying things you shouldn't, it was Carly. Sometimes Heather had marveled that Carly had lasted as long as she had in a ballet company, where dancers, especially women, were expected to stay quiet and do as they were told without asking questions. Carly wasn't especially good at either of those things, but she was a very good dancer, so the company had always granted her a long leash. Still, she and Heather both knew if it weren't for Carly's hot head and big mouth, she'd probably have been promoted out of the corps by now.

Heather couldn't muster a reply or even a smile. She just nodded into Carly's shoulder and let the tears roll down her face.

Heather awoke on the couch to the sound of Carly's apartment buzzer screaming erratically from the kitchen. Her head was pounding, and her tongue felt like a piece of tree bark stuck to the roof of her mouth. She groped in the direction of the coffee table until her hand found her phone. She squinted against the bright light as she flipped it over.

It was 11:14 PM.

The buzzer squawked again, and Heather groaned. Was she still drunk? Was she still drunk and also already hungover, somehow?

Carly stumbled out of her bedroom and past the couch, Heather's blanket snagging on her thigh as she made her way to the kitchen. She put her elbows on the counter and leaned her shoulder against the buzzer.

"Who is it?" she groaned. It sounded like the wine hadn't quite worn off for her, either.

"I know she's up there, Carly," came an unmistakable voice. *Jack.* Heather sat up on the couch, suddenly wide awake, and her head throbbed in protest. Carly looked over at her, eyebrows raised. Heather shook her head as vehemently as she dared. She didn't want to talk to Jack. What would she even say? She didn't want to give him the chance to talk her out of her decision.

"She's not here, Jack," Carly declared into the speaker. "And I wouldn't let you in if she was."

"Yes, she is." Jack sounded angry and exhausted, and Heather's skin prickled. She knew that tone. It usually meant there was an explosion coming. "Let me up, I want to talk to her."

"Don't you have a girlfriend to go home to?" Carly snapped.

Heather's heart twisted in her chest at the idea of Jack going home to Melissa. Or worse, of him bringing her home to the apartment they'd shared, the place where they'd planned to live together as husband and wife.

"Goddammit, Carly!" There was a loud thud, and static crackled into the kitchen. It sounded like he'd slammed his hand against the glass on the intercom panel. "I have a right to talk to her!"

Before Carly could respond, Heather pulled herself off the couch and crossed the living room quickly, a little unsteady on her feet but one thought perfectly clear in her mind. She leaned close to the intercom box.

"You have no rights here. Goodbye, Jack Andersen. And fuck you, forever."

Chapter 2

Sydney, two months later

Kirribilli. *Kee-ree-bee-lee? Kai-ri-billai?* Heather stared at the address in the email on her phone. She turned the word over in her mind, wondering how badly she was about to butcher it aloud.

"Where you headed?" the cab driver asked, tossing her suitcase into his trunk. The still morning air was chill and damp, as though it had rained overnight.

"Uh, Kirry-billy?" Heather ventured, wincing and shrugging inside her denim jacket.

"No worries," the driver said, sliding into the front seat and starting the engine. Apparently, she hadn't butchered it so badly as to make herself unintelligible to an Australian. She shrugged again, opened the car door, and climbed inside.

It wasn't until the driver had pulled out into a line of cars that she realized the car was on the left side of the road. Her stomach flip-flopped as she stared at the oncoming traffic, then at the driver, who was sitting on the right-hand side of the car. She knew intellectually, of course, that Australians drove on the left, like the English. But after a full day in transit, she had to remind herself through her fatigue that she was not destined for a head-on collision.

"Bad traffic this morning," the driver said over his shoulder, "but it'll be better once we get through the city."

Heather nodded, gazing out the window at streets lined with eucalyptus trees, their long leaves hanging down lazily over the sidewalks. It was still early—she had gotten through immigration and customs by 7:30—but the sun was already high and bright in the pale and cloudy blue sky.

"How far is it to Kirry-billy?" she asked, wondering how long she would have to wait until she could wash twenty hours in an airplane off her skin and fall into bed. She'd managed to sleep a little on the flight from Los Angeles to Sydney, but she'd been wearing the same clothes for more than thirty-six hours, and she felt grubby and exhausted.

"Kirra-billy," he corrected.

"Kirra-billy," Heather repeated. "Kirra-billy, Kirra-billy. It's pretty when you say it right."

"Yep. It'll be about twenty minutes, maybe thirty."

A crowded high-rise skyline soon came into view. As the taxi wound through what looked like the outskirts of a downtown area, Heather took in a strange statue planted in the middle of a sloping green lawn. There were two massive matchsticks sticking up out of the ground, at least twenty feet high. One was new and straight, all gleaming blonde wood with a perfectly round red top. The other was blackened and shriveled, slumping next to its pristine neighbor. Burned out and broken down. Heather could relate.

The last two months had been the hardest of her life. It was one thing to end a seven-year relationship with the man you thought you were going to marry. It was another to have to work with him, his shiny new girlfriend, and all your colleagues who knew exactly why the relationship had ended. The blazing rush of power she'd felt at leaving Jack and the reflected glow of Carly's undisguised pride in her had faded quickly. She'd been left with a heartbreak that felt like a physical injury, like the time she'd pulled the muscles between four of her ribs doing a lightning-fast renversé a few years ago. Heather knew she'd made the right decision, but some mornings, when the alarm went off and she remembered where she was and what she'd done, she had to lie in a ball on Carly's couch and recite a mental list of all the reasons that was true.

After that first night at Carly's, Heather waited until Jack left for his weekly dinner with his parents across the park—thank God she'd never have to attend one of those again—before she and Carly went back to the apartment to collect her things and move most of them to a storage unit. Jack had already dumped some of her stuff haphazardly into boxes, and the ZZ plant that had once thrived on her bedside table looked as though it had been watered only with vodka and piss since she left.

As Carly cleaned out her shelves in the medicine cabinet and Heather scooped the little plant up, wondering if it could be salvaged, she noticed an empty spot in the gallery wall next to the window. He'd taken down the framed photo of the two of them, taken by the company's official photographer from the wings the night they'd gotten engaged.

When the company returned to work after a short summer break, Jack made it clear to everyone he was moving all the way on. On their first day back in the theater, he and Melissa walked into company class hand in hand, and Heather had felt multiple sets of eyes swing across the room and land on her. She kept her face impassive and her gaze fixed on her feet as she sat on the floor wrapping her toes, wishing she could melt into the marley floor and disappear forever.

It continued on like this all summer. Jack and Melissa stood next to each other at the barre, whispering and giggling in between exercises like infatuated teenagers. Mr. K, who usually demanded silence in his classes, didn't seem to care, and Heather spent every morning holding her humiliation at bay, trying desperately to focus on her dancing.

But it was impossible. Her colleagues observed her closely, waiting to see what would happen on today's episode of the in-house soap opera they had been watching for the past few weeks. Heather had a lot of practice concealing inner turmoil and pain for the benefit of an audience that would be disappointed by anything but outer perfection. Ballet audiences didn't want to think about the broken toes and herniated discs that made ballet possible; they just wanted to watch their Sleeping Beauty sparkle and smile and spin across the stage. But this was different.

It felt as though her colleagues *wanted* to see her armor crack, wanted to watch the anguish leak out of her as Jack and Melissa laughed at an inside joke at the barre across the room. Once the ballet gossip blogs caught wind of the breakup, things got even worse: Whenever a ballet fan spotted her in the street or in the dancewear store across from the theater, she'd watch their faces light up with recognition, then dim into patronizing pity. *America's Brokenhearted Ballet Sweetheart.*

By the start of August, Heather could barely sleep. She'd lie awake at night listening to the sirens and late-night roadwork outside, dreading the morning as shame and self-doubt simmered in her chest. She had spent so many years thinking of herself as Jack Andersen's Girlfriend, the lucky woman on his arm. Now she was just . . . Heather.

"Mr. K never would have promoted you if you hadn't been with me. If it weren't for me, no one would know who the fuck you are."

Some nights, panic clutched at her throat, and she'd imagine losing all of it. Mr. K would decide promoting her had been a mistake, and while he couldn't demote her, he could choose to cast her in fewer and fewer dances until she got the message. Quietly, she'd slip out of the company. No Jack, no job, no working alongside her best friend.

On those nights, she clenched her jaw to hold back her tears. She'd wake up tucked in a tight ball a few fitful hours later with a pain in the side of her face, drag herself off the couch, tend to the struggling plant, and dress mindlessly for company class.

One night, she'd been lying awake on the couch, scrolling through her phone in the dark after yet another fruitless attempt at sleep, when Carly had arrived home, knocking a stack of mail off the little table in the entryway as she came through the door.

"Honey, I'm home," she'd said to Heather in a tipsy stage whisper. "Sorry I woke you."

Heather sighed, kicking restlessly at the blanket and sitting up. "You didn't. How was your date?"

"He spent the first twenty minutes explaining ballet to me." Carly rolled her eyes. "Because he watched his sister dance in a few local *Nutcracker*s twenty years ago."

Heather scoffed. Dating male ballet dancers was hard, but she'd learned from Carly over the years that dating male civilians wasn't much easier. Most of them had no idea how time consuming—how all-consuming—a ballet career was. More than one guy had asked Carly what her "real" job was, and some of them were only interested in finding out just how flexible ballerinas truly were. For a while, Carly had told men she met at bars that she worked in marketing.

"And how was your evening?" Carly asked, plopping herself onto the arm of the couch.

"The same," Heather said dully, fiddling with the blanket. The same as every other sleepless, anxious, tight-chested night since she had moved out of Jack's apartment.

"Did you hear back from Moscow?"

Heather nodded, then shook her head glumly.

"Another no? What's wrong with these people?"

"They don't want me without Jack," Heather said.

Since she had been promoted to principal, a number of companies had invited her and Jack to join them for a month or two as guest artists. But Jack had never wanted to leave New York—probably, she realized now, because it would mean leaving behind whoever he was secretly screwing—so they'd always turned the offers down. But now the fall season was approaching. Casting would go up any day now, and what if Mr. K cast her and Jack together? The idea of having to rehearse *Swan Lake* or *Firebird* for hours a day with the man who had dragged her heart up and down Broadway filled her with dread. Every time she tried to imagine dancing with him on stage, her Odette falling in love with his Siegfried, panic rose in her chest, threatening to flood her whole system.

So she'd reached out to a few of those companies, asking if their offers still stood. The Moscow Ballet had given her the same answer as all the other premiere companies: they were very sorry, but they weren't interested unless Jack came with her. She'd been so thrilled to receive their invitations last year, and it was humiliating to realize that they'd never really wanted her—not enough to take her on her own merits, anyway.

"This is crazy. You're Heather Fucking Hays, principal dancer at NYB, not some random dancer they've never heard of." Carly pushed Heather's legs off the couch and slid down to sit next to her. "Who gives a crap if Jack comes too? Surely they have some dude they can pair you with in London, and Paris, and Moscow."

"Don't forget Berlin." They'd all said no. They'd all said she was nothing without Jack. *"If it weren't for me, no one would know who the fuck you are."*

"Maybe I shouldn't try to leave. Wouldn't I just be running away? Letting them win?"

"Listen," Carly started. Even through the haze of a few drinks, Heather could hear she was trying to be serious. "You're miserable. You wouldn't be *running away*; you'd be removing yourself from a shitty situation. Which, I'm sorry to say this, could soon get a lot shittier. Mr. K will probably cast Melissa with Jack, and it'll get a ton of press attention. Do you really want to spend the fall season trapped here with those two?"

"I know," Heather sighed, "you're right."

"I know," Carly echoed, with a wiggle of her eyebrows, her voice playful again. "I'm always right."

"Which doesn't actually solve my problem: there's no company that wants me. Apparently, I'm nothing without Jack." Heather tried to match Carly's light tone but couldn't quite pull it off. The words felt a little too true tonight.

"That's bullshit," Carly said. "And I'll tell you so as many times as I have to, until you believe it. You're not the problem here; they are."

Heather nodded limply, but Carly wasn't done.

"Listen to me, because I'm always right. You've got it backward, and so do all these companies: *Jack* is nothing without *you*. That asshole is lucky he gets to breathe the same air as you. He might be the bigger star, but that doesn't make him better than you, okay?"

"Okay," Heather managed.

They sat in silence for a while, and Heather checked the time on her phone. It was almost midnight. In a few hours she'd have to get up and go uptown for another morning of trying to concentrate on dancing, while her ex-fiancé and her replacement traded smitten smiles during degagés. Just like she'd done today, and the day before.

Heather had been about to suggest they both get some sleep when Carly gasped and turned to her, delight visible on her face even in the semi-darkness.

"There's one company we forgot," she'd said excitedly. "Better than any of those places. Well, farther away, anyway. And I bet they'll say yes."

A sparkle of light on water interrupted Heather's memories. The taxi had wended its way through the city and now, out the right-hand side of the car, she saw Sydney's famous, dazzling harbor for the first time. Sunlight bounced off the calm water, and large boats crisscrossed on their way to a big central wharf, leaving long trails of white water behind them. And then there was the iconic Harbour

Bridge, a huge, elegant gray arch teeming with cars, connecting two crowded shorelines. Despite her fatigue, Heather grinned. This place was her new home for the next month.

"Are we going over it?" she asked the driver.

"The Bridge? Yeah. Your first time in Sydney?"

"It is," Heather said, craning her neck to see more of the water.

"Then you'll want to look up as we cross. It's a hell of a view up through all that steel."

But as the cab rolled onto the bridge and under its graceful steel arch, Heather looked to the right, and gasped. Beneath her, on a piece of land jutting out into the water, sat the Sydney Opera House, home of the Australian National Ballet. Its iconic off-white sails curved into the blue sky, and through her exhaustion, Heather felt a thrill of anticipation as she gazed down at the bizarre, beautiful building. That theater was going to be her home for the next month.

But first, a shower.

Marcus sat on the swaying bus as it trundled over the Harbour Bridge, staring glumly out the window. Jammed into the seat with his backpack on his knees, he tried to keep his crutches from falling onto the woman next to him. When he could stand, he'd never noticed how packed the morning buses into the city were. Now that he had to hunt for a seat every morning, he felt rather claustrophobic.

The Opera House came into view, its sharp white peaks like jumbled teeth in the bright winter sun. Marcus turned away and focused instead on the brightly colored pattern on the upholstered seat in front of him. He put a hand on his knee and squeezed it tightly, trying to calm the flutter of anxiety he felt in his gut every time he looked at the building now. It helped, a little.

As the bus rolled into the city, Marcus reached over the beleaguered-looking woman sitting beside him with an apologetic grimace and pressed the red STOP button. The bus crawled to a halt amid the morning traffic, opening its doors with a loud exhale, and his seatmate pivoted to let him pass. Awkwardly, he hiked his backpack over one shoulder and made his way off the bus, heading down the hill towards work. He didn't particularly enjoy these slow, crutch-supported walks to the dance studios, but it was a relief to move a little more freely after so many months immobilized and in pain.

Twenty-five minutes later, Marcus eased himself into the lobby of the ANB, sweating slightly. Crutching downhill was still work, and the last leg from the bus stop was down a steep flight of a hundred and fifty sandstone stairs. Sharon, the company's head physiotherapist, said it was good for him, but he was willing to bet she'd never tried it herself.

Marcus passed the dance studios, nodding to his colleagues as they hustled past him on their way to morning class. He tried not to envy his friends as they disappeared into Studio B to claim a spot at the barre. If he let himself think too hard about what his life used to be like—what it felt like to start every morning with fluid, pain-free pliés, what it felt like not to miss his dad every second of every day—he'd get dragged back down into the deep chasm of grief he'd only just begun to climb out of.

It had been a year since Marcus had shredded his left Achilles tendon, since that awful night on stage at the Opera House when he'd landed a tour jeté and felt a previously unimaginable pain rip through the back of his ankle. Sometimes, in his dreams, he still heard the audience's horrified gasps, and then the little groan of shock and confusion that fell out of his body as he hit the floor in agony. He could still see the panic in Alice's eyes as she watched him from the wings, suddenly on his hands and knees when he was supposed to be standing tall and proud and ready to dance the next section of their pas de deux.

He had been hurt before, every dancer he knew had been. But most of his injuries had been from overuse, little aches that ballooned into more serious problems over time. Despite the little injuries, and the short bursts of rest and rehabilitation he'd been through before, he'd always felt . . . kind of invulnerable. He had been young and strong; he'd always bounced back. But he hadn't seen this one coming, and it had knocked all the wind out of him.

The surgery to repair the busted tendon hadn't gone well, and they'd had to go in a second time. And now, his rehab was moving more slowly than he'd imagined. Six months in—six months of hoisting himself around on crutches with his foot hanging uselessly in a boot—he was growing restless. This was the longest he'd gone without dancing since he was eight years old. Now, in his early thirties, every month counted, because who knew how much time he had left before the rest of his body gave out and he had to figure out what the hell to do with the rest of his life? He'd had a glimpse, now, of what life without ballet looked like, and it looked pretty fucking grim.

"Morning, Marcus," called Sharon as he crutched his way into the clinic and shrugged his backpack onto the bench beside the door. The room was quiet, and like the dance studios, it had floor-to-ceiling mirrors along one wall. There were several massage tables, a Pilates reformer, and a large shelf in the back stocked with resistance bands and medicine balls. In another corner, a rack of kettlebells stood next to a small collapsible ballet barre.

"Morning, Shaz," he said, gently testing his weight on his foot and deciding to limp his way to her. "Not bad, eh?" he asked, when he reached her, holding on to the massage table for balance.

"Not bad at all," she said. Her short, blonde ponytail swayed along with her vaguely impressed nods. "I reckon we can start you walking without crutches pretty soon."

Marcus beamed. "Really?"

"Nothing too major," she warned. "I want to take it nice and slow. The slower you come back, the faster you come back."

"I know, I know," he grumbled, his little shot of excitement already fizzling out. It was Sharon's mantra, one she'd been trying to drill into the company's dancers for fifteen years. *The slower you come back, the faster you come back.* It rarely worked. Most of his colleagues started taking dance classes because as kids they couldn't sit still, and most of them still couldn't. Others felt like they couldn't afford to rest, even when they were injured. Especially the women. There was so much competition for jobs and for roles, and an endless supply of talented young dancers looking for a spot in the company.

Marcus didn't think ANB was going to let him go on account of his injury; since Peter became artistic director, they didn't do things like that anymore. But he had other reasons for wanting to get back on stage, even if the very sight of the theatre made him queasy.

"I know you know," Sharon said, levelling her no-nonsense gaze at him as he climbed onto the table and lay on his back. "I want you back at full strength too, believe me. So let's take a look at it and maybe today we'll get you walking. And *maybe* some very gentle pliés."

Marcus smiled to himself as she got to work, manipulating his left ankle. It had been the worst fucking year of his life, grinding dutifully through physio despite a grief so heavy it sometimes felt like it was pinning him to his bed in the morning. But maybe the worst was over.

From down the hall, he could hear the pianist for company class playing a Chopin étude. His colleagues were dancing. And soon, he'd be able to join them.

Chapter 3

Heather woke in a weak gray light and felt a momentary jolt of panic. Where was she? *When* was she? She opened her eyes and scanned the dim bedroom. Her suitcase lay open on the floor, and she was lying fully dressed atop the still-made bed. Then she remembered: She had taken that much-needed shower, pulled on some jeans, plugged in her phone. She must have lain on the bed while she waited for it to charge . . . and now it was evening.

She'd slept right through her first day in Sydney.

Sitting up, Heather pulled her damp hair from her face, and it only took a moment for her to realize she was absolutely ravenous. She rolled herself off the bed, feeling every one of the fourteen hours of the flight from L.A. in her hip flexors, then slipped on her sneakers and grabbed her phone, tossing it in her bag as she left in search of food.

Kirribilli, as it turned out, was a quaint and leafy old suburb built on a hill above the water, tucked right under the Harbour Bridge. The little house provided by the company was a narrow two-story sandstone row house, with a dark-green front door and three terracotta pots of riotous hot-pink geraniums on the tiled front porch. Inside, Heather had found a small, sun-drenched living room at the front of the house, and an equally small but recently renovated kitchen in back.

Heather walked a short way down her quiet street and soon found herself on a narrow main drag where shops and cafes crowded along the hill. Farther down was the harbor, now an inky blue under the cloudy twilight sky. She headed up the street, relishing the cool evening air against her skin, thinking she might wander a bit before deciding where to have dinner. But the very first restaurant she walked past was a tiny Thai place, and the scent of tom yum soup and green curry made her stomach rumble with desperation. She could explore later.

One large plate of pad thai and a cold light beer later, Heather sat contentedly at her sidewalk table, gazing down the hill at the shifting, shimmering water. For the first time since Carly had entered her apartment that awful Sunday morning two months ago, Heather felt truly relaxed.

What time was it in New York? Too late to call Carly? She screwed up her face, trying to do the math, then gave up and searched her bag for her phone. She checked the time and saw it was nearly 9:00 AM in New York.

Heather, 6:47 PM: Made it to Sydney fine. Exhausted but it's gorgeous here.
Carly, 6:49 PM: 👍 The couch misses you
Carly, 6:50 PM: And I miss you ❤️
Heather, 6:50 PM: I miss you too.
Carly, 6:53 PM: Gotta get on the subway but glad you made it okay
Carly, 6:53 PM: Love you, don't forget your promise: I want lots of photos of hot Australian dudes 😘

Heather laughed. Carly had, indeed, made her promise to send photos of hot Australian dudes as Heather was loading her suitcase into the cab to JFK.

> *Heather, 6:53 PM: Don't forget YOUR promise: I want lots of photos of my plant.*

A moment later, a photo of her potted plant appeared. Heather spotted a few promising new leaves sprouting in the sunlight.

> *Carly, 6:54 PM: I've named her ZZ Pot. She also wants photos of hot Australian dudes*
> *Carly, 6:54 PM: I should probably water her more if she's going to be this thirsty* 😄

Heather smiled ruefully. She wasn't sorry to be away from New York for a while, but she was going to miss Carly. She pulled up her mother's number, and after a moment of hesitation, tapped out a quick text. Her mom hadn't taken the news of the breakup well, probably because Heather hadn't told her Jack cheated. Even before Melissa, Heather never had the heart to spoil the press-friendly fairy tale that made her mother so happy and so sure of her daughter's future. As far as Linda Hays knew, her sensible, predictable daughter had walked away from a stable seven-year relationship with the biggest star in American ballet, a man whose family had enough money to make sure she never wanted for anything—for no good reason.

> *Heather, 6:57 PM: Landed safely in Sydney, all is well here.*

She didn't wait for a reply.

Heather had just signed the check when her phone vibrated and a long, unknown number appeared on the screen.

"Hello, this is Heather."

"G'day Heather, it's Peter McGregor at ANB," said a voice with a broad Australian accent.

"Mr. McGregor, hello!" Heather sat up straight and snapped into obliging-and-attentive-employee mode. As the artistic director of the company, this man was now her boss, even if only temporarily.

"Oh, please, call me Peter, all the dancers do."

"Uh, okay, Peter." It felt strange to call an artistic director by his first name, and she certainly couldn't call him "Peet-ah," which was how he pronounced it. But this fit with what she knew about Mr. McGregor's—nope, *Peter's*—tenure at ANB. He'd been put in charge a few years ago and had set about reforming the company to make it more dancer friendly, doing his best to remove the strict hierarchy that defined so many ballet companies.

In the gate lounge at JFK, Heather had scrolled through articles about him and ANB, which had helped distract her from the enormity of the snap decision she'd made. One of Peter's first acts had been to install an on-site counselor alongside the physical therapy team. As he'd told the *Sydney Morning Sun*, he believed dancers' mental health was inextricable from their physical health and wanted to eliminate the stigma attached to seeking mental healthcare. He'd brought in lots of women choreographers to create new dances for the company, pledging that for at least his first five years, the company would perform more works by women than by men.

Heather had stared in shock when she read that, and then counted quickly on her fingers—it only took one hand to name the few women choreographers whose works she'd performed at NYB in the last five years. Little wonder, then, that Carly's instinct had been correct: of all the companies Heather had approached, ANB was the only one willing to hire her without Jack. For that, she was extremely grateful.

"How was the flight over?" Peter asked. "I know it can be grueling."

"It was, but I've spent the day resting and the house is lovely, really," Heather assured him. "Thank you for arranging all this at such short notice," she added quickly. *Thank you for throwing me a life preserver when I was drowning.*

"You're welcome, and we're just delighted to have you joining us. We're planning on announcing our newest guest principal artist in a press release tomorrow." Heather could practically hear his wide smile. He'd assumed leadership determined to turn ANB into a world-class company, and it sent a little thrill through her to think she might suddenly be part of that plan. Her, alone. Heather Hays, the world-class artist, not Heather Hays, Jack Andersen's girlfriend.

"If you're feeling up to it, you're welcome to join company class at ten o'clock," he went on. "You can take it nice and easy and just do barre if you like, but you can meet the company and I can arrange a tour of the studios and a bit of the city."

"That sounds great, thank you."

"Wonderful. I'll see you tomorrow morning, then. Company class is in Studio B. Enjoy your evening."

"Yes, see you then. Thank you again."

Heather hung up and let out a shaky breath. This was really happening. She was really here, far away from Jack and the company and the mess that was her life in New York. Gathering her things, she set off back toward the house. On the corner of the main drag, she stopped and gazed at the hulking gray bridge, which sprouted out of its pale-yellow sandstone approaches and curved over the calm, dark water. Headlights whizzed across, red and gold, and a train slid slowly alongside them, glowing from within.

Davo, 6:12 AM: Call me when u wake up

Marcus rolled groggily out of bed and walked the short distance to the kitchen, where the coffee machine was already gurgling. His stomach clenched with anxiety as he dialed his brother's number.

"Hey," Davo answered brusquely.

"You rang?" Marcus replied.

"Yeah, I did. Listen," Davo said, in his usual stern and serious tone. Marcus could picture him stepping out of whatever house he and his crew were working on, maybe slipping into the back garden for some privacy. "I'm going over to Mum's for dinner Sunday night, you should come too. We can try again."

Marcus leaned against the counter and sighed. Since their dad had died, this was the only thing Davo wanted to talk about with him: his campaign to convince their mum she should sell the family home and downsize.

"Don't you think she's got a point?" he asked cautiously. "Yeah, the place is getting to be too much for her, but she doesn't have to move out right away. We could hire a cleaner, or something."

Davo tsked impatiently, and Marcus heard his brother's kelpie Banjo bark in the background. "That's just a short-term solution. And it's not just the upkeep, it's the stairs, too. They're really steep, and there's no bathroom downstairs, so she's gotta go up and down all day."

Marcus sighed. Solving that problem would be much more expensive than hiring a cleaner. He thought about the little brick house where he and Davo had grown up. The Campbells' home was small, especially compared to the luxury homes that started springing up on the Northern Beaches in the last decade as even people with plenty of money started getting pushed into middle-class suburbs. Still, Marcus had had a hard time getting up those stairs on crutches, and his mum's osteoarthritis wasn't getting any better. He and Davo had both noticed it was getting harder for her to get around the house, and to keep the place in decent nick. And now that his dad was gone . . .

"I just don't want to rush her," Marcus said, determined to stop his thoughts drifting in that direction. "She's had a hard year, like we have, and moving is really stressful."

"Yeah, but the market's having a great year, so if she moves fast, she can get a really good price."

Marcus sighed again, trying not to think about what modern monstrosity a new owner would inevitably build once they bought his childhood home and knocked it down. There was no stopping Davo once he got an idea into his head, but Marcus really wished he would be a little less terse with their mum as he was shooing her out the door of her own house. The last time he'd brought this up with her, she nearly burst into tears. Marcus couldn't let his brother go over there on his own. "I'll be there on Sunday, but I need to get out the door now. I'll text you later."

"Yep, seeya," Davo said quickly and hung up.

Marcus returned slowly to his bedroom and pulled on yesterday's jeans, rolling up the left leg and strapping on his boot. He poured as much of the steaming coffee as he could into a travel mug, stashed it in his backpack, seized his crutches, and headed out.

An hour later, Marcus crutched his way down the central hallway at ANB. For what felt like the thousandth time, he bypassed the studios for the physio room, where Shaz was finishing up with another dancer. Pausing in the doorway, he called, "I'm here, I'm just gonna go change."

Down at the end of the hallway, Marcus shouldered his way into the men's locker room. After yesterday's session, Sharon had been satisfied that he was ready to practice walking and pliés again today. Finally, *finally*, he was moving in the right direction.

Marcus sat on one of the locker room benches and carefully unwrapped his boot. He slid out of his jeans and gently worked his left foot into a pair of navy tracksuit pants. He'd just slid his right foot in and stood up to pull them on when he heard the door swing open behind him, followed by a loud gasp.

"Ohmygod," a woman exclaimed as he whipped his head around. "I'm so sorry, I thought this was the women's locker room!"

Marcus hastily pulled his pants up over his arse and crotch, then turned around to face her, too intrigued to be embarrassed. But she had turned back towards the door, and had her hands over her eyes, which seemed a little redundant to him.

"You can turn around," he said, amused. "I'm fully clothed now."

She didn't move, her shoulders shrugged up towards her ears in obvious embarrassment. Marcus examined the back of her head, where a mass of dark brown hair was pinned in a sleek French twist. She was in a snug, deep-red warm-up jacket, and with her hands raised to her face, he could see the wings of her shoulder blades outlined clearly through the clinging fabric. Judging by her crinkly plastic garbage-bag pants and worn canvas slippers, she was ready for class. But she clearly wasn't a company member, or she wouldn't have come barging into the wrong locker room. Was she a guest teacher, or maybe a visiting choreographer? Even standing there with her hands over her face, she filled the run-down, dimly lit change room with a presence he couldn't ignore. He didn't know who she was, but something deep in his gut told him he wanted to.

She lowered her hands slowly and turned to look at him, her face a mask of pure mortification, and he stared. Instantly, Marcus recognized that face, those big brown eyes and those high cheekbones. He'd seen them on Instagram, on YouTube, on the cover of *Barre* magazine.

It was Heather Hays. *The* Heather Hays. Of New York Ballet.

What was The Heather Hays of New York Ballet doing here? And had The Heather Hays of New York Ballet just copped a look of his bare arse?

Well, Heather thought, *that's one way to start your first day as a world class artist: walking in on an ass-naked coworker.*

Even through her embarrassment Heather couldn't help but notice it was a very nice ass. She'd only caught a glimpse before she'd spun and covered her eyes, but what she'd seen had been impressive, even by ballet standards, sitting high and round above hamstrings so defined they looked like bridge cables under his tanned skin. Whoever this guy turned out to be, she'd never be able to forget that under those sweatpants he had a perfectly sculpted butt.

Now, he was staring at her, and she willed herself to stop thinking about his ass and provide him with an explanation for her presence in what was very clearly not the women's locker room. Face hot, she forced herself to speak.

"I'm so sorry," she managed. "It's my first day here, and I was in a rush. I didn't look closely enough at the sign on the door."

"It's okay," he said, his awkward attempt at a smile making deep crinkles appear around his green eyes. "The women's locker room is next door." He tipped his head toward the wall and looked at her expectantly. When she continued to stand there, her feet frozen to the floor, he fidgeted in the awkward silence and ran a hand through his thick, light brown curls. Without meaning to, she followed his hand with her eyes, kept watching as it settled casually on his hip.

"Right!" she blurted, realizing only once the word was out of her mouth that she'd spoken way too loud. "Yes, sorry, I will . . . go there," she finished weakly.

"All right, then," he said with another smile, genuine this time, like he was suppressing a laugh. His eyes sparkled with mirth, and the effect was so attractive she almost forgot to be embarrassed. Almost.

Heather's face burned again, and she gave her head a tiny shake. It was hopeless. Between the jet lag and the surprise—and surprisingly perfect—butt, she felt like her brain had been totally scrambled.

"I'm going now," she announced needlessly as she turned her back on him and scurried out of the room as fast as she could.

She waited until she was safely next door in the women's locker room before she groaned in horror.

"Not off to a great start," she muttered as she dropped her bag on a bench and hurried to one of the several mirrors to check her hair one last time.

"What's not off to a great start?" came a voice from the other side of the lockers.

Heather suppressed another groan. Why hadn't she checked the room was empty? She was still scrambling for a plausible reply when a petite dancer came around the corner, her shiny black hair in a low bun.

"Holy shit," the woman said. She was half a head shorter than Heather, who was surprised to hear so deep a voice come out of so small a person. "Are you Heather Hays?"

"Uh, yes?" Heather asked. "Yes," she repeated, more firmly this time.

"Wow," the woman said, looking at Heather, plainly impressed. "Shaz hinted the new guest artist was a star, but I didn't think she meant a *star.*"

Heather's already flushed cheeks went even hotter. "I'm not—I mean, I'm just . . . I'm Heather. What's your name?"

"Alice Ho," the woman said, holding out her hand and delivering an enthusiastic handshake.

"Nice to meet you," Heather said.

"Nice to meet *you,*" Alice grinned. "Everything okay?"

"Oh, yeah, I'm just jet-lagged and a little out of it, and my bun's loose," Heather said quickly. She was not about to tell Alice about the incident in the men's room.

"I've got spare pins, if you need 'em," Alice gestured over her shoulder.

"Thanks, I'm okay. I just need a second."

"All right, well, there's pins and hairspray in my locker. And tampons. Yellow one in the middle. It's never locked, so help yourself, everyone else does."

Heather gave Alice a grateful smile as the other woman pulled the door open and left. If only Alice had been the first person she'd met at ANB and not Butt Guy, she thought as she walked to one of the full-length mirrors and adjusted a few bobby pins. She wobbled her head back and forth, testing the security of her bun, and then the wobble turned into a dispirited shake. Five minutes at ANB and she'd already embarrassed herself.

She stared at her reflection, taking in her slightly puffy eyes and pale cheeks, and tried to recapture some of the confidence she'd felt when she'd arrived this morning, before barging into the men's room. She was Heather Hays, world-class artist. *A star*, Alice had said. Heather didn't think of herself that way, but she knew even stars weren't allowed to be late to class, especially on their first day. Satisfied she looked neat enough, she headed out into the corridor and into Studio B.

Just inside, a man she recognized from her research as Peter stood by the grand piano, shuffling through papers on the glossy black wood. He looked up when she entered, and his face broke into a toothy smile.

"Heather, welcome!" he called, opening his arms and gliding toward her across the rubbery black dance mat. In his accent, her name sounded like *Heathah*, like she was from Boston. He had a tall, upright frame, and he was thicker around the middle and thinner on top than he had been when he was one of ANB's principal dancers. He wore a tight black T-shirt tucked into snug black jeans, with a pair of chunky dance sneakers that told Heather he'd be teaching company class this morning.

Peter gave her two quick air kisses by way of greeting, then stepped back and gestured around at the large, airy studio. "Welcome to ANB. I'm delighted you're here." *Hee-yah*, it sounded like.

"I'm delighted to be here," Heather smiled back, taking in the high ceilings and the glittering water beckoning just outside the window. This was nothing like the studios at Lincoln Center, where the largest rehearsal rooms were half underground and the thick stone edifice blocked out all but the brightest sunlight.

"Everyone," Peter called to the dozens of dancers who sat chatting in clusters around the room or stood stretching at one of the many barres. They fell silent and turned toward him expectantly. "Everyone, this is Heather Hays, principal dancer at New York Ballet. She'll be joining us as a guest artist for the next month. She's rather jet-lagged, so she'll be settling in slowly. But we're very lucky to have her with us and I'm very much looking forward to seeing her on our stage in a few weeks. In the meantime, please welcome Heather to ANB!"

Heather managed a small wave and a toothless smile, feeling suddenly shy as the dancers gave a short but enthusiastic round of applause. It seemed Peter had kept her arrival a secret until now, because some of the dancers looked extremely surprised at the announcement. Pleasantly surprised, but still. She glanced around the studio, but was relieved to see no sign of Butt Guy. In the back of the room, though, she spotted two young-looking dancers exchanging open-mouthed looks of delighted awe, and at the barre closest to her, a handful of women grinned at her welcomingly. Alice gave her a little wave from the back corner. Heather felt her own smile widen as she took in the room. For the first time in months, she didn't mind that a studio full of dancers was staring at her.

Peter took his place at the front of the room as the dancers arranged themselves in evenly spaced lines at the barres. Heather chose a spot on the wall that wasn't too close to the mirror, and a moment later Peter nodded to the pianist, who began to play a slow and meditative tune.

Heather glanced around and quickly slid her feet into first position, trying to quiet her mind. *Shoulders down, chin lifted. Spine long, ribs closed. Left hand on the barre.* That was one comfort, Heather thought as she took a deep breath and exhaled into a gentle demi-plié: no matter where you were on the planet, ballet class always began the same way.

It was steady and predictable, even when nothing else was.

Forty-five minutes and many tendus later, Heather had removed her jacket and her warm-up pants and was sweating through her pale-blue leotard. As the pianist played a punchy tango, Heather gripped the barre tighter than usual and concentrated on her grand battements, hoping it was the final combination. Throwing her legs into the air, she felt a lingering stiffness in her muscles and ligaments, a reminder of the long flight. Front, side, back, side, the familiar pattern she'd been following since she was five years old. Right leg, then left leg.

She tried not to think about all the time she'd spent doing these same exercises next to the man she had planned to marry, or the fact that she'd unwittingly spent months—years, maybe—doing them just a few feet away from the women he'd been screwing on the side. *"He doesn't deserve to breathe the same air as you."* Well, now he wasn't. She was here alone, and she had one month to prove to ANB, and the rest of the world, that she was enough on her own.

Heather gritted her teeth through the last few battements and breathed out shakily as the music stopped, then gathered up her clothes and wiped the sweat from her neck. As the dancers moved the barres from the middle of the studio and the women swapped their ballet slippers for pointe shoes, Heather made her way to the door. Peter intercepted her.

"I hope that wasn't too onerous for your first day," he said, taking in her flushed face and her sweat-splotched leotard.

"No," she breathed, "it felt good. A few more days of that and I should be ready for a full class."

"No need to rush," Peter replied, gesturing for her to proceed out of the studio and into the hallway. He led her past framed posters advertising decades' worth of company performances. "Flying across the world does a number on your body, so please take your time. In the meantime, I've arranged for one of our company members to show you around. Sydney's a big city and it's not built on a grid, so it can be hard to get around at times."

"I don't want to inconvenience anyone," Heather said quickly. "I know everyone's busy—"

"It's no trouble," Peter interrupted, his tone firm and genuine. "Unfortunately he's recovering from an injury, so he isn't rehearsing." Peter turned right, and Heather followed him into what looked like a physical therapy suite. A man in dark-blue sweatpants stood on the far side of the room, doing slow, tentative pliés at a small collapsible barre.

"Marcus," Peter called across the room, "come meet Heather Hays."

The man turned, and Heather stifled a groan as he limped carefully toward them. It was Butt Guy.

Chapter 4

Marcus stared at Heather Hays, who stood mute in the doorway next to Peter, and felt momentarily lightheaded. Her cheeks were flushed pink from what he knew from experience had been a hard barre, and the colour made her brown eyes glow brighter than they had in the locker room. Her once-sleek hair frizzed out from her temples and nape, and beads of sweat gathered along her sharp collarbone. He moved towards her slowly, but she looked at him like he was a speeding freight train bearing down on her.

"This is Marcus Campbell, one of our soloists," Peter was saying jovially. The sound of his boss's voice jolted his attention away from Heather Hays's wide eyes and sweat-dampened skin. "Marcus, this is Heather Hays. As I've just informed the company, Heather will be spending some time with us as a guest artist. She recently finished the spring season with what I'm told was a sublime *Giselle*, dancing with . . . uh . . . well . . ." Peter trailed off uncomfortably.

With her ex-fiancé who had cheated on her, Marcus knew. Everyone knew. The ballet world was really fucking small, and everyone knew somebody who had done a summer intensive with somebody who had competed at YAGP with somebody. His own best mate from ballet school had spent most of his career dancing in European companies, with colleagues from Argentina and South Korea and Ukraine. The ballet gossip machine was fast, efficient, and, unfortunately, a global operation.

Marcus saw a tiny flutter of alarm in Heather's golden-brown eyes, and she looked away, down at the carpet and blinking a few times as Peter spoke.

"I thought it might be helpful for you to show Heather around Sydney a little, just to help her get settled. It would be a big favour to me and the company," his boss was saying.

Marcus looked at him in surprise.

"Is that all right with you?" Peter asked. "Sharon's okayed it," he added, as if he'd read Marcus's mind.

"No, yeah, fine," Marcus said, vaguely. Peter was taking pity on him, trying to make him feel like he was still useful to the company even though he hadn't been able to dance in a year. If it had been any other task, he would have been insulted, would have begged off by claiming physiotherapy would take all day. But Sharon had eliminated that excuse. *Besides,* he thought, chancing a glance down at Heather's flushed face, *would it be so bad to spend a day or two crutching around the city with her?* He wasn't starstruck or anything, but she was The Heather Hays, after all.

"I don't want to inconvenience you," Heather said hastily. "I'm sure this is taking plenty of your time and energy." She gestured at the physio room. Was she trying to get him out of this? Was she trying to get herself out of it?

"No worries at all," Marcus said, pulling his face into a pleasant and obliging smile. "I'm done for the day." He nodded at Peter, who smiled back and then glanced down at his smartwatch.

"Well, that's that," Peter said breezily, "I'll leave you in Marcus's hands, Heather, and we'll have you settled in in no time." He turned and left, leaving Heather and Marcus standing in awkward silence, he in the empty physio room and she hovering just outside of it.

"Thank you, again," Heather said, after a long, silent moment. "I'll just go get my bag. It's, um, in the locker room."

"The women's locker room or the men's?" Marcus asked, before he could stop himself. He'd always been a bit of a shit stirrer, but it had been a while since he'd made a joke without thinking about it. He'd just wanted to crack the uncomfortable tension, and the words had slipped out.

It worked, though. Her face broke into a wide grin, and the sight of it left him a little breathless. She had been striking enough just standing there, sweaty and wilting slightly after a hard class. But now she was dazzling, her eyes lit up with a mixture of mirth and mortification, and he couldn't help but grin back. Her full, arched eyebrows shot up in response, and he felt the movement deep in his gut.

She put her face in her hands for a moment and let out a tiny groan, then looked up at him again, still smiling.

"I wouldn't usually say yes to being a tour guide, but you clearly need one," he teased, encouraged by her expression. "Left to your own devices, who knows how many half-naked men you'll walk in on?"

She groaned again, but this time it was tinged with laughter. The sound was delicious. "I will be right back, and then we can start pretending that never happened."

"Pretending what never happened?" he called after her as she disappeared towards the locker room.

Minutes later, Marcus was in the hallway with his boot back on and his backpack on his shoulders. Heather approached, now wearing a baggy wool jumper tucked into the front of her pale, snug jeans. She had taken out her bun and put her long dark hair in a low, loose ponytail. She was still a little flushed, and Marcus averted his eyes as she came towards him, swatting away the kind of thoughts he knew he shouldn't be having about her.

He lifted one of his crutches in greeting. "I'll be moving a little slowly. I hope that's all right."

"Fine with me. I am, too. Peter does *not* mess around."

"Yeah, his barres are brutal. But not as brutal as the rest of his class," he added cheerfully. "Would a coffee help?"

"Maybe? I don't even know what time it is in my body. I think it's dinner time. But coffee sounds good."

They made their way into the lobby, where there was a small and bustling café. One wall of the café was almost entirely windows, giving everyone who sat at the round white tables a stunning view of the Harbour Bridge and, if you craned your neck, the Opera House. Marcus didn't crane his neck, and instead watched as Heather gazed around, apparently awestruck.

"Pretty remarkable building, hey?"

"I'll say. But I guess I assumed the company rehearsed at the Opera House."

"Only during tech week. This place used to be an active wharf, but they converted the warehouses in the '70s and turned a bunch of them into arts spaces. We share this wharf with a big Aboriginal dance company, and there's a theatre company a few wharves down." Though, lately, some of the arts spaces had been converted again, this time into luxury apartments, all glass and steel hovering over the water.

Heather nodded as he talked, then yawned widely.

"I suppose my first act as your tour guide should be to introduce you to Australian coffee," Marcus said as they joined the café's queue.

"Oh, I've had an Australian coffee," Heather said, her accent curving tightly around the vowels in *Australian*. "You mean a flat white? Starbucks makes those."

Marcus feigned an expression of horror. "Starbucks?! On behalf of the Australian people, I beg you not to drink that crap. I don't know what Starbucks thinks it's making for you over there, but I guarantee you it's not a proper flat white."

She shrugged and looked at him, nonplussed. Maybe he'd over-sold the coffee a little.

"Order me whatever you think is best," she said, pulling out her wallet and fishing out some cash.

"My shout," he said, waving her money away and turning to the barista. "G'day, Gina! May I please have a flat white, and one for our American visitor, please? It's about time she knew what a decent coffee tastes like." He gestured at Heather with his thumb and flashed Gina his best attempt at a charming smile. He knew he was show-ing off a little, but he couldn't help it. It wasn't that he wanted to impress Heather, he just wanted to do a good job at the task Peter had assigned him. After all, it was the first useful thing he'd be able to do for the company in almost a year.

And, okay, he wanted to impress Heather.

Heather sipped her coffee, which, she had to admit, was nothing like the giant foamy drinks from Starbucks. This one had a thin layer of dense, rich foam at the top, and strongly flavored milk underneath. It was delicious, and she could already feel the caffeine perking her up.

Rather than sit inside, she and Marcus decided to sit out on the low wooden railing at the edge of the long finger wharf. The air was chilly, but the sun was strong, and she turned her face toward it, wrapping her hands around her warm green cardboard cup. Marcus eased himself down to sit and dangled both feet over the end of the wharf. Heather watched the water slosh gently around the pylons and wondered if she'd ever want to take a ballet class on dry land again.

A few minutes later, she'd drained her cup. "That was perfect."

"I'm telling you, Starbucks has been lying to you." Marcus sipped his coffee and barely concealed a triumphant little smile that revealed a charming dimple in his right cheek. His eyes sparkled, green and gold, like the water below. Butt Guy had an undeniably nice face to go with his undeniably nice butt.

"Now that I know the truth, I'll never go back," she promised, taking his empty cup and tossing both in the trash. "Thank you for that. What's next?"

"If you're up for a bit of a walk, we could go over the bridge," Marcus said, looking down at her with hope on his freckle-strewn face. He had a few days' worth of scruff, but it wasn't enough to conceal his square, solid chin. The light breeze caught strands of his hair and played with it, and she smothered the sudden urge to reach up and do the same.

That is absurd, she told herself. *You did not come halfway around the world just to start crushing on the first cute boy you meet.*

"Are you up for it?" she asked, glancing at his crutches.

"Oh, yeah, it's basically the only exercise I get these days, once Shaz is done with me."

"You sure it's not too far out of your way?"

"They've put you up in Kirribilli, right? I'm in Neutral Bay, one suburb over. I can always get you home and then get on a bus."

Slowly, they walked along the water toward the bridge, past a finger wharf that housed a luxury hotel, and another that looked like fancy condos. The harbor glittered, and Heather stopped to watch two large boats, dark-green on the bottom and pale-yellow on top, pass each other beneath the bridge.

"Commuter ferries," Marcus said as one boat slid out of view behind the other, then reappeared. "You can drive across the harbor or take a bus or a train, but nothing beats taking a boat to work."

They made their way around the headland, pausing under the bridge and leaning on the high iron fence at the edge of the sidewalk. In the wide band of the bridge's shadow, it was chilly, and Heather shivered slightly as she examined the underside of the massive structure. She could hear the rattle and thunk of cars passing overhead.

"That's Kirribilli," Marcus said, pointing straight across the water. "And that," he said turning to the right and pointing unnecessarily at the iconic white structure hanging off the edge of the next peninsula, "is the Opera House."

Heather heard a note of unhappiness in his voice, a flatness that wasn't there before. She glanced at him curiously and saw him gazing over at the building, looking anxious. She wondered.

They resumed their progress around the headland and walked in silence for a few minutes.

"What happened to your ankle?" she asked.

"Total Achilles rupture. I landed a tour wrong." He paused. "On stage."

Ah, Heather thought. *That explains that.* It was a common injury for men. Women tended to get sidelined by repetitive stress injuries in their toes and feet, because they spent so much time on pointe. But men were far more likely to blow out their ankles or knees from jumping, and their shoulders from lifting their partners.

She'd never been injured on stage before, but she'd seen it happen, and it had been simply awful. It was one thing to get hurt in rehearsal, surrounded by friends and colleagues. It was another to do it in front of an audience. Enough to traumatize you, even if the injury itself healed.

Plus, she thought, studying his profile as they walked, he wasn't young. Early thirties, maybe? An injury like that could have ended his career, and even if it didn't, he probably didn't have that many dancing years left. It was harsh, but it was also the reality of their profession.

"That's awful, I'm sorry. What kind of timeline did they give you?"

"Sharon says once I get basic motion back, it could be pretty quick. But it's been slow going so far," he said. Then he sighed and added, with grim determination in his voice, "but I've got other reasons for wanting to get back on stage."

Heather opened her mouth to ask but stopped herself. She didn't know this man, and years of dating Jack had taught her that asking questions someone didn't want to answer was a recipe for a fight. She decided to change the subject.

"How do we get up to the bridge?"

"We'll head up the hill through The Rocks," he replied. She must have looked perplexed, because he explained, "It's the name of the old neighborhood on this side of the bay. It's mostly for tourists now, but it's where the British started building when they arrived to set up their colony. Well, they tried to build farther south, near the airport, but the land was bad, so they came here instead."

Marcus led them around the headland and along shaded, sloping streets lined with squat sandstone buildings that looked old, but very well maintained. There were shops selling opal jewelry and sheepskin rugs and galleries with indigenous art in the windows. Tourists wandered, some toting selfie sticks and others lapping at large cones of what looked like gelato. They crossed a crowded commercial street and continued up the hill, tracing a path Heather knew she would never remember but one Marcus seemed to know well.

Soon, they found themselves on a steep street, at the bottom of an equally steep set of sandstone stairs. Tourists milled around in small groups, and Heather stepped aside quickly as a man in sweatpants and a tank top reading SYDNEY SWANS came jogging toward the stairs. She watched as he took them two at a time, gained the top, then disappeared.

"Sydneysiders are big on lunchtime workouts," Marcus explained. "That guy will be back at his desk wearing a suit in an hour, I bet." He was sweating slightly from the climb, and she noticed he'd unzipped his sweatshirt a few inches. His well-defined traps reached down his neck and across his shoulders as he leaned against the crutches, and she spotted a few determined chest hairs peeking out from under the fabric of the hoodie. Once again, she batted away a sudden and totally unprofessional urge to trace the lines of muscle with her fingertips.

"This is the last big climb," he said, and she realized she'd been gazing at his chest for slightly longer than was appropriate. She snapped her eyes up to his face.

"You don't have to reassure me," she said with a smile. "You're the one doing this on one leg."

"Yeah, but I do it every day." He smiled back. Then he paused for a moment, his eyes sparkling with mischief. "Wanna race?"

"Are you kidding me? I'm not racing a man on crutches, that's not fair."

"Well, that's very noble of you. How about we make it a fair fight, then? You . . ." He paused to think. "You have to run backwards."

"Up the stairs?"

"Yeah," he said, a grin creeping over his face. "Unless . . ." He raised his eyebrows and widened his eyes. "You don't want to *lose* to a man on crutches."

"Fine," she said, unable to keep a flirtatious lilt out of her voice. She waited for a group of tourists to clear the last few steps, then arranged herself with one foot on the landing and the other on the bottom stair. "Ready when you are, Sir Limpsalot."

Marcus let out a bark of a laugh, and the surprising sound of it sent a thrill of delight spiraling through her. She stood up a little straighter, wondering if he made that sound often, or if it was a rare, special occurrence. He joined her at the base of the steps, playfully jostling his shoulder against her bag.

"Ready?" he asked, and she nodded, meeting his eyes for a brief, stomach-flipping moment, and then fixing her gaze firmly straight ahead. "Set . . . go!"

She scrambled backward, glancing over her shoulder and realizing almost immediately what a terrible idea this had been. What if she sprained her ankle goofing around on her second day in Sydney? She picked her feet up high to clear each step, holding her breath as though that would keep her from tripping and falling backward. Marcus sped past her on the other side. She tried to move her feet faster, but it was no use. She was going to lose.

"Noooo!" Heather squealed. A tourist at the bottom of the stairs turned to look up at her, clearly baffled.

When she arrived at the top, panting, Marcus met her with a triumphant smile.

"Sir Limpsalot," he said, "is pretty fast."

She caught her breath, brushing her hair back out of her face and tightening her ponytail.

"Well done," she said.

"It wasn't really a fair matchup," he conceded, with a glance down at the crutches. "God knows I've had enough time to get good at moving around on these things."

"Still, a proper tour guide would have let me win," she said.

"Ah, well," he said, shaking his head ruefully, "I'm a volunteer tour guide. You get what you pay for."

Marcus couldn't remember the last time he'd smiled this much. By the time they reached the middle of the Harbour Bridge, his cheeks actually ached. They paused at the midpoint, because Heather said that the first time she'd come over the Bridge she'd meant to look up but had gotten distracted. So they paused a few minutes, the wind whipping up their hair as the cars roared past on the roadway, taking in the hundreds of lines of steel intersecting overhead.

On a normal day, he'd be walking alone, trying to get home as fast as possible, trying to break a sweat. Trying to feel like his body was still the tool he needed it to be. Today, though, he was happy to move leisurely, Heather strolling beside him. It wasn't that he'd normally ignore the beauty of the harbour—it was hard to miss, even if you'd grown up around it and commuted over it to work every day. But he usually had other things on his mind.

Now, he noticed the way the Bridge vibrated under his feet and through his crutches, how the mirrored sides of the high-rise apartment buildings across the roadway reflected the sky and turned the towers blue. And he was hyperaware of Heather, of her presence next to him, her movements in his peripheral vision. As they'd lined up to race at the bottom of the steps, he'd even caught a trace of her scent: lavender and the sweat of a hard class. His pulse had spiked as he'd crested the top, and it still hadn't settled, even though he'd slowed to an easy pace. He knew he shouldn't, but he couldn't stop glancing over at Heather every few moments—and each time he did, he felt his pulse kick again, until their stroll felt more like an interval workout.

As she admired the Bridge, Marcus tried to follow her gaze instead of tracing the long expanse of the skin of her neck with his eyes as she tipped her head way back. The line from her chin to the hollow at the base of her throat made a smooth, graceful curve.

At the very centre of the Bridge, two enormous flags fluttered in the brisk breeze.

"What are they?" she called over the din of the traffic.

He leant closer to make himself heard, and as he did so, his upper arm just happened to press gently against her sharp shoulder. Heat radiated down his arm and into his chest from where their bodies met, and he resisted the urge to flex. Just. Marcus held his breath, wondering if she'd lean away, break the contact, but she stayed and turned towards him to hear his reply. *Barre* magazine hadn't done her justice, hadn't captured the way her mahogany eyes sparkled with curiosity and interest, or the clever, skeptical arch of her eyebrows.

Marcus reminded himself to inhale so he could answer her question.

"The blue one is the Australian flag. The red, black, and yellow one is the Aboriginal flag. The fight to get it up there permanently took years."

She reached into her bag and pulled out her phone, taking a photo of the flags through the gaps in the elaborate crisscrossing steel. Then she turned and took a few of the harbour and the Opera House across the water, and they continued on until they reached the other side of the Bridge.

"How far are we from Kirribilli?" she asked before giving in to an enormous yawn.

Marcus gestured with his chin towards the top of another set of sandstone stairs. "We're here."

Down the stairs, they found themselves on the neighbourhood's main drag, across the street from a bottle shop and a little Thai restaurant.

"I can't believe you do that every day," she yawned again, her shoulders drooping a little. "That's a long walk."

He shrugged. "I didn't just get off a plane from the other side of the world. And I didn't take a ballet class, either." He tried, but failed, to keep any bitterness out of his voice. "Plus, sometimes I take the bus or the ferry."

A third yawn.

"I'm sorry, am I boring you with my thrilling tales of Sydney's public transit system?"

"No!" Heather said, with a little shake of her head. "I think I just need a nap. I know I'm not supposed to, with the time difference and everything, but I'm beat."

"Of course. I can walk you home, and we can continue our tour of Sydney tomorrow, if you like." She looked surprised for a moment.

"Unless," he said quickly, worrying he'd overstepped, "you think you've got it from here."

"No." She smiled, and he felt his heart quicken. "That sounds great. What have you got planned?"

She'd caught him off guard. "Uh, nothing yet. But you should probably know about the best beaches, right? We'll do a beach tomorrow."

Tired as she was, when Heather lay down on the fluffy white comforter, she couldn't sleep. She slipped her feet under the knit throw rug draped across the bottom of the bed and tried to let her mind go blank, but it was no use. Her body was buzzing, and despite her fatigue, she felt restless and fidgety. A result of the long flight and the jet lag, obviously. Certainly nothing to do with an unpaid tour guide with eyes the color of Sydney Harbour.

She sat up and sighed, scanning the small bedroom with its shining red-brown floorboards and floaty white curtains, then heaved herself up and to the bathroom to splash some water on her face. Watching herself in the mirror, she realized that even in her short time outside, she'd managed to get a mild sunburn. The tip of her nose was rosy, and her forehead looked a little pink, too. This Australian sun was no joke, even in winter. She added sunscreen to her mental list of things she should've packed. She would certainly need it if Marcus was taking her to a beach tomorrow.

Unbidden, the sound of Marcus's surprised bark of a laugh popped in her mind. Had Jack ever laughed at one of her jokes like that? If he had, she couldn't remember it.

It didn't matter. Marcus was showing her around because Peter had asked him to. He was being friendly because he was a friendly person, and again, because Peter had asked him to. He had seemed deflated at the idea that she might not want to go to the beach with him tomorrow because . . . well, she couldn't put that one on Peter.

She poked at her forehead and her chin, watching the skin turn white, then flood pink again. She had what Jack's mother Christine called "a stage face," meaning, Christine had explained, that her large eyes and sharp chin looked good from a distance, but not up close. She had said this in a very matter-of-fact kind of way at Thanksgiving dinner in the high-ceilinged Upper East Side apartment where Jack had grown up, a few years after Jack and Heather had started dating.

"It's like the costumes," Christine had said, cutting her turkey and then leveling a cold, toothy smile across the wide table at Heather. "If they look good on stage, they look ghastly in the dressing room." The woman even cut her food gracefully, Heather remembered thinking in awe, before she realized Christine had just insulted her.

"I mean that as a compliment," Christine had reassured her after a pause in which Heather had sat, speechless, wondering how on earth she was meant to respond. "It will be a boost to your career, I suspect." Christine's eyes sat wide and innocent beneath her oddly immobile forehead. She smiled tightly again, and her cheeks didn't budge. "Then again," she added, "so will dating Jack."

Heather remembered the effort it had taken to give a small polite nod while she waited for Jack to say something, to tell his mother she was out of line. He hadn't said a word.

She had never looked in the mirror again without thinking about that casual barb. She inspected her reflection for another moment, gave herself one more poke, then turned off the bathroom light.

Nobody wants a stage face. Especially not cute, bark-laughing Australians with perfect butts.

Chapter 5

The next morning, Heather entered the correct locker room on the first try. She smiled slightly as she filled up her water bottle at the fountain, remembering the look of surprise on Marcus's face as he'd found her standing in the doorway yesterday. For a split second, she allowed herself to picture what she'd seen just *before* he'd turned around—that butt, those sinewy thighs dusted with pale brown hair, that inviting muscular dimple at the base of his spine—but then she cleared her throat and, reluctantly, cleared the image from her mind.

Her bottle filled, she changed into a leotard and pulled a pair of tights over it. After sliding a few extra pins into her bun, just to be safe, she headed to Studio B. Even half an hour before class, there were already a dozen dancers here, some doing sit-ups with headphones in, others on the floor stretching or standing at the barre doing calf raises. One woman was on the ground, supporting herself on her forearms as she worked her quads with a narrow foam roller, wincing.

Heather returned to the same spot she'd taken at the barre yesterday and was about to start her usual warm-up routine—jumping jacks, crunches, then a series of stretches, always in that order—when someone called her name. She looked to see Alice walking toward her, in a baggy ANB sweatshirt and leggings, her long hair in a low ponytail.

"Hi again," Alice said. "Are you feeling better this morning?"

"Much," Heather said, starting her jumping jacks.

Alice joined in, and for a moment Heather thought she might be making fun of her, but Alice's face held no trace of mockery.

"How many?" Alice asked, a little breathlessly.

"Forty, then thirty crunches," Heather said, the voice distorted by her jumping.

"Yes ma'am. Are you settling in okay?"

"Yeah, though I'm a little daunted by the idea of taking a full class with Peter today. He's intense." Jumping jacks done, Heather lay on the floor with her knees up and started crunching.

"Oh, he won't teach today," Alice said, imitating her. "He only teaches once a week, and anyway, Thursday is company day."

"What do you mean?"

"The company members take turns teaching Thursday class," Alice said. "And lucky for you, today is my day."

"Oh, so you're a principal?"

"No, I'm in the corps," Alice said, managing to combine a shrug with a crunch.

"Oh, wow," Heather said vaguely, but then she remembered something she'd read in the press coverage she'd found: Most companies occasionally let principal dancers teach morning class, but Peter believed in giving all company members, even those in the corps, a chance to practice leadership. Especially the women, he'd told the paper, since most ballet companies were still run by men.

"So everyone in the company really teaches?" she asked Alice. She counted out her three final crunches, then climbed to her feet to stretch.

"Not everyone, but anyone who wants to. Peter thinks dancers should be ready for a life after they can't perform anymore."

Heather nodded, thinking about what Marcus had told her about his injury yesterday. Dance careers were all-consuming, but they could end in a split second. Then you were left adrift with no other skills or work experience. But then her thoughts slipped sideways, and she found herself wondering what Marcus was like when he taught the company on his assigned Thursdays. Was he quiet and serious like he'd been under the bridge? Or was he mischievous and lighthearted like when they'd raced up the stairs? She pushed her thoughts of him away—again—and focused on Alice, who had climbed to her feet and mirrored her calf stretch.

"Would you want to run a company one day?"

Alice shrugged again. "Maybe. It's a lot of work, and none of it looks that fun. But I do like to teach."

"Are you going to go easy on us?"

"Never," Alice grinned. "I hope you've had your Weet-Bix, Miss America, because I make Peter's class look easy."

Alice was true to her word. Heather had never done frappés so fast, or ronds de jambe en l'air so slow. By the time barre was over, she was drenched in sweat, and could only imagine what Alice had in store once they started dancing in the center. But as hard as Alice's combinations were, and as fast as she had the accompanist play as they all flitted frantically across the floor in petit allegro, the mood in the studio was more relaxed than in any ballet class Heather could remember taking.

Dancers were chatting and laughing between exercises, smiling as they took their turn sweeping across the floor in groups of three and four. Alice cracked jokes from the front of the room, correcting her colleagues' small mistakes and yelling out praise when one of them did particularly well.

"Yes, Nikki!" she called exuberantly, clapping as one of the younger-looking dancers finished an especially clean series of pirouettes.

"That's what I'm talking about, Matty!" she cried as a stocky guy stretched his arabesque longer than Heather would have thought possible and floated his leg down weightlessly behind him.

The studio had been chilly when Heather arrived, but after ninety minutes of dancing for Alice, the air was warm and pungent with sweat, the mirrors starting to fog. Alice dismissed them with a round of applause, and Heather stood a few feet from the open door, panting and enjoying the relief of the cool air on her skin.

Alice approached, grinning.

"How often do you teach?" Heather panted.

"Lucky for you, not that often," Alice said.

"No, I loved it," Heather said, truthfully. She wondered why NYB didn't let more of its dancers teach. She'd never thought about it before, but at home, almost every class was taught by Mr. K, or a ballet mistress, and the atmosphere was entirely different. Dancers barely spoke in class, and they definitely didn't laugh out loud. They had been trained since they were tiny children to quietly obey a teacher's orders, and it had never occurred to her that they were still doing it, even though they were adults and professionals now. There was something joyful about being taught by a peer, about learning from an equal.

"Did you really love it?" Alice said, looking skeptical, and a little bashful.

"Truly," Heather said firmly. "You're a natural. An absolutely ruthless natural."

Alice let out a joyful cackle, and Heather was reminded of Carly. She felt a sudden pang of homesickness, or rather, Carlysickness.

"I should get going," Alice said. "I want to grab a coffee before my rehearsal starts. When do you start rehearsing?"

"Next week, I think," Heather replied as they both made for the door. "In the meantime, I'm trying to get the hang of the city. Did you grow up here?"

"Nah," Alice said, retrieving her bag from under the piano, "I'm from Bendigo." Heather must have looked confused, because Alice added, "middle of Victoria, about two hours from Melbourne?" Heather made a mental note as they walked out: *Mel-ben, not Mel-born.*

"Ah, okay," she nodded. "And how long have you been with the company?"

"This is my sixth year. I joined right out of the school."

"And she's been killing us with her classes ever since," came a voice from behind them. Heather turned to see Marcus sitting on a bench, sipping a coffee and watching them with a fond smile.

"It's not my fault you can't hack it, old man," Alice called playfully over Heather's shoulder. She walked over to Marcus and looked him up and down. "Speaking of old men, is that a cane?"

Heather tore her eyes from Marcus's face to a metal cane with a curved rubber handle propped against the bench.

"It's only for now," Marcus grumbled, "and only if I need it. Shaz just cleared me for walking. Look ma, no crutches." He gave them sarcastic jazz hands.

"It's very stylish, but you should probably add a top hat and tails and get the full Fred Astaire look," Alice said with a smirk. Heather glanced from Alice to Marcus, her stomach squirming unpleasantly. Were they flirting? Or was this a big brother–little sister dynamic? It shouldn't matter to her, obviously. But still, she was curious.

Marcus rolled his eyes at Alice, and then stood, leaning gently on the cane. How did he manage to make leaning look that good? Even with his foot in his bulky boot, he looked Astaire-esque: graceful and at ease, as if he'd already integrated the cane into his body. She let her eyes linger on his broad shoulders and his strong, slender fingers wrapped around his coffee cup, and wondered for the first time what kind of a dancer he was, when he was well. Was he long lines and fast feet? Big bravura pirouettes and explosive jumps? She realized with disappointment that it would be months until he'd be back on stage, so she'd never know.

"You ready for the beach?" he asked Heather, and she nodded. Her muscles ached from Alice's merciless adagio combination, but at the thought of spending another afternoon with Marcus, her skin began to buzz again.

"Alice is gonna lend us her car for the day." Marcus stuck out his hand, and Alice dug into her bag, rummaging for a moment before pulling out a jangling set of keys.

"Are you sure you can drive with that thing?" she asked, looking down at the cam boot.

"Yes, Mum, I am sure."

"Hey, that's a compliment, because your mum is awesome." Alice looked over her shoulder at Heather. "And are you sure you want to spend the day with him?"

Heather gave a small, awkward smile that she hoped concealed the return of yesterday's restless energy, which had begun coursing through her body the moment she heard Marcus's voice.

"Uh, well," she said, deciding to join in on the playful ribbing. "I don't want to, but Peter's the boss, right? Come on, tour guide." She cocked her eyebrows at him, and the grin he gave her in return made her breath catch in her throat. Alice handed over the keys.

"Have fun, Fred and Ginger," she called as Heather and Marcus headed toward the lobby.

Marcus had thought long and hard about which beach he should show Heather. Sydney had dozens of ocean beaches, stretching along the coast from the centre of the city in both directions. The huge and convoluted harbour was dotted with dozens more beaches, sheltered ones, where the water was flat and peaceful. Some were a kilometre long, and others were tiny, tucked away in hidden bays even some locals didn't know were there. Marcus had grown up down the street from one of the city's best surf beaches, Freshwater, but it was too far from the studios to bring Heather there. Too close to home, too.

From the esplanade at Balmoral Beach, you could see right out past North Head, the headland that formed one side of the harbour's snug mouth. Past the calm water lapping at the golden sand, past the clusters of sailboats anchored offshore, North Head's steep, forbidding face towered over choppy water at the edge of the open ocean. At the turn of the century, Balmoral had been a destination for Sydney's well-to-do and fashionable, who would stroll along the esplanade with their parasols and wade into the water in their Victorian bathing dresses. These days, it would be packed all summer with scampering children, leather-skinned retirees, and teenage boys trying not to stare at the occasional topless sunbather.

Marcus pulled Alice's car into an open parking spot across from the fish-and-chip shop and climbed out as gracefully as he could.

"Is there somewhere I can change?" Heather asked as he pulled his cane from the back seat. Marcus realised she was still wearing her leotard, tights, and garbage-bag pants.

"Yeah, of course, there are public toilets just down there," Marcus said, pointing down the wide esplanade to a small green building. He eased himself across the grass and sat on a bench to wait.

A steady stream of people passed by as he waited. There was a white-haired man walking an old, stiff-legged dog, and a trio of chattering mums in expensive-looking yoga pants with babies strapped to their fronts. Here and there tourists wandered past, periodically lifting their cameras from around their necks to snap photos of the calm blue water and the striking view right out to the heads. The water wasn't warm enough for Marcus to want to swim, but a few brave souls were out for a dip. He watched one of them glide by in a dark wetsuit, envious of how elegantly they moved through the water.

"New York City is on the water, too, but it just smells so good here." Heather was back, dressed in black leggings, a white T-shirt, and a faded denim jacket. Her hair was loose, and she shook out the kinks caused by a tight bun and a sweaty class. With some difficulty, Marcus averted his eyes and surveyed the beach rather than watch her run her hand through her hair. She sat down next to him, folding her legs underneath herself.

"Sadly, we can't offer the exciting garbage odours of a big city like New York. All we have here is fresh air, stunning views, strong coffee, and excellent fish and chips." He gestured to his right at a little building, which seemed to stick out of the water on stilts. "Down at that boathouse, you can buy overpriced baked goods *and* rent a kayak. We can go have a look if you want. I haven't checked with Shaz, but I think she'd be okay with me walking on the sand."

"Why do you call her Shaz? Isn't her name Sharon?"

"It's how Australians do nicknames. Either you add an *O*, so Dave becomes Davo, or Rob becomes Robbo, or if the name has *A-R* in it, it gets a *Z*. So . . . Harry becomes Haz, or Carol becomes Caz."

"And Sharon becomes Shaz."

"Yeah, or Shazza."

"Our company PT's name is Dr. Rajendra, and I'm trying to imagine what would happen if we called him something like that. I don't even know his first name."

"Yeah, but I doubt Shaz would even answer if I walked into physio and called her 'Dr. Murphy.'"

Heather laughed and shook her head. "I had no idea I'd need a dictionary to survive here. This morning was hard enough, trying to decipher Alice's French with an Australian accent." She paused for a moment, then added, "Alice seems pretty great."

Her voice was light and casual. Almost as if, Marcus thought, she was trying very hard to keep it that way.

"She's pretty great," he confirmed. And then, because it suddenly seemed very important to clarify what he'd meant, he said, "She's like my little sister. A pain in my ass, and willing to beat the shit out of someone for me."

Heather raised her eyebrows, looking sceptical. "Oh, she's small," Marcus assured her, "but she's mighty. You saw her in class today. You do not wanna fuck with Alice Ho."

It was true, Marcus thought. Okay, so he'd never actually seen her beat someone up, or threaten to, but Alice was one of the fiercest and most loyal people he knew. When she'd joined the company, she'd been serious and quiet, the way so many girls were when they graduated from ballet school. But after a few months, she'd grown comfortable, and Marcus had realised that while she was dead serious about ballet, she was not a naturally quiet person.

She'd been his partner in a few ballets that year, when they were both in the corps and dancing peasant roles in *Swan Lake* or playing courtiers at the Capulet ball in *Romeo and Juliet*. They'd spent hours together in rehearsal and slogged through night after night of performances under the hot lights at the Opera House. They'd been friends ever since. When the company toured, they would often buddy up, sitting next to each other on planes and finding the best spot for dinner in whatever city they were in. Alice was fun to travel with, because she could make a joke or a game out of just about anything. A few years ago, the company had gone viral because they'd spent a long layover at Singapore airport filming themselves doing big pas de deux lifts and pretending to do barre on the moving walkways. The whole thing had been Alice's idea.

"And you two aren't . . ." Heather's cheeks flushed an enticing pink as she trailed off awkwardly, confirming his suspicions about her earlier comment. Excitement and dread warred in his chest, and he suppressed a groan at the unfairness of the situation. Here he was with The Heather Hays, with her wide eyes and expressive brows and deliciously pink cheeks. The first woman he'd even noticed in over a year. Here they were, dancing around the question, and he had to be the one to stop the music. He fidgeted with the handle of his cane, putting off the moment of truth.

"We're not," he said finally. "Even if we were into each other— which we're not—we wouldn't dare violate Pas de Don't."

Heather looked at him quizzically. "Is that more Australian slang?"

"No, it's what the dancers call the company's fraternisation policy. One of Peter's many reforms: he's got a strict no-dating-within-the-company rule."

"What?" Heather scoffed. "How does that even work? Every company I've ever heard of has multiple married couples in it."

"Oh, so do we. They were exempted when Peter made the policy. I mean, he couldn't exactly make them split up, could he? But no new relationships allowed."

"And what happens if you break the rule?"

"You get fired," he said simply.

She stared at him. "Are you serious?"

"Deadly," he nodded. "I think Peter witnessed some fairly full-on sexual harassment when he was a dancer, and you know how many MeToo scandals there've been in ballet in the last few years. Peter takes that stuff really seriously. He says a no-dating policy makes for a more professional and harmonious work environment." He probably wasn't wrong, Marcus thought. It was pretty awkward being in a rehearsal with two dancers you knew had just started hooking up or watching people in the middle of a nasty breakup trying to playact as lovers on stage.

"So he's actually fired people who got caught?"

"Yep, two guys from the corps got busted fooling around last year, and he sacked them on the spot."

"Is that even legal?"

"It's ballet," he shrugged. "Peter's a reformer and everything, but . . . legally he can still fire us for just about anything if he wants."

Heather cocked her head to the side and frowned. "Why didn't I know anything about this?" she asked. "I read up on the company and all Peter's reforms, but I didn't see anything about . . . Pas de Don't."

"Probably because the dancers hate it. I mean, it's well intentioned, but it makes our lives pretty difficult. It's hard to date outside of ballet, you know?"

"Pretty hard to date inside ballet too," Heather retorted.

"Uh, yeah, that too," Marcus said quickly, hearing the bitter edge in her voice and hating it. "Anyway, Alice and I are just mates. Friends, I mean. I'm, uh, I'm not seeing anyone right now. Very single."

He glanced over at her and saw an unnameable expression on her face. Relief?

"But if you were to date someone, they'd have to be outside the company," she said flatly, turning to meet his eyes. "Those are the rules."

"Those are the rules." He held her gaze for a few long seconds, wondering if his face was betraying any of his disappointment. Then, seized by an urge to move and put some physical distance between them, he pulled himself to his feet. "Shaz says I should practice walking as much as I can."

They strolled slowly along the esplanade in silence. Just as he had yesterday, he felt hyperaware of her next to him, not least because her shoulder kept brushing against his arm. Was she touching him on purpose?

"Sorry," she said, with a small shake of her head. "Walking on the left is going to take some getting used to. My body wants to be over there." She pointed to the other side of the wide footpath. So, no, she was not touching him on purpose. *My body wants to be over there. What else would her body want?* he wondered, before swatting the question away. *Don't go there*, he thought. She'd just broken off an engagement and was only in the country a short while. Plus, Pas de Don't. It was hard to imagine anyone more off-limits than the woman walking beside him.

"You can ask about it, if you like," she said, interrupting his thoughts.

"About what?" he asked guiltily.

She looked up at him and pulled her sharp chin down firmly, her eyes meeting his with an expression that plainly said, *Cut the crap.* After a confused moment, he realised what she meant.

"About how my fiancé screwed a corps member behind my back and how, when I found out, I fell apart and ran away to the other side of the world," she said, matter-of-factly. Her voice was steady, but Marcus noticed that, as she spoke, she crossed her arms tightly across her chest and pressed her forearms against her stomach. She turned away from him and looked out at the water.

"I did hear something about that," he said. She gave him that look again, holding his gaze a little longer this time. Her eyes bore into his, challenging him. "Okay," he conceded. "Everyone heard something about that."

"No secrets in ballet. Well," she scoffed, "*almost* no secrets."

"Fuck that guy," Marcus shrugged. "He's a tosser. Men in ballet think they're God's gift to dance. I mean, no offence to what's-his-face," he said, as if every male ballet dancer in the world didn't know Jack Andersen's name, "but as long as a guy can do half a pirouette and is willing to wear tights, they'll put him on stage and let him do whatever he wants off of it." Marcus knew Jack Andersen could do at least eight perfect pirouettes, on both sides, if you asked him to. And the Prince of American Ballet didn't just wear tights, he looked like the very concept of tights had been invented for him.

Marcus had looked at the guy's Instagram feed the previous afternoon, when he'd gotten home from dropping Heather in Kirribilli. He had never seen anyone so . . . symmetrical. Jack Andersen looked like he'd been genetically engineered in the same lab that made the Hemsworth brothers. He was bronzed and blue-eyed, and his straight teeth were a bright American white. It was easy to see why the role that had made him a star was Apollo, the sun god. Marcus couldn't imagine that anyone looked more like the princely ideal of the danseur noble than Jack Andersen.

But he'd also spent six years listening to Alice talk about how well men in ballet were treated, and how badly a lot of them treated women. And as special as Heather's ex was, in this regard, he doubted he was any different from the assholes Alice complained about. From what Marcus had heard, he was probably worse.

He looked over at Heather and found her watching him, her mouth open in surprise.

"What?" he said, bringing his hand to his cheek. "Do I have something on my face?"

"No," she chuckled. "That was just a bit unexpected."

"Well, it's true," Marcus said, relieved.

"And you think you're better than that, do you?" she said, her eyebrows raised skeptically again. He liked the shape they made as they lifted. So arched and expressive.

"Well, as we've established, I'm not allowed to sleep with or marry a colleague," he said placidly. They walked past a huge Moreton Bay fig tree, its sprawling branches reaching out over the esplanade, casting patchy shadows on the sand below. "But if I were, I certainly wouldn't sleep with one when I was about to marry another. And if you ask me, that's a pretty low bar."

Heather blinked a few times, then glanced back out at the water. "Yeah, it is," she said softly, as if more to herself than him.

"He wasn't always a . . . whatever you just called him," she said after a moment. "He could be attentive and loving when he wanted to be. Or when it suited him, I guess. And he really was, at the start. It wasn't until later that I started to feel like he was—"

"A tosser?" he interrupted. "Come on, you can say it."

She managed a small smile. "Yeah, okay, he was a . . . tosser," she said, saying the word slowly, as though she was speaking it for the first time in her life. Which, he realised, she probably was.

"A complete tosser?" he pressed.

"A complete, total, absolute, utter *tosser*," she confirmed, loudly enough that an elderly man on a nearby bench startled and stared at them. She gasped and clapped her hand over her mouth, and Marcus snorted.

They continued in silence for another minute, then she spoke again. "It's a good rule, Pas de Don't. No mess, no drama, just a . . . 'harmonious and professional work environment.' Maybe every company should have that rule." She gave him a wry, half-hearted smile.

It was a good rule, Marcus thought to himself as they approached the boathouse café. Then again, he had never met someone who made him want to break it.

Heather sat on a bench on the boardwalk and watched the water as they ate in contented silence. The wind whipped her hair around her face and stung her eyes a little, but it felt glorious, invigorating.

Marcus had suggested they eat lunch here and had acquiesced when she insisted on paying for him this time. She had vetoed his suggestion of fish and chips, rolling her eyes slightly at the mere thought of all that deep fried food, no matter how much of a "classic Aussie beach meal" it was.

"You know I can't eat that," she said simply.

"I shouldn't either," he conceded, with an impish shrug, "but as your tour guide, I had to offer."

So they settled on sourdough sandwiches instead, with coffees to go. Heather had learned how to order a coffee the way she liked it, and now knew that if she asked for a skim flat white "with one," the barista would stir the sugar in for her.

While she ate, taking her time with the avocado and alfalfa sprouts, Marcus practiced walking without the cane. He rolled his weight carefully over his left heel, watching his feet in the grass as he paced slowly back and forth. Heather tried to keep her eyes on the water, but she couldn't stop herself from sneaking looks at him.

She'd spent so much of her life around men with rippling muscles that they had become almost unremarkable to her: virtually every male dancer she knew was lean and cut in a way that male models could only dream of. But not every male dancer had a cheeky smile and full, soft-looking lips. Not every male dancer had deep-green eyes that sparkled when he made a joke or widened in delight when he laughed at one of hers. The golden flecks she'd noticed yesterday seemed brighter today, especially when he laughed. His eyes were warm and inviting, and for some reason she liked how it felt when they landed on her.

He would literally lose his job if he got caught with you, she thought sternly, *and you would too.* ANB had been the only company willing to hire her without Jack by her side. She'd already humiliated herself in front of one major ballet company, and the last thing she needed was to get kicked out of this one. *You're here to dance,* she reminded herself. *You're here to prove you still exist without Jack.*

Heather finished her sandwich and stood, pulling out her phone to snap a photo of the view. She took a few shots of the beach to her right, where a few dozen anchored sailboats bobbed lazily just offshore. Carly would like that view, she thought.

She looked over her shoulder at Marcus, who was still pacing, his back to her. Carly would like *that* view more.

"Hey, Marcus?" she called, and as he turned to face her, smiling, she took a photo.

"Not bad, right?" he gestured out at the water. *Not bad,* she thought, *and the beach is nice, too.*

"It's gorgeous. But I guess I thought Australian beaches were all about surfing."

"Lots of them are," he said, walking slowly back to the bench and collecting the cane. "But sometimes you just want to take a nice calm dip, you know?"

"Do you know how to surf?"

"I used to. I grew up near a surf beach, and my dad taught me and my brother when we were little. But once I got serious about dancing, it just seemed too risky."

"Figures," Heather said. "My teacher told my mom she couldn't buy me Rollerblades, and my friend Carly's parents weren't allowed to take her skiing." Her mom had probably been secretly relieved at the prohibition, Heather realized years later. Rollerblades were expensive. Skiing, of course, had been out of the question. "Do your parents still live near the beach?"

His face tightened, and he dropped his eyes to the grass.

"My mum does," he said slowly. "My dad died. About ten months ago. Lung cancer." He swallowed and kept his gaze on the ground.

"I'm so sorry," she said quietly.

With what looked like considerable effort, he pulled his eyes up to meet hers. The glimmer of mischief she'd seen several times was gone, and his mouth was an unsmiling line. She recognized the expression from yesterday: it was the way he'd looked as they'd rounded the tip of the headland under the Harbour Bridge and she'd caught sight of the Opera House.

Then she remembered what he'd told her about his injury: it had happened about a year ago. What a hellish year it must have been for him. Before she could stop herself, she put a tentative hand on his shoulder and gave it a light, cautious squeeze. He didn't react, seemingly lost in his thoughts.

"Did you hurt your Achilles before or after?"

"Before." His voice was thick and hoarse, and she resisted the urge to put her arm all the way around his broad shoulders. "A few days before he was meant to come see me dance. He'd been crook for a while, and—" he stopped and swallowed hard, then took a deep breath. "And we all knew it was probably the last time he'd see me dance. And then . . . he didn't get to."

"I'm sorry," she said again, knowing even as she said them how pointless and insufficient the words were. What an unimaginable series of catastrophes.

"Yeah, thanks," he shrugged. "It's been a rough year, but at least this is healing," he added, kicking his left foot up gently.

"You looked pretty good just now," she said, trying to inject some brightness into her voice. "Oh God," she said, realizing quickly what she'd said. "I meant, I don't mean—not *good*-good, I just," she floundered, "you were walking well, and it didn't look like it hurt too much." What was wrong with her? He'd just told her his father had died, and now she sounded like she was hitting on him. She was making such a mess of this.

He smiled weakly at her. "You're more graceful than this on stage, right?" he said. His smile widened, his eyes unmistakably sly.

"God, I hope so," she replied, with a relieved smile of her own. "Otherwise Peter has made a very expensive mistake."

"We'll just blame it on the jet lag," he said, standing up. "Speaking of which, should we get you home?"

"Oh, sure," Heather said, a little surprised and, if she was honest with herself, a little disappointed. Awkward moments and painful memories aside, she'd been having a good time with him. He was funny and earnest, and he didn't seem to mind when she contradicted him. With Jack, she'd expended so much energy trying to keep him happy, alert to any conflict she needed to smooth over. But she didn't feel the need to do that with Marcus.

It doesn't matter, she told herself as they gathered their trash and walked back to the car. *You're here to dance. And besides, why would anyone risk getting fired just to go out with you?*

Marcus was silent as he drove up the steep hill from Balmoral. They didn't speak as he turned on to Military Road, followed it through Mosman's commercial area, and along the peninsula back to Kirribilli. Occasionally he glanced over at Heather, who stared wordlessly out the window at the posh shops lining the busy thoroughfare.

He tried to remember the last time he'd had two good days in a row. Two days when he'd smiled without it feeling like work, when he'd had the mental energy to think of a joke to crack before the conversation had moved on without him. It had been months since he'd sat with someone in a silence that felt comfortable, not heavy with grief or fear or unspoken bitterness. It had been even longer since he'd felt a physical pull towards someone, since he'd felt the kind of thrilling awareness of a woman's body that he'd felt just driving with Heather in the passenger seat.

It was a relief to find he was still capable of it. And it was a slight shock to discover that, without even realizing, a large part of him had given up on ever being able to do it again. It felt like realizing only after he'd slipped on a warm jumper that he'd been cold this whole time.

When they arrived at Heather's place, he watched her unbuckle her seatbelt and gather her things, her delicate fingers fumbling slightly with the button. As she bent to grab her bag, her ponytail fell over her shoulder against her cheek, and he had to grip the steering wheel to stop himself from sweeping it back for her. *Don't be stupid*, he told himself. *As if The Heather Hays is going to break company policy for you.* Even if she'd looked as disappointed as he felt when he'd told her about Pas de Don't, he needed to keep his hands out of her hair, and the rest of his body as far away from her as possible. He knew this, and now she knew it, too. But as she put her hand on the door handle, he threw caution to the wind anyway.

"What do you want to do tomorrow?"

She looked at him, seemingly surprised. "How many days of tour guide duty did Peter ask you to do?"

"Well, I guess he didn't really specify. But Sydney's a pretty big city. Lots to see."

"Please don't feel like you have to do this. I don't want to be a burden."

"It's not a burden. Really," he added, because she looked unconvinced. "I'm having a good time." *For the first time in a long time.*

"Okay," she said finally. "I'll take your tour guide services for one more day."

"Any requests?"

"Um, this is kind of touristy, but I would love to see a koala bear."

"That is pretty touristy. But I'll see what I can do."

She smiled and got out. He watched her walk over the nature strip and open the low wrought-iron gate of the little terrace house, the late afternoon sun finding bronze threads in her long dark hair as she moved. For the first time since that terrible night at the Opera House, Marcus realised, he was looking forward to tomorrow.

Chapter 6

Carly, 2:25 AM: 👀 *THAT'S your tour guide??* 👀
Carly, 2:25 AM: Is he into women?
Carly, 2:26 AM: If yes, you should tie his kangaroo down, sport 🦘🔥

Heather scoffed and shook her head. She had been right: Carly liked the photo she'd taken of Marcus at the beach yesterday, and overnight she'd filled up Heather's inbox with emoji proof of her appreciation, as well as photos of her ZZ plant, whose leaves were perky and glossy green. Heather pulled her phone from the nightstand and rolled back to the middle of her bed, yawning widely. For the first time since arriving in Sydney, she'd managed to sleep through the night.

Heather, 7:47 AM: Yes, pretty sure he's into women.
Heather, 7:48 AM: But ANB has a firm "no dating" rule. And they're serious about it. Apparently two guys got fired last year.

She looked up at the molded ceiling, tracing the floral pattern absentmindedly while she waited for Carly's reply. She ached all over, but it was a pleasant kind of pain, a reminder that she'd worked her muscles hard in Alice's class yesterday. She had just pulled one knee up to her chest to stretch out her hips and hamstrings when her phone vibrated.

> *Carly, 7:50 AM: Booooo. Maybe you should try breaking the rules for once, then* 😬

Heather shook her head and rolled herself out of bed. Of course Carly would say that, she thought with a smile. The easiest way to get her best friend to do something was to tell her that someone, somewhere, had made a rule saying she couldn't.

Heather, on the other hand, had always been a rule-follower. She didn't always want to be, but it was hard to make it in ballet if you weren't. And there were so many rules: rules for how to do your hair, for what color leotard to wear, for how to stand and walk and place your feet and bow to the teacher at the end of class. Some of them existed for good reason. Some of them were there because they'd always been there. Heather always tried to obey both kinds, even when it irked her, because she knew that's what her mother expected from her.

Her mom could never have sent Heather to the company school if she hadn't been offered a full ride, and Heather had learned early on that the best thing she could do—the best way to make her mother's life easier—was to keep her head down, do as she was told, and work her ass off. Linda had enough on her plate working, taking night classes, and raising a daughter on her own, a daughter who happened to have a talent for a very expensive after-school activity. She didn't need the added worry about whether that daughter was getting kicked out of ballet class for doing cartwheels, which Carly had definitely done.

Twice.

Heather loved Carly to pieces, but Carly had rich parents who could buy, bargain, or donate her out of basically any problem. While Heather had spent her teen years collecting quarters for the subway, Carly's parents gave her a fat wad of cash to pay for cabs. She'd always invited Heather along for the ride. Even now Heather was always welcome in the Montgomerys' huge apartment on the Upper West Side, where the rooms were furnished with priceless antique furniture and the walls were crowded with modern art. The Montgomerys even had enough room on the second floor to build Carly her own small ballet studio so she could practice any time she wanted.

Once Heather and Carly had gotten their company contracts and moved out of the dorms, Carly had returned her father's credit card and made a point of not accepting any more money from her parents. Heather knew perfectly well that with their help, Carly could have spent her first few years in the company living in a much nicer apartment than the one they'd shared, but she'd insisted on only looking at places in Heather's budget. Still, Carly had grown up safe in the knowledge that her parents' money would always be there if she needed it.

Yes, it might be fun to try breaking the rules for once, but we can't all cartwheel through life. She decided not to reply.

An hour later, Heather had completed her morning routine. She'd eaten a bowl of cereal and a banana. She'd twisted her hair up into a braided bun and applied her usual daytime makeup. Sure, she had deviated a little from her usual makeup sequence and spent a little more time on it than she would have for a regular company class. As she'd applied a second coat of mascara, she'd told herself it was simply because she wanted to conceal the lingering jet lag and look presentable for her new colleagues; after all, she was still making first impressions. For the same reason, she'd dabbed lavender oil on her wrists and pressed them against the sides of her neck, something she usually reserved for going out to dinner.

But there was no point lying to herself, she realized as she locked the front door. As she glanced up at the hulking bridge, her stomach fluttered with nerves that had nothing to do with company class, and she strode toward the bus stop, buzzing with anticipation that had nothing to do with seeing a koala bear for the first time.

Just a few leotards. That's what Heather had said. She was down to her last clean one, and hadn't packed enough for a month, she'd explained, even though she was usually so careful and organized about packing. So, she'd asked, could they stop by a dancewear shop on the way to the zoo and pick up just a few leotards?

Marcus perched awkwardly on a plastic display platform, next to a headless mannequin dressed in a hot pink leotard and arranged in first position. Techno music throbbed overhead, threatening to give him a headache.

When they'd walked in almost an hour ago, the woman behind the counter took one look at Heather and was totally starstruck.

"Oh my God," she'd gasped, "aren't you Heather Hays?"

"Um, yes," Heather had started, "and I need a few leot—"

"I can't believe Heather Hays is in my shop right now," the woman blurted, raising her perfectly manicured hands to her impeccably made-up face. "This is absolutely mental."

She'd rushed around the counter to shake Heather's hand, and Marcus watched as Heather quickly masked her surprise and greeted the woman politely, asking her name and inquiring about her background in dance. He could tell she'd done it before, and watching her, he remembered that in a dance-mad city like New York, she must get recognized on the street fairly often.

The woman, whose name was Izzy and who had been a dancer her whole life until she quit because of a back injury but who still loved to go see ANB and couldn't wait to see Heather perform with them—she told Heather all this in one long, breathless sentence— had showed them some of her new stock, then took Heather's bag and jacket to a fitting room.

"I wish I could offer you a sparkling water or something," Izzy said, like she was running a couture boutique, and Marcus had suppressed a laugh. He'd been to Dancewear Central dozens of times and no one had ever offered him a beverage of any kind. He watched, amused, as Heather wandered around the shop, Izzy at her heels, peppering her with information about each leotard brand.

Soon, Heather had disappeared into the dressing room to try on what, to Marcus's dismay, looked like several dozen leotards.

"I'll be as quick as I can," she'd said to him apologetically on her way in.

"Take your time. You're making Izzy's day. I think she's going to propose soon."

"Shut up," she replied, with a grin and a roll of her eyes, and closed the dressing room door behind her.

Marcus sat patiently, trying not to think about Heather undressing over and over again, mere metres away from him. She was off-limits, and today was his final day of showing her around. Starting next week, she'd be in rehearsals all afternoon and she wouldn't have time to see the sights with him. He knew he should feel relieved, but all he really wanted was to get over to the zoo, so he could see the look on her face when she saw a real-life koala.

Eventually, after Heather had tried on seemingly every leotard in the shop, she called to Izzy that she'd found a few she wanted to buy.

Izzy rushed to the door, holding a white tutu skirt.

"Do you need a rehearsal tutu?" she asked loudly.

Say no, Marcus thought, *the company has ones you can borrow. Say no.*

"Oh." Heather sounded surprised. "I guess I do. I left mine in New York." Marcus swallowed a groan.

The door cracked open, and Izzy slipped the wide, stiff skirt through to Heather.

"It's free if I can take a photo of you in it for our Instagram feed," Izzy said, hopefully.

"Uh, sure. Thank you, that would be great. Marcus, just one more thing and then we can go, okay?"

"No worries," he called back, trying to ignore how good his name sounded coming out of her mouth.

He glanced around the shop, noting that the tiny boys' and men's section had hardly expanded in the decades since he'd first come here with his parents, his dad clutching the school-issued list of clothes and accessories Marcus would need. Davo had spent the whole afternoon snarking impatiently, and eventually his dad had ordered him to go across the way to the sporting goods shop and wait for them there.

Just then, Marcus's phone vibrated in his pocket. Speak of the snarky devil.

Davo, 1:30 PM: U right to go see mum tomorrow?

Marcus sighed. He'd allowed himself to hope Davo would be too busy this weekend to push on with Operation Sell the House. He should have known better. Once his brother decided to do—or not do—something, he didn't let anything stand in his way.

Marcus, 1:31 PM: Yeah no worries, what time?
Davo, 1:32 PM: 4?
Marcus, 1:32 PM: Works for me.

"Wow, it fits you perfectly," Izzy said, clearly awestruck.

Marcus looked up, and for a moment he forgot how to breathe. Heather stood in the doorway wearing a forest green leotard with a deep scoop at the front, the mirror behind her revealing a panel of delicate green lace in the back. She'd pulled the practice tutu on, and Izzy was right: it fit her slim waist perfectly. She wasn't wearing tights, and Marcus stared, realizing that he was seeing her bare legs for the first time. They were taut and muscular, and even as she let Izzy fluff the skirt out, they were turned out in a loose fourth position. He spotted a birthmark just above her left knee, a small patch of darker skin, like she'd spilled milky coffee on the inside of her thigh.

"How does it look?" she asked him.

Marcus gaped, aware she was waiting for his answer but unable to find the appropriate words. *Perfect. Better than I let myself imagine. Ruinously beautiful.* None of those would do.

"Yeah, good," he finally managed, hardly knowing what he was saying.

"Okay, this'll just take a minute," Heather said, and she followed Izzy to the area reserved for pointe shoe fittings. One wall was fitted with a mirror and barre, the other wall taken up by floor-to-ceiling shelves crowded with glossy shoes. The tutu bounced gently around her hips as she walked.

Marcus watched, still a little dazed, as Heather took the barre with one hand and rose up into sous sus, one strong leg tucked behind the other and the balls of her feet pressing against the floor.

As Izzy directed her, crouching and kneeling to find the perfect angle, Marcus watched Heather move slowly through a series of positions—coup de pied, retiré, and then a slow, high developpé in second. Each of them was technically perfect, the result of decades of practice, but the way Heather's face lit up with joy as she moved made it look as though she was discovering each position for the first time. For a split second, as she balanced on one leg with the other foot level with her shoulder, she caught his eye, and there went his breath again. Then she lifted her hand off the barre and brought both arms to high fifth, beaming at him as she did. In that moment, there was nothing in the world but Heather Hays's radiant smile. No pounding techno music, no chatty, enthusiastic photographer. Just Heather, with her graceful arms, strong, steady legs, and the smile that stole all the air from his lungs.

"Perfect, that's the one!" Izzy exclaimed, and Heather brought her hand back to the barre and came down from relevé as fluidly as she'd gone up. Marcus gave his head a little shake, reminding himself again that Heather—and her smile, and her milky-coffee birthmark—were totally off-limits to him.

She hurried back to the dressing room, and Izzy followed behind, taking the leotards Heather had chosen to the register to ring them up. Marcus sat back and dug his hand into his pocket to check the time again. At this rate, they'd never make it to the zoo.

"Darn it," Heather muttered through the dressing room door.

"You right?"

"Uh, yeah," she said quickly, her voice faint and muffled. "I'm just . . . dammit! I'm just stuck in this thing."

Marcus put his hand on his cane and started to stand, then thought better of it. He couldn't very well invite himself into her dressing room, even if it was to help her.

Seconds ticked by, and he heard Heather groan impatiently, which somehow managed to be endearing.

He stood but didn't move towards her door. She made the little sound again, and he smiled to himself. He should alert Izzy, who could rescue her.

"Do you need some help?" he asked, right as she said, "Can you please help?"

Marcus froze, then gave himself another little shake and walked over. She wasn't asking him to undress her, she was asking him to help her get undressed, and there was a world of difference between the two. Still, he hovered awkwardly outside the door for a moment, and glanced over his shoulder at the cash register, where Izzy was folding the leotards into pale pink tissue paper. He tapped quietly with his knuckles.

The lock slid back, and he pushed the door open gently to sidle inside. "Thanks," she said, sounding relieved.

Heather stood with her back to the mirror, craning her head over her shoulder and examining the back of the tutu. In the mirror, he could see the skin of her upper back through the dark green lace, and as she twisted her body, he watched the tight fabric cling to her small, pert breasts and her narrow, muscled waist.

"They're these tiny hooks and eyes," she murmured, without looking at him. She brought her hands to the waistband and twisted it at the point where it closed. "I think they're just really snug because it's new."

Marcus's mouth had gone too dry to manage a reply. She was so close, and she smelled like lavender and heat. Half of him wanted to throw open the door and get as far away from her as he could. The other half wanted to slam the door and lock them in here together forever. Instead, he closed the door carefully, hoping Izzy hadn't noticed his absence or seen where he'd gone. He propped his cane in the corner and leant against the wall.

"Let me try," he said quietly, and she turned and backed up towards him. He bent down, keeping his hips propped against the wall, and took a closer look at the closure on the skirt. This close to her, he could smell her shampoo. He slipped his fingers carefully inside the waistband and felt his mouth go even drier as his heart began to race. The fabric of the leotard was soft against his hands, and he tried not to think about this one thin velvety layer being the only thing between his fingers and Heather's bare skin. For one short, idiotic moment, he let himself imagine he was undressing her, not just helping her. The thought made blood rush in his ears, and his hands shook around the closure.

Marcus leant closer still, applying pressure to the top hook and pushing it out of the eye.

"That's one down," he said, his voice low, victorious. He looked up at the mirror and saw that her eyes were glued to him, watching his hands as he worked. She lifted her gaze, and their eyes met in the mirror. He was suddenly aware that she'd been holding her breath this whole time.

"Breathe," he said, straightening and giving her a tiny, cheeky smile. "We'll get you out of this. You will not have to go to the zoo in a tutu."

She exhaled slowly, her ribs relaxing above his hands. Then she turned to face him.

* *

Heather stood in the dressing room, which felt spacious before Marcus slipped inside, bringing warm air and a faint musk with him. Maybe it was the jet lag, or the comforting way he'd joked with her. She didn't know, exactly. All she knew was she wanted to kiss him now. And before she could second-guess herself or remind herself of the rules that prohibited exactly that, she'd spun, swiftly and decisively, to face him.

Now, though, it felt like she was moving through honey. Slowly, gathering her courage along the way, she raised her chin to meet his eyes. He was looking at her, his hands still at her waist, loose but impossible to ignore, his eyes green and golden and full of unmistakable surprise.

Her heart hammered against her ribs, pumping heat and panic and desire through her. They stood, unmoving, her eyes locked on his. As the seconds stretched, the panic threatened to take over. He didn't want to kiss her; he was looking for a polite way out of this unbearably awkward situation, and in a second, he would open the door and call Izzy to help extricate her from this goddamn skirt.

But then his hands tightened at her waist, and he pulled her gently towards him, flattening the tulle of the tutu as he drew her body against his. She raised her arms and pressed her palms to the walls on either side of him, steadying herself, then rose on the balls of her feet to brush her lips lightly, carefully, against his. They were as soft as she'd imagined.

Marcus was still for a moment, and all she could feel was the tulle prickling the tops of her thighs and the heat radiating from his skin. Then he opened his lips and captured her mouth, lowering his head and kissing her steadily, insistently. He ran one warm, flat palm up her back and settled it between her shoulder blades, bringing her closer and holding her there as she slipped her tongue into his mouth. She tasted spearmint and a hint of coffee, and when his tongue answered hers, Heather let out a tiny, involuntary moan of relief and wanting.

He tilted his head to gain more access to her mouth, and Heather moved her hands from the wall to his solid, muscular chest. He inhaled sharply when she touched him, and then let out his own small groan of arousal. The sound made Heather's nipples harden against the thin fabric of the leotard, and desire gathered between her legs, pulsing demandingly as she grabbed a fistful of his T-shirt.

The feeling of air against his skin seemed to knock Marcus out of the dreamlike moment, and he pulled away, straightening and loosening his hold on her slightly. He gazed down at her, looking slightly dazed, and Heather realized she was panting. She hadn't felt lust like this in years. Her hand shook slightly as she released his shirt.

"We should get you out of this skirt," he murmured.

Heather nodded, unable to form coherent words. *Yes*, she thought. *Get me out of this skirt, out of this leotard, out of this skin if you have to.* Then she remembered where they were: in a fitting room, in a dancewear store, mere feet away from a very attentive manager who would surely be wondering why Marcus had vanished and why Heather hadn't emerged yet.

She nodded again, more fervently this time, and turned back so Marcus could undo the rest of the closures. Her heart was still pounding, and feeling his hands slip back under the skirt's waistband didn't help. But now her arousal was laced with anxiety: she needed to get control of herself, and he needed to get out of the fitting room before his absence was noted.

"Just undo one more," she muttered over her shoulder. "I can probably pull it off after that."

He made a small assenting noise, and she felt his breath on her bare shoulder.

"There," he said a few seconds later. His warm hands left her waist, and she instantly wanted them back. "That should do it."

"Thanks," she said with a reluctant smile.

Marcus picked up his cane and unlocked the door, easing back out as carefully as he'd come in. As the door swung shut, Heather shimmied the skirt down and let it drop to the floor. Standing there in only the leotard, she turned to look at herself in the mirror. Her cheeks were flushed pink and her nipples were clearly visible through the clingy green fabric. Her own chest rose and fell rapidly in the mirror, and the memory of Marcus's hand, flat and firm and warm between her shoulder blades, made her want to check if he'd left a mark.

Instead, she changed hastily back into her street clothes. *Stupid, stupid*, the icy voice hissed in her ear as she pulled on her jeans. *Are you trying to get fired? Are you trying to get him fired? He only kissed you out of pity, anyway, Stage Face.*

She had to be the world's biggest idiot. She had thrown herself at her coworker, basically launched herself at him in a confined space he couldn't escape, when just a day earlier he'd told her about the consequences of that kind of behavior. Heather took a deep, steadying breath, and then looked back at her reflection. They couldn't do that again. She couldn't do that again. No matter how badly she wanted to.

She collected the skirt, making sure to straighten out any incriminating crumples of tulle before she escaped the fitting room.

Chapter 7

Shopping bags in hand, they rode the escalator down to street level in prickling silence. Heather avoided his eyes, staring into the shopping bag and, as far as Marcus could tell, hardly breathing. She hadn't said a word to him since she'd emerged from the changing room, fully dressed and with the treacherous tutu pinned under one arm. She'd avoided his gaze as Izzy ran her card, and as Izzy asked for a hug—then a handshake, then another hug—before they left.

Marcus couldn't keep himself from looking at her, trying to catch her eye. He needed to know if she was as shaken as he was. He hadn't kissed anyone in a while. Well over a year. But he was fairly sure he'd remember if he'd ever been kissed like that in his life.

When they reached the bottom of the escalator, they entered a street teeming with people in suits rushing from their offices to the food courts and back again. Marcus stared at the crowds for a moment, surprised to see the lunch rush was still out. They'd only been in the dancewear shop for an hour, but that hour seemed to change everything. He'd gone in with a plan: they'd grab a few leotards, then go to the zoo, see a koala, eat an overpriced ice block, and go their separate ways. Making out in the dressing room, feeling the muscles of Heather's upper back undulate beneath her skin, and extricating himself with what he hoped was not a visible hard-on had definitely not been on the agenda.

He'd known, even as he was pulling her into his arms, that it wasn't a good idea, for so many reasons. She was fresh off a very public breakup with ballet royalty, and even if she weren't, this wasn't a risk either of them could afford to take. He'd spent the last year working with Sharon to get his strength back so he could do his job, and he'd have to be an idiot to jeopardize that by kissing her.

But he also would've been an idiot *not* to kiss her, not when she was so close and smelled so sweet, and her waist fit so perfectly in his hands. The sight of her face, with its unmistakable mix of nervousness and determination, had overpowered all his objections. And then her lips had touched his, and something in him had broken open in relief and recognition. All the reasons he'd spent the last few days repeating to himself had vanished from his mind.

Now, though, they were out here in the bright sunlight, and even if he couldn't bring himself to regret what they'd done, he knew it couldn't happen again.

Marcus glanced back at Heather and caught her looking at him, finally meeting his eyes. A shallow line gathered between her eyebrows, and it looked like every single one of her muscles was tensed. He took a breath to speak, but she beat him to it.

"I'm sorry," she said. "That was wrong of me."

"You're right," he said, with a solemn nod. "You should have gotten Izzy to give me a free dance belt."

Heather stared at him for a moment, looking baffled, then her face cracked into a smile. God, she was beautiful with her face lit up like that. It was thrilling to think he, of all people, could make her light up. But as quickly as it had appeared, the smile slipped away, and the crease between her eyebrows returned.

"You know what I mean. I shouldn't have done that."

"Well, we both did it," he replied. And if it wouldn't cost both of them their jobs, he thought, he'd happily do it again. Probably several times. Ideally without forty-seven layers of tulle in the way.

"Still, I started it," she said to his collar, shaking her head as though she was annoyed with herself. Or with him? Had she not enjoyed it, at least? It had certainly seemed like she'd been into it, but maybe he'd misread the situation. She pulled her gaze up to his. "I started it, and I'm sorry," she repeated firmly.

"Heather, it's okay, it was . . ." What was he going to say, exactly? Hot? Breathtaking? The sweetest, most intense kiss he could remember? Marcus groped around his brain for the right words, but she interrupted his thoughts before he could find them.

"It was a mistake," she said. "We just got caught up, and . . . and it won't happen again. It can't happen again."

A cloud slid over the little patch of sunlight that had bloomed in his chest at the sight of her smile, and he drew himself up a little straighter, taking a step backwards. A mistake. Of course. Marcus fidgeted with the hem of his sweatshirt. Of course it hadn't been real. Of course she regretted it and couldn't imagine it happening again. And even if she wanted it to happen, he reminded himself yet again, she was right: it couldn't. His pride was a little bit stung, but it was for the best.

She was watching him closely, waiting for him to speak, he realised. He cleared his throat.

"Well, um, it's probably a bit late to go to the zoo now," he lied, "so why don't we call it a day?"

"Sure," she nodded, sounding disappointed. She looked up and down the crowded street. "Is there a bus we can take? Isn't there a train station nearby?"

He led the way through the crowd of the city's central business district. Disappointment throbbed in his chest, but he tried to focus on the positive. He was moving faster than he had the previous day, which was lucky, because the roving packs of private school boys out for their lunch breaks were too busy joking and giving each other shit to notice him until it was nearly too late.

"Sorry, mate!" one of them yelled over his shoulder after Marcus dodged out of his way and wobbled perilously.

"Are you okay?" Heather asked, grabbing his free arm to steady him. A pleasant heat shot through him at her touch and lingered when she pulled away.

"Yeah, I'm right," Marcus said, shaking his head and looking down at the cane. "I'll just be glad to be shot of this thing."

"What did Sharon—er, *Shaz*—say today?"

"She said I can go back to class next week, if I'm careful about it," Marcus replied as they headed towards Wynyard Station, where a dozen buses would be lined up to take people over the Bridge and out to Sydney's sprawling northern suburbs. "Just barrework, and not too much of it."

"That's great, though," Heather encouraged.

It *was* great, Marcus thought. So why didn't it feel great? He'd spent months hoping for permission to go back to class, pushing himself through all the exercises Shaz assigned him, even when they were painful and difficult or repetitive and boring. He should have been delighted by his progress. But after what had just happened, the thought of being in the same studio as Heather for forty-five minutes every morning suddenly had him feeling something close to dread.

Sitting across from her on the half-empty bus, Marcus was careful to keep his knee from touching hers and tried not to stare at her mouth as she gazed out the window at the North Sydney skyline, chewing on her bottom lip.

It was fine, he thought. Well, it would be fine. His first few classes back might be a little weird, but this was for the best. They'd be friendly colleagues, just like they'd been a few hours ago. She'd no doubt be pulled into rehearsals soon, and he could get back to concentrating on his recovery, and—his heart gave an anxious little flip—on his mum. And he would forget, or at least pretend to forget, the way goosebumps had risen on Heather's neck and shoulders when he'd bent down to unclasp the tutu.

Heather spent the bus ride in anxious silence. When they'd boarded, she'd blocked the seat next to her with the tutu and the shopping bag. It seemed wise, given what had just happened, to put some space between them. The tutu bag sat hot pink and huge next to her, and she resisted the urge to scowl at it. None of this would have happened if the damn skirt hadn't gotten stuck. She'd be at the zoo petting a koala bear right now. She wouldn't know what it felt like when Marcus's tongue swept across her lower lip. But now he sat opposite her, and she worked hard to keep her eyes from wandering toward him.

Kissing him had been a mistake. A stupid, spur of the moment mistake, and she was proud of herself for apologizing quickly and making it clear it wouldn't happen again.

But you want it to, a sly, Carly-ish voice whispered, and Heather bit her lip. *Maybe you should try breaking the rules for once.* She remembered the sight of her own flushed cheeks in the fitting room mirror and the feeling of the soft fabric brushing against her suddenly rigid nipples, and she bit down a little harder.

She wished the last hour had never happened. Wished she didn't know what Marcus's mouth tasted like. Wished she hadn't made things so weird and awkward with the one friend she had in Sydney so far.

Besides, she was here to dance, she reminded herself yet again. To prove what she could do on her own. To show the gossips of the ballet world she'd earned her place at the top. She was not here to fool around in fitting rooms with the first hot guy she met. She definitely wasn't here to get that man fired and herself humiliated—again.

They would be friends and nothing more.

Friends and nothing more. She repeated it a few times, the way she had learned to do when trying to memorize a particularly challenging piece of new choreography. Usually, the message would sink into her body after a while, and she'd commit it to muscle memory. The same thing would happen with Marcus, she thought.

Her mental mantra was interrupted when Marcus reached for the railing next to his seat and pressed the stop button. The bus pulled into Milsons Point station, and they clambered off, making their way down along the Kirribilli main drag, past a butcher, a gelato shop, and a quaint little church. Marcus really was moving better, she noticed. She wasn't walking at her usual out-of-my-way-I-have-somewhere-to-be New York City pace, but she was striding fairly normally, and with help from his cane, he was keeping up just fine.

They turned onto her shady, quiet street, and she breathed an almost unconscious sigh of relief. It had only been a few days, but this place already felt like a refuge, if not like home. She had looked up the name of the parrots that nested noisily in the tree outside her house and learned they were called rainbow lorikeets, which was apt, given their blue heads, green wings, and yellow-orange chests. They were in the tree now, screeching and fluttering from branch to branch, feeding out of the fluffy red flowers that she had learned, also from her research, were called bottlebrushes. The ground under the tree was scattered with fine red filaments, as though someone had shredded crimson fabric and sprinkled it on the grass.

"I love these birds," she said, grinning up at the tree. "They're so unapologetically bright."

"Yeah, but don't ever park a white car under one of those trees," Marcus replied as another tuft of red fell to the grass. "My brother and I used to wash the neighbors' cars when we were kids, and I can tell you, it's a nightmare getting that stuff off."

One of the lorikeets screeched loudly, as if in response to Marcus, and she giggled. This didn't have to be awkward, she thought, relieved. They would be friends, and it would be fine. As they walked up the short pathway to the house, she repeated it a few more times. *We will be friends. It will be fine.*

For the best, really.

"Do you mind if I come in for a sec?" Marcus asked.

Heather felt her eyebrows shoot up her forehead. He wanted to come inside? After they'd just agreed what happened in the dance-wear store could never happen again?

As if he'd realized too late how his question sounded, Marcus added quickly, "I need to use the bathroom."

"Oh, of course," she said, fumbling with the keys for what felt like several minutes. *Of course*, she repeated as he followed her inside. *Friends, and nothing more.*

Inside, she dropped the keys on the front table and slung the tutu bag over the banister.

"Wow, this place is swish," Marcus said. He stood in the hallway and peered into the living room, taking in the plump pale-yellow couch and the sleek glass coffee table topped with an orchid in a gold pot. Heather was already looking forward to spending tomorrow morning lounging on that couch, drinking coffee and prepping her pointe shoes for the next week.

"I don't know what I was expecting company housing to be, but it wasn't this. I love it here," she said, realizing she really meant it. "The bathroom's down there," she added, gesturing down the hallway to the back of the house, where there was a bathroom so tiny she thought it might once have been a closet.

Marcus disappeared, and she took her packages upstairs and tossed them on her bed. She had just put away the last leotard when she heard the toilet flush, followed by Marcus's footsteps. For a long, nervous moment, Heather listened to the sound of his feet on her floorboards, wondering if his heart was hammering like hers was. *Of course it's not, Stage Face.* Checking her hair in the mirror, she slid the drawer shut and hurried downstairs.

Marcus was in the living room, taking in the molded ceiling and the plush off-white carpet. Heather watched as he reached down and touched the orchid, rubbing one of the velvety petals gently between his fingers. She considered clearing her throat, but she wanted to keep watching him. Gripped by curiosity, she wondered again what kind of a dancer he was. Or had been. Was he an attentive pas de deux partner? Did he make his partners feel steady, or did he always keep them slightly off balance? A few more seconds ticked by, and she realized with a jolt that if she watched him any longer, she would have officially crossed over into creepiness.

"Thanks again for taking me shopping," she said, a little louder than intended, and Marcus whirled around, whipping his hand away from the flower as if it had burned him. "And thanks for being my tour guide. I'll make sure Peter knows how good you were."

He raised his eyebrows in surprise, and her mouth dropped open in horror.

"Not like that, oh my God. I didn't mean it that way. I mean, not that you weren't goo—oh my God." This was a mess. She was a mess. "I won't tell anyone about . . . about what happened. I promise. I'm sorry."

"I get it, okay?" he snapped. "You've made yourself extremely clear."

Heather flinched, and he ran his hand through his hair, looking frustrated.

"I'm sorry," he sighed. "You're right. Let's just pretend it never happened."

Heather couldn't think of anything to say that wouldn't make this worse, so she just nodded. Thankfully, Marcus saved her by gesturing toward the door.

"I should get going," he said, and she nodded in agreement and opened it for him.

"I'll see you Monday morning," she managed as he sidled past, and she barely heard his reply before she shut the door, leaned her back against it, and slid down to sit on the floor.

Pretend it never happened. Sure, she could do that.

Chapter 8

Just before four the next afternoon, Marcus got off the 139 bus in front of the Harbord Returned Servicemen's League and made his way down the hill towards his childhood home. It was a trip he'd made hundreds of times, thousands, maybe, but lately the destination had begun to feel a little like an entirely different suburb than where he'd grown up. The old RSL club had been razed a few years ago and resurrected as a gleaming five-storey behemoth with a gym, a spa, and four different restaurants. Above the dog-friendly outdoor beer garden were several floors of apartments for the retired fifty-five-plus crowd, and Marcus didn't want to think about how much those units cost. Then again, as he paused on the cliffside and gazed over Freshwater Beach, he had to concede that waking up to a view like that would be worth a small fortune.

And that's what people were paying for houses in this neighbourhood these days. Marcus shook his head at the modern minimalist white compound that had replaced the small brick house where a family friend had once lived. It looked like the paint had barely dried. A few doors down was another old brick home with a second storey under construction, house wrap rippling in the wind. Tomorrow morning the contractors and their crews would return, and the street would be full of battered utes and the sound of power tools—the sound of Marcus's childhood. His dad had had a battered white ute, complete with a scruffy Heeler mix named Pip. She'd been an impressively sedentary animal—she would've made a useless cattle dog—but his dad had loved her from the moment he set eyes on her at the pound. He'd loved this neighbourhood too, with its laid-back, beachy atmosphere and its small brick and fibro homes. *The closest thing to heaven*, that was what his dad had called Freshwater Beach.

The wind clawed at Marcus's hair as he made his way downhill. Even with the cold gusts buffeting him sideways, he felt stable and strong, despite gripping his cane a little harder than usual. It had been a bit of a comedown to put the boot on this afternoon after spending the morning walking carefully around his apartment. But Shaz had said yesterday he still had to wear it any time he left the house, and he wasn't brave enough, or stupid enough, to disobey her.

The sounds of Freshwater Beach wafted to him on the salty air. He could picture the beach perfectly, on the other side of those houses, the way the dark waves rolled in steadily, reliably, their deep blue giving way to a warm teal as they approached the sand. The way they crashed on the beach and dissolved into fizzing white foam, which stretched back from the shore like fragile lace before disappearing into the pale green shallows. Seagulls picked their way along the beach, scavenging for abandoned chips, unbothered by the occasional jogger padding along the denser sand near the water's edge. Even on a windy winter day like today, there would be surfers out, left to their own devices to stay between the red and yellow flags while one or two surf lifesavers sheltered in the little hut on the grassy dunes at the back of the beach. And even though the cafes wouldn't be packed with sweating, sun-pink beachgoers,

Marcus knew the kiosk inside the surf club would still be serving up hot coffees and toasted cheese sandwiches from inside their cramped kitchen.

He hurried, aware he was late. After all these months, he still hadn't gotten into the habit of leaving himself more time to get around. When he turned onto his old street, sweating lightly against his T-shirt and hoodie despite the brisk breeze, Marcus saw Davo's own white ute—freshly washed and not even a little bit battered—already parked outside the house.

Marcus let himself in through the front gate, noticing that the front fence had some thick vines growing on it that he hadn't seen there before. The grass inside the gate, which his dad had taken so much care to mow every second Saturday afternoon, was looking a little overgrown too, and as Marcus made his way carefully over the uneven paved path to the front door, he could see weeds sneaking up between the rough grey stones.

The little gold sign next to the front door was still shiny, though. When they'd moved in a few years before Davo was born, his parents had named the little brick house Sand Castle, a sly joke about how small it was, and a nod to the beach just down the road. Lots of old Sydney houses had grandiose names etched on old-fashioned signs, but theirs was the only one he knew that was mostly in jest. One of his childhood chores had been to polish the sign once a week, and his mum had taken over the task once he'd moved out.

"I'm here, sorry I'm late," he called, pushing open the unlocked front door and slipping inside. He heard a single bark from the back of the house, and then Davo's glossy red kelpie, Banjo, came trotting down the hallway to investigate the new arrival.

The familiar smell of home enveloped Marcus as soon as he shut the door behind him, a mix of eucalyptus floor disinfectant and his mother's sweet floral perfume. The piney scent of his father's aftershave, which used to waft from the bathroom and down the hall, was gone, replaced by another, less comforting odor: the sharp smell of the essential oils his mum rubbed on her joints when her pain got especially bad. The house was quiet, and he could hear his mother's voice and Davo's deep rumble floating down the hallway.

"Hello, darling," his mother said with a smile as he entered the kitchen, Banjo trailing behind him. The back of the house got all the sun, and the pale pine table gleamed in the light that streamed in through the wide windows.

"Don't get up," he said quickly as she moved to stand. Ignoring him, she rose from the chair—slower than Marcus had seen her move in a while—to give him a hug. She pressed her cheek against his chest, and he dropped a kiss onto the top of her grey bob. He had outgrown her during a growth spurt when he was about fourteen, and had hoped he would keep getting taller, but he'd topped out at just under six feet. He'd been disappointed at the time, but it turned out to be the perfect height for ballet. Davo, on the other hand, towered over the entire family at six-foot-five, just like he did now as he, too, stood to greet Marcus.

"How ya goin'?" Davo asked, giving Marcus a nod and a brief clap on the shoulder.

"Yeah, not bad," Marcus said as Davo headed for the fridge. He pulled out a beer—his mum must have bought a six-pack of Davo's favourite, because she didn't keep beer in the house for herself—and held it up to Marcus.

Marcus shook his head. "Nah, I'm right. Just water, thanks. Haven't been drinking since the surgery." He left it at that, as though he were abstaining to speed his recovery. In truth, he would have loved a cold Carlton, but since he wasn't in class and rehearsal all day, he couldn't afford the calories. But he sure as hell wasn't going to tell Davo that.

Davo gave a characteristic shrug and pulled a glass from the cupboard, and Marcus was surprised to notice a few greys at his temples. Davo was pale and freckled like their dad had been, with dark hair and watery blue eyes. Marcus, meanwhile, had always taken after their mum. "How is it?" Leanne gestured at his boot. She had settled herself back in her usual seat at the kitchen table, her back to the windows. Marcus noted that both he and Davo had defaulted to their habitual places, the ones they'd sat in for dinner thousands of times as kids. At the head of the table, a fourth chair sat empty. Marcus stared at it for a moment, remembering. Then he looked away, cleared his throat, and answered his mother's question.

"It's getting there," he replied, nodding his thanks to Davo as he plopped down a glass of water in front of him. Davo sat, leant back in his chair, and nursed his beer in silence. Marcus patted Banjo's velvety ears for a few seconds before she settled at Davo's feet. "I'm only in the boot when I'm out and about now, and I'm allowed back in company class next week."

"That's wonderful news," Leanne said, looking relieved. "And I hear there's an American star joining the company. Heather something?"

Marcus coughed in surprise and narrowly avoided spraying water across the table.

"Yeah," he gulped as his mum watched him curiously. "Heather Hays. From New York. She's here to dance *Giselle*, I think."

"Is that the one with the swan?" Davo asked dismissively, the last word loaded with derision.

"*Swan Lake* is the one with the swan," Marcus answered dryly. "*Giselle* is peasant boy meets peasant girl, boy turns out to be a duke who's engaged to a duchess, girl goes mad and dies of heartbreak."

"Sounds like a laugh riot." Davo shrugged, and Marcus tightened his grip on his water glass. Typical Davo, he thought. He never missed a chance to remind Marcus of how little he thought of ballet.

"But that's just the first act, right?" Leanne jumped in, her voice not quite bright enough to defuse the tension. "She comes back as a ghost."

"Uh, yeah, she becomes one of these ghosts who trap men in the woods and force them to dance until they die. But she saves the duke, because she loves him."

Davo gave him a slow, unimpressed nod.

"There are worse ways to spend your afterlife," Leanne said. "Why be a friendly ghost when you can be a . . . what are they called?"

"A *wili*," Marcus supplied. Davo looked away and rolled his eyes, and irritation bloomed hot and prickly in Marcus's chest.

"A wili, right," his mum said, meeting his eyes with a familiar encouraging smile. "One of these days I'm coming back as a wili. And what about you, David, how's work?"

Probably great, Marcus thought. If the construction he'd seen on the way here was any indication, it was a good time to be a contractor.

"It's fine," Davo replied. Leanne looked at him and raised her eyebrows expectantly. Davo had never been the chattiest guy, but these days he was downright monosyllabic.

"We're finishing up a big home over in Potts Point," Davo added reluctantly, "and the neighbour across the street likes it so much he's hired us to do his place, too." Leanne looked impressed. Potts Point was one of the city's wealthiest suburbs, and Marcus was sure Davo was charging those people an arm and a leg for their renovations.

"Well, that's wonderful news too," Leanne said, smiling at them both. "And it's lovely to have you both here together again. What's the occasion?"

Busted, Marcus thought. He should have anticipated this. His mum was no fool, and he should have realised she'd know something was going on if both he and Davo turned up together for a scheduled visit. Especially since the last time they'd done it, Davo had introduced the idea of moving her out of the house.

Marcus looked across the table at Davo, eyebrows raised. *This was your idea*, he wanted to say, *you start*.

"I think—we think—you're wrong about staying in the house," Davo said.

Leanne cocked her head and blinked a few times.

"What he's trying to say is we're worried about you," Marcus said, resisting the urge to kick his brother under the table. He knew Davo was speaking out of concern for her, but come on. He forced himself to meet his mother's eyes. "Because living alone in this house seems to be getting harder for you. And I know you said you're not ready to sell just yet, but we think you should reconsider. Or . . . consider reconsidering."

"Nonsense," Leanne said calmly. "I'm doing just fine here. The garden's a bit of a mess," she added, gesturing behind her at the back of the house, "but that doesn't bother me at all."

"Yeah, but," Davo tried again, "the house is pretty big for one person, and it's hard to move around. The stairs, and everything . . ."

"I move around perfectly well, thank you," Leanne corrected him, her calm tone giving way to crispness. "The doctor's got my knee pain under control and says it should be fine for a few more years. I'm certainly not about to move out of my home over a little joint pain." She'd spent most of her life as a nurse, but she would have made a very good ballet dancer, Marcus thought with a twinge of irritation. *This thing I'm doing hurts me? Who cares, I'll just keep doing it because I love it!*

This was going about as well as it had last time—except now, she was ready for them. "But what about the toilet upstairs?" Davo asked, shifting in his seat.

"What about it?" she shrugged. "I've been managing my own bowels for quite a while now, m'dear, and I'm quite sure I can keep doing it, stairs or no stairs."

Davo opened his mouth, but nothing came out. Marcus met his brother's eyes and gave him a little shrug.

They didn't have to convince her today, he reminded himself, they just had to float the idea again. Davo wanted this settled as soon as possible, efficiently and without fuss. There was a reason his clients liked him: he got the job done, fast and clean. But their mum seemed pretty dug in, just as she had the first time they'd raised this with her.

Marcus was about to say they should drop it when Davo tried again. "Mum, I really think it's a good time to downsize. Move somewhere a bit smaller where you can move around more easily. A unit somewhere."

"And where would that be?" Leanne inquired, though Marcus knew from experience it wasn't really a question that expected an answer. Her green eyes were wide and her brows were raised sceptically in her sun-lined face. She had grown up in a time before sunscreen became a way of life for Australians, before public schools started requiring kids to wear hats to go outside and play, and he knew she'd already had a few sunspots burned off her shoulders.

"Um," Davo started, pointlessly, because they both knew from her tone what was about to happen.

"There isn't a unit somewhere," she answered her own question, predictably. "At least, not somewhere near here or near my friends or near anything else in my life. You think it's hard for young people to buy a home in Sydney? Try being a senior citizen on a fixed income, especially one who took a few years off work to raise her children." She looked at her sons and raised her eyebrows still further.

Marcus felt his cheeks flush, and guilt crawled in his ribs. Why had he let Davo talk him into this again? What had he thought would happen, that she'd suddenly change her mind and start chucking things out on the front lawn for a garage sale?

"Look," Davo put his elbows on the table, looking almost as guilty as Marcus felt as he leant towards his mum. "We don't want to gang up on you, but—"

"Then don't," she said, her tone crisp again. "This is my home. I love it here, just like I did when Richard and I bought it thirty-five years ago." Her eyes flicked to the head of the table as she spoke, and her voice cracked a little. She paused for a moment and swallowed before continuing. "I'm delighted you boys are here together and that you seem to agree on something for a change, but I will leave when I'm good and ready, which won't be any time soon. Now, David, will you please start the barbeque?"

There was no point in continuing to argue. Not just because Marcus recognized her And That's My Final Answer tone, but because he'd heard the shake in her voice when she mentioned his dad. He didn't want to upset her any further.

She was right, he thought as Davo rose moodily from the table and went to fetch the lighter for the barbeque. The Sydney housing market was a nightmare, and people like him and Davo couldn't afford to buy anything bigger than a one-bedroom apartment without handing over a small fortune. Flats in Manly, the suburb built around the next beach over from Freshwater, were going for a million or more. For all the fuss people made about how hard it was for first-home buyers to break into the property market without help from rich parents, he'd never given much thought to how hard it must be for older people, especially women. He didn't know how much his dad had left his mum when he died, but he knew it wasn't a mint. His dad had done all right as a builder, and better as a contractor once he got too old to haul cement and go up on roofs. They'd never been rich, and they certainly weren't wealthy.

But they'd had this house. This squat brick three-bedroom just a few blocks from the best beach in the city, maybe the country. This house where, as a kid, Marcus used the railing of the back verandah as a barre and shared a thin wall with Davo all through their teen years.

Marcus gathered cutlery for dinner and pulled plates from the cabinet above the dishwasher, realizing too late he'd collected four of everything out of sheer habit. With a stab of grief that hit him in the sternum and slid down into his gut, he put the superfluous knife, fork, and plate back in their proper places.

In truth, he wasn't sorry she'd dismissed their idea out of hand again. It was too soon to leave this place, to walk away from his dad's beloved home. Whoever bought the house would knock it down and build something totally obnoxious in its place. He pictured the faceless, charmless white edifice he'd passed on his way down the hill and shuddered.

After he'd set the table, he opened the back door and stepped out onto the verandah, where Davo stoked the fat barbeque coals with obvious frustration. From behind, he looked strikingly like their dad. He looked like him, was in the same line of work as him. And he'd inherited his spot at the barbeque.

Davo kept stabbing at the coals as Marcus joined him next to the bulbous old grill on its rusted, spindly legs. Their father had refused to upgrade to a newer gas machine, insisting the meat wouldn't taste as good without the charcoal.

"She'll come around," Davo said eventually.

"I mean, it's fine if she doesn't, isn't it?" Marcus replied.

Davo gave the coals another shove. "She can't stay here forever."

"Yeah, but you heard what she said. Where would she go?"

"I dunno." Davo closed the lid of the barbeque with a scrape and clang. "But if she stays here, she's gonna hurt herself. Maybe she already has."

"You said that last time, but she'd tell us if something had happened, and—"

"No," Davo interrupted, "she wouldn't. She'd keep it to herself and keep telling us everything was fine."

Marcus paused. It was true that their mother was a stoic, uncomplaining woman. He'd seen her cry right before and after their dad had died, but since then, she'd done her best to carry on with life as usual, taking her daily dip in the ocean pool at Freshwater Beach and meeting her girlfriends for morning tea at the same local café once a week. She liked her routines, she said. She'd been living with her osteoarthritis for nearly a decade now, he reasoned. Maybe it had simply become part of her routine, too.

"I just don't think we need to rush this," Marcus said to his brother, fiddling with the hem of his sweatshirt. "It's her home, after all. Our home."

"Your home," Davo snapped.

Marcus stared at his brother, taken aback. His instinct when Davo got stroppy was to cut the tension with a joke, but his brain seemed to have frozen. He was about to ask what he'd meant when their mother rapped on the glass sliding door, beckoning him inside. Not sorry for an excuse to leave Davo alone with the barbeque, he went in, feeling the boot scrape against the wooden slats of the verandah as he went.

"What's up?" he asked as he slipped back into the kitchen. His mother had donned an apron and stood at the counter, chopping vegetables and tossing them into a large salad bowl.

"Spin the lettuce for me, would you please?" She gestured over her shoulder where a pile of wet green lettuce sat in the salad spinner next to the sink. Marcus put the lid on and realised instantly why she'd ask him to do this for her: her hands and shoulders couldn't manage the motion. Was that a new development?

"Mum," he started, but she interrupted him.

"I've already got the update on your brother's life," she said breezily over the sound of her knife dismantling a red capsicum. "As much as he'll tell me, which is not much." Once finished, she shook out her hand and joined him near the sink. Marcus nodded, unsurprised. Davo had never been one to volunteer information about his life.

"So," she said, reaching for the tap and running her hand under a stream of warm water, "now it's your turn. What's going on? Physio's going well, that's good. How's Alice?"

"She's fine," Marcus said with a small smile. "She's Alice. She's been great with . . . with all of this."

"And what about your love life?" His mother turned off the tap and dried her hand gently with the bottom of her apron. "Are you seeing anyone?"

Marcus paused. He thought about yesterday, about Heather's lips, soft and warm and parting against his own. Then about how stupid and risky it had been to kiss her in the first place—how much it had stung when she herself had pointed that out.

On the bus today, he hadn't been able to resist pulling up the shop's Instagram account to see the photo Izzy had taken. Perhaps it was the angle or the way Izzy had edited the shot, but Heather looked even stronger and more graceful than she had when she'd posed for it. Her legs were long and powerful, and the shadows that wrapped around her left foot as it pointed and curved around her right ankle made her arch look steep and dramatic. The sunlight from the shop window turned the tutu into an ethereal disc encircling her hips and . . .

She was stunning. Stunning and perceptive and endearingly awkward when flustered, which was fairly often. And not for him.

Then, against his better judgment, he'd clicked on Jack Andersen's profile, again. His most recent post, a video taken after a company class, showed Heather's ex completing a series of should-be impossible jumps, which he landed cleanly, before flashing the camera a devastatingly handsome grin and bursting into photogenic laughter.

Marcus cleared his throat.

"No one to speak of," he told his mum. It wasn't really a lie, he reasoned. But then, judging from the look she gave him as she returned to the chopping board, she didn't really believe it.

Chapter 9

Heather spent the weekend exploring her new neighborhood on foot. On Saturday morning, once she'd bought herself a flat white from a café on the main drag, she'd wandered the leafy streets of Kirribilli, taking in the grand old mansions that dwarfed her little row house and catching glimpses of the glittering harbor between their roofs.

As she walked, she'd snapped photos and sent them to Carly, who'd responded hours later with heart emojis—and a gentle reminder that she'd requested photos of beautiful men, not beautiful homes.

Heather had bit her lip, wondering if she should tell Carly about the beautiful man she'd kissed in the fitting room on Friday afternoon. But she decided against it and pushed thoughts of Marcus's mouth, and the cheeky dimple right next to it, out of her mind.

Let's just pretend it never happened, he'd said, and she'd agreed. She'd been trying all weekend. Really, she had. She'd been trying not to think about the way his hands tightened around her waist, the hunger he communicated through his fingertips as he pulled her toward him. She had been failing, miserably.

On Sunday, she'd walked farther afield and found a beautiful secret garden tucked away on the hillside above the water. She'd spent an awestruck hour there, wandering among the native trees and beautiful sculptures. From a bench in the garden, she enjoyed yet more views of the sparkling sapphire water, with hardly any other people in sight. It reminded her of the few rare spots in Central Park where, if you lay down on the grass, you could pretend the skyscrapers and the clogged city streets weren't right beyond the trees, that you weren't surrounded by millions of other people.

She'd also sat down with the company manual she'd found in a kitchen drawer and read it cover to cover. In addition to the reforms she'd read about in the press, she found policies about skin-tone tights and shoes—*dancers may wear tights and shoes matching their skin tone and women will be provided with tights in the colour of their choosing*—and about hair—*hair length, colour, and texture may be of the dancer's choosing, and dancers are not required to obtain permission from management before altering their hairstyles.*

And there, on page twenty-seven, in black and white: *Romantic or sexual fraternisation between dancers is strictly prohibited and will result in immediate dismissal from the company.*

Pas de Don't.

Heather had seized a pen and underlined the passage, trying to remind herself of what was at stake. It wasn't just a thrilling, muscle-melting kiss in a fitting room. It was her career on the line.

By the time she'd fallen into bed on Sunday night, she was pleasantly fatigued by the sun and the walking, and she'd woken up this morning feeling rested and ready to start rehearsing. Then she'd remembered. She'd have to see Marcus again today. She wouldn't be able to avoid him; now that he was cleared to dance, he'd be back in company class. She'd thought about him in the garden, and as she shopped for groceries, and as she sewed ribbons onto her pointe shoes for the week. And now she was trying not to think about him, again, as she sat in a deep lunge on the floor of Studio B, stretching out her hip flexors before class.

"Good morning, Miss America," Alice said cheerfully as she entered the studio and saw Heather.

"Hi, Alice," Heather replied, with what she hoped looked like a normal, friendly smile and not an I-was-just-thinking-about-your-best-friend's-mouth smile. "How was your weekend?"

"Not bad." Alice tossed her dance bag under one of the barres in the middle of the studio and joined Heather on the floor. She wore her baggy black ANB sweatshirt over her leotard and tights, and her hair was up in a high, loose bun.

"Me and my brother braved Ikea, for a new couch." Alice spoke like a lot of Australians did, Heather noticed, with what sounded like a question mark at the end of most sentences. *Me and my brother braved Ikea? For a new couch?*

"Do you live together?" Heather asked. "Does he dance, too?"

Alice shook her head. "No, he works in IT. He did ballet for a little while, when we were kids, but the teasing was just too much. It was bad enough being one of the few Asian kids at school, but being a Chinese boy who did ballet? A nightmare."

Heather shook her head in dismay. She'd heard stories like that before, of boys who loved ballet but were driven out of it by bullying. There had only been a few boys at her little Yonkers dance school to begin with, and by the time she left for the NYB school in the city, they'd all dropped out.

"So, anyway," Alice was saying, "he dropped ballet and took up footy instead."

"Footy . . . is that what Australians call soccer?" Heather asked.

"Nah, we call soccer soccer. Footy is Aussie rules football, and then there's also Rugby union and Rugby league."

"Wait," Heather said, switching legs before looking at Alice, confused. "There are three kinds of football here?"

"Four. Union and league are two different codes. And Will was annoyingly good at all of them. What about you?" Alice asked, reaching into her bag and pulling out a container of hairpins, "how was your first weekend in Sydney?"

"Pretty good," Heather said as she rolled onto her back and pulled one knee up to her chest. "I think I'm getting my bearings now, although I almost missed my stop this morning." *Because you stopped counting the bus stops and started thinking about Marcus.* "Marcus was very helpful."

"Ha, I bet he was," Alice said through clenched teeth. Heather's stomach lurched. Did Alice know what had happened? She looked over and was relieved to see Alice had bun pins between her teeth and was pulling them out one by one to stick them in her hair.

"Speaking of which," Alice said, with a glance at the studio door. "Here's the helpful man himself."

Heather willed herself not to sit up too quickly, despite the bolt of excitement that shot through her body. She sat up slowly, deliberately, trying to look nonchalant, as if Marcus's arrival was neither here nor there to her. But she couldn't stop her eyes from flying to the studio door, where Marcus had just walked in with his cane and his boot, his brown hair disheveled from the wind. Was it possible he'd become more attractive since Friday? Or had she just failed to commit his sharp jawline and muscled forearms to memory?

Marcus glanced around the studio, looking a little nervous, then his eyes fell on Alice and Heather. For a fleeting moment, he and Heather made eye contact. His eyebrows gave the slightest flick upward, and he gave her a friendly smile. *Friends, and nothing more.*

"Oi!" Alice called happily. "Welcome back!" She beckoned him over, and he deposited his cane against the studio wall and joined them. He sat next to Alice and gave her a quick one-armed hug.

"Good to be back," he said to her. "It's about bloody time." Even from five feet away, Heather caught his scent, that same faint musk she'd noticed in the fitting room, and she hastily busied herself with her pointe shoes, rummaging in her bag for her gel toe pouches.

Marcus unwrapped his foot from the boot and pulled on a pair of canvas slippers. From the corner of her eye, Heather watched his calf muscles flex under his olive skin as he worked his feet into the shoes. He snapped the crisscrossed elastics against the tops of his feet with what looked like immense satisfaction, then rolled his sweatpants back down and got carefully to his feet.

Heather stole a look at Alice, who was in downward dog, pedaling out her own calves, then glanced up at Marcus hopefully.

"How was your weekend?" she asked. Had he also spent the last two days trying, and failing, to pretend nothing had happened on Friday?

"It was fine, thanks," he said neutrally. He placed one hand on the barre and bent his knees slowly, first one and then the other. He moved tentatively, and Heather felt her cheeks flush with embarrassment. Of course he hadn't spent the weekend thinking about her, and of course he wasn't anxious about seeing her this morning. He had more important things on his mind: it was his first morning back at work in a year, a day he'd been working towards for months. He was focused on that. He was here to dance, and so—she reminded herself yet again—was she.

Alice, who had lowered herself into a plank, twisted toward Heather.

"So, what's your favorite part of Sydney so far?" she said, her voice a little distorted by the strange angle of her neck.

"Uh, well," Heather said, racking her brain for a bland answer. *Marcus's forearms*, she thought. Not the bland answer she needed. "The people," she said, instead, and was surprised to realize it was the truth, if not the whole truth. "Everyone's really friendly and welcoming, and I already feel so at home here. And the harbor is like nothing I've ever seen. I had no idea how beautiful it would be. Being able to dance on top of it every day is such a privilege."

Alice walked her toes up to her hands and stood folded in half for a few seconds before rolling up and smiling at Heather. "Yep, it's pretty special. But there's plenty of Sydney that isn't on the water, and you should see that, too. And the mountains. The harbor's nice, but you can't beat the Blue Mountains for views."

"I'll keep that in mind," Heather said. She should start a list, she thought, of all the places she wanted to go, if there was time between rehearsals, performances, and whatever press commitments Peter and the company were lining up for her. She reached into her bag and retrieved her phone, intending to write herself a note, and saw Carly had texted.

Carly, 9:47 AM: Casting email for the first half of the season just went out . . . Mr. K cast Melissa in a bunch of dances with Voldemort.

Heather stared at the screen. Even Carly's new nickname for Jack—apparently she'd tired of "Asshole McGee" and "Dipshit von Fuckface"—couldn't soften this blow.

"If it weren't for me, you'd still be stuck in the corps with Carly."
Well, it seemed Melissa wouldn't be stuck in the corps for long.

Carly, 9:48 AM: And his goons have been talking shit about me under their breath in class . . . But my meditation app says I should inhale deeply and think of a tranquil forest or something 😵

Heather sighed. She knew exactly who Carly was talking about. Samuel and Brett were Jack's closest buddies, and if Jack had been badmouthing her and Carly to them, it was hardly a surprise they'd taken matters into their own hands.

She shuddered, then glanced around her to see if anyone had noticed. Marcus stood at the barre rotating his bad ankle in slow, careful circles, and Alice was on the floor putting on her shoes and catching Marcus up on her Ikea ordeal. Marcus grinned as he listened to Alice's animated story, but, Heather realized with a jolt, he'd been watching her, too.

Their eyes met again, and he gave her a questioning little frown. *You okay?* he mouthed.

Gratitude filled her chest. She gave him a tiny nod and an even tinier smile, then turned back to her phone and tapped out a hasty response.

> *Heather, 9:58 AM: Well, I hope Melissa's up to it.*
> *Carly, 9:59 AM: Really? Because I hope they both fall into the orchestra pit*

Heather chuckled. As she typed, Peter and the pianist arrived, and the chatter in the studio tapered off.

> *Heather, 9:59 AM: As long as Samuel and Brett go too. Hang in there, I love you. Gotta go, class starting.*

She hit send and stashed her phone in her bag.

Heather stood, took her place at the barre, and arranged her feet in first position. Peter began the class, and she fixed an attentive smile on her face, trying to chase Jack's voice from her head.

That was over. She was here now. And she was here to prove what she could do on her own.

"Good morning everyone," Peter called, and received a murmur of greeting in response. Marcus faced the front of the room, and his thrumming anxiety, which had receded while he chatted with Alice, came rushing back.

He had thought about this day for months. Longingly, sometimes despairingly. When his scans revealed he'd completely ruptured his Achilles, when his surgeon told him what kind of recovery time he was looking at, Marcus had wondered if he was ever going to dance again. A tiny part of him still did. Plenty of men didn't come back from this kind of injury, even when the surgery went well. In the exhausted, grief-stricken days and weeks after his surgeries, and after his dad's death, he'd wondered whether it was worth trying to come back. Maybe it was enough to walk again, to get enough function back to jog and swim and live a normal, active life. Maybe he didn't need to spend months getting back into ballet shape, especially in his early thirties. Even if he did manage to regain his dancing strength and range of motion . . . how long would he really need it?

When he tried to reconstruct those first few months now, Marcus could only conjure a swirling blur of physical discomfort, punctuated by occasional spikes of anguish and stretches of blank numbness. He had a few firm memories that stood out, sharp and crisp against the fog. Most of them were inconsequential—a too-salty canapé at his father's wake, or the first time he'd laughed out loud at a sitcom joke after a week of mindlessly watching Netflix in bed—but one of them was not.

A few weeks after the funeral, he'd ventured downstairs to the mailboxes in the lobby of his building, where his mail had been piling up for who knew how long. As he'd stood there, balanced awkwardly on one leg and one crutch while he fumbled with his keys, one of his elderly neighbours tottered past, leaving the scent of her hairspray in her wake. It smelled like childhood ballet concerts, Marcus had thought, the moment the smell reached him. Like letting one of the backstage mums lacquer him with Aqua Net as he squirmed against a scratchy rented costume in a crowd of similarly restless kids. Like creeping into the wings and peeking at the audience even though his ballet teacher had forbidden them to. It smelled, he had realised with a hard swallow, like his parents greeting him in the theatre lobby after the performance. It smelled like a tight hug from his dad, beaming with pride and awe at watching his younger son on stage.

It wasn't like Marcus had decided, in that moment in front of his mailbox, that he would dance again no matter what. It wasn't nearly so dramatic. But when he looked back on it now, he realised he had been looking for a reason to at least try. *You only fail if you never try*, his dad had told him before his first ballet competition, when Marcus was beside himself with nerves. And he knew how proud his father would be to know Marcus was, in fact, trying.

Now that the day had arrived, though, he was antsy with doubt. The pianist began a slow tune for their pliés, and Marcus took it gently, not bending his knees too deeply, and doing a demi-plié when the rest of the company went down into a deep grand plié. Over their heads, Peter caught his eye and gave him a nod of approval. Clearly, Sharon had talked to the boss and told him Marcus would be back in class but was under her very strict instructions to limit his range of movement for now.

The slower you come back, the faster you come back, he reminded himself as, all around him, his colleagues dipped into enviably deep grand pliés and he simply bobbed up and down in his shallow demis. He had come this far, and there was no reason to think he wouldn't keep getting stronger. Still, he felt out of place today, in this room full of his perfectly in-shape colleagues.

Against his better judgment, he let his eyes drift over to Heather, who was wearing what he recognized as one of her new leotards, a slate grey V-neck with short sleeves. She had her garbage-bag pants pulled up high on her waist and her hair in a low bun. Around her neck, she'd wrapped a plush deep-red scarf.

Trying not to be too obvious about it, he watched her as she swept her right arm down in a wide arc, her gaze following her hand as it travelled in front of her body and up over her head. It was the most elementary of ballet movements, a grand plié in second position, but she made it look like breathing. Beautiful, otherworldly breathing. Her arm swam through the air, floating around her body, and energy seemed to flow seamlessly from her shoulder to her elbow, down through her wrist and into the knuckles of her long, slender fingers.

Marcus had spent thousands of hours of his life in ballet class, and he'd stood behind many of his colleagues over the years, observing their technique in hopes of learning what to do to get better—and what not to do. But watching Heather, he couldn't see a single thing that was wrong. As he watched her rearrange her feet into fourth and readjust her hand on the barre, he felt his pulse quicken, and not because of the tiny pliés he was attempting.

Was he surprised to discover that one of the highest-ranked women at one of the world's best ballet companies was a beautiful dancer? No, he wasn't. Was he a little breathless just watching her warm up? He definitely was. Compared to this, watching her strike a few poses in a dancewear shop was nothing. Even doing something as mundane as a set of pliés, even in those unflattering garbage-bag pants with her long neck swallowed by a scarf, Heather Hays was unquestionably gorgeous.

The rest of barre passed in a blur. Marcus did what he could—some tendus, some petit battements, and some grand battements on his good leg. To his surprise and satisfaction, he wasn't in any pain. His ankle felt stiff, like there was a blockage keeping him from bending his knee too deeply or rising too high on demi-pointe, but Sharon had said that was normal at this stage of recovery. He tried to keep his eyes off Heather, which wasn't easy, especially when, after Peter had them repeat a rond de jambe exercise and the dancers on both sides of him were panting audibly, she unwound her scarf and peeled off her pants. He had a feeling he'd looked at her just a little too long that time, because when he turned away, he spotted Alice watching him curiously. He gave her a breezy grin and waggled his eyebrows playfully. She replied with a quick, close-mouthed smile.

When the music stopped, the dancers sharing his barre picked it up and transported it to the back of the studio. Marcus gave Alice and Heather a quick wave, collected his cane and bag, and slipped out the door. On his way to the change rooms, Sharon stuck her head out of the physio room.

"How'd it go?" she asked, taking in his flushed cheeks and damp T-shirt.

"Yeah, good." He ran a hand through his sweaty hair. "I took it easy, I promise." He heard the grumble in his own voice and silently reprimanded himself. He wouldn't have made it half this far if not for Sharon and the rest of the physio team.

"Well, as long as it doesn't hurt this afternoon or when you wake up tomorrow morning, you're right to keep going back," she said, ignoring his tone. "Come and see me on Friday morning and we'll check your range of motion, okay?"

"Okay," he nodded, giving her a grateful smile. "Thanks, Shaz, really. I know we've got a ways to go yet, but thanks."

"You're welcome, love," she said, with real affection in her voice. "I'll be glad to see you back on stage. We all will."

After class, Heather took a short break, changed into a dry leotard, and snuck out for a coffee. Between the cafes on the Kirribilli main drag and the one in the lobby, she was getting accustomed to drinking at least two flat whites a day. Soon the freckled barista at the company café would know her order by heart, she thought as she tipped her head back to capture the last cold milky drops from the bottom of the to-go cup.

She arrived in Studio C feeling thoroughly caffeinated, if a little reluctant. It was the first day of rehearsals for *Giselle*, a ballet she'd be happy to never dance again. On top of the piano, she found a piece of paper with her name printed at the top and was surprised to see that it was the week's rehearsal schedule. Her entire week had already been mapped out: the act one pas de deux today and for the next few days, and in the middle of the week a session with the dancers who'd trade off playing Myrtha, queen of the wilis. Then some solo rehearsal time on Friday.

"Peter?" she asked, once he'd settled in a chair at the front of the room, his back to the mirror and a notebook on his lap. "I assume this schedule is subject to change? Is there an email that goes out the night before, or . . . ?"

"Oh, no," Peter said with an affable wave of his hand. "We don't do that anymore. It was one of the first things I changed when I took over. You'll get your rehearsal schedule at the start of the week, and we'll stick to it. This way you can plan your week more than a few hours ahead."

Another of Peter's famous reforms. It certainly wasn't the way she was used to rehearsing: at NYB, she never knew until the evening what the next day would hold after company class finished at noon. It was hard to have a life outside of ballet when the company dictated your schedule—and didn't tell you what that schedule would look like until the night before. And even then, Mr. K could call an emergency rehearsal any time he wanted. Once, Heather had been in the middle of a haircut downtown when her phone had buzzed, calling her back to Lincoln Center for an unscheduled rehearsal. She'd rushed out of the salon with her hair wet and half cut, then had to return later in the week so the very perplexed stylist could finish. Evidently that wouldn't be a problem at ANB.

But a few hours later, Peter's reforms were the last thing on her mind, and she found herself wishing she'd asked for an extra shot of espresso in that flat white. She was exhausted, and rehearsal wasn't going well.

It wasn't her partner's fault. Justin Winters was a principal dancer with a thick Australian accent, close-cropped blond hair, incredible feet, and a few inches on Heather. He seemed nice enough, if a little starstruck by her. He was a steady and capable partner, and unlike some of the men she'd rehearsed with, he'd made an effort to freshen both his armpits and his breath before they started working. He was more deferential than any partner she'd ever had, too. Whenever Peter told them to try a lift or an assisted pirouette again, Justin would ask, "You right?" before placing his hands on Heather's body, which she quickly figured out was Australian for "Are you okay?"

Still, something felt *off*, and all three of them could sense it. The first few times they ran through the pas de deux, they were behind the music every time. When Peter pointed this out, they overcorrected, and the next two runs felt rushed and frantic. Maybe she and Justin needed a few more rehearsals to get to know each other and learn how to read each other's little nonverbal cues.

Or maybe, that cold, treacherous voice whispered, *you're the problem. Maybe you don't deserve to be here at all.*

Heather tried not to think about how easy it had been to dance with Jack, how well they knew each other's cues. No, how well *she* knew *Jack's* cues. He'd been a fine partner, but if she was honest with herself, they'd worked well together because she was so attuned to him, even when it wasn't reciprocated.

After almost an hour and a half, they had run the pas de deux six times, and neither Justin's armpits nor hers were anything resembling fresh anymore.

"I think that's enough for today," Peter sighed at last, and the rehearsal pianist shuffled her sheet music away almost immediately. "Thanks, Kimberly," Peter called as she pushed her stool under the piano and slipped out of the room.

Heather walked slowly over to her bag and eased herself onto the floor. Everything ached, and as she untied her ribbons and slipped her feet out of her pointe shoes, she resisted the urge to groan. Peter thanked them for their hard work, then gathered his things from the top of the piano and headed for the door. The moment he was gone, Justin flopped dramatically onto the floor in the middle of the studio and lay flat on his back with a loud moan. Heather laughed.

"My sentiments exactly," she said. "He's relentless, isn't he?"

"Yeah, but he's nice about it," Justin said to the ceiling. "And if you ask for a rest, he'll give you one. Plus, he'll never let you dance hurt."

That was another difference between ANB and NYB, Heather thought as she packed her water bottle and pointe shoes back into her bag. Mr. K would never make someone dance hurt if they didn't want to, but he wouldn't stop them, either. A few years ago, a fellow principal had insisted on dancing the second half of the season with a stress fracture in her metatarsal, and she'd come off stage in tears every night. Mr. K hadn't said a word, and none of the dancers had suggested she take a break to let it heal.

Justin peeled himself off the floor and crossed the studio to collect his bag from under one of the barres, then turned back to face her.

"Listen, I'm sorry about today, I'm usually a little more on the ball than that."

"It's okay. We've got time to figure it out."

"Yeah, I know, I just . . . well, I have to say I'm a little intimidated," he said sheepishly, ducking his head. "I mean, you're kind of a big deal."

Heather guffawed in surprise, and he blushed.

"I'm not laughing at you," she reassured him hastily. "I just don't think of myself as a big deal. I'm just a dancer, you know, and . . ." *And apparently I slept my way to the top anyway*, she thought, her smile faltering.

"Okay then, you're just a medium deal," Justin said. "Either way, I promise it'll be less weird tomorrow."

The next morning, Marcus was relieved to wake up without any pain in his ankle. He was pleasantly sore in his legs and hips, but thankfully, his ankle felt just as it had yesterday. And so he went back to company class, for more gentle pliés and more tentative tendus. He was so pleased with his progress, so happy to get reacquainted with his body in this way, that he'd even managed to keep his eyes off Heather throughout barre. Mostly.

Unfortunately, keeping his eyes off Heather was not an option right now. As barre ended and he'd been on his way out, sweating but deeply satisfied, Peter had stopped him and spoken in a rushed, low voice.

"We had a few hiccups in yesterday's rehearsal with Justin and Heather. Nothing major, but I think Justin could use some help. Can you sit in for a few days, if Sharon can spare you?"

Marcus's stomach lurched, and he felt some of the morning's elation drain away. So much for staying away from Heather. It had been hard enough to dance across from her this morning. He remembered watching a bead of sweat slide down her throat into the hollow of her collarbone, and his stomach gave another nervous jolt.

"Yeah, no worries," he'd managed, hoping he sounded nonchalant and obliging, and Peter had nodded his thanks before returning to the rest of the company.

So now he was sitting at the front of one of the smaller rehearsal studios, watching Justin and Heather run through the first act pas de deux. Peter scrutinized their every move with his characteristic squinted gaze and cocked head.

When Marcus had arrived at rehearsal, he'd stood quietly by the piano, fiddling with his cane and avoiding Heather's eyes while Peter briefed them on the plan for today: to borrow the expertise of someone who'd danced Justin's role far more recently than Peter himself had. Marcus didn't really buy it. Justin had danced the role of Albrecht plenty of times—after all, the company wasn't about to place their new American star in inexperienced hands. Marcus suspected this was another of his boss's attempts to make him feel useful even though he couldn't dance properly yet, but it made him anxious. Those who couldn't do taught, but Marcus wasn't ready for his doing days to be over yet.

Still, as Peter explained the plan, Justin looked relieved. Heather looked as though Peter had just informed them they'd be bungee jumping off the Harbour Bridge. She hid it well, but he could see the panic flicker in her face, the way her eyes widened ever so slightly as Peter spoke. She bit her lip and shot Marcus a fleeting glance, and he was quite sure they were thinking exactly the same thing: this was going to be awkward as fuck.

Perhaps this was why Peter had implemented his deeply unpopular policy, Marcus thought as Heather placed her hand in Justin's and stepped up onto one of her pointe shoes. This would be a lot more awkward if he and Heather had dated and broken up or were sleeping together, right? It would be pretty damn difficult to focus in rehearsals if he knew exactly how smooth Heather's skin was under her leotard, or what it was like to wrap his hand around one of her strong, lean calves. Or what she sounded like when she—

Jesus, stop it. Marcus surreptitiously pinched his thigh through his tracksuit pants. Wincing, he forced himself to concentrate on Peter's corrections.

"Justin, make sure you're giving her as much stability as you can through that left hand." Peter gestured with his own left hand to Justin, who knelt on the ground and offered Heather one open hand with which to support her one-legged balance. "It's looking shaky, and we don't want that. Marcus, any notes?"

Marcus looked up from his stinging leg to find three sets of eyes on him.

"Uh . . . no, yeah, it's looking shaky," he repeated quickly, "and we don't want that." Peter raised his eyebrows, and Justin shot him a look that very clearly said, *Mate, what the fuck?*

Marcus felt his cheeks heat with embarrassment, and he glanced apologetically at Peter. His boss had supposedly brought him in to be useful, to pass along whatever nuggets of wisdom he'd accumulated from dancing the role of Giselle's unfaithful duke. And all he'd done so far was sit here lusting after Heather. He had to pull himself together.

"Sorry," he muttered, then he cleared his throat. "Justin, if you press your back foot into the floor, it'll create more tension through your whole trunk, and your arm and hand will be more stable."

Justin looked over his shoulder at his back foot, then murmured something to Heather, who nodded. He held out his left hand to her again, and she stepped back up onto pointe, placing her hand in his. She bowed forward into a deep penché, until her face was level with Justin's and her free leg pointed directly at the ceiling. It was graceful and seamless, and, Marcus noted as he checked her supporting leg and Justin's outstretched arm, it was rock solid. Not a shake in sight.

"That's *much* better," Peter said, sounding very pleased. Justin flashed Heather a quick grin, which she returned before bringing her leg down. Envy poked Marcus unpleasantly in the gut at the sight of their shared smile.

They tried the penché one more time, then moved on to the next section. This part required a lot of assisted pirouettes, with Justin standing behind Heather with his hands at her waist. From where Marcus sat, he could barely see his friend, and he couldn't avoid looking at Heather. He couldn't avoid the sound of her breath in the small, otherwise silent studio—a deep breath through her nose as she prepared to spin, and then a relieved little puff out as she completed her final rotation and Justin stopped and steadied her. Marcus couldn't stop his mind from drifting to the last time he'd been close enough to Heather to hear her breathing change.

He shifted uncomfortably in his seat, then glanced at the clock. There were ten minutes left in this rehearsal. He could make it through another ten minutes, he thought as Heather and Justin exchanged notes in a mix of muttered words and abbreviated steps. Marcus kept his eyes on Justin and gave his thigh another pinch, determined to stay focused. Then Heather slipped her fingers into the neckline of her leotard and pulled the fabric out a few times, as if she were scooping cool air onto her skin. God, ten minutes was a long time.

Heather and Justin both took their places, and he placed his hands at her waist. Meeting his eyes in the mirror, she gave her head a little shake, then moved his hands closer to her hips. She placed her palms flat over his fingers and pressed them against her body. Marcus gritted his teeth. This was torture.

"Don't be afraid to hold a little tighter, okay? It's better than the alternative," she said quietly, but Marcus heard every word. He shifted in his seat again.

"Marcus, why don't you show Justin how you'd do it?" Peter asked. Heather froze, and her eyes flew from the mirror to Marcus's face.

"Oh, no, he's getting it all right," Marcus said quickly.

"Please," Peter pressed, encouragingly. "Let's see what he can learn from you." Marcus swallowed a groan. He knew his boss thought he was doing him a favour, knew he was just trying to make Marcus feel valued and included. But, Marcus thought as he eased himself up and made his way over, this could not have been less helpful.

As Marcus pushed his sleeves up his forearms, Justin stepped aside so he could watch. Heather stood stiffly, avoiding his eyes, and he could see two pink spots on her cheeks that he was fairly certain weren't due to exertion. She clearly didn't want him anywhere near her.

Marcus stepped behind her, her lavender and sweat scent enveloping him again. Wisps of her dark hair escaped her bun, and clung, damp and wavy, to her neck. In that moment he wanted nothing more in the world than to gently sweep them away with his fingers, to brush his lips across the skin there. Would she want that? Would it make her shiver? Moan? Reach behind her and pull him hard against her?

Jesus, fucking stop it, he chastised himself. *Focus.* Marcus cleared his throat, and Heather jumped at the sound. He gave his hands a little shake, then placed them low on her waist, right where she needed them. Even through her leotard, he felt the warmth of her skin, and the tautness of the muscles. Was she holding her breath again?

"I've got you," he said, his voice more gravelly than he expected, and he felt her soften as she released a puff of air. She rose up on both pointe shoes, then extended one leg low in front of her.

"Ready?" she muttered back.

"Whenever you are," he said, nodding.

She stretched her leg out farther, then pulled it in tight, the motion rotating her entire body into several dizzyingly fast pirouettes. His hands worked at her waist, keeping her steady and spinning, his fingers spread wide so he touched her in a dozen different places as she moved. It had been months since he'd danced with a partner, let alone a new one, but he could feel she was perfectly balanced over the box of her pointe shoe, spinning seamlessly. With every rotation, the lavender-scented air thickened around him, pressing the scent of Heather and the breeze of her motion against every inch of his bare skin. Time slowed, and if someone had asked him, he wouldn't have been able to say if he'd been holding her for an hour or a minute.

"Just six," Peter called suddenly, "it's just six pirouettes here."

Marcus heard Heather's gasp, and he moved a hand quickly at her waist to stop her motion.

"Sorry," he whispered, pressing his palms against her to make sure she was secure and balanced. He thought—no, he could have *sworn*—he felt a tiny, almost imperceptible shiver, and the thought made his heart race. He kept his hands where they were, not certain he'd ever find the will to remove them from her.

"Excellent, you two, that looked lovely," Peter said, and Marcus gave him a half-hearted smile. Excellent, except for the bit where he forgot where he was, and who Heather was, and how totally off-limits she would always be. He dropped his hands from her like he'd been caught stealing and shoved them into his pockets.

"Justin, did you see how wide his fingers were spread on her torso?" Peter asked. "Why don't you give that a go and see how it feels? Heather, can we try it one more time?"

Heather nodded, and Justin resumed his place behind her. Marcus hastily returned to his seat as Justin and Heather set up for the pirouette again, but he barely noticed how it went. His head was still full of her scent, and his fingers still tingled with the memory of her body stiffening and relaxing under his touch.

Chapter 10

"Very nice, Heather, very nice," Peter called approvingly across the studio. "Thank you," he gestured at the pianist, who stopped playing at once. Heather stopped too, holding her ribs and taking deep, steadying breaths. The solo at the end of first act of *Giselle* wasn't technically difficult, but there was a lot of running around the stage, and it took a lot of work to make going mad look graceful.

"Make sure you really sweep that left arm nice and wide," Peter said, putting his notepad down on the piano to demonstrate. "You want to make sure the entire audience feels her despair, not just those people who are lucky enough to sit close." He flashed an affable smile at the reporter perched on a plastic chair at the front of the studio furiously scribbling in her own notepad. Peter had introduced her as Ivy Page, of the *Sydney Morning Sun* arts section, the journalist who reported Heather's arrival at the company.

Ivy had shaken Heather's hand with a hasty and somewhat flustered-sounding "Wow, so great to meet you," and then added quickly that she was a big fan, and, of course, a former ballet dancer.

If there was one thing Heather knew about journalists who covered ballet, it was that most of them had done ballet as children and saw journalism as a way to stay in the ballet world after they stopped dancing. They all loved ballet, but they weren't always kind to ballet dancers: a few years ago, a prominent dance reviewer had written some snarky remarks about an NYB dancer's weight, and then had doubled down on his comments even after the dancer publicly revealed she'd struggled for years with an eating disorder.

As for Heather's own interactions with the press, they'd loved the idea of her and Jack, the golden boy and the scholarship kid. She'd loved it too, at least at the start. The interviews would go well enough—Jack would charm the reporter and sing Heather's praises—but when she saw his words in print, they always left her feeling unsettled.

"She's working hard to become the artist I know she'll be one day," he'd once been quoted for a cover story about them for *Barre* magazine. Heather had glowed at the praise when he said it. But when she'd seen the words on the page, they didn't have the same effect. They made her feel small and condescended to. And when she'd mentioned it to him, he'd gotten defensive.

Can't you see I was complimenting you, Heather? What's wrong with you?

Heather had eyed Ivy cautiously as the reporter had arrived and slipped off her heels at the studio door to preserve the flooring, flashing Peter a bright smile. Now, Ivy sat at the front of the studio in her dark-blue jeans, black blazer, and leopard-print T-shirt, her light-brown bob tucked behind her ears and her glossy black plastic glasses catching the sunlight.

Ivy took what looked like very thorough notes as they rehearsed the act one finale, in which Giselle discovered that the man she thought she was going to marry wasn't who he said he was—and he was engaged to someone else. The act closed with Giselle dying of madness and a broken heart, while her mother sobbed over her dead body. Albrecht, whose lie had just been revealed in front of the whole village, looked on in horror, then fled the scene.

Later in the ballet, he would beg for her forgiveness, and she would give it to him, even though it wouldn't bring her back to life. She'd be doomed to spend the rest of eternity as a forest spirit, and he'd get to go back to his castle and marry his noble fiancée.

"Just one more time, I think, Heather," Peter said after she caught her breath and sipped some water. In the back of the studio, Katarina Antonov, an ANB principal dancer who would dance Giselle on the nights Heather didn't, padded around in sweatpants and thick socks, marking the choreography to jog her muscle memory; she'd have her own rehearsal with Peter once Ivy left.

Heather took her place downstage, and the pianist started the tremulous and unsettling Mad Scene music. On stage, Heather would pull her hair out of its bun to signal to the audience that Giselle was coming undone in her grief. Thankfully she didn't have to do it in rehearsal. After a few minutes, as the music reached its crescendo, she threw herself on the ground on her back, her head lolled to the side and her legs crossed at the ankles, toes pointed. Even in death, Giselle had to have nice feet.

"Lovely, lovely," Peter called as Heather rolled up to standing, brushed off her leotard, and checked the security of her bun. Peter gave a few taps of applause, and Ivy joined in, beaming. Heather bobbed a little curtsy, and Ivy slipped her notebook back in her handbag and stood.

"That was wonderful, thank you so much for letting me watch," she said to Heather. Heather gave her a polite, wary smile, and thought about the nickname she'd heard Justin use for her. "Poison Ivy," he'd called her yesterday, when Heather had mentioned she'd be sitting in on rehearsals. That didn't bode well at all. Or perhaps she and Justin just had some bad history.

It had been a long, hard week of rehearsal, but Heather was starting to feel like it was paying off. She and Justin were way more in sync than before, and Peter had decided one rehearsal with Marcus had been enough to get them on the right track. Thank goodness for that. She'd been a mess after that one session, her muscles wound tight and her mind full of the sure but gentle way his hands moved over her torso, and the heat that radiated from his body into hers. Even after she'd rushed home, thrown her leotard in the hamper, and taken a long shower, she could smell him on her skin, the same enticing musk she'd inhaled in the fitting room.

I've got you, he'd whispered, and even now, days later, the memory of his low, reassuring words made goosebumps erupt across her shoulders.

She definitely did not need Marcus showing up to any more rehearsals.

She'd managed to have nothing but brief and friendly interactions with him all week. And if her eyes sometimes drifted in his direction during company class, that didn't really count as being distracted by him. Just like if she sometimes lay awake at night and thought about the way his breath had flickered over the back of her neck right before she'd spun in his hands, well, that didn't really count either.

Heather joined Peter and Ivy as they stood conferring. Ivy was petite, and though Peter wasn't an especially tall man, he practically towered over her. Still, she held herself with an undeniable authority, like she knew exactly who she was and what she was capable of. Heather found it equal parts enviable and daunting. Something told her this was one reporter who wouldn't have bought the half-true fairy tale she and Jack had spent years constructing.

After a brief, polite conversation with Peter and Ivy, movement in the doorway caught her eye. Alice waved at her from the hallway. She was back in her floppy ANB sweatshirt and had already pulled her hair out of its all-day bun.

"Are you still coming out to dinner tonight, Miss America?"

"Yes, please," Heather smiled gratefully. If not for Alice's invitation, she'd be spending another night sitting alone on the couch with a container of takeout noodles, like she'd already done several nights this week.

"Great! I'll take you to one of my favorite places. Can't let Marcus have all the tour-guiding fun, right?"

"Right," Heather agreed with a smile. Friends! She was making friends.

Alice was already starting down the hallway. "It's called Café Luxor, on Military Road. Meet us at 7:00?"

"Uh, us? Who else is coming?"

"Oh, I invited Marcus," Alice called over her shoulder. "He loves this place. He'd eat there every night if he could. And I'll bring my brother so you can meet some nondancers for a nice change. I gotta run, see you tonight!"

Alice disappeared around the corner, leaving Heather standing in the doorway with her mouth agape. Dinner with Marcus? After she'd spent all week trying to avoid him, and mostly succeeded? She glanced over her shoulder to where Peter and Ivy were still deep in conversation. This wasn't a violation of Peter's policy, was it? Surely it was acceptable to have dinner with Marcus if Alice and her brother were there? It would just be three colleagues and an IT guy out at dinner. Nothing untoward or fireable about that. She was simply going to dinner with two of her colleagues. One of whom she happened to want to make out with.

It would be fine, she told herself as she collected her bag and headed for the lobby. As long as Alice and her brother were there, it would be just fine.

"You can't go wrong with the lamb," Marcus said absently, studying the menu in the dim light of the votive candle. He glanced up and saw Heather gazing around, looking a little overwhelmed by the eclectic decor of Café Luxor. There were Moroccan fabrics and Sri Lankan art hanging on the ochre yellow walls, and a wooden statue near the entryway that Marcus thought might be Jamaican. The menu was as global as the decor, and the spices emanating from the kitchen at the back had hit him in the face the moment he walked in the door.

He watched her surreptitiously while she took the place in. Her hair was in a loose plait down her back tonight, and she'd swapped her usual small gold studs for a pair of dangling gold tassel earrings that brushed against her neck and caught the light when she moved. The restaurant was crowded and warm, but it was a cool, breezy night. When he'd met her outside, she'd been wearing a denim jacket and high-heeled ankle boots. The jacket hung over the back of her chair now, and even in a simple snug scoop-neck black sweater dress, with her sleeves pushed up along her forearms, she looked radiant.

She also looked pretty damn uncomfortable.

"Did Alice say when they'd get here?" she asked, her eyes darting to the empty seats on either side of her for maybe the tenth time since they'd sat down.

Marcus flipped his phone over on the table again. No new messages. "No, she just said she'd be here as soon as she could and we should order without her."

Heather bit her lip, frowning, and Marcus resisted the urge to check his phone yet again. When Alice said she was organizing a dinner for Heather, he'd said yes so quickly she'd looked startled by his enthusiasm. But he'd gotten the distinct impression she was inviting a group of people. A big, raucous table full of his colleagues with plenty of physical space between him and Heather. A table this small, with just four people around it, was way too intimate for his liking. And without their third and fourth wheels, well, it was awfully date-like. Which made it dangerous. What if someone from the company saw them? Word would get back to Peter fast, and they'd both have some explaining to do.

"I'm sure they'll be here in a sec," he said, reassuringly, and she nodded, turning her attention to the menu. The menu, the decor, the empty table settings: she looked at everything but him. That wasn't a surprise, given how studiously she'd been avoiding him this week.

After that torturous rehearsal, she'd given him nothing but polite nods and brief close-mouthed smiles whenever they'd crossed paths.

Marcus knew it was silly to miss hanging out with someone he barely knew, but he did. The few days they'd spent together had been really *good* days, and he hated the idea that one stupid, ill-advised kiss had ruined it. Sure, they couldn't go on dates or make out in any more dressing rooms, but now, it seemed, they couldn't even be friends. He doubted very much she would have agreed to this dinner if she'd known it would just be him and Alice and Will.

"Alice said you like this place?" Heather asked, glancing up from the menu and addressing his collar.

"Yeah, it's a local institution. Been here as long as I can remember."

"I guess I never really thought about what Australian cuisine was. Turns out it's . . . everything?"

Marcus laughed, and a smile flickered over her face. "Sounds about right. I guess if you want a traditional Aussie meal you could have a meat pie or a sausage roll, but why eat that when you can eat . . ." he scanned the menu, "locally caught prawns cooked in Portuguese piri piri?"

"That does look tempting," she agreed, "but did you say lamb?"

"Lamb's what Australia does best," he said. "I can personally vouch for the Moroccan slow roasted lamb shanks." He reached across the small round table and pointed it out on her menu. As he leant forward, she stilled, holding herself rigid until he settled back into his chair again. God, this was awkward. Where the fuck was Alice?

He flagged down a waitress and ordered some olives and roti wraps to start, and Heather ordered a glass of red wine. After a moment's hesitation, Marcus ordered one, too. He was back in the studio dancing for the first time in months, he'd walked to the restaurant, albeit slowly, with his cane but without his boot. And he was here with a beautiful woman—although she, to be fair, didn't seem to want much to do with him. Still. He might as well treat himself.

"Should I clear these settings for you?" the waitress asked, bending down to gather the cutlery in front of an empty chair.

"No!" Heather exclaimed, and the waitress jumped, taken aback. "Sorry, we're just . . . we're definitely expecting more people. They'll be here soon."

The waitress nodded and disappeared.

"That embarrassed to be seen alone with me, huh?" He'd meant to break the tension, but the words had come out sulky instead of light and teasing. Heather's eyes widened, and she opened her mouth to reply, but the waitress returned with their wine and olives.

They sat in stiff, awkward silence as she emptied a carafe between two squat wine tumblers. Marcus was suddenly hyperaware of the raucous, friendly conversations occurring at almost every table except theirs. The candle flickered through the pale-crimson wine, and Marcus murmured his thanks before the waitress retreated.

"I'm not embarrassed," Heather said quietly, once they were alone again. She fiddled with her wine glass, but for the first time that night, she actually looked at him. Her brown eyes were wide and serious, and this close up, he could have counted each of her long dark lashes. "I also didn't know this was going to be a cozy dinner for two. So while I'm sure the lamb is delicious, I'm not sure it's worth my job. Or yours."

"I'm sorry," he muttered. "That was a dickish thing to say."

"Thank you," she said, eyeing him as she took a sip of her wine. Still, at least she was still looking at him. No, she was studying him, cool and a little reproachful. He'd take it. Even being on the receiving end of Heather's annoyed, assessing gaze, or her *cut the crap* look, felt like winning a prize.

"On the plus side, we probably look miserable enough that no one would ever mistake this for a date."

She laughed, and a warm, satisfied feeling fizzed in his veins. At least she didn't look miserable now.

"Or it's the world's worst first date," she said. She took another sip of wine, swallowing quickly, then gave him a conspiratorial smile that made his mouth go dry. Heather glanced around the restaurant again. "Who here do you think is on an actual first date?"

Marcus grinned, then cast his eyes around as discreetly as he could.

"Bingo. Your seven o'clock."

Slowly, Heather twisted in her seat, as if she were looking around for the server. A second later, she turned back to face him, looking sceptical.

"No way. He looks old enough to be her dad."

"Which for some men is actually a selling point."

"Ew." Heather wrinkled her nose endearingly.

"Okay, let's hope she's his daughter. Oh, I see another one." He tipped his head towards two middle-aged men sitting in upright silence, picking reluctantly at their food and avoiding each other's eyes.

Heather followed his eyes, and for a few seconds he watched her watch them. "Yikes. That's either a very bad first date or a very bad last one."

"Or both," he added, and she giggled.

"Okay, new game: what's the worst date you've ever been on?"

"Easy. Year 11, Sasha Perkins. We went to Warringah Mall for lunch and then to the movies. She kept calling me 'Iceberg' for some reason, and when I got home I realised I'd had a giant piece of lettuce stuck in my braces the whole time."

"Oh *no*," she laughed, taking an olive and popping it in her mouth. It left a smear of shining oil on her bottom lip, and Marcus worked hard not to stare at it.

"Oh, yes. That one scarred me for life. I couldn't eat Caesar salad for years. What about you? Worst date ever?"

"I haven't been on that many dates. I guess I've kind of dated vicariously through my best friend. Carly has enough bad date stories to write a book about them."

"A field guide to fuckboys?"

"Yes. Knowing Carly, she'd call it . . . *Bangs of New York*." She smiled, like she was proud of the pun.

"That is an instant bestseller," he said, grinning.

"Once, she went home with a guy and discovered he had an entire room devoted to his antique doll collection. Just hundreds of musty old doll faces staring at you from every surface."

"And that," he said, "is a serial killer."

"That's what I said!" Heather exclaimed, propping her elbows on the table. "But she stayed the night anyway."

"She stayed?! That's . . . brave."

"Well, that's Carly."

"What's she like? Apart from brave, and lucky to be alive?"

Heather's smile turned a little sad. "She's the best. I think some people would say she's an acquired taste, but I love her. She's loyal, and she's funny."

"And she's not afraid of creepy antique dolls, which is an important quality in a best friend."

Heather laughed again, and Marcus wondered if it was possible to get drunk on a sound.

"I don't think she's afraid of anything," Heather mused, fiddling with her glass again. "Ever since I've known her, she's been totally comfortable with herself, even when we were gawky, pimply teenagers. She's not afraid to be exactly who she is. She's Carly, take her or leave her, you know? I wish I could do that. . . ." Her voice trailed off, staring into her wine.

Marcus watched her, hungry to know more but afraid to ask. He was no longer impatient for Alice and Will to arrive. They could take another half an hour, for all he cared, if it meant more time laughing and joking and listening to Heather.

"I'm trying to be more like her," she said to the wine, then she raised her head as though willing herself to look him in the eye. A determined little frown creased her forehead. "More myself, take it or leave it. I spent so many years making myself into someone else's idea of me. I think I was so grateful he wanted me, I didn't notice he didn't want all of me. He only wanted the parts that were quiet and obedient. And I just . . . let him have the parts he wanted and buried the rest."

Marcus watched her face twist with regret as she spoke and resisted the urge to say what he was thinking, which was that the loud, disobedient parts of Heather, the parts that had her yelling "tosser!" at the beach and kissing him in fitting rooms, were his favourites so far. He knew she expected a response, and he opened his mouth to say something—anything but that—but was interrupted by a flurry of movement a few feet away.

"Hi hi hi! I'm so sorry, Will was late getting home from work and we got stuck in traffic!" Alice rushed to their table, hair windswept and keys still in hand. "We got here as fast as we could and he's parking the car. Did you order without us? Did you get the lamb?"

Marcus stared up at Alice, slightly disoriented. He knew he should be relieved she'd finally arrived. Instead, he felt crestfallen.

"No, we just ordered some starters," he said, glancing at Heather. Her elbows were no longer on the table, and she sat up straight, looking at Alice with an inscrutable expression.

"Oh, good," Alice sighed, dropping her bag onto the ground next to the empty chair and plopping down into it. "What did I miss?"

Marcus started, "Well—"

"You didn't miss anything," Heather said quickly, reaching for her jacket and bag, "and actually, I should go. Sorry, Alice, I appreciate the invitation, but I'm not feeling well. I'll see you on Monday."

Before Alice could reply or Marcus could object, she stood and walked out the door.

"Heather, wait!"

Heather winced and turned to face Alice.

"Are you okay? I'm really sorry we were late—"

"No, it's not that," she reassured Alice quickly. "I'm just really tired. Long rehearsal week."

Alice frowned up at her, looking concerned. Heather wished she'd come up with a less clichéd excuse. She'd just started making friends with Alice, and now she was messing it all up.

"Okay, well, do you want to get some dinner to take away at least?"

"No, no, I'll be okay, but here," Heather rummaged in her bag for her wallet. "Take this, to cover my wine and appetizers."

Alice took the twenty dollar bill but otherwise didn't move. She was watching Heather, concern now mingled with curiosity. "Do you want Will to drive you home? He probably hasn't even found a park yet."

"No, I . . . I think a walk in the night air will be good for me," Heather said weakly. "Bye, Alice. I'll see you on Monday. And thanks for inviting me out."

Heather gave her an awkward wave, then turned and walked away as fast as a person who was meant to be tired reasonably could.

She pulled her denim jacket tight across her body in a fruitless attempt to keep out the chilly evening breeze buffeting her as she stalked along Military Road. Cars and buses rumbled alongside her, loud, but not loud enough to drown out her thoughts as she put as much distance as she could between herself and Café Luxor.

She'd known going to dinner tonight was a mistake, even before Alice's traffic problems had left her alone at a small, dimly lit table with Marcus for almost an hour. She'd spent the week trying to resist the magnetic pull she felt toward him, and she'd succeeded, even when he had his hands on her in rehearsal and she could feel his pulse pounding in his fingertips, echoing through her body. But she'd shown up tonight and undone all that progress.

What was worse, she thought, flipping her braid over her shoulder in frustration, was that for a few minutes there it hadn't felt like a mistake at all. It had felt like . . . well, it had felt like a really good first date. They'd been talking comfortably and teasing each other, enjoying each other's company, making each other laugh. If Alice hadn't arrived, she would have kept talking. She had wanted to keep talking. She would have told him about all the ways she'd let Jack change her, all the parts of herself she'd shut down and shut away in order to be with him. All the invisible, inviolable rules Jack made that she'd learned to follow, even when it didn't feel right. She'd have told him everything, and he would have listened to every word without judgment.

She couldn't blame the wine; she'd only had a few sips. It was him. *He* was intoxicating. And kind, and easy to confide in, and quick to apologize when he made a mistake. And absolutely off-limits to her.

Heather pulled out her phone, her stomach growling, and sighed. No Moroccan lamb shanks or Portuguese prawns for her tonight. Fifteen minutes later, her rideshare car pulled up in front of the Thai place near her house, and she climbed out, thanking the driver with a sigh. Another night of pad thai alone on the couch, then, just like she'd done three other nights this week. Maybe tonight she'd get adventurous and order the shrimp instead of the chicken.

While she waited for her food, she checked the world clock on her phone. It was just past 6:00 AM in New York. Carly definitely wouldn't be up yet.

Heather, 8:04 PM: Call me when you get up?

Her thumbs hovered over the screen as she wondered whether she should say more. What would she say? "FYI, I just accidentally went on a really good first date and fled the scene as soon as I realized what was going on"? She gave her head a little shake and was about to text Carly it was nothing serious—even though she wasn't sure that was the truth—when, to her surprise, the phone vibrated, and Carly's photo popped up.

"You're awake early," Heather answered.

"'Awake' is a strong word," Carly croaked, and Heather smiled. She felt better just hearing her friend's voice.

"What did you do last night?"

"I drank a little champagne," Carly said coyly, and Heather could hear the rustle of sheets in the background. "Okay, sparkling wine, not real champagne, but still. I was celebrating."

"Did Samuel and Brett actually fall in the orchestra pit?"

"Not yet," Carly growled. "But yesterday Jack cornered me after class and demanded to know what you're doing in Australia."

"Are you okay?" Heather asked quickly. "What did you tell him?"

"Oh, I'm fine. I just smiled sweetly and told him I hadn't heard from you because all those fine Australian men were keeping you so busy."

Heather scoffed, then felt her cheeks heat with embarrassment. Carly didn't know how right she was. "Did you really say that?"

"No, I told him to fuck off forever, like I've been wanting to do for seven years. It felt amazing! His face went *purple.*"

Heather let out a shaky breath. Her best friend could stand up to Jack and his cronies, but Heather wished she didn't have to face them on her own. "Okay," she said, grateful for an excuse to change the subject, "are you going to tell me what you were celebrating, or should I keep guessing?"

"You'll never guess, I could hardly believe it when I found out."

Now Heather was really curious. "What's going on?"

"Well, it's not definite yet, but Mr. K finally agreed to do some women's empowerment initiative this season, because they've been getting so much shit for not hiring women choreographers, you know?"

Heather nodded. There had been a series of outraged op-ed columns in the last few years, every time NYB announced yet another new season with basically no ballets made by women.

"So yesterday one of the women choreographers came to company class to figure out who she wants to use in her ballet, and it sounds like she wants me for a principal role! Baby's first principal part!"

"That's great! Oh, I'm so happy for you," Heather grinned. It was unusual for a corps de ballet dancer to be picked for a principal role, but Carly deserved this. In truth, she had deserved it a long time ago.

Across the counter, a waiter slid a plastic bag toward her, and she put her hand over the phone to thank him.

"I'm in the second cast, so I think it'll only be for Wednesday nights and matinees," Carly was saying as Heather stepped back onto the sidewalk, "But still, exciting, right?"

"So exciting," Heather said, "I'm so proud of you." As her friend talked and Heather rounded the corner onto her street, she felt her shoulders relax. For a moment she forgot why she'd wanted to talk to Carly in the first place.

"They're doing this big press rollout about all the women choreographers they've hired," Carly continued. "Well, all two of them. But they're making a big fuss about it, after all the pressure they've been under. I'm going to be in the photo shoot and everything! It's totally nerve-racking, but—"

"You'll be brilliant," Heather interrupted her, and she meant it. "And everyone else who dances the role after you will spend the rest of ballet eternity trying to do it as well as you will." Carly laughed, sounding delighted and a little relieved.

Heather let herself into the house and hustled back to the kitchen as Carly talked about how cool the choreographer seemed and how she hoped the new work was something interesting and innovative. Heather set her food down on the counter next to the fridge, then froze in horror.

"Ohmygod," she breathed, staring, too shocked to properly form words.

"I know, right?" Carly said, oblivious.

"NononoIgottago," Heather gasped, and slowly, moving as carefully as she dared, she hung up and took a step backward.

There was a spider in her kitchen. A huge, hulking spider, with a bulbous body that, even from a distance, she could see was covered in dark brown fur. Its legs were hunched up around its round, revolting body, but they looked so long that, when fully extended, the creature would be bigger than her hand. Heather stared at it, open-mouthed and appalled, her heart hammering in her chest.

New York City roaches she could handle. Rats parading along subway platforms proudly dragging entire slices of pizza behind them were no big deal. But a giant hairy spider casually perched on her toaster, ready to pounce any moment, waiting to kill her in her sleep?

Hell. No.

What was she supposed to do about this? Did Australians keep some kind of giant bug spray in their houses? Should she call 911, or whatever number Australians called when they called 911? She had looked it up before she came, but her brain had been temporarily wiped blank by panic. Without thinking, and without moving anything except her eyes and her right thumb, she swiped through her phone and called the only person she could think of who could help.

He picked up on the first ring. "Hello? Heather?"

"Marcus," she whispered. Any loud noises or sudden movements and she was going to die right here in this chic little kitchen.

"Hello? Hello? I can't hear you. Uh, Heather, did you mean to call me?"

"Marcus," she managed to say, a little louder this time. "Come over. Right now. I need your help."

Heather's words echoed in his head as he climbed out of the taxi as quickly as his ankle would allow. His phone had rung just as he'd left the restaurant after a hasty meal with Alice and Will. They'd split the famous lamb shanks, but he hadn't enjoyed them like he usually did. His unfinished conversation with Heather—and the look on her face as she'd rushed away—ate at him. After Alice returned to their table, she'd spent the whole meal throwing him suspicious, curious looks, as if she knew she'd interrupted something important.

Which, of course, she had. After a week of wanting to be close to Heather again, he had finally gotten time alone with her. She'd been confiding in him, telling him things he was willing to bet she wouldn't tell just anyone. Then Alice showed up and the moment evaporated.

"*Right now. I need your help.*" He'd called her back as soon as he was in the car, anxious to know what had happened to make her voice breathy and desperate like that, but she hadn't answered. Was she hurt? Shit, what if she'd injured herself and couldn't dance? What if someone had broken into the house?

He walked up her front steps faster than he should have and rapped on the door. It opened instantly, and there she was, still in her sweater dress and earrings, her plait a little looser now, her big brown eyes wide. "What's wrong?" he asked, a little winded. "What happened?"

For a moment Heather simply stood in the entryway, her chest rising and falling with rapid breaths. She looked terrified. Marcus looked her up and down and was relieved to find she wasn't hurt.

"I'm sorry," she whispered, "I shouldn't have called you. But I didn't know who else to call."

"It's fine, I'm glad you did. What happened? Are you okay?"

"Spider," she said, still whispering.

"What?"

"There's a spider," she said, a little louder, waving one hand behind her. "In the kitchen. It's huge and just sitting there waiting to kill me, and I watched it crawl from the toaster to the counter, and—" she broke off and shuddered with her entire body.

Marcus stared as he processed this information, then let out a relieved laugh. She watched him in disbelief as he stepped into the house and closed the door behind him.

"Shh!"

"Heather, it's a spider, it can't hear us," he said at a normal volume. "Show me where it is."

"It was in the kitchen a few minutes ago, but I've been hiding here, so I don't know where it is now." She glanced up at the ceiling, as if she expected to find it dangling above her.

Marcus rested his cane against the door, then walked into the kitchen and looked around. Crouched on the counter was a fairly large huntsman spider. It wasn't the biggest he'd ever seen, though in fairness to Heather, it was probably the biggest *she'd* ever seen. But it was definitely not going to kill her.

"It's just a huntsman," he called, "they're harmless."

He heard her scoff, and he poked his head out into the hallway.

"I was worried you had a redback or a funnelweb or something; those could really do you in."

"How is naming other deadly creatures helpful right now?" she hissed.

"Okay, okay, sorry," he said, suppressing a smile. She didn't sound that scared of the spider anymore, just annoyed with him. "I promise you, this is not a deadly creature. This guy's more afraid of you than you are of him."

"That's bears," she retorted, crossing her arms tight across her chest.

"Yeah, but bears can actually kill you. A huntsman can't. Look, I'll show you. Can you get me a plastic container and a piece of cardboard?"

She nodded, then tiptoed past him into the kitchen, edging along the wall and keeping her eyes averted from the spider. She pulled a takeaway container and a piece of junk mail out of the recycling bin and held them out to him.

"Thanks. Now watch this. I promise you I wouldn't do this with a venomous spider. But huntsmen are really common, and I did this a tonne in the house I grew up in."

Marcus advanced towards the spider with the container in one hand and hovered it a foot above the counter. Then he brought it down fast, trapping the spider beneath it. It started and its legs made a scraping, crunching sound against the plastic. Behind him Heather gave a small, disgusted whimper. Holding the container down firmly, Marcus dragged it towards the edge of the counter where he held the cardboard in his other hand. In one quick motion, he pulled the container off the counter and covered the bottom with the junk mail.

"Can you open the front door, please?" he asked, and Heather scurried out of the room as he flipped the container over. He followed her to the front, where she waited with the door thrown open. Once out onto her little verandah, Marcus crouched down next to the bushes and set the container down, taking the cardboard with him as he stood again.

"That's it?" Heather called.

"That's it." He shrugged, facing her. She'd closed the door almost completely and peered out through a narrow crack. "He'll see himself out."

"What if it comes back?"

"Then you know how to escort him out."

Heather scoffed again. "Or I can just move to a new house."

"Or you can call me again." He smiled. Heather paused, and he realised what he'd said. An uncomfortable silence stretched between them. He was about to assure her he hadn't meant it like that when she spoke.

"Um, thank you. For saving me."

"Yeah, no worries. Any time." Another silence. "Did you eat dinner? You missed some pretty good lamb."

She sighed from behind the door. "I ordered some takeout, but now I think I've lost my appetite forever." She opened the door a little wider. "Do you . . . would you . . . could you stay? Just for a bit? In case it comes back? Or has friends?"

Marcus paused, staring at the cardboard in his hand to buy time. He should just go home. He'd done what she'd needed him to do. She was never in any real danger, and she definitely wasn't in harm's way now. Staying here would only make it harder to pretend he didn't want her.

"Spiders don't have friends," he said softly, throwing her a rueful smile.

She paused, then opened the door wider still, her shoulders hunched and tense. "Please, Marcus?"

The sound of his name in her mouth decided it. The Heather Hays—gorgeous, talented, funny, loud, disobedient Heather Hays—was asking him to come inside and keep her company on a dark, windy, spider-infested night. He was kidding himself if he thought he had the strength to say no.

"Okay, Heather. Just for a bit. In case it comes back."

A relieved smile broke over her face, and her shoulders dropped as she pulled the door open to let him inside.

"Do you want a drink? I want a drink, or five."

"Sure, but I can't get too drunk. What if I have to save you from another poisonous monster?"

"You said it wasn't dangerous!" she exclaimed as he sidled past her. "I don't know how people live like this." She shook her head and disappeared into the kitchen, returning a moment later with two bottles of light beer and a bottle opener. Marcus was still standing in the entryway with his hands in his pockets. She handed him one and switched on the living room lights.

"You can sit if you want," she said, gesturing towards the plump, pale-yellow couch, but Marcus was too nervous to sit, so he wandered into the living room, feeling stilted and ungainly. He forced himself to stand still and at least try to look relaxed. This was just a beer. Just a beer with a colleague. A colleague he'd kissed once and desperately wanted to kiss again. Hard and deep, for as long as she'd let him.

Heather fumbled with the bottle opener, and her fingers slipped on the condensation. "Sorry, I'm still a bit shaky."

"Here, let me," he said, putting his hands out, and she brushed her hair out of her face before offering him both the bottle and opener. For a second, he didn't move away, and they stayed like that, their hands loosely joined around the items. He looked down into her breathtaking face and told himself to pull away. *Now.*

There's a policy against this, and it exists for a reason.

He would pull his hands away, he told himself. Right after he ran the pad of his thumb lightly over the heel of her hand. Just once. Just to know what it felt like. He held her gaze, watching her watch him, and stroked the soft, smooth skin of her palm. A tiny movement, and the sound she made in response, the quiet intake of breath, was just as small. But it nearly undid him. He watched her as she bit her lip, watched the plump pink skin dimple and flush dark under the pressure of her teeth. He watched her as a small frown creased her forehead, and as she gave a tiny, decisive nod. Then her fingers tightened and he watched, perplexed, as she tossed both bottle and opener onto the couch.

"Cartwheels," she whispered, and then she kissed him.

He stepped towards her so fast he knocked over his own bottle. It clattered onto the glass coffee table, but he barely heard it. Heather Hays was kissing him again, and nothing else in the world mattered. He grabbed her hip in one hand and her face in the other, pulling her into him, kissing her back, hard. She gasped in surprise against his mouth, but a second later she looped her arms over his shoulders and pressed herself against him.

The kiss felt like oxygen, like he would be lightheaded if his mouth ever left hers. He explored her lips with his, first one, then the other, then his tongue slid between them. Her mouth was hot and hungry, her lips achingly soft and full but determined to match his urgency.

There was no trace of the slow caution he'd felt in her kiss in the changing room. This time, she was fierce and focused, as if she'd been craving him for days, just like he'd craved her. The thought shot through him, hot and triumphant, as her body pressed and arched against him, fluid and strong and so much better than his brain had allowed him to remember.

Heather ran her hands through his hair and traced her fingers down the back of his neck. He growled approvingly into her mouth and pushed his hips harder against her. She did it again, like she was relishing the response she'd provoked.

As quickly as he could without hurting himself or tripping over her feet, he walked her backwards until her shoulders hit the hallway wall a foot from the staircase up to her bedroom.

She gasped as her shoulders made contact, and he broke the kiss.

"Is this okay?" She'd just had a scare, and he didn't want to push her too far or too fast.

"Better than that," she breathed, and he grinned, turning his attention to the side of her neck, kissing steadily down the steep slope of muscle along her shoulder until his lips met an infuriating fabric barrier. Her sweater still carried the scent of the cafe's spices. He dipped lower, exploring the smooth, sensitive skin above her sternum and the tops of her small, perfect breasts, feeling her quiet moans vibrate through her and into his mouth. Goosebumps rose every place his lips and tongue touched.

"Too many clothes," he muttered against her collarbone, and he felt her quiet laugh rumble through her rib cage.

Without a word, she reached up and undid his topmost shirt button. He resisted the urge to kiss her again and instead watched her, his heart pounding as her fingers worked their way down his chest and pulled the shirt out of his jeans. He extricated himself from his shirt and tossed it aside, then pulled her against him, the fabric of her sweater dress soft and ticklish on his bare chest. The feel of her lean, muscular body and small breasts pressed against him was blissful.

He kissed her again, and her hands roamed his chest to trace the ridges of his stomach, skimming lightly, torturously, over the sensitive skin just above his belt. He groaned with frustration and desire, sliding his hands down to her firm, round ass and pulling her hard against him so she could feel exactly what that did to him. She did it again, and he grinned against her mouth.

Breaking the kiss again and looking down, he realised she was still fully clothed, boots and all. He desperately wanted her out of this dress, wanted to peel it off and wrap her legs around his waist.

Resisting that urge, he instead slid his hand to the back of her thigh and pulled her leg out to rest her foot on the lowest step.

She gasped, and his eyes flew to hers.

"Do you want me to keep going?" he asked.

"Yes," she breathed, returning his gaze, and relief flooded him.

He moved his hand slowly up her leg, keeping her steady with his other, holding eye contact as his fingers slid over the smooth, taut skin of her inner thigh. Her eyes stayed locked on his as he touched her, her fingers tightening on his upper arms as his fingers pushed the hem of her dress up higher, and higher still.

When his hand disappeared under her dress and brushed against damp, soft lace, he moaned at the sensation and nearly closed his eyes against the surge of want slamming through him. But he kept watching her, holding her gaze, observing her face as he slipped the fabric aside and touched her hot, sensitive flesh. She gave in first, dropping her head back and whimpering as he stroked her. His fingers slid between her delicate folds, tracing loops and circles and approaching her clit before backing away. Heather whimpered louder this time, digging her knee into his thigh and rocking her hips against his fingers. More than happy to give her what she wanted, Marcus slid a finger carefully inside her—fuck, she was so slick and so hot—and settled the heel of his hand against her. She gasped at the pressure, clutched at his arms as she began to grind against his firm hand and his thrusting finger.

The hallway was silent except for the distant rumble of traffic sliding over the Bridge a few blocks away and Heather's quiet but increasingly urgent moans. Marcus's aching erection strained against his jeans, but there wasn't a chance in hell he'd interrupt this, not when she was making those delightful, deliriously sexy sounds, not when she seemed to be right on the edge. Marcus slid a second finger inside and Heather grabbed at his hips, leaning forward, pressing her forehead into his shoulder as she shuddered around him, her breaths landing hot and sharp on his bare chest.

After a moment she lifted her head and leant back against the wall, still panting, heat radiating from her skin. He removed himself from her underwear and held her thigh, unwilling, and possibly unable, to stop touching her.

"So worth it," Heather breathed with a dreamy smile.

"Worth what?"

"Worth living in a death trap with a poisonous eight-legged monster."

Marcus laughed his surprised bark of a laugh up to the ceiling of the quiet house. Through the deep fog of an orgasm that had threatened to buckle her knees, Heather registered again how good it felt to make him laugh like that.

"Well, I'm a full-service exterminator, ma'am. The spiders go, and you come." Marcus's eyes lit up and his hands slid to her bare hips, pulling her against him. She could feel him through his jeans, rock hard and ready. She couldn't help letting out a tiny moan as their hips met and his erection pressed against her again.

"I think there are probably some more spiders around here," she managed as he kissed her neck again, "so I might need you to do that again."

"Oh no, not that, anything but that," he growled playfully in her ear, and this time she was the one laughing.

Had she and Jack ever laughed like this during sex? If they had, she couldn't remember. She certainly couldn't remember him laughing at her jokes; in fact, he'd been embarrassed by her attempts at humor. Once, after he'd been promoted to principal and she was still in the corps, they'd gone out to dinner with Samuel and Brett and their girlfriends, and she'd made some goofy pun about an item on the menu. When all four of them stared at her as though she'd suddenly spoken in tongues, Jack placed a hand gently on her forearm and jumped in to rescue her—or so she thought.

"Sorry," he'd said to them, sounding genuinely apologetic, before casting her a fleeting, irritated glance. "She was trying to make a joke. She does that sometimes."

Heather sighed, suddenly exhausted. Marcus pulled away from her earlobe and leaned back to look at her.

"Everything okay?"

"Yeah," she replied quickly. "Just thirsty. I'm going to get a glass of water."

"I'll get it," he said, pulling away and making his way toward the kitchen. Heather followed, admiring the way his back muscles shifted beneath his skin as he walked, and noting a spray of freckles across his shoulder blades that matched the ones on his forehead. Heather leaned against the counter, enjoying the view of his rippling shoulder muscles as he reached into an upper cupboard, pulled out a water glass, filled it at the sink, and handed it to her.

She gulped at it gratefully. She hadn't realized how parched her throat had been. Marcus watched her intently, and when she set her empty glass down, he filled it again and slid it back toward her. She looked at the blue and yellow striped glass, which had left a thin wet streak behind where he'd pushed it across the counter. She must have stared a moment too long, because he took a step toward her and put one hand on her waist.

"You sure you're okay?" he asked, more concerned this time.

"Yeah," she nodded, "I just, I, um . . ." She paused, avoiding his eyes by looking at the hollow of his throat, trying to choose the right words. She suspected there was no combination of words that wouldn't disappoint him. He waited.

"It's been a really long day. Rehearsal with Peter was hard, and the spider . . . I'm tired. And I know you probably don't want to hear this right now but can we just, could we . . . not? I mean, can we stop for tonight?" She winced apologetically. "I'm sorry," she added quickly.

Marcus looked confused, and she instantly regretted saying anything. He'd just made her come, and he was clearly very revved up, so she should just return the favor.

"Sorry," she repeated into the silence.

"Please don't apologize," he said quietly. "Of course we can stop." He shifted uncomfortably.

"Are you sure?" With difficulty, she raised her head and searched his face for annoyance or frustration. To her surprise, she found none.

"Uh, yes?" he said slowly, as though she was missing something very obvious. "You don't, like, owe me anything."

For a moment, Heather didn't know what to say. In her experience, men—well, Jack—expected to get off in a situation like this, especially if she already had.

"Okay. Do you want to go?" She knew what he was going to say, but she wished he wouldn't say it. Obviously this could never happen again. *It shouldn't have happened at all*, she scolded herself half-heartedly. But once he left, it would all be over.

He took a step toward her, put his hands on her hips, and pulled her against him. "Not really," he murmured into her hair. "I mean, what if that spider did make some friends?"

A relieved giggle escaped her mouth. Apparently she didn't know what he was going to say. She didn't know him that well at all. But, she thought, taking his hand and leading him out of the kitchen toward the stairs, she really wanted to.

Chapter 11

The next morning, Heather woke to the sound of a door snapping shut. Her eyes flew open, and she was greeted by weak morning sun creeping into her bedroom. Squinting and screwing up her face, she listened hard. Was that the front door? Had Marcus . . . left? She sat up quickly, dread swimming in her stomach. His side of the bed was warm but empty, and his clothes were gone.

"Damnit," she muttered, disentangling herself from the sheets. What an unbelievable mess to have made for herself. Twenty-four hours ago, she'd been doing a perfectly fine job at keeping her distance from Marcus. Now she'd accidentally had dinner with him, and very deliberately kissed him, and—she shivered at the memory—come hard against him and felt his rock-hard cock through his jeans. Then, most intimate of all, she'd spent the night sleeping soundly next to his still, warm body. In the space of just a few hours, she'd managed to endanger their jobs, her reputation, and any hope of a normal, professional friendship with him. And now he was gone, vanished before she could even wake up.

"*Damnit,*" she said a little louder, flopping onto her back and scowling at the ceiling. Last night had been . . . well, in hindsight it had been stupid, and embarrassing, and clearly not worth the risk of anyone at ANB finding out. But while it had been happening, while he was touching her, kissing her like he was starving and her mouth was a feast? That had been something else entirely.

"Damnit, damnit, damnit," she chanted under her breath. "Stupid, stupid, stupid."

"Everything all right in here?" Marcus appeared in the doorway, holding a cardboard tray with two to-go coffee cups. Heather froze, then sat up slowly. His hair was damp, and raindrops sparkled on the shoulders of his wrinkled shirt.

"Hi," he said slowly, frowning at her. "You okay?"

"I'm fine . . ." Heather trailed off. "Um, I thought you'd snuck out."

"I did, but only to get us coffee." Marcus shrugged. He sat on the bed and held a cup out to her.

"Oh, thanks," she said and smiled up at him, suddenly wishing she'd used his absence to brush her hair and wipe the sleep out of her eyes. Marcus looked perfectly tousled and handsome, but she was pretty sure she looked disheveled and sleepy. Heather took the cup and stared down at the lid. In blue pen, the barista had scrawled, "SF +1." A skim flat white with one sugar. He'd remembered her coffee order.

"Anyway, why would I sneak out?"

"I don't know." She fiddled with the plastic lid, brushing off raindrops and flipping the flimsy lip back and forth with her thumb. "Isn't that a thing guys do?"

She thought of the time, a year after they'd joined the company, when Carly had woken up in the apartment of a guy she'd been dating for a few months and found him gone. His roommate, who she'd found sitting on the kitchen counter eating cold mac and cheese right out of a crusty-looking pot, had told her the guy had left on a three-week vacation. It was the first Carly had heard about it. She never heard from him again.

"I'm sure there are some guys who do that, but I'm not very sneaky right now, and I probably wouldn't get away with it." He gestured down at his foot. He lifted his cup up and bumped it lightly against hers. "Cheers."

Heather took a fortifying sip and sighed. Two weeks in Sydney and she was already addicted to whatever Australians put in their coffee.

"Speaking of getting away with it," she said quietly.

"Nice segue." He smirked, and she suppressed a smile.

"Last night," she tried again, "things kind of got out of hand." He raised his eyebrows and smirked harder in reply.

"Oh God, worst possible choice of words." She put her hand over her face. "I just mean, last night was exactly what we were trying to avoid. What we cannot be doing. And it can't happen again. We need to just . . . pretend it never happened."

He reached out and pried her fingers away from her face. She expected him to drop her hand, but he kept his fingers loosely tangled with hers and looked at her closely, the morning light making the golden flecks in his eyes shimmer and dance.

"Please don't take this the wrong way," he said gently, a kind smile crinkling the corners of his eyes, "but that's the worst fucking idea I've ever heard."

She squawked in surprise and then coughed to cover the unflattering sound. He released her hand and ran his fingers through his hair, then went on.

"We've tried 'pretend it never happened,' and it hasn't worked. We didn't even last a week. In fact, I think 'pretend it never happened' made things worse. I couldn't stop thinking about you."

Her stomach did an inelegant little sauté, and she couldn't conceal her smile this time. "I couldn't stop thinking about you either," she said quietly, unable to meet his eyes. "But this has to stop. We have to stop. You know how this ends. We get caught, we both lose our jobs, and I . . ." *I go back to New York even more humiliated than when I left*. The woman who screwed her way into one job then screwed herself out of another. It was too awful to contemplate, let alone say out loud.

"Or it ends when you leave town," he countered hopefully. "No one finds out, we keep our jobs, and we have a fun time together while we can. It wouldn't be forever; it would just be for now."

"*Or*, everyone finds out, and we're both humiliated and unemployed, and for what? A fling?"

Marcus sat up a bit straighter, as though her words had stung, and she wished she'd spoken a little less vehemently.

"Listen, I'm not going to pressure you into something you don't want to do," he said softly, sounding far less confident than he had a moment ago. "I know this situation is . . . complicated. I know what's at stake. But I had a good time last night. I have a good time whenever I'm with you. And listen," he glanced around as if hoping he'd find the right words somewhere in her bedroom, "life is short, and it can fall apart in a fraction of a second. I like spending time with you. And I think you like spending time with me. So it's actually pretty simple."

"Nothing about this is simple," Heather retorted, though a part of her wanted to trust he was right. Another part of her didn't care if it was messy and risky, thought it might even be fun and sexy to sneak around. Break the rules for once in her life, like Carly was always telling her to do. Cartwheels.

"I just don't want—" she started, then stopped when he lifted her coffee from her hand and set both cups down on the bedside table.

Marcus sat on the edge of the bed and faced her, his thigh pressing lightly against hers. Then he leaned forward and kissed her. A gentle brush of his lips, but it sent heat and want rushing through her, and she could barely contain the whimper that formed in her throat. He pulled back far enough to meet her eyes as he spoke.

"You've told me all the things you don't want, Heather. I want to know what you *do* want." She swallowed hard, her pulse suddenly racing. "Tell me what *you*"—he emphasized the word—"*want*."

Heather was sure he could hear her heart throwing itself against her ribs, and her tangled thoughts tumbling over each other in her head. But he just watched her and waited.

And in the split second between leaning forward and claiming his soft, lush mouth with her own, she glimpsed a flash of something—delight, surprise, disbelief, *something*—in his green and gold eyes.

Relief and reckless desire shot through Marcus in equal measure. He kissed her back, slipping his tongue between her lips and meeting hers—gently at first, but when she twisted towards him and looped her arms around his neck, he grew bolder. One of his hands found her waist and flattened against her rib cage, holding her firmly, possessively. In that moment he wanted nothing more than to let it roam all over her, to explore every one of her gentle curves and her smooth expanses. Now. But before he could do that, she pulled away and scooted backwards, putting a foot of bed between them.

"Rules," she said breathlessly. "We need rules."

"I thought we'd just decided we're breaking the rules."

"Well, yes, but in order to get away with that, we're going to need . . . other rules," she said, her tone increasingly businesslike. "The first one's obvious: we don't tell anyone, at ANB or anywhere else."

"First rule of fuck club is you don't talk about fuck club," he said, nodding, and she swatted his arm, grinning.

"Yes, but we're not calling it that. Let's see. . . . I guess the second rule is no touching at work? No sneaking around or secret kissing in the lounge or anything. At work, we're colleagues and that's it."

"Right, except if you happen to walk in on me half naked in the men's room, and who would ever do something like that?" She swatted him again, but this time he grabbed her hand and pulled it up to his mouth.

"I'm serious," she insisted, but she sighed and bit her bottom lip as he kissed the inside of her wrist hungrily.

"So am I," he said against her skin. She smelled like lavender and sleep.

"The quicker we figure this out, the quicker we can get back to what we were doing," she said matter-of-factly, and he dropped her arm and sat up straight, eyebrows raised expectantly. She laughed and shook her head, and the sound was like a mouthful of hot, strong coffee, warming his insides and making his heart beat just a little faster.

"What's rule three?" he asked, folding his hands chastely in his lap. For all his jokes, he wanted her to trust the choice she'd made. And he was enjoying watching her plan this little rebellion.

"Rule three . . . I think . . . no photos."

He frowned, surprised. "Like, naked photos? I wouldn't want to do that anyway. Not that I judge people who do; I just think it's too risky."

"No, I mean no photos at all. I don't take any of you, and you don't take any of me. And obviously no photos of us together. That way, if someone looks at our phones there's no evidence of anything inappropriate."

"Okay." He nodded slowly. "That makes sense." Though it was a lot of subterfuge he wished he didn't have to think about.

Marcus wondered how many other dancers had pulled this off—and how many had thought they could pull it off, only to get caught and fired. Had his colleagues in the corps had this very conversation last year, only to find themselves in Peter's office, being kicked out of the company? Maybe Heather had been right, and this was far more complicated than he'd been willing to admit. He studied her as she sat on the bed, her pointed chin raised almost imperceptibly, her face a picture of determination bordering on stubbornness. It was easy for him to imagine that expression taking over her face in the middle of a difficult rehearsal, when the pirouettes weren't working but she was hell-bent on making them. It was so endearing, he thought, it would be worth a little sneaking around to see more of it. More of this face, more of her.

"One last rule," she said. "Obviously nothing out in public. No dates out where anyone could see us, like last night. That's a pretty easy way to get busted."

For a moment, he was confused by the sharp edge in her voice, then understanding dawned. Of course Heather knew how to sneak around, even if she'd never done it herself. No telling, no touching, no taking photos—that was how her fiancé had hidden his affair, until he hadn't.

"Got it," he said. "These are good rules. Shake on it?" Marcus held out his hand, and she gave it a firm shake, nodding decisively.

He released her fingers, but she held onto his hand and pulled herself towards him. A second later she was straddling his lap, and Marcus toppled over in surprise, falling onto his back on the bed. Heather went down with him, bracing her hands on either side of the bed and giggling. He was surrounded by her, defenseless against the heat rolling off her skin and the addictive sound of her laugh.

He pulled her down against him, and, cupping her face with his hands, claimed her mouth. She tasted like coffee still, and he groaned with relief as her tongue slicked against his, matching his urgency. He broke the kiss and brought his mouth to her neck, pulling the collar of her pyjama shirt aside to gain access to more of her.

"Fuck this," he muttered. He seized the bottom of her shirt and pulled it over her head, then wrapped one arm around her waist and rolled them over. Then Heather Hays was beneath him wearing nothing but pyjama pants and a lace bralette.

"Sweet Jesus, you're so beautiful," Marcus breathed, trying to take in all of her and feeling slightly drunk from the attempt.

Her body was a finely honed tool, all muscle and taut skin, gentle curves where her breasts swelled around her sternum and her slim waist gave way to narrow but unmistakable hips. Marcus had seen her in class, seen her sweat through a skin-tight leotard, but he had barely allowed himself to imagine her like this. Half naked, her hair a wavy, tangled mess, her breasts rising and falling with every rapid breath. The thin, pale green fabric of her bra did nothing to conceal her nipples or disguise their hardness as they strained against the lace, all but begging to be stroked and sucked and rolled between his teeth.

Marcus wasted no time, returning his lips to her neck and nipping gently at the soft, smooth skin there, loving the way Heather moaned and ground her hips against him in response. While he explored her neck with his mouth, he cupped one of her breasts gently, holding his hand against her until her back arched, urging him on. His cock hardened at the sensation of her pressing more of her soft, pliant flesh into his palm, and he obeyed her request, sliding his thumb over her breast and brushing it lightly, delicately, over the lace that covered her puckered nipple.

Heather whimpered, and the sound made him want to stay here all day, teasing one nipple and then the other, listening to her moan and gasp and feeling her body arch helplessly under his. But she seized his shirt and unbuttoned it hastily, and a moment later he was shrugging it off, desperate to remove his clothes so he could get his hands back on her.

Marcus leaned down to kiss her again, but Heather put her hand on his chest and pushed him up to kneel over her, shirtless and breathless. Taking her time, she surveyed him the same way he'd run his eyes over her. As he watched her face, she actually, literally, licked her lips. He had never felt more wanted.

"Sweet Jesus," she said, sounding like she was working very hard to keep her voice steady, "you're pretty beautiful yourself." Then she hooked two fingers into the waist of his jeans and pulled him back down, kissing him fiercely and sliding her fingers into his hair.

It was electric bliss, the way Marcus's hot, damp skin brushed against her while the cool bedding pressed against her exposed back.

His hips pinned hers to the bed, the weight of him at once thrilling and comforting as their mouths met, and she plunged her tongue back into his mouth. She ran her hands over his arms, relishing the way the muscles of his shoulders flexed under her fingers as he supported himself. He responded by grinding against her, and it was delicious torture, the way his erection rubbed against her cleft through several infuriating layers of clothing. Her entire body pulsated with need, and nowhere so much as between her legs, where her underwear was already beyond damp and well on its way to drenched.

His mouth left hers and landed on her jaw, then the side of her neck, and she arched her upper back, urging him downward until his lips hovered over the lace of her bra, and she could hear her breath coming in desperate gasps. Then, with one easy motion, Marcus slipped the flimsy fabric down and flicked his tongue over her nipple. A bolt of pleasure shot through her, and her eyes fluttered closed as she slid a hand back to Marcus's hair. Her fingers tangled in the loose curls as his tongue flicked again, harder and more insistently this time.

Then, to her dismay, he stopped. Her eyes flew open. He was looking at her, his dimple deep as a cheeky smile played on his lips.

"Oh, I'm sorry," he murmured, "were you enjoying that?" She stared, unable to muster a response. "Did you like it," he breathed, and he slid his other hand up her rib cage to rest just under her other breast, his fingers unbearably close to her most sensitive flesh and his breath dancing over her skin, "when I was playing with your nipples?"

Heather gaped at him, then words returned to her.

"You absolute shit stirrer!" She shoved him playfully on the shoulder, her glare undermined by the giggle that escaped her. Marcus let out that bark of a laugh she was coming to crave so much, and she wanted to pull him back down against her. But a second later, his weight was gone, and he knelt on the bed.

Heather sat up quickly, wanting to close the space between his body and hers, and pressed her lips against the ridges of his abs before trailing her fingers over the skin above his belt. Marcus groaned, and she grinned against his skin, wondering if she'd ever heard a sexier sound in her life.

Marcus slipped off the bed and stood over her, breathing hard, his lips slightly swollen and flushed a deep reddish pink. She scooted forward and reached for the button of his jeans, but he stopped her. For a moment, she was confused: Did he not want to have sex? She bit her lip.

"Is something wrong?" Heather watched his face, wondering if she'd broken the mood and ruined the moment.

"Not at all," he said, with a hard, audible swallow. "There's just something I really want to do right now."

Then Marcus lowered himself carefully and knelt on the sheepskin rug at the end of the bed. He leaned forward and, dropping a kiss onto her collarbone, hooked his fingers into the waistband of her pajama pants.

"Can I take these off you?" His voice was husky with need again, and she thought she felt his fingers trembling against her hips.

Heather met his eyes and nodded, then decided to make herself perfectly clear. "As long as you take the panties, too."

She had never seen him move so fast. She had barely lifted her hips when he peeled the pants down her thighs and slid them over her pointed feet, tossing them haphazardly onto the floorboards. The Marcus who moved slowly and cautiously was gone, replaced by a man who wasted no time spreading her thighs and settling himself between them, who moaned loudly when he caught his first glimpse of what waited for him there.

"Fuck, Heather," he groaned. Heather had never much cared for cursing, had especially hated the way Jack wielded curse words like weapons when he was angry. But she found she didn't mind when the words were in Marcus's mouth, and his mouth was on her.

She refused to think about Jack in this moment. Refused to think about how, on the rare occasions he went down on her, she'd feel like she needed to come as fast as she could so he wouldn't get bored or annoyed. About how, after she did, he would hastily wipe his mouth on the sheet and act like he deserved some kind of medal.

Heather pushed that out of her mind and focused on Marcus. Marcus, who ran his tongue between her folds, coming within torturous millimeters of her clitoris but never quite touching it, who hummed in satisfaction every time she gasped. When he ran one hand up over her hip and slid it under her bra to gently pinch her nipple, Heather clutched at the comforter and stifled a moan, only to remember she wasn't in an apartment with neighbors on all sides, but in a house, where she could be as loud as she pleased. She whimpered and arched her back, thrusting toward his face, desperate for his tongue on her clit.

"Oh God, please," she moaned, and Marcus obliged. He sucked on her clit, gently at first, letting his lips and tongue play over it, lightly, lazily, like he was planning to spend all day there and saw no point in rushing. Heather released her grip on the comforter and ran her hands through his hair, tracing her fingertips up the back of his neck the way she knew he liked. He groaned, and the vibrations rocketed through her, bouncing off every nerve ending. She did it again, and he growled against her, sucked her harder, rolling her nipple between his finger and thumb. She felt light-headed and woozy, and yet somehow hyperaware of every sound he made, every movement of his fingers and lips.

Heather rolled her hips against his face, feeling the heat and pressure spiral through her muscles as her orgasm approached, desperate for it to arrive but already sorry it was coming so soon. Marcus pulled his hand away from her breast and placed both palms on her hips, spreading his fingers wide and digging into her flesh to hold her to him, and she knew that if she wanted to come again, he would make that happen as many times as she wanted.

That flash of realization sent her careening over the edge. The orgasm ripped through her, and she cried out to the ceiling as she held Marcus's hair tight, bucking against his mouth. Her heart hurled itself against her ribs. She was out of her body, and yet she could feel every cell alight with heat and pleasure and hunger for more.

As her climax subsided, the world came back into focus. Her rasping breath slowed, and Heather's entire body, down to her gums, tingled and buzzed. She loosened her grip in Marcus's hair and pushed her melted body up on her elbows.

Marcus stared at her, his lips and chin glistening. As she watched, he licked his lips, and then dropped light, tender kisses on her inner thighs. The sensation set off an aftershock of pleasure, and she gasped in surprise and delight.

"That was fucking incredible." He grinned. Heather could only nod. Her brain was too scrambled to find the words to tell him that "fucking incredible" didn't begin to cover it, that she couldn't remember ever coming so hard, that if ballet didn't work out, he should open some kind of school and teach workshops on what he'd just done to her.

When her words returned, she didn't say any of that. What she said was "Thank you."

He tipped his head to the side, looking vaguely perplexed.

"Thank you?" he repeated.

"I, uh, yes?" she said slowly. "Thank you for doing that."

He stared at her in disbelief. "This again?"

Her delirium had well and truly evaporated now. "What do you mean?" she asked, scooting up the bed and away from him.

Marcus sighed and slowly stood, testing his weight on his left ankle.

"Heather," he said, his tone firm but kind, "you don't have to thank me for doing something I've wanted to do since the first day I met you. It wasn't some kind of favor to you. I mean, it wasn't only for you. You don't have to thank me for doing something that turned me on so much I might actually die of blood restriction if I don't get out of these jeans."

Her cheeks burned, and she wanted to avert her eyes, but Marcus started undoing his fly and she couldn't look away. He unzipped his pants and slid them down his legs, revealing gray boxer briefs that had ridden up high on his thighs for an unobstructed view of his glorious legs, all muscle and sinew and light brown hair on olive skin. A moment later, his jeans fell to the ground, and he stepped out of them, kicking them across the floor, visibly relieved.

She felt as if she owed him an explanation, and she opened her mouth to speak, but stopped herself. Marcus wasn't Jack, and she wasn't about to let the memory of her ex ruin this for her. So she said nothing.

Instead, Heather met his gaze, crossed her arms over her body, and pulled her bra over her head, tossing it somewhere in the general direction of his jeans. Marcus gritted his teeth and stared at her, eyes dark with concentration and lust, and she let her gaze slide down his body, over his lean, sculpted torso to his briefs, which bulged so insistently it made her mouth water.

And then his phone rang.

Chapter 12

Marcus was going to die.

He was going to die right here in Heather's bedroom at the tender age of thirty-one, naked except for his boxers, and the paramedics wouldn't be able to zip the body bag over his crotch. *Here lies Marcus, dead of sexual frustration and blood loss to the brain. Rest in Penis.*

"This better be a fucking emergency," he growled into the phone. Heather lay on the bed, naked and waiting, desire clear on her flushed face, and Marcus decided that if he didn't die, if he somehow survived this ordeal, he was going to kill his brother instead.

"It is a fucking emergency," Davo shot back. "Mum's at the hospital. She's fallen and hurt herself in the house, apparently there was a lot of blood. I'm on my way now."

The arousal drained out of Marcus faster than he'd imagined possible. He turned towards the bedroom door, seized by a sudden urge to run, coupled with a completely contradictory urge to crawl back into bed and hide. Heather sat up. Moments ago, she'd been loose and relaxed, but now there was new tension in her body that matched his own.

"Marcus, did you hear me?" Davo had him on speakerphone and was half shouting in the car.

"Yeah, shit, yeah, sorry, I heard you. How . . . how bad is it?" He pushed away the image of his father, half-conscious in his hospital bed, weak and ghostly pale under the fluorescent lights.

"I don't know, just get there as fast as you can. You're closer than I am."

"Okay." Marcus nodded, but his neck felt strangely disconnected from his head, like his skull wobbled in midair. "Fast as I can."

Davo ended the call, and Marcus let his hand fall to his side.

"What is it?" Heather asked. She was already up, grabbing his jeans from the floor and tossing them onto the bed.

"It's my mum, she's had an accident and she's at the hospital. I need to go, I need to . . ."

Marcus trailed off as panic stole his words. He hated hospitals. Hated the sound and the smell of them, hated the waiting and the way the lights made everything too sharp and too bright. Blood pounded in his ears as he pulled on his jeans with trembling hands. What had happened to her? How bad was it? Had she hit her head? Disastrous scenarios unfolded in his mind's eye: His mum on her living room floor for hours, alone with a broken hip and unable to call for help. Or worse, unconscious and bleeding and undiscovered for who knew how long.

He ran his hand anxiously through his hair and blinked hard, trying to banish those images and think clearly.

"Shirt, where's my shirt?" he muttered.

Heather pulled his shirt off the floor, then held it out to him, looking at him closely with her forehead creased in concern. "How far away is the hospital?"

"In Manly," he said distantly. Then, realizing she probably had no idea where Manly was in relation to Kirribilli, he added, "Over the Spit Bridge, about half an hour if I don't hit traffic."

Heather gave a tight nod. "I'll come with you."

"You don't have to, it's fine. I'm fine."

She shook her head firmly and walked over to the chest of drawers, pulling out underwear and a shirt. "You're not fine, you're freaking out. I'm coming with you."

Marcus buttoned his shirt with shaking fingers. "You don't have to," he said again, but he didn't know why he was resisting. The sight of her putting her clothes on filled him with a gratitude that rivaled his excitement when he pulled them off her. If he had to go back to the hospital, at least he wasn't going alone.

"And you didn't have to come over here and save me from a harmless spider, but you did." She twisted her hair up into a high, messy bun, then walked over and finished buttoning his shirt for him. "I'll call a car."

Thirty minutes later, Marcus entered the emergency room and tried not to think about the last time he'd rushed to a hospital. He clenched his hands into fists, pushing down the panic that crawled up his throat at the memory of that night. The nauseating pain, the fear, the lack of answers from the paramedics who had loaded him into the back of the ambulance at the stage door, then rolled him into a room just like this one.

Anxiety crawled in his chest, and he had to will his legs to keep moving, to carry him into the buzzing waiting room. Just as there had been the last time, there were crying children and hacking coughs and a blaring TV, and just as it had last time, the onslaught of sound made his brain feel waterlogged.

His mother's voice pulled him out of his spiral.

"There you are!" she called, and he whipped around to see her sitting in an otherwise empty row of blue plastic chairs. She wore what looked like a pyjama shirt and a sarong wrapped around her waist. On her feet, she had a pair of untied walking joggers, with no socks. He couldn't see any obvious injuries from here, not even bruises or scratches.

"Mum, what happened?" He walked to her as fast as he could, trying to see as he did if her arm was broken or if she was bleeding anywhere. Aside from her unusual outfit, he couldn't spot anything amiss.

"It's not a big drama, love," she said evenly. "I just fell and cut myself."

"Where?" he asked, scanning her again. Now that he looked closer, he could see some reddish brown under her fingernails.

"In the living room."

"No," he said, frustrated now, "where did you cut yourself?"

"Oh, my thigh," she answered matter-of-factly, gesturing at her right leg. "I was getting off the couch, and I fell. Knocked over a vase on my way down, and one of the shards got me, right through my PJ pants. Blood all over the rug, I'm afraid, but I was planning to replace it sooner or later. Now I suppose I'll have to do it sooner."

Marcus glanced at her leg, and she pulled the sarong up to reveal a large white gauze pad bandaged to her thigh, just above her knee.

"Are you in pain? How long have you been sitting here?"

"An hour or so. And it hurts a little, but it's nothing I can't handle." She shrugged. She was so calm in the midst of the beeping and the crying, but of course, she'd spent her professional life being calm around beeping and crying.

"They couldn't see you sooner? I mean, if the cut was deep, doesn't it need to be cleaned, or stitched, or . . ." Marcus trailed off, the whirlpool of panic in his chest starting to slow and settle.

"The triage nurse already had a look at it." She shrugged again. She really did seem completely unruffled. "You know as well as I do that if they needed to fix me up sooner, they would have. It's just a gash, love. My leg's not going to fall off."

"Okay," he sighed, nodding a few times and lowering himself into a chair opposite her. "Okay, so you're fine."

"I'm fine." She smiled, and then her eyes moved from his face, and Marcus glanced over his shoulder. Heather hung back, watching the scene from five feet away.

"Oh, sorry," Marcus said hastily, more to himself than to either woman. "Heather, this is my mum, Leanne. Mum, this is my friend—"

"Heather Hays," his mum finished, sounding surprised. "From New York. I recognise you from the paper."

Heather stepped forward, fidgeting with the sleeve of her sweater. "Hi, Mrs. Campbell. It's nice to meet you. I'm glad you're okay."

"Leanne, please, and come make yourself comfortable. Well, as comfortable as you can be in these chairs."

Heather nodded and sat in a seat next to his mum.

"So, Heather, what brings you to the emergency department this fine Saturday morning?"

Heather hesitated for a fraction of a second, then gave her a pleasant smile. "Marcus has been showing me around the city, and we were about to set off when he got the call."

His mum looked Heather up and down, taking in her messy hair, then looked at Marcus, who looked even more rumpled. "Where were you planning to go?" she asked, sounding sceptical.

"The zoo," Marcus said quickly, hoping he sounded more relaxed than he felt. He'd never been good at lying to his mum. He had a useless poker face, and she had a finely tuned bullshit detector. It was not a good combination. "Heather's keen to see a real live koala."

"I know it's touristy," Heather said, with a self-effacing eye roll, "but . . . I am a tourist."

"And Peter asked me to be a tour guide," Marcus added. He chanced a quick smile in Heather's direction. The first test of their rules and they were doing fine. A little sweaty, but fine.

Leanne looked over at the sliding glass doors, which revealed a grey sky threatening more rain, then back at Marcus.

"Might not be the best day for the zoo," she said. As if to emphasize her point, a thunderclap rolled overhead, and the rain began to pour.

"We can go some other day," Heather jumped in. "And Alice has told me I should try to get out of Sydney if I can. She mentioned the Blue Mountains?"

"She's right, it's beautiful up there, even this time of year." Leanne shifted in her seat and winced.

"Mum, are you sure you're okay?"

"I'm *fine*," she said adamantly, and turned back to Heather. "And I don't want to talk about Sydney. I want to hear all about New York. I've never been, and I've always wanted to. What's it like?"

Marcus watched as Heather raised her eyebrows in surprise, and then thought for a moment. "It's a lot. It feels like you're on all the time, like you're going at full speed every second of the day. Which means you never get bored, but you also never get a moment to rest. And it's a huge city, obviously, but sometimes it can feel very small." She fidgeted with her sleeve again. "Sometimes it can feel like you don't have enough room to move properly. Like you're trapped."

"Did you grow up there?"

"Kind of. My mom worked in Manhattan, but we lived just outside the city, in Yonkers, which some New Yorkers will tell you is *not* New York City. But then I moved to Manhattan when I was fourteen, into the dorms at the company school."

No wonder she talked about her friend Carly like a sister, Marcus thought. They must have lived together during their teens, in addition to taking classes together all day at the school. They'd grown up together. They were basically family.

"And do you like dancing with your company? It must be hard bloody work." Leanne looked at Heather with kind, interested eyes, and seemed to have no idea what a complicated question she'd just asked.

Heather bit her lip and paused for a moment before answering. "I did like it," she said carefully. "But it's really nice to have a break from it all. I like the pace of life here, and I like what Peter's trying to do with ANB. But it's hard bloody work wherever you are in the world," she added, and Marcus couldn't resist smiling.

The stereotypically Australian phrase sounded sweet and strange in her American accent.

Thank God she'd insisted on coming with him. Awkward questions from his mum aside, her presence made sitting here a lot easier. With their conversation to focus on, he didn't have to think about his last visit to an emergency room, or about all the time his father had spent in the oncology wing of this very hospital. Marcus caught Heather's eye across the aisle, and she gave him a tiny, reassuring smile. It sent fragile spirals of warmth and calm through him, the same ones he'd felt when she'd reached across the back seat of the car and given his hand a brief, gentle squeeze.

"Mum, are you okay?" a breathless voice said from a few metres away. Marcus looked up to see his brother walking towards them, his clothes splattered with rain and his face clouded with anxiety. Marcus felt his smile falter and fade.

Leanne smiled at her eldest son cheerfully. "Everything is just fine, thank you, David. It's just a cut and some bruises. You really didn't need to come all the way over the Bridge or call your brother out."

Davo sighed heavily and looked up at the ceiling, and Marcus could tell from the slump and ease of his shoulders that he was relieved.

"Christ, I was so worried. You said something about blood everywhere. You're sure you're all right?"

"Yes, though I'm afraid the living room looks a bit like a crime scene. I might need some help cleaning it once they stitch me back up. Come sit down, I've just been hearing all about life in the Big Apple from your brother's new friend."

Davo saw Heather for the first time, and Marcus watched as his brother stood a little taller and pulled his hands from his pockets.

Heather stood and extended her hand. "I'm Heather. Nice to meet you, and I'm sorry it's under these circumstances," she said. Davo shook her hand, taking her in.

"I'm David. You must be a ballet dancer, if you're a friend of Marcus's," he said. "And is that an American accent I hear?" Marcus's shoulders tensed under his shirt. Of course his brother could manage to speak about ballet with some semblance of respect when there was a beautiful woman involved.

"It is." She smiled at him politely, then cast a sparkling conspiratorial grin at Marcus. "Although I'm working on my Australian slang. Do they call you . . . Davo?"

"They do," Davo chuckled, settling himself into the seat next to her. Marcus kept his eyes on the floor to avoid glaring at his brother.

"Leanne Campbell?" a woman's voice called from across the room.

"That's me," his mother called back, raising one hand in the air. "This shouldn't take long," she said to Marcus and the others.

A young nurse in light pink scrubs approached, holding a clipboard. "We're ready for you now, I can take you back," she said to Leanne. "Can you walk on your own?"

"I most certainly can," his mum replied. She made to stand, and Marcus and Davo both flinched. Marcus leapt to his feet and offered Leanne his hand.

"Would you all relax? I'm fine." Marcus did his best impression of the sceptical squint she'd just given him, and she shook her head at him.

"All right, all right," she relented, placing her hand in Marcus's and leaning on it as she rose to her feet. "You can go, if you want, I'll be right to get myself home."

Marcus rolled his eyes as he sat down. "Yeah, right. We'll be here, Mum," he said to her retreating back.

Once she was gone, Heather stood, and Marcus saw Davo's eyes flick up and down the back of her body with naked interest. Marcus gritted his teeth.

"I'm going to get myself another coffee, would anyone like one?" she asked.

"Yes, please," Marcus said quickly, and Davo nodded gratefully. Heather picked up her shoulder bag and headed around the corner, where a sign advertised a café with "hot coffee and lite bites." He'd never been so glad to see her go.

Marcus and his brother sat in silence for a few moments. With Heather and his mum gone, he was more aware of the sounds of the waiting room, and he shifted against the hard plastic chair, trying to get comfortable.

"Guess it wasn't a fucking emergency," Davo said eventually.

"Guess not," Marcus agreed, "but I'm glad you called me. I wouldn't want her waiting here alone."

"Yeah, me neither. And maybe this'll make her see reason about the house."

Marcus shook his head. Davo was nothing if not single-minded. "Don't you think you should give it a rest for now? She's just had a fall, and she's shaken up."

"Right, she's just had a fall, because she's not safe on her own in the house anymore. This is the perfect time to talk to her about how to stop this from happening again. What if something worse happens next time?"

"It's not a good time."

"She could've broken a hip. She could've hit her head and blacked out, or—"

"But she didn't," Marcus said, unwilling to tell Davo he'd been gripped by the very same fears. "I agree we need to talk to her, but not now. Let's get her home and get the place cleaned up, and we can bring it up in a little while. Just don't badger her about it right away."

"Fine," Davo agreed tersely. Another moment of silence, in which the TV in the corner played an ad with a grating jingle and a small boy with what looked like a broken arm asked his father if hospitals had lollipops like doctor's offices did. When Davo spoke again, there was a sly lilt in his voice.

"So, tell me about the lovely Heather."

Marcus clenched his jaw. He'd rather go back to arguing about the house. "She's a guest artist at ANB," he said shortly, hoping his tone would ward off any follow-up questions.

"Straight?" Davo asked, sounding hopeful.

"Yes."

"Single?"

"Technically," Marcus gritted out.

"She's hot."

You have no idea, Marcus wanted to reply, but he said nothing. He reminded himself of the rules he and Heather had laid out barely an hour ago. He couldn't tell his brother to back off without breaking Rule #1 and blowing the entire arrangement when it had barely begun. But he really needed Davo to back the hell off.

"I'm gonna ask her out," Davo declared, not bothering to ask Marcus the obvious question. As if he couldn't imagine Heather would be interested in his little brother. As if a ballet boy like Marcus couldn't possibly pull a woman like her.

"I don't think that's a good idea." Marcus kept his voice steady, but he squeezed his thigh, trying to quiet the anxiety that bubbled in his chest from the moment Davo laid eyes on Heather.

"Why not? She's hot as shit. If that's what ballet girls look like, maybe I should've come to more of your concerts."

But you didn't, did you? Marcus wanted to say. *Because Mum and Dad had to drag you every year and you rolled your eyes the whole time.* Besides, Davo had never had a problem getting women to date him. And he'd never understood—had never tried to understand—how demanding a ballet career was, even though Marcus spent every weeknight in the studio growing up, and every school holiday at all-day dance camp. He'd made it clear from Marcus's very first concert that he thought ballet was pointless.

"She's not a 'ballet girl,' okay, she's . . . she's one of the best dancers in the world." *Also, she's mine.*

"Ah, I get it," Davo said, the sly tone returning. "I can't ask her out because you've got a crush on her."

"Piss off," Marcus shot back, loud enough that the dad across the room threw him a disapproving look. He lowered his voice. "It's not like that. My boss asked me to show her around town."

"Well, I can do that. I'll show her anything she wants to see."

Marcus wanted to deck him. His heart was pounding, and gripping his thigh wasn't helping anymore. *Ask her, then,* he wanted to say. *See if she wants to go out with someone who has no respect for what she does for a living. Who doesn't understand what a miracle her hot as shit body is.* But when words tumbled out of his mouth, he said:

"She's not gonna go out with you. She only dates dancers, the more famous the better. Was your face plastered on every ballet magazine and dance shop last season? No. It wasn't. So if you wanted to pull ballet girls, maybe you should have taken dance classes with me after all."

Marcus's voice, hot and possessive, carried across the room to where Heather stood holding the tray of coffee cups in both hands.

She'd almost rounded the corner back into the waiting room when she'd heard his voice, a low rumble that carried under the cacophony of the waiting room. Davo had been needling Marcus about asking her out, what sounded like friendly brotherly teasing, and Marcus had denied that there was anything going on between them. Forcefully, sounding more annoyed than she'd ever heard him.

And suddenly, there'd been nothing friendly or brotherly in his voice. *"She only dates dancers, the more famous the better."*

Heather's breath caught in her throat, and she stood rooted to the scuffed linoleum floor. Her skin prickled with a discomfort she recognized but couldn't name—then the back of her neck tightened at the memory of Jack slinging his heavy arm around her shoulders. Claiming her, speaking for her, taking credit for her success at NYB. Using her like a prop, like she was barely more human than the wooden lyre he danced with when he played Apollo. Suddenly her mouth was bitter with more than coffee as she remembered all the times she'd consented to it, the way she'd let herself be used even when a part of her knew better. All the little pieces of herself she'd given away in exchange for the sparkly fairy tale and the promise of stability.

She couldn't believe she'd been foolish enough to think a secret fling with Marcus would be any different from a public relationship with Jack. The hurt was exactly the same. But this time she didn't have to accept it, or explain it away, or pretend it was fine even when it wasn't.

Pulling her shoulders down and raising her chin, she marched into the waiting room, where Marcus and Davo now sat in stony silence, their arms crossed over their chests, eyes on the floor.

Marcus looked up at her and gave her a weak, relieved-looking smile she didn't return. She set the tray down on an empty seat and plucked her own cup out of it.

"Enjoy," she said coldly.

"Thanks, what do I owe you?" Marcus sighed.

She stared down at him, willing herself not to cry before she could get out of there.

"Nothing. You owe me nothing, just like I owe you nothing."

Marcus looked up at her, confused. "Are you okay?"

"I'm fine. Tell your mom I hope she feels better soon."

"You're leaving?" He looked more concerned than confused now. "Where are you going?"

"To find a dancer to go out with. The more famous the better."

She didn't wait for his response. She turned sharply, splashing coffee over her shaking fingers, and walked out into the rain.

A few blocks away, Heather ducked under the awning of a newsagent and pulled out her phone, her hands shaking slightly. They were still shaking when the car arrived, and when she unlocked her front door thirty minutes later.

She'd asked the driver to turn up the radio, but the pulsing pop music hadn't drowned out the memory of Marcus's words. He might as well have told his brother she'd screwed her way into her job. *"If it weren't for me, no one would know who the fuck you are."*

Hot rage bubbled in her stomach as she marched up the stairs to her bedroom, and only intensified when she saw the bed, unmade and rumpled after a night of restful sleep and a morning of pleasure with Marcus. She'd been so stupid. Stupid to trust him, stupid to think he'd be any different than Jack. For one insane moment, she wanted to call Jack and rage at him the way he'd raged at her so many times. She'd tell him that everything Carly had said about him over the years was true: He was a narcissist, a small, insecure man who felt best about himself when he was making other people feel their worst. That he'd broken her heart a thousand tiny times, always mending it just enough that she'd stay and let him do it again. She'd list everything he'd ever done to hurt her until he felt the same shame she felt. Until he apologized for how he'd treated her.

She threw her phone on the bed so she couldn't give in to temptation. Jack didn't apologize. Or if he did, he did it so dramatically, so woundedly, that she ended up feeling like the one who'd messed up.

This time, though, she *was* the one who had messed up. It had been a mistake to kiss Marcus, a mistake to call him for help, and a mistake to agree to sneak around with him. She'd been kidding herself to think she could trust him, and a fool to think she could get away with doing cartwheels, when in her heart she'd known it would only get her in trouble. Stupid to think he was immune to believing the rumors the ballet world whispered about her.

Well, that was over now. No more cartwheels. No more sneaking around. For the next two weeks, she was going to do what she'd come here to do: dance. And as for Marcus, well, he'd said it himself. She only dated famous dancers—and he was neither of those things. So they were done. She stripped off her clothes and turned on the shower.

By the time she'd rinsed the last of his scent off her skin, she almost believed it.

* *

The sky was dark by the time Marcus trudged into the lobby of his apartment building. He was ravenously hungry and desperately in need of a shower. Davo had driven them all back to the Sand Castle, and the two of them had spent over an hour cleaning up the living room. There'd been shards of glass scattered everywhere—he'd even found a few pieces in the kitchen—and a splash of blood on the sofa that had taken a half hour of soaking and scrubbing to remove. His mum had been right about the rug; it was destined for the tip, and her bloodied pyjama pants had gone into the bin, too.

They had asked her if she wanted them to stay and cook her dinner, but she'd shooed them out, insisting she was just fine on her own.

"It's just a few stitches," she'd said impatiently when they objected.

"Six," Marcus had retorted, putting the dustpan and broom back in the laundry closet. "Six stitches. That's more than a few."

"I'll put my feet up and rest, I promise, and I've got some leftovers to reheat," she'd said grudgingly. "You two have done enough."

At least she'd been sitting on the couch at that moment, though Marcus was sure that would only last for a minute or two after he and Davo left.

It had been easy enough not to think about Heather while he was cleaning or making sure his mum had supplies to last the next few days. But now that his hands weren't busy, now that he wasn't fussing over her or interpreting Davo's grunts, he couldn't get the image of Heather's furious face out of his mind. People always said disappointing someone was worse than making them angry. But that didn't account for making someone both disappointed *and* angry. And that's exactly what he'd seen in Heather's face and heard in her low, livid voice.

He hated how he'd spoken to Davo. His skin crawled with shame when he thought about how easily he'd allowed himself to be baited into speaking that way about Heather, into acting like someone he wasn't. Or hoped he wasn't. He wished she hadn't heard it, but it would have been shameful even if she hadn't. Most of all, he thought as he let himself into his empty apartment, he hated how easily his brother was able to get under his skin, how efficiently he could locate and push all of Marcus's buttons.

It had been that way for years. Davo had never understood Marcus's passion for ballet and had always found ways to let him know he found it silly and embarrassing. When they were kids, their parents had resorted to bribing Davo to come to one ballet concert a year, and soon after Davo hit his teens he had plenty of excuses not to show up. He was working at the supermarket, or training with his rugby team, or doing just about anything except watching his brother dance. For the first two years of high school, Davo pretended they weren't even brothers—he'd told anyone who asked that Marcus just happened to have the same very common surname as him. He'd been that embarrassed to tell his mates his little brother took ballet classes.

When their dad had died, Marcus had half hoped the shared loss would give them something to bond over, something to wipe away some of the unpleasantness that had come before. There weren't a lot of silver linings when your dad died of cancer, but it had seemed possible. Instead, it had only made things worse. Davo became more distant, and, when they'd actually seen each other, more dismissive of Marcus's work.

Still, Marcus thought as he tested the temperature of the shower and then stepped under the stream, there was no excuse. He was a grown man. A grown man who loved what he did for a living and saw the value in it, even if his brother didn't. He didn't need to impress Davo anymore. And he definitely shouldn't have talked about Heather like she was some kind of reward for being a man in ballet. Even if the idea of Davo asking her out made his stomach churn. He heaved a deep sigh, watched the steam billow and swirl towards the ceiling, and made a plan.

An hour later, he rang Heather's doorbell and held his breath, partly from nerves and partly because the scents wafting from the bag made him lightheaded with hunger.

She opened the door quickly and purposefully, but she raised her eyebrows in surprise when she saw him. She wore a pair of black leggings and a loose wool sweater, and her hair hung in damp waves around her shoulders.

"Oh, I thought—you're not dumplings. I mean, I thought it was my dinner." Heather gave her head a little shake, and her jaw tightened. "What do you want?"

"I want to apologise," Marcus said quickly. "What I said wasn't okay. And I'm really sorry. I wanted to come after you and say that, but I couldn't without Davo getting suspicious about . . . about us." *If there even is an us anymore.* "And you don't have to accept that or believe me, or do anything at all, but I promise it won't happen again."

Heather said nothing, and once again, Marcus found himself waiting. Watching her think. Hoping.

"Is your mom okay?" she asked eventually.

"She's fine. Six stitches, but she's home and not in any pain."

"Okay." She nodded.

He waited.

"I trusted you." Her voice was quiet, steely. "You know what a huge risk we're taking, and what could happen if we're found out. But I trusted you, and I thought you felt the same way about me. And you couldn't trust me to say no if your brother asked me out. You had to go swing your dick around and tell him I'm a gold digger."

He shrugged his shoulders in discomfort. It was nothing he hadn't said to himself for the last few hours, but hearing Heather say it made him feel a hundred times worse.

"I know, and I'm really sorry." He'd completely fucked this up. He hadn't even managed to make whatever they had last a full day. He knew, like everyone else in the ballet world knew, how badly her trust had been broken, and how recently. He hated that he'd done it again.

Heather studied him reproachfully, like she'd done at the restaurant last night.

"Don't ever talk about me like that again. I'm not some kind of prize for men who deign to take dance classes, and neither is any other woman in ballet. I'm not a prop, and I'm not a trophy, and I can speak for myself. If Davo had asked, I would have told him I'm newly single and not looking." The finality in her voice was unmistakable. *Not looking.* And definitely not looking to give him another chance.

Marcus sighed, exhaling what felt like the last traces of hope. "I know you can speak for yourself. It's one of my favourite things about you, actually. I really am sorry, Heather." He held out the warm plastic bag. "I'm gonna go, but you should take this. It's lamb shanks from Café Luxor, since you missed out on them last night."

He prompted her to take the bag, suddenly exhausted by the whiplash of emotions he'd cycled through that day: excitement, desire, panic, relief, rage, and now a dull sense of resignation that sat heavily in his stomach.

Heather looked at it then back up at him, and her expression softened.

"Smells really good," she said. She opened the door by a few centimetres, wide enough for him to hand it through the gap.

"They'll keep till tomorrow, if you're having dumplings tonight."

She nodded, her brown eyes still fixed on his face. Then she opened the door wide enough for him to walk through. "Did you get enough for two?"

Heather couldn't remember the last time she'd had a meal this sublime. The lamb fell off the bone onto her plate and all but dissolved in her mouth. The couscous, which had started off salty and spicy, soaked in the lamb's flavorful sauce. The little dining table in her kitchen was even smaller than that of Café Luxor, but it was just large enough to fit two plates. And cramped enough that her knee kept bumping against Marcus's thigh as they ate.

Her muscles still buzzed slightly with the adrenaline that surged through her when she'd found Marcus standing there, looking contrite. She hadn't expected to see him until Monday morning, when she'd been ready to treat him cordially and like any other coworker—just as they'd agreed. But then he'd showed up looking miserable, like he'd been berating himself all day for what he did.

She was proud she hadn't let him off the hook. Hadn't let the expression on his face sway her from saying exactly what she needed to, from unloading the angry thoughts that had been chasing each other around her head since she left the hospital. It hadn't felt good, exactly, but it had felt true. Like she had excavated a part of herself that had been hidden for a long time and held it up to the light. It felt familiar in her hand, this part of her, even if it bore the permanent marks of the years it had spent underground, buried in the dark.

And then he'd offered her a real apology. Not a "sorry you felt that way" apology, or a "sorry you misunderstood me" apology. Not an apology that was really a guilt trip to make her feel like *she* had hurt *him* by telling him he'd done something wrong. A real apology. What a novel concept, she thought, swallowing another sumptuous mouthful.

Soon, too soon, her shank was picked clean of meat, and all that remained were a few preserved lemons. Marcus still ate, and for a moment, she enjoyed watching the way his tanned forearms flexed and released as he cut the meat off the bone. When he ran his tongue over his top lip to catch some stray sauce, she let her eyes follow it, and a different kind of hunger skittered through her, warming her skin. She crossed her legs and, this time, bumped the whole table. The plates jumped and clattered, and Marcus sat up with a start.

God, she was so smooth.

"Sorry," she said, jumping up and trying to cover her blunder. "Do you want some water, or a beer?"

"I could murder a beer after today," he said, gratefully.

She filled a glass of water for herself and pulled a beer from the fridge.

"I've been researching koalas," she said as she set the drinks on the table and sat back down.

"What, today?"

"Yeah, I needed a distraction. I was mad, and I thought looking at some cute animals might help."

"And did it?"

"A little. They're pretty cute. But apparently they sound like pigs. I always thought they'd make some sweet little squeaking sound, but they grunt and snort and it's . . . not cute."

"You still want to cuddle one though, don't you?" Marcus took a swig of his beer and groaned with relief, and Heather resisted the urge to cross her legs again.

"I absolutely do," she smiled across the table. "Preferably one that doesn't grunt too loud. And I learned that the word 'koala' means 'no water,' because they can survive so long without drinking."

"Huh, I've always heard they're drunk from the oil in the gum leaves," he said, holding up his beer, then taking another swig.

"That's a common myth. They're just loud and cranky while stone cold sober."

"So you're telling me," he said, standing and clearing their plates, "koalas have been falsely labeled as the winos of the animal kingdom?"

"It sounds like it. Koalas clearly need a better publicist." She said nothing for a moment as he rinsed the dishes and put them in the dishwasher, then rummaged in the bottom of the takeout bag. Heather stood and joined him at the counter. He stilled as her hip brushed against his side, and she heard his intake of breath when she lifted her hand and traced her fingers down the back of his neck.

"I took a gamble on their dessert options"—his voice was husky as he pulled out plastic packages—"and got you a Portuguese tart. They're really good, and it was this or rosewater ice cream, which I thought might melt on the way, so . . ."

Marcus fell silent when Heather turned her back to the counter and hopped up onto it. For a long moment they looked at each other, and she cataloged the spray of freckles over his forehead and the way the dim kitchen light darkened his eyes to the color of moss. Seconds ticked by, and the cold press of the countertop against her thighs warred with the heat pulsing between them. Then Heather realized: he was waiting for her to ask for what she wanted. The thought made her feel reckless and alive—and at the same time, entirely safe and cared for.

Heather smiled to herself, then scooted sideways, pushing the takeout cartons along the counter until she was in front of him, their eyes level and her knees between him and the counter. Marcus fixed his gaze on her face, his pulse jumping in his throat. He didn't move when she placed her arms on his shoulders, but she heard his breathing quicken, fast and frantic in the quiet. When she let her legs fall open, he kept his eyes on her face, but released a sound that was half hiss and half moan.

"Marcus?" she murmured.

"Heather?" he rasped back.

"Would you please kiss me? Now?"

"Fuck yes," he breathed.

Marcus closed the space between them and pulled her hips against his. The thin cord of his restraint seemed to quiver and snap, and when their lips met, it was less a kiss than it was a clash, their tongues colliding and her teeth grazing roughly against his bottom lip. She tightened her arms around his neck, pressing herself against his chest, wanting to devour and be devoured.

He skimmed his hands up her body, his fingertips flitting over her breasts, teasing maddeningly before returning to her hips. Heather sighed in frustration and seized one of his hands, returning it to her breast. Asking for what she wanted. Mercifully, he answered by stroking her nipple through her sweater, sparking white hot pleasure that burst and scattered through her body. His mouth moved to her neck as he rubbed his thumb firmly and steadily over her, and Heather rolled her hips against him, desperate for contact and friction.

Marcus moaned into her neck as she ground against his hard length, and for the first time, Heather understood the kind of frenzied lust that made people do uncomfortable, unhygienic things like screw on a kitchen counter.

She broke the kiss before it could come to that and pulled his hand from her body, panting. She hopped off the counter but didn't release him until they were in her bedroom. She peeled off her sweater and leggings, hurling them onto the floor, then sat on the bed, sliding back towards the pillows, pulse hammering as she watched him unbuckle his own jeans.

Marcus plunged his hand into his pocket and pulled out his wallet, extracting a condom with fumbling fingers before shoving his pants down his legs. Then he stopped and let his eyes rake up her bare legs, over her hips and breasts, before he met her gaze. She bit her lip, and he took a deep breath.

"Are you sure this is what you want?" he asked. His voice trembled, like it took enormous self-control to form each word.

Heather had never wanted anyone or anything more, had never ached so undeniably to be touched and kissed and filled and held.

"I'm sure," she said, and she almost laughed at how insufficient the words were. "I want you, right now."

Heather reached back and unhooked her bra, then slid her panties off her hips. In the few seconds it took her to toss them onto the floor, Marcus had pulled off his boxer briefs and crawled onto the bed, where he knelt between her legs and handed her the condom. His uncut cock hung hard from his torso, thick and heavy.

Her fingers shook around the condom wrapper, but she ripped the foil open on her third attempt. Looking into Marcus's face, she saw him watching her hungrily, and she hurried to roll the rubber down, relishing the firm heat of him under her fingertips and the way he groaned quietly in his throat as she ran her hand over the base of his shaft.

The moment she was done, Marcus lifted one hand to her face and pulled her toward his mouth. She kissed him back hard, impatiently, letting her hands roam his lower back and his ass, that perfect, firm ass she'd been thinking about since the moment they met. Then she broke away and let her shoulders fall back on the bed, dragging him down with her. Finally, *finally* this was happening, she thought, wrapping her hand around his cock and guiding him into her.

She gasped at his girth as he entered her slowly, carefully. Her muscles stretched deliciously to accommodate him as he held still for a moment. Then she thrust her hips upward to take the last inch of him.

They groaned in unison. In relief. In mutual recognition that this was better than either of them had dared imagine. It was slick, hot heaven, the way he filled her, the way she melted around him. Marcus braced his hands on either side of her shoulders and set a slow, steady rhythm, thrusting hard and deep, then deeper still when she wrapped her legs around his waist.

"Jesus fuck, Heather, you feel so good," he gritted out, and she clenched around him, eliciting another groan that rumbled through his body and echoed into her own.

He sped up and swore again, his breath more ragged now. She ran her hand up his back and into his hair, then pulled him to her chest until his mouth found her nipple. His tongue flicked against her again, and she whimpered to the ceiling, holding tight to his hair as he sucked and licked at the sensitive skin, lavishing attention on one breast, then the other, sending hot waves of pleasure through her muscles as he thrust hard and steady into her.

Marcus lifted his head and kissed her. For a moment she missed his mouth on her nipple, but a second later, he'd slid one hand between them and was teasing her slick folds with gentle but determined fingers. Heather gasped against his mouth at the sensation, and he answered with a hungry moan, stroking her firmly with the pad of his thumb, drawing tight, firm circles around her clit that made her throb around his rigid cock. He stayed there, circling and thrusting, his breath growing harsher and more desperate, and Heather's moans rose in pitch as she felt her orgasm build.

Marcus broke the kiss and pressed his forehead against hers, stroking her relentlessly.

"That's it, baby, come for me. Come with me." The urgency in his voice unraveled her, pulling her under.

"Oh God, Marcus, I'm—" She lost the ability to form words, coming with a silent scream as her climax shook her body and he drove into her.

"Fuck, Heather, that's it," he growled, and with his next thrust, he came, his forehead pressed to hers and his arm trembling over her head. His breaths were deep, shuddering exhales, and she held tight to him, one hand in his hair and the other on his lower back, feeling his muscles release as his orgasm subsided.

She relaxed her grip on his hair but left her hand buried in his curls, enjoying the gentle sensation of his chest expanding and contracting against her body as his breath returned to normal. Marcus lifted his head for a minute, only to lower it again and groan against her skin.

"I promise I'm not going to thank you," she whispered to the ceiling, "but I am going to thank Shaz."

He raised his head sharply. "What? Wait, why?"

"Because," she replied, a sly smile creeping over her face, "she clearly got you your full range of motion back."

Marcus guffawed, and she lifted her head to grin at him. He smiled back at her, sure he looked as dazed and glassy-eyed as he felt.

In the days since their first kiss, he'd wondered—a few thousand times, conservatively—what it would be like to sleep with her. How it would feel to bury himself inside her. It had crossed his mind—a few hundred times, actually—that if it ever happened, he might be setting himself up for disappointment. That the reality might fall short of the now very well-worn fantasy.

He'd never been happier to be wrong. He could never have imagined the thrill of her fingernails brushing against his scalp just before he came, or the head-spinning pleasure of feeling her entire body surrounding him, inside and out, when she wrapped her smooth, strong thighs around his waist, her milky coffee birthmark pressed against his ribs.

And now, she cracked jokes while he was still inside her, and he laughed as he reached down to secure the condom before he pulled out. Marcus wanted to kick his past self for ever imagining sex with Heather could be anything other than mind-numbingly, bone-meltingly good. What a ridiculous idea. The fantasy, it turned out, had fallen far short of the reality.

Once he'd disposed of the condom, Marcus pulled on his boxers and joined her on the bed. They had fallen onto it without even pulling the doona back, and he scooted up to slip his legs under it.

Heather had sat up, and for a moment he watched her, noticing the slight sway at the bottom of her long, sinewy back and the shimmering white ribbons of stretch marks on the sides of her breasts. She lifted her hair off her neck and tried to run her fingers through it, but strands of it stuck to her damp skin. The rest was a tangled disaster. When she raised her arms, her breasts lifted and swayed, and Marcus felt his cock stir again despite his exhaustion.

She turned and caught him watching her. "Do you want a glass of water or something?" she asked.

"Not if you have to get out of bed to get it," he replied, pulling her toward him. She lay on her side and rested against his chest.

"I think getting out of bed would be unavoidable," she said as he traced loose circles on her upper arm.

"Then I guess I'm never drinking water again, like a koala," he murmured, "and you'll get to stay here forever."

Heather lifted her head to look at him, her pointed chin pressing gently into his chest. She smiled contentedly; her warm brown eyes seemed to glow in her still-flushed face. Marcus's heart gave an unfamiliar little squeeze.

"Oh no," she whispered, "not that. Anything but that."

They lay there a while, Heather's long tangle of hair tickling his skin pleasantly, and every few seconds he was tempted to look at her, or sit up and check she was real. That he was really post-sex cuddling with The Heather Hays. A series of words that would instantly lose him his job if anyone overheard them. He knew that. She knew that. But in this moment, with her fingers idly brushing up and down his forearm, he couldn't bring himself to care.

Marcus felt the cool rush of air on his skin when she inhaled to speak, and he looked down at her curiously.

"I'm sorry," she said, not quite meeting his eyes.

"What for?"

"I overreacted this morning, when I heard you and Davo. I know you were just trying to keep us out of an awkward situation. I just . . ."

She trailed off, biting her lip and frowning, as if she were looking for the right words. Marcus waited until she found them.

"I spent so long not speaking for myself. Letting people believe things about me, say things about me, that weren't really true, because it made it easier to be with . . . with him. But it made everything else harder. It made it harder to be a good friend to Carly, and it put distance between me and my mom. It even made it harder to dance, I think, because I wasn't really dancing as myself. And I want to be myself now."

Marcus watched her face as she spoke, wondering if Jack Andersen had any idea how much damage he'd done—and if he'd care.

"I don't think you overreacted, but it helps to know why you were upset. I'm sorry, again."

"I know." Heather held his gaze, and there was no blame in her face, no anger. There was so much more he wanted to ask her, so much more he wanted to know.

"Were you yourself the day we met?"

"Yes," she smiled, tentatively.

"And when you called me to save you from a spider that couldn't kill you even if it tried?"

"Definitely."

"And just now?"

Her smile widened, and she propped herself on an elbow, taking in his mostly naked body with obvious appreciation. "Oh, yes."

"Then I think you should keep practicing being yourself. It's not that late. You can probably practice two, three more times tonight. And some more practice in the morning, just to be safe."

Heather opened her mouth to speak—to call him a shit stirrer, he suspected—but then she kissed him, and for a while, there were no words spoken at all.

Chapter 13

The following Wednesday, Sharon gave Marcus permission to stay for all of company class. She prohibited jumping, of course, and he still had to keep his pliés and fondus shallow, but Marcus didn't have to pack up and leave once barre was over. He wished he could take his first classes back in private, or at least away from his colleagues, so they wouldn't see him wincing and wobbling his way through his first adagio in over a year. Certainly, he wished Heather couldn't see it—but he wished his dad could. He would have been proud Marcus was trying, and that trying had gotten him this far, after spending the last year wondering if he'd ever dance again.

"You look good," Alice said as they stood on the side of the studio, watching a group of dancers run through the tough-as-nails adagio Peter had set today. Heather was in the middle of the pack, and from here Marcus could see all the muscles of her shoulder blades rippling between the straps of her navy-blue leotard.

"You're full of it," he retorted under his breath, reluctantly tearing his eyes from Heather's steady, languid developpé and flashing Alice a wry smile. "I look like crap, but it's good to be back."

Alice looked him up and down appraisingly, then raised one eyebrow. "Yeah, okay, you look like crap. But you'll get it back, especially if you don't rush. What's Shaz always saying?"

"The slower you come back, the faster you come back," they droned in unison.

"Plus," Alice said, scrutinizing him again, "you seem pretty happy lately. What's going on with you?"

Marcus pretended to watch his colleagues again, careful not to let his gaze fall on Heather this time.

"What do you mean?" he asked, even though he knew exactly what she meant.

"I dunno," she said, shrugging. "I just thought . . ."

"I'm just glad to be back and properly on the mend," he said easily. "Sharon said if this keeps up, I might even come back stronger than I was before." He turned back to face Alice. "Nice, right?"

She tipped her head sceptically, but then said, "Yeah, nice."

Alice looked as if she wanted to say more, but she didn't have the chance. Heather's group finished the adagio combination and cleared out of the centre of the studio to make room for his and Alice's group. Marcus hung back, not wanting to call attention to himself or his low extensions and trembling supporting leg.

He hadn't enjoyed lying to Alice's face. On Monday, she'd asked about his weekend, and he'd told her about his mum's fall and trip to the hospital, editing out what he'd been doing when he'd gotten Davo's call, or what had happened that night. Alice hadn't seemed to notice the highly redacted story. But she had noticed that, in the last few days, he'd probably smiled more than he had in the last year combined.

Alice had been so steadfast and reliable in the last year, so solid and so *there*, when he had felt like he was slowly disappearing from the world. Marcus wished he didn't have to hide the truth from her. Because the truth was he *was* happier lately, and he wanted to tell Alice exactly why. He knew she'd be happy for him. But even telling his best friend was asking for trouble. He trusted Alice to keep their secret . . . but still, accidents happened.

As he lifted one leg into attitude and pivoted on the other leg in a slow and painstaking promenade, Marcus could see Heather out of the corner of his eye, leaning against a barre at the side of the studio. She was chatting with Justin, who replied discreetly under his breath just like Marcus and Alice had been. Heather smiled and nodded in response, and Marcus felt a tiny knot of jealousy burrowing itself into his stomach, where it joined the guilt he'd felt at lying to Alice.

At last, the adagio ended, and Marcus closed his feet in as tight a fifth position as he could manage. His heart raced, and every muscle in his upper legs ached and twitched. He had enjoyed this part of class, before. Had appreciated the way the slow and contemplative pace disguised the gruelling work of lifting his legs into the air and holding them there, suspended by nothing but his own hard-earned strength and muscle control. Now, his muscles had atrophied, and so much of that strength had dissipated.

It would come back to him, he told himself, retreating from the centre to seize his water bottle and gulp at it while his heart rate slowed. *Stronger than ever*, Shaz had said. Across the room, Heather had paused in her conversation with Justin. She caught his eye and he saw the tiniest frown appear between her eyebrows. It was a question, but not one he could answer here in front of Peter and all his colleagues. He kept his face impassive but chanced a nonchalant nod, then looked away, pretending to watch the group dancing in the centre.

Marcus didn't dance much for the rest of class. After adagio, Peter set half a dozen jump and pirouette combinations, so Marcus put his bad foot up on the barre and stretched as his colleagues leapt and spun around him. It was thrilling, after so many months away, to watch dance up close again. He'd spent so long avoiding the company's performances, because watching other people dance when he couldn't only depressed him. When he'd gone to the ANB building for physio, he'd walked past the open studio doors as quickly as he could, averting his gaze from all the dancing happening inside those rooms he wasn't well enough to be in.

He'd missed live dancing, he realised, missed the intimacy and the humidity of a studio full of sweating, working bodies. And now he was back. Now he could watch Heather fly across the room, soaring into a grand jeté and hitting a perfect hundred-eighty-degree split in the mirrors. She was petite, but her jumps swallowed up metres of the studio, carrying her from one side of the room to the other with just a few quick strides. When she landed, it was near-silent, controlled, and breathtakingly precise. It was hard to keep his eyes off her, but looking around, he realised he wasn't alone: half his colleagues were watching her, too. Pride swelled in his chest as he watched them watch her, as in awe of her talent and skill as he was.

None of them knew she'd woken up in his bed this morning. She'd come over last night and he'd cooked, because she'd said she was sick of eating takeaway. He'd made one of his favourite winter meals, pasta with pumpkin and sausage. It had all gone well enough, until he'd gotten distracted kissing her and let the sage leaves burn in the pan. While the smoke cleared, they'd taken their bowls of pasta out onto the balcony and enjoyed his view of the Bridge. He'd told her about how his first full class back had felt, and she'd caught him up on her rehearsals with Justin. He'd had the distinct pleasure of watching Heather enjoy a meal he'd prepared—and then they'd gone inside, for other distinct pleasures.

But now they were at work, and Marcus had to pretend he hadn't watched her step out of his shower this morning, her wet hair twisted into a long, dripping rope over one shoulder, trailing droplets down the tops of her breasts and into one of his towels. Heather's penchant for planning turned out to be essential to their sneaking around: she'd downloaded the city bus schedule and cross-referenced it against a list he'd given her of other dancers who lived in the area, then determined which bus stops and routes were safest for them to take in order to leave each other's houses and get to work on time without risking being spotted. Today, they'd taken different buses to the studios so that they arrived a few minutes apart. They'd said their polite hellos at the start of class and taken their places at barres on opposite sides of the room.

It had been like this every day this week, even when they didn't spend the night together: he'd spend his bus ride buzzing with anticipation at seeing Heather again, only to arrive at work and remember that whatever happened in his bed last night, or whatever joke she'd made that had him spluttering around his mouthful of rigatoni, here they could only exchange professional pleasantries in the café and polite goodbyes at the end of class. It was maddening, but it was also kind of fun.

"It's like being a spy," he'd said this morning as they prepared for work in his bathroom.

"A sexy ballet spy," Heather had agreed, meeting his eyes in his mirror as she slid the final pin into her bun. "Makes me want to buy a watch just so we can synchronize. Should we have a secret hand signal?"

"I showed you my secret hand signal last night, and I don't think it's appropriate for a public place."

She'd giggled and rolled her eyes, and for one crazed moment he'd wanted to wrap his arms around her, pull her back into his bed, and keep her there all day, class and physio and rehearsal be damned.

Thank God it was almost the weekend. Marcus would get two uninterrupted days with her, away from prying eyes. And three uninterrupted nights. He'd asked her to go away with him for the weekend, but he hadn't told her where, or what they'd be doing when they got there. All he'd given Heather to go on was that she should pack something warm to wear and tell him if she had objections to sleeping on the ground. She'd looked slightly alarmed at that, and pressed for more details—specifically, if she should be worried about spiders—but Marcus was determined to surprise her, and eventually she'd agreed to go with him.

His thoughts were interrupted by a sharp poke to his shoulder.

"Oi, space face," Alice said, with another prod. "Class is over. What planet were you on?"

Marcus blinked and looked around, then hastily pulled his foot off the barre. Some of his colleagues collected their bags from the sides of the studio and headed for the door, while others sat under the barres, gulping breathlessly from their water bottles. A few of the guys mucked around in the middle of the room, attempting difficult pirouette combinations while their friends recorded them on their phones.

"Sorry, I got distracted. It's a bit overwhelming, being back."

"Uh-huh," Alice said sceptically, and he walked over to his bag and rummaged for his second water bottle, glad for the excuse to avoid her eyes. "Hey, what are you doing this weekend? Want to come over for dinner with me and Will?"

Marcus took his time swallowing, trying to think of a plausible lie. "I'm going to check on Mum. She put on a brave face last weekend, but I think she was pretty shaken up. And Davo won't let go of this selling the house thing, so I need to be there in case he brings it up with her."

Alice shrugged. "Okay, well, that's not your whole weekend, right? You should come hang out with us. Will's been getting really into that British baking show. He won't stop making cakes, and I can't eat them all myself."

"I can't, I'm sorry. Next weekend, maybe. And actually"—he inwardly winced, hating that he followed a lie with a request for a favour—"I was wondering if I could borrow your car. Just so I can get out to Mum's a bit more easily. Weekend buses are so slow."

Alice shrugged again, but this time it looked more like she was shooing a fly from her shoulder.

"Yeah, fine, whatever you need," she said, and his stomach sank at her annoyed, disappointed tone. "I'll give you the keys on Friday, okay?"

"Thanks," he said. "I appreciate it. I appreciate everything you do for me."

"Uh-huh," she said again, stooping to retrieve her bag. As she headed for the studio door, he thought he heard her grumble something that sounded a lot like "You better."

As a younger dancer, Heather had never understood the appeal of a ballet like *Giselle*. The heroine went mad and died at the end of act one, then spent all of act two trying to save the man who broke her heart and got her killed. And then he got to go off and marry his duchess, and she had to spend eternity as a woodland ghost? It didn't seem fair.

Not that she'd been sorry to be cast in the role last year. It was an iconic ballet role, one little girls dreamed about dancing, and she'd loved the challenge of finding something modern and relatable in an eighteenth century German peasant teenager that would allow her to understand the character a little better. When she'd been promoted and proposed to on a night when she performed the role, it was harder to roll her eyes at the ballet.

Now, of course, she understood Giselle a little *too* well. A foolish woman who thought she was living in a fairy tale, who threw herself into the arms of a man who wasn't who he said he was? A silly girl who thought she was about to get everything she'd ever wanted, who instead went a little mad when she learned the awful truth? It all cut a little close to home.

If Heather never had to dance another step of *Giselle* for the rest of her life, she'd die happy. It was Thursday afternoon, and she'd spent the last hour running through a particularly challenging scene in the second act in which Giselle was raised from her grave by Myrtha, the queen of the wilis, and initiated into the ghostly sisterhood. The choreography called for lots of long, slow, controlled extensions, and there were only so many times she could lift her foot up to her ear before she *actually* wanted to murder a man in the woods.

"Lovely, Heather, lovely," Peter called from the front of the studio. "Really stretch that last developpé as long as you can." His voice was a little more clipped, a little less friendly, than usual. Opening night was just over a week away, and they only had one more day of rehearsals in the studios before they moved to the Opera House and began rehearsing on the stage. Understandably, he was a little tense.

Still, Peter gave Heather an encouraging smile as she finished the section and the accompanist stopped playing. That was one thing she appreciated about Peter: he didn't take his feelings out on his dancers. She stood in the middle of the studio with her hands on her hips, panting. Thankfully he took pity on her.

"That's looking really good. You can take a break if you want, and come back in"—he glanced at the clock over the studio door—"fifteen minutes?"

Heather nodded gratefully, grabbed her trash-bag pants, and made for the door as he turned to Anabelle, the dancer who was playing Myrtha. A coffee would help, and then she was going to lie on the floor of the dancers' lounge with her feet up on a couch. Once she had her flat white in hand, she headed back down the hallway and let herself into the lounge.

Marcus sat up on one of the couches as she entered, and she checked to make sure the lounge was otherwise empty. A second ago she'd been exhausted. Now her stomach did giddy backflips at the sight of him.

"Hi," Heather whispered, closing the door behind her quietly and walking over to him. Instead of tights, he was back in the sweatpants he wore for physical therapy—sweatpants he'd pulled on this morning, when they'd woken up together in her bed. His bare feet were propped on a pillow, revealing the long silver-pink scar at the back of his ankle. She'd seen it up close this morning, when she'd returned to bed with a to-go coffee in each hand. He'd let her run her hand over it gently, feeling the slightly raised skin under her fingertips as he explained why his first surgery had failed.

"Hi," Marcus replied. His curls were slightly mussed from lying down, and he gave her a sleepy smile as she approached. He yawned wide.

"Boring you already, am I?"

He rolled his eyes, then smiled at her. "I was napping. Justin's class nearly killed me this morning, and I had a late night last night."

Heather's eyes widened in warning. Despite glancing over her shoulder, she bit her lip to keep her smile from becoming a grin. Last night had been . . . Well, she hadn't known she was capable of coming so hard, or so many times.

"I'm sorry to hear that," she said evenly. She took a sip of her coffee. "I hope you get some rest tonight." He wouldn't. She'd make sure of it.

"Oh, me too." He yawned again and gave her the tiniest of winks.

She wanted to leap over the back of the couch and kiss him. They'd spent four of the last five nights together, and she must have kissed him hundreds of times in the last few days, but it was always the same: the touch of his lips to hers, the way he ran his hand up her neck to cup her cheek, felt both electric and deeply soothing. She wondered how many kisses it would take for that feeling to wear off.

Instead of kissing him, however, Heather took another sip of coffee and offered him a polite smile before walking around to the couch opposite his and flopping onto the floor. She groaned as she put her feet on the couch, feeling the swelling drain out of her toes and ankles as blood flowed easily down her legs. She could feel Marcus's eyes on her, but she kept hers on the ceiling.

"Does that feel good?" he asked, his voice neutral, and she bit her lip again. He'd asked the same question in a very different tone last night, when he'd teased and tasted her neck, her collarbone, her shoulder, flicking his tongue over her skin for what felt like an hour until she was breathless and writhing, desperate for him to take off her panties and touch her.

"Yes," she said, just as neutrally. *Yes*, she'd moaned, when he'd finally lowered his mouth to her clit and slid a finger inside her, stroking her until she came so hard she might have blacked out.

Her feet felt cooler and less swollen, but her cheeks were hot with the memory, and she grew wet remembering the feeling of his tongue swirling around her swollen, throbbing clit. This wasn't technically a violation of Rule #2, but it sure felt like one. Heather took a few deep breaths, trying to settle her heart rate.

She sat up and faced him. He still lay on the couch, watching her, and she could tell from the look on his face that he was thinking about last night, too. Or perhaps looking forward to tonight. *Only a few more hours*, she thought. Then they could be together again. But until then, they had to keep it professional.

"How's your ankle feeling?" She'd managed not to watch him too closely in class, but on the few occasions she'd glanced at him, Marcus looked stronger and steadier than he had even a week ago. He still skipped jumps and pirouettes, but now he moved without the hesitation he'd had when she met him, when he'd walked like he worried his body would fall apart at any moment.

"Pretty good. The rest of me is still struggling, but Shaz says I'll get there. And who's going to argue with Shaz?"

"Not me." Heather gave Marcus another polite smile, but she wanted to hug him, or at least squeeze his hand. He'd worked so hard to get here, and even though she'd only been around to see the very end of that work, she was proud of him.

She wanted to tell him that, but it would have to wait until tonight. She was due back in the studio in two minutes, and if she stayed here even that long, she might do something stupid. Reluctantly, Heather eased herself to her aching feet. "Break's over," she groaned.

"Have a good rehearsal," Marcus said, his voice giving no hint he'd be seeing her shortly after.

"Thank you," she said quietly. Heather started for the door but stopped as she passed the arm of the couch, unable to resist when he was this close to her. Quickly but gently, she put her hand on his head and stroked it, just once, letting her fingers tangle for the briefest moment in his loose curls.

His sigh was still in her ears when she closed the door behind her.

Chapter 14

Heather's ears popped as they wound their way through the mountains. Marcus hadn't told her where they were going, insisting he wanted to surprise her, but the compass on the dashboard of Alice's car told her they were headed west, away from the coast and out past the edge of Sydney. Almost an hour ago they'd reached the foot of the Blue Mountains—which, Marcus had explained, were named for the haze that hovered over them, the product of tens of thousands of eucalyptus trees releasing their oil into the air—and kept driving. Marcus shuffled occasionally through a playlist of what he said was classic Australian rock, rolling down the windows and singing along off-key to a song about flame trees. She didn't know where they were going, but she liked that they were going together.

The fact that they were escaping the city to be together in public made Heather wonder, yet again, about the wisdom of what she and Marcus were doing. Well, no, not exactly: she knew damn well what they were doing was unwise. She'd known it the other day, when she'd stolen a second of physical contact with him, unable to be so close without touching him. It was a stupid risk. This entire exercise was a stupid risk. But every time she thought about ending this, her heart would sink, her ribs would ache, and she'd glance down to find her knuckles white from gripping too tightly to whatever she happened to be holding.

Sure, it was unwise, she told herself, but the alternative somehow seemed even worse. Despite the risk, she felt safe with Marcus. Safe, and entirely herself, far removed from the humiliated emptiness she'd felt before she came to Sydney. Heather couldn't bring herself to give it up. And so here she was, in Alice's car, Marcus's hand resting gently on her thigh as he reminisced about the one time he'd been to New York on tour with ANB. He and Alice had taken the express train instead of the local and found themselves fifty blocks north of where they needed to be—and very late for a dress rehearsal.

As they drove farther up the mountain, giant eucalyptus forests hugged the winding road, and a series of signs announced their entrance into each mountain town. Some had English-sounding names like Glenbrook and Springwood, and others had what Heather now recognized as Aboriginal names like Bullaburra and Katoomba. They wound past churches, old pubs, and antique shops, the road and the train line tracing their way up the mountain in parallel as Heather leaned her head against the window and let the winter sun warm her face.

Finally, shortly after they entered a town called Blackheath, Marcus turned off the main road and drove along a winding street down into the giant green valley below.

"Nearly there now," Marcus said, glancing at her with a mischievous smile.

"Nearly where?"

"Nearly at the surprise location you've managed not to ask me about for the last"—he checked the clock on the dashboard—"hour and a half. You've done so well, don't ruin your streak now."

Heather stuck her tongue out at him, and he returned the gesture. The car slowed as the incline increased, and Marcus turned onto a narrow dirt road.

"But seriously, where are you taking me? Wait . . ." Heather looked around at the dense forest on either side of the bumpy road. A dirt road into the forest, and sleeping on the ground? She looked at Marcus, realization dawning. "Are you taking me *camping*?"

"Not exactly." He took his eyes off the road briefly to look at her. "Why, do you not like camping?"

"I wouldn't know, I've never been. It's kind of hard to get away for the weekend when the company has four shows between Friday night and Sunday afternoon."

"Well, we're going to ease you in gently," Marcus said. "This isn't even really camping, it's glamping. In fact, I think lots of actual campers would be offended if you called this camping."

"And we're out here all weekend?" she asked. It was pretty here, Heather thought, but what were they meant to do with their time when they weren't sleeping on the ground or cooking on an open fire? She was about to ask when a small, packed-earth parking lot appeared on the side of the road, and Marcus pulled into an empty spot.

"I think you're going to like being out here all weekend," he said, turning the engine off and turning toward her. He was alight with what looked like excitement and satisfaction, as if delighted he could finally unveil his surprise. "You see, this isn't just camping. It's camping in a national park."

"Okay . . ." Heather said, not really following.

Marcus pulled her close, and the feeling of his warm, firm body against hers knocked the breath out of her. Heather looked into his twinkling, mischievous eyes, and felt her stomach do that now-familiar saut de chat.

"And in this national park, there's a wildlife conservation center"—his smile grew—"where the parks service is working with the traditional owners of the land to prevent bushfires. And to reintroduce a particular species of wildlife into the bush out here."

"*Okay* . . ." Heather repeated, but this time, she was smiling, too, a little bubble of hopeful suspicion forming in her chest. She searched his face for confirmation of her hunch.

"And that species is the *Phascolarctos cinereus*, also known as the koala. Or as you call it—incorrectly, by the way—the 'koala bear.' So we're out here all weekend to glamp and go on bush walks and see koalas in the wild. Since we never made it to the zoo, I figured you might—" The rest of his sentence was lost to the hard, grateful kiss Heather planted on his grinning mouth.

Marcus took a deep breath of bush air and looked around the small clearing they'd been taken to after checking in at the conservation centre. The air was cooler up here than it was in Sydney, and the sunlight had to struggle down between the thick trees to reach him. He zipped his hoodie up, glad he'd told Heather to pack something warm to sleep in.

This really wasn't camping at all, he thought. The five tents in the clearing were sturdy, semi-permanent structures that looked reassuringly wind- and rainproof. And although he'd warned her they'd be sleeping on the ground, their sleeping bags had in fact been rolled out on thin but comfortable looking mattresses on low wooden platforms. A short walk away, along a path marked by solar-powered lanterns, Heather had been very pleased to find an all-gender restroom block with flushable toilets and fully stocked soap dispensers.

Marcus sat on one of the several benches around the firepit in the middle of the clearing. It was so still here, away from the bustle and noise of the city. They were right on the edge of the national park, and the immenseness of the bush made him feel the same way he did when he stood with his feet in the water at the beach. On the edge of something huge and alive, something thrilling and endless and indifferent to his presence. He closed his eyes and listened to the scattered chorus of birdsong.

Marcus could hear a magpie croaking melodically above, some parrots chattering, and somewhere in the distance a couple of kookaburras laughing their famous maniacal cackle. His dad had loved that sound. He'd always been tickled by how human and unhinged it was, and any time he'd heard it, he'd laughed in reply—even when there were people around and Marcus and Davo were embarrassed. The laugh rang out again, closer this time, and a wave of grief washed over Marcus, briefly draining the air from his lungs and the strength from his muscles. His dad would never hear that cackle again—and Marcus would never again have the chance to be embarrassed by his dad laughing back.

He heard footsteps approaching and turned to find Heather returning from the restrooms, wiping her hands on her jeans. For a moment, Marcus just watched her, let the sight of her—out in this place with him, because of him—soothe the parts of him that ached.

Marcus worried she might not want to come this weekend. That she might decide it was too risky to keep doing . . . whatever it was they were doing. He'd been sure she'd say it wasn't a good idea and was slightly taken aback by the depth of his own relief when she said she wanted to. And he'd never imagined the thrill of victorious satisfaction he'd felt as he watched the realization dawn on her face that she was about to see koalas in the wild and up close. She'd gasped in delight, and she glowed with anticipation, and his heart squeezed at the sight of it. It was better than any curtain call, better than the way she smiled after she came. And he'd made it happen.

Heather caught his eye as she approached, and he noticed the clutch of people following close behind her.

"All right, everyone," called the man at the front of the group, who had checked them in when they'd arrived. "Make yourselves comfortable on the benches, if you would." He'd introduced himself as Craig and was dressed in khaki, the centre's logo embroidered on his chest pocket, and well-worn leather work boots.

Heather sat next to Marcus. Their thighs touched, and he realised with a jolt that this was the first time they'd been able to sit that way in public. He scooted a little closer, and she pressed her leg against his, shooting him a sideways smile. On his other side, a man sat with his two young daughters, dressed in matching outfits, and next to them a tourist couple who Marcus had heard muttering to each other in what sounded like French.

"Welcome to Blue Mountains National Park," Craig said, giving them a crinkly smile. Under his wide-brimmed hat, he had straggly sun-bleached hair and a deeply tanned face, as though he'd spent most of his life working outside. "We're here as guests of the traditional owners of this land, the Dharug and Gundungurra people, who have lived here for tens of thousands of years, caring for the land and waters you see around you."

Craig gave them all a moment to look around the clearing. Marcus took in another deep breath of the air, smelling the gum trees and the hints of old woodsmoke from the firepit behind him.

"Now, there are some ground rules I need to go over before you get settled into your tents and I set you loose in the park," Craig went on. He gestured to the bush behind him. "This is a fragile wild ecosystem. There are lots of creatures living out here, minding their own business. Most of them are harmless, but a coupla them are deadly when disturbed. We're visitors in their house. So as long as we're polite visitors, and we don't get in their way, there won't be a problem."

Next to Marcus, Heather gave a tiny gulp. He reached over and took her hand, squeezing it gently and revelling in the fact that he could. Craig went on.

"That means if you're walking out in the bush, you need to stay on the track unless you're with me or one of my colleagues. No littering, no picking any plants or flowers, and absolutely no touching or approaching wildlife, no matter how cute and cuddly. If you're going to take photos or videos of creatures you see out here, the zoom lens is your friend. If you're close enough to snap a selfie, you're too close. If you see something you think might be dangerous, like something that creeps or crawls or slithers along the ground, walk away slowly, don't make any sudden movements, and come find me and tell me where you saw it. All right? If you can follow those rules, we can all have a good time out here, and I won't have to suck any poison out of any spider bites."

"Gross," the younger girl whispered. "Awesome," her sister breathed.

Heather gave a little shudder, then turned to Marcus with wide, horrified eyes. "Slithers along the ground? There are snakes out here? Are they harmless like the huntsman?"

"Uh, sure," he lied. "Let's go with that." Her eyes widened even further.

"We'll be fine, don't worry. I'm the spider whisperer, remember?" Marcus waggled his eyebrows, and she bumped her shoulder playfully against his.

"You've got time for a short bush walk this afternoon, and then dinner's at 5:30," Craig continued. "We'll do a bit of stargazing after dinner, and then it's early to bed. Koalas are early risers, and we want to catch them first thing in the morning."

Marcus sensed rather than saw Heather grin with excitement. He turned to her and smiled back, loving that he didn't have to avert his eyes and pretend he'd barely noticed her, the way he'd had to all week.

"Want to go for a walk?" she asked, looking down a path with uneven ground. "Can you handle this?"

"Yeah, if we take it slowly," he nodded. "I brought my cane, but I don't think I'll need it. Might just have to hold on to you if I'm feeling weak or wobbly."

"Well, if you must," Heather sighed, pretending to be put-upon. Then she stood and offered her hand, helping him rise from the bench. They slowly headed toward the visitors' centre, where a small sign gave them the choice of two tracks, one for a long loop and the other for a short walk to a lookout over the Megalong Valley.

They chose the second one, and Marcus held Heather's hand even though he didn't need it for balance, even as his fingers grew sweaty against hers.

The air was cool and still around them, the leaves of the gum trees barely moving as they walked in silence down the sun-dappled track, which sloped gently upwards on its way to the lookout. Marcus's ankle felt strong and steady underneath him, and the rest of his body felt solid and alive in a way it hadn't felt in months.

Still, they were both sweating slightly by the time they gained the top of the path, and Heather had released his hand to tie her sweater around her waist. Now she was a few paces ahead as the path brought him around the corner to the edge of a cliff, and he stopped and stared at the sight before him. Heather faced the giant sweeping valley, her back to him as she gripped the railing and looked out at the craggy rock formations that poked out of the thick green forest below. Out here away from the tree cover, the breeze played with her hair, fluttering her long ponytail gently as she took in the entire valley.

For the first time since that day in his lobby all those months ago, the day he'd decided to throw himself into his recovery so he could one day dance again, Marcus felt a sense of perfect, unnameable clarity. Heather belonged here, in this sweeping place, in the warm golden sunlight of the fading day. And he belonged with Heather.

Slowly, Marcus joined her, and let his hand rest gently on the railing beside her so she knew he was there. Then he wrapped his arms around her waist and rested his chin against her head, pulling her against him and leaning her shoulders into his chest.

"It's beautiful out here," Heather said quietly.

"You have no idea," Marcus murmured, and she turned to kiss his cheek.

He squeezed her gently around the waist, and they stood there in silence watching the shadows creep and lengthen in the valley. Marcus refused to think about everything he'd lost and could still lose. He wouldn't think about Heather's ex, or her looming departure, or the fact that standing this way out in public could get them both fired. In this moment, none of it could touch them. In this moment, he could pretend this never had to end.

Heather lay on her back on the picnic rug Craig had provided and took in the night sky. The air was chilly, but her scarf and wool socks kept out the worst of the cold, and a cup of after-dinner tea, sweet and milky, left her insides thoroughly warmed.

Heather and Marcus had returned from the lookout to find Craig starting a fire in the pit. The little light it threw off and the glow of their small solar lanterns weren't enough to dim the stars scattered across the dark sky. Now, the night was quiet but for the breeze in the gum trees and the crackling fire. Heather took a deep breath and let her body relax against the packed dirt.

On a blanket a few paces away, the two sisters matched in purple plaid pajamas and fleece robes. As Craig settled onto his own blanket and pulled on a beanie, Marcus returned from the bathroom and lay down next to her, his arms folded under his head and his thigh pressed gently against hers. Warmth blossomed through the fabric of her leggings where they touched.

"How's your ankle?" she whispered.

"Not bad," he replied. "I'm not going to outrun any snakes on it, but I feel a lot better than I did a few weeks ago."

"You don't need to outrun the snake; you just need to outrun one human. As long as it's not me."

Marcus chuckled and turned to look at her. She could barely make out his face, but she could see he was grinning. He shook his head.

"What?" Heather asked.

"Nothing," he replied, the smile in his voice clear, "I just—"

"All right, ladies and gents," Craig started, and Marcus fell quiet. "If you look up and give your eyes time to adjust, I can give you a tour of the southern sky tonight. In winter we've got several planets visible to the naked eye, including Saturn and Jupiter. I'll be sure to show you those, but let's start with the most famous of the Australian constellations, the one that appears on our national flag. Can anyone tell me what it's called?"

"The Southern Cross!" the younger girl called loudly. Her sister shushed her.

"That's right." Craig pulled out a laser pointer and switched it on. "If you look at this very bright star here"—he directed the pointer into the air—"and follow this line of stars down, you'll see the cross right there, quite low in the sky tonight. Four large points here"—he drew a long cross with the pointer—"and one little one on the side here. That's how you know it's the real Southern Cross, and not the false cross that sometimes tricks people."

It never really occurred to Heather that the southern hemisphere had entirely different stars from the northern hemisphere. She supposed if she'd stopped to think about it, she wouldn't expect to see the northern lights in the southern sky, but then, she'd never stopped to think about such a thing. In New York, she rarely saw the stars anyway.

Marcus nudged her. "He's talking to you," he whispered, and Heather sat up.

"Sorry," she said. "What was the question?"

"What's your star sign?" Craig asked, sounding a little miffed she hadn't been listening.

"Oh, uh, Sagittarius, I think? December second," Heather replied quickly. "But I don't think any of that stuff is real."

"Well, neither do I," Craig said, "but the stars are real." He unfolded a piece of paper and laid it on his lap, then shone the pointer onto it. "Sagittarius," he said, consulting the map closely and then pointing the light upward to the left of the Southern Cross, "is right here. The Archer."

Heather looked up politely and nodded.

Craig consulted the paper again. "Incidentally, that means you're 'adventurous, impulsive, and brave.'" He looked at Marcus, who had sat up at her side. "Is that true?"

"Yes," Marcus replied, at the same moment Heather scoffed, "No."

They turned to look at each other. Despite the dark, Marcus's eyebrows were raised in what looked like surprise. She frowned slightly, trying to read his expression, and he gave a little shrug, as if to say, *What? It's just the truth.*

"Well," Craig sounded amused. "Sounds like you two are very compatible."

Marcus gave a good-natured chuckle, but Heather said nothing. Her throat felt tight, and tears prickled her eyes. She stared at her knees in the dark, willing the tears away. At the sound of Marcus's answer—no, at the sound of the certainty and admiration in his voice when he answered—two startling realizations had tumbled, one after the other, into her mind. The first, which had made the tears threaten, was that for all the compliments Jack had ever given her—he had praised her looks more times than she could count, especially at the beginning—he had never called her adventurous or brave. The second, the one that tightened her throat, was the realization that somewhere beneath her routines and her rule-following, she might in fact be both those things.

Heather had always been capable of cartwheels.

When Craig's presentation finished up a few minutes later, he handed each of them a flashlight and told them to turn in for the night. "Early start, remember," he warned as they climbed to their feet and headed toward their tents. "We'll be on the koalas' schedule in the morning."

When they'd arrived at the campsite, Marcus thought the mattresses in the tents looked pretty comfortable. Now he was actually lying on one of them, though, he realised how wrong he'd been. He shifted in his sleeping bag, trying to pull more of it beneath him to cushion his hip against the hard wooden platform. It didn't help much.

"I'm sorry," he whispered to Heather. "This isn't great. Are you going to be able to sleep?"

"Maybe," she whispered back. Her voice sounded a little strained, like she was in real discomfort. "But if I do, I'm just going to have nightmares about creepy crawlies, so it's probably for the best. The koalas better be extremely cute tomorrow."

"You don't need to worry about that; I put in a special request for extra cute koalas," Marcus replied.

"Oh, really?" she asked, turning from her back onto her side. In the darkness, he could just make out the silhouette of her head propped on her hand and her sleeping bag pulled up to her armpits.

"Yeah, they made all the un-cute ones leave before we got here," Marcus said, smiling. She shifted again, and his face fell. "I'm sorry this isn't as glam as you were promised."

"No, I'm glad you brought me," she whispered. "This place is great."

"It really is," he said, allowing himself a sigh of relief. "I haven't been up here since I was a kid. When we were little, we'd come up here once a year for a school trip, and it was always the best day of the year."

"What did you do out here?"

"We learnt about photosynthesis and leaf litter and the native wildlife and stuff. And when we got older, about Indigenous culture and history." Marcus thought about the kookaburras, and the old memory lapped in his chest. "Dad would take the day off work to chaperone, and he was always the only dad who came. Just him and a bunch of mums making sure no one fell off a cliff or got lost in the bush."

Heather laughed quietly, before a heavy silence filled the tent. Marcus could hear the two girls giggling in their tent a few metres away and what sounded like Craig rolling up the picnic blankets. After a moment, Heather turned onto her stomach, closing some of the space between them, and put her chin on her folded forearms.

"Do you want to tell me about him?"

Perhaps it was because the tent was so dark, or perhaps it was because they had sworn each other to secrecy. Marcus couldn't say why, but he did. He wanted to tell Heather about his dad. He wanted to tell Heather so many things.

"He was a good man," Marcus sighed. It sounded simple and empty, the kind of platitude people had repeated to him at the wake and in the weeks that followed. He tried to elaborate. "He wasn't shy, but he was pretty soft-spoken. I think I heard him yell maybe four times in my entire life, and one of those times was when I came home from school with a fat lip from a kid who liked to bully me for doing ballet."

"He yelled at you?" Heather sounded alarmed.

"No, he yelled at Davo. He said Davo should have stood up for me instead of letting the kid and his mates carry on. Then he took us both back to school to make the principal promise it would never happen again."

"Wow. How old were you?"

"About eleven. Davo was fourteen. He just wanted to be cool and hang out with his rugby team. He didn't want his weirdo little brother showing up at school and making his life difficult. Dad wasn't having it. He told Davo—" Marcus swallowed, the decades-old memory making the bridge of his nose tingle and burn. "—He told him he was proud of having a dancer in the family, so Davo should be too."

"Did it work?"

"Kind of. Davo made it clear after that that anyone who gave me any shit would have to answer to him and his rugby mates, though I think it was less about sticking up for me and more about the chance to beat the crap out of someone." Marcus shook his head. "And then when Davo left a few years before me, some of the boys tried to start up again. But by then, I knew I wanted to dance professionally, and I knew I probably could if I kept training and didn't get hurt. So it didn't bother me when they teased me, you know, because I knew where I was going. And I did my last two years of high school at the ANB school, dancing basically full-time.

I made real friends there, guys who got ballet and got me. Never had to see those kids again."

"You were lucky," Heather said.

"Yeah," he agreed quietly. "Plenty of boys don't get that kind of support from their families. My uncle used to tease me about ballet every time he came over. He'd have a few, and then start making jokes about me wearing a tutu or a tiara or whatever." Marcus rolled his eyes. "Oh, always as a joke, you know, 'don't take yourself so seriously, don't get offended.'" To this day, the memory made his skin prickle with the same hopeless frustration he'd felt as a kid, because how could you argue with an adult, and how could you argue with a joke?

"But Dad would always tell him to cut the shit, and Uncle Gary would, most of the time. I think Dad realised there were going to be lots of reasons for me to drop out of ballet, and he didn't want a lack of support from him to be one of them." Marcus swallowed again, harder this time. "He never let me forget he had my back and that he was proud of me. And now he's gone, and it's just me and Davo."

Heather didn't say anything in response, and Marcus shifted on his pillow, wondering if he'd let the conversation get too deep. But after a moment, her sleeping bag rustled and she placed one hand between his shoulder blades, sliding her palm lightly, reassuringly, over his hoodie. He felt his shoulders release under her touch, and the rest of his body stilled. He closed his eyes and breathed deeply into his back, into her hand.

"I think he would have liked you," Marcus murmured. "He liked stubborn women. It's why he loved my mum so bloody much."

Heather gasped and pulled away, a cold patch blooming where her hand had been a second ago.

"I'm not stubborn," Heather whispered, sounding faux-scandalized. He could just make out her face in the dark, her eyes wide and her mouth open in objection.

"Yeah, you are," he said, reaching towards her in the dark and pulling her against him. He wanted her hand back on him, wanted more of her warmth. Heather gasped again, this time with what sounded like surprise and delight. "No one becomes a principal dancer without being bloody stubborn. You can argue all you want, and you don't have to believe in horoscopes—I sure as shit don't—but I think you're adventurous and brave, too. And a little impulsive. If you weren't, you wouldn't be here. And I'm really, really glad you're here."

"I can't argue with you without sounding stubborn," she whispered, and her warm breath flickered across his face.

"That's a real shame, because I love when you argue with me," he whispered back, and he leant forward and kissed her.

In another world, in another lifetime, perhaps Heather could have been convinced to like camping. There were New Yorkers who loved to get out of the city and go on hikes, who left Friday evening to hike state parks, carrying tents on their backs, returning Sunday afternoon sunburned and stinking and glowing with the smugness that came with being outdoorsy. Her schedule had never permitted her to try, but now, Heather knew it wasn't for her.

Her hip felt like one enormous bruise, and her neck had practically frozen solid in the twisted position she'd found herself in when she woke up Saturday morning. For a moment she lay on the thin excuse for a mattress with her eyes closed, grateful that, aside from her nose and cheeks, she was warm. The morning light seeping in through the fabric of the tent bathed everything in a faint green glow, and last night's silence was replaced by birdsong. Heather listened intently, picking out a plaintive cawing and an exuberant, chattering chirp. She could hear what sounded like human movement outside the tent, too.

Barely a foot away, Marcus was deep in sleep, looking otherworldly in the pale green light. He lay on his side, his curls mussed on the pillow and his lips slightly parted. She noticed for the first time that he had a thin white scar above his top lip. She thought about last night's whispered conversation and wondered if that had been a bully's doing.

Heather would never envy Marcus's grief at losing his father, but it was hard not to let a sense of wistfulness nip at her when she thought about how fiercely the man had insisted on the value of his son's ballet training. Heather had never met her father, and since she'd never known his presence, she hadn't thought much about his absence. But she knew enough to realize how much easier her mother's life would have been if he hadn't left when she was five months pregnant, and if he'd paid child support like he was supposed to.

Heather had grown up knowing her mother was doing her best to do the work of two parents. She'd tried to be understanding when her mother didn't have time to help out backstage at *The Nutcracker* like the other moms, or when she needed reminding yet again what a particular French term for a ballet step meant.

There had certainly been times when Heather was grateful not to have a pushy, over-involved ballet mom—the horror movies and reality shows exaggerated the intensity of dance moms, but only a little bit. When she and Jack started getting serious, Heather had let herself imagine she might end up with a ballet mother-in-law, someone who had walked this career path and understood it intimately. She imagined Jack's mother giving her advice, regaling her with anecdotes about what it was like to debut the roles Heather now danced at NYB a generation later.

But then Christine had turned out to be, well, Christine. A woman who looked down her surgically reshaped nose at Heather, and thought Heather was so obviously beneath her son. Who had all but told Heather to her face that she thought she was using Jack to get ahead in the company.

"That was quite a sigh," Marcus mumbled, and Heather started.

"Good morning," she said, propping herself up on her elbow and pushing thoughts of Jack's mother away. Slowly Marcus winced and stretched his body straight in his sleeping bag. "How'd you sleep?"

"Ow," he groaned.

"Yeah," she laughed. "Same."

"I am . . . so sorry," he half moaned, half yawned. Marcus eased himself up onto one elbow, wincing again.

"I forgive you, but I don't know if Sharon will. That can't have been good for my hips or your ankle."

Marcus huffed a tired laugh, and smiled, the crinkles around his eyes deeper than normal and his eyes the color of the valley outside. She smiled back, and saw his eyes drop to her lips, and then to her chin. His gaze lingered there, and she felt her cheeks heat as her smile faded.

Heather glanced away and studied the seam of fabric just above her head, but she could feel Marcus watching her closely.

"Hey," he said, "what's wrong?"

"Nothing," she lied.

He sat up tentatively. He didn't say anything, just looked at her, expectantly, and waited.

"You were staring at my chin," Heather sighed, finally. "And I hate my chin. It's too pointy and sharp and . . . I have stage face."

He glanced at the offending facial feature, then met her eyes again, a hint of a smile on his face. "What the fuck is stage face? Is it a medical condition? Oh my God, is it contagious?"

Heather rolled her eyes. "It's when . . . it's this thing someone said to me once, that my face doesn't look good up close, but that means it looks good on stage."

Marcus stared at her, a frown crumpling his forehead and his mouth half open. "Someone said that about your face . . . to your face?"

She nodded. "She wasn't wrong, and it's not like I haven't heard hard feedback about my body before. I mean, it's ballet." Basically every visible part of her was fair game. Teachers had been assessing her legs and hips and pinkie fingers since she was a child. Random people on Instagram posted zoomed-in, disembodied photos of her feet in pointe shoes. Why should her chin be any different?

"She *was* wrong, but hang on a second, a teacher said this to you?"

"No, my ex's mom," Heather said, quietly. Her would-be mother-in-law. The former reigning queen of American ballet.

"Well, she sounds delightful."

Heather shrugged. "It's over now."

Except it wasn't, not really. Even if Christine would never be her mother-in-law, even if she never saw the woman again, that barb still snagged in Heather's mind every time she looked in the mirror. She couldn't watch Marcus watch her without thinking about it.

Marcus looked at her intently for a moment, a small crease between his eyebrows. Then he cupped her face gently in his hand. She resisted the urge to glance away again, willed herself to hold steady under his gaze.

"Do you know what I thought the very first time I saw you?" he asked, his voice quiet and deadly serious.

Heather smiled ruefully. "What is this woman doing in the men's locker room?"

"Well, yeah. But after that?"

She gave her head a tiny shake, pressing her jaw into his hand.

"I thought, 'This woman has a face shaped like a heart. And it's so beautiful I can barely stand to look. But if she'd let me, I'd want to look at her up close every day.'"

Heather opened her mouth to reply, but she was too stunned to speak. He'd said that so frankly and guilelessly, as though it were a self-evident truth. *Water is wet. What goes up must come down. Heather Hays has a face like a heart.* There was no agenda, no strategy, and he wasn't going to turn around and twist the compliment into something cruel to throw her off balance. And Heather knew he'd tell her as many times as she needed to hear it. Until she could look in the mirror and believe it.

Her eyes welled with tears, and she blinked them away with a small smile. Deep in her chest, a tight knot of anxiety began to loosen, and she thought suddenly of a curled new leaf on a plant, unfurling slowly in the light. She took a long breath, feeling a few more leaves unfurl as she closed her eyes and pressed her cheek into his large, warm palm. Contentment crept through her, radiating from his hand and settling into her aching muscles. A few minutes ago, she'd have said she never wanted to spend another moment in a tent. Now, she would have happily lain here with him all day.

Marcus released her cheek, but only to trace his index finger around the edges of her face, grazing her hairline gently as his hand made its progress across her skin. Heather opened her eyes and gazed up at him, riveted by his warmth and determination as he charted the path from her forehead to her temple, down her cheek and along her jawline, until his finger came to rest on her chin. Then he ducked his head and gently kissed her there.

"Stage face, my ass," he murmured, and she let out a watery giggle, tipping her head back so his lips met her throat.

Outside the tent, a bell clanged, and they both jumped.

"Must be time to get moving," Heather said regretfully. She disentangled herself from his arms and her sleeping bag, then groaned. Now that she no longer had the distraction of Marcus's hands and mouth, she was reminded of just how poorly she'd slept and how sore she was.

"These tents looked so comfortable in the brochure," Marcus said, grimacing. "We can sue for false advertising."

Heather laughed. "I don't think that'll be necessary, but maybe you should hand over date planning to me next time."

"Hey, I'm just glad to hear there'll be a next time after this." Marcus rubbed the shoulder he'd slept on, then reached stiffly toward the corner of the tent and unzipped the entrance flap.

"Not if there isn't coffee out there," Heather grumbled as she eased herself carefully into a sitting position. Her hamstrings complained as she did, and her lower back felt like it was made of cement. She officially hated camping. And glamping.

* *

Marcus staggered out into the sharp morning light. The two sisters appeared to have slept perfectly well, or at least well enough to run around the firepit playing some kind of game as their father sat on a bench, nursing a steaming metal mug.

"Where'd you get that?" Marcus called to him.

The man gestured to the other side of the clearing, where some-one—likely Craig—had set up hot water and instant coffee. Behind him, Heather let out a whimper of longing, and Marcus took her hand.

"Come on, let's get you caffeinated."

As they walked, Heather laced her fingers between his and swung their hands a few times through the cool air. Marcus gave her a gentle squeeze, and then, on the third swing, he pulled her close and gave her a spin. She laughed as he pulled her into him, suddenly chest to chest, one hand firm on her lower back.

"You wanna dance?" Heather asked, gazing up at him, anticipation in her tired, beautiful face.

"With The Heather Hays?"

"I'm just Heather up here." She shrugged, smiling, eyes sparkling with invitation.

In that moment, another fleeting but perfectly clear thought dashed through Marcus's still-groggy brain. It would be worth spending another year with Sharon if it meant getting strong enough to dance with Heather. It would be worth grinding through tedious exercises and enduring the pain of rebuilding his atrophied muscles to perform with this woman, this dancer, this unexpected ray of sunshine. The image of the two of them flashed before his eyes, him and Heather on a real stage, in front a real audience, and not in joggers.

For a few seconds, they swayed, moving together in silent rhythm. When Marcus spun her out, she responded by stepping in front of him, into the highest fifth position relevé her shoes would allow. Then she took a step forward and set up for a pirouette. Marcus put his hands on her waist, ready to spin and steady her.

Heather turned, her shoe scraping in the packed dirt, and after three rotations Marcus stopped her, holding her tight and secure. It was just like rehearsal with Justin and Peter, except here, no one was watching them. No one was scrutinizing or judging or watching for signs of inappropriate fraternization. It was just him and Heather and the music only they could hear.

Heather stepped away from him again, this time into a low arabesque, and again Marcus caught her waist and held her there.

"Penché?" he asked, and she hesitated.

"Slowly. I'm cold, and I just spent the night on the world's thinnest mattress."

Marcus chuckled and squeezed her waist in understanding, then she lowered her body towards the ground, diving carefully forward until her free foot pointed to the sky. After a few seconds, Heather pulled up, and once again Marcus felt her muscles working beneath his hands and marvelled for a moment that he was in fact dancing with Heather. The woman everyone else thought of as The Heather Hays. On packed dirt at a campsite, on the way to get weak instant coffee, but still. He hadn't danced a pas de deux in over a year, but this had been more than worth the wait.

When she was fully upright, Heather spun out from him, tight chaîné turns taking her a few feet away until he caught up with her. She stopped and swept one leg up into an attitude derrière, beaming as he took her hand and walked around her, turning her on one leg in a slow promenade. After a few seconds, she wobbled, and before Marcus could catch her she lost her balance and came down from relevé, laughing.

"That's all I can do before coffee. Is your ankle okay?"

"It's fine," he said. Better than fine, actually, Marcus realised as she gave him a relieved smile, kissed him quickly, and made a beeline for the coffee. Sure, he hadn't moved much, and it wasn't like he'd just performed some huge jumps or anything, but his Achilles hadn't complained at all. He'd barely thought about it. He'd been so focused on Heather, on making sure she was placed properly over her leg and stable in her pirouettes. And it had felt easy, like they'd been dancing together all their lives.

Heather handed him a mug full of milky coffee, and he sipped it gratefully. It was no flat white, but it was hot and caffeinated, and today it would do. They walked back to the fire hand in hand, and even though he knew better, Marcus let himself wonder what it would be like to dance with Heather Hays for the rest of his life.

After making sure they all had water and appropriate footwear, Craig led everyone down the longer, scenic path. The girls and their father were at the front, the sisters chattering with each other and peppering Craig with questions. The French couple walked serenely behind them, and Heather and Marcus followed slowly at the back of the pack.

"Are you sure your ankle can handle this?" Heather asked, watching the weak morning sun slide over his face as he moved. The night's chill hung in the air, and the forest smelled of damp soil.

"Yeah, no worries," he said. "If I can handle pas de deux before breakfast, I can definitely hack this. Plus, I can't leave you out here on your own. Don't trust you not to steal a koala when no one's looking."

Heather giggled and took his hand. Her body still buzzed from dancing with him, as if it had been the opening night of some huge production, not a simple improvised pas de deux in the middle of the bush. Dancing with Marcus felt strangely intimate. They'd slept together, and sex with him felt like dancing, when all the steps came easily and the music sang in her bones. Sex with Jack had felt like a hard class she always wanted to overanalyze later to figure out how she could do better.

But actually dancing with Marcus? Feeling him listen to her body and understand it with almost no words? Knowing he wouldn't judge her if she wobbled or messed up? That made her feel far more exposed to him, and far closer to him, than anything else they'd done.

As they made their way down the gully, Craig turned and picked his way along the track backward, telling them all about the effort to turn the national park into a koala sanctuary. The koalas were thriving here, Craig told them proudly, and their numbers were slowly growing: the first crop of babies—joeys, they were called—had arrived this year. The two girls squealed when Craig delivered this news, and Heather barely stopped herself from joining them.

"It's hard to say where they'll be from day to day, so we might spend the morning getting cricks in our necks trying to find them," Craig warned. "But generally, we've found them around about here, so keep your eyes on the track, but make sure you're looking up, too."

Everyone slowed, craning their necks at the trees around them while trying not to trip on the uneven path. They walked this way for about ten minutes, descending deeper into the valley. Heather's neck, already sore from last night's restless sleep, was starting to complain when she heard a triumphant "Aha!" from the front.

Craig stopped and held a finger to his lips as the rest of the group halted. Then he pointed toward the treetops on the side of the path. They all followed his hand with their eyes, and one of the girls gave another quiet squeal.

At first, Heather wasn't sure the koalas were even there. There was no movement except for the long gum leaves swaying in the breeze, and the occasional flicker of foliage disturbed by a bird in the branches. It was only when Heather looked closely at the ash-brown trees that she saw the round gray lumps wedged into places where the trunks and branches met. As she and Marcus stared upward, she realized the lumps were expanding and deflating ever so slightly. Breathing. If Craig hadn't told her where to look, she would have missed them entirely. Looking more closely, she could just make out the outlines of ears and a squished face on one of the nearby lumps: the koala had its back pressed against the tree, its head drooped down toward its stomach, like a rotund old man snoozing in a recliner.

Slowly, the koalas began to wake. One of them unwedged itself from the join of the branches and stretched out its arms to grab hold of the tree. It moved along the branch, painstakingly slowly but with total stability, gripping the bark with its small, clawed hands until it reached a tuft of leaves. As Heather watched, her mouth open in awe, it pulled the tuft with one hand and thrust the leaves into its jaws.

"Dad, look!" one of the girls shrieked, and her father shushed her. "Look, a baby joey!" she said in a stage whisper, pointing at a tree on the other side of the path.

Heather followed her finger, and sure enough, a smaller gray lump was attached to one of the koalas. As the larger animal started to climb through the tree, Heather pulled out her phone and held it up, zooming in just in time to see the joey raise its head and look over the forest with dark, beady eyes. Its ears were impossibly fluffy and entirely too big for the rest of its head.

"Oh *God*, it's cute," she whispered. Marcus rubbed her back, and she noticed he was grinning with what looked like delight and self-satisfaction. But he wasn't looking at the treetops. He was looking at her.

"It's well and truly time for brekkie," Craig said in a low voice as Heather saw several more koalas digging into the gum leaves of their respective trees.

"Breakfast," Marcus translated, under his breath.

"No, I got it," she smiled at him. "My tour guide's taught me well."

Marcus chuckled, his eyes on the trees. "Why koalas?"

"What do you mean?"

"Why were you so dead set on seeing koalas?"

"Oh," she said, glancing over her shoulder to where the two girls gazed at the trees and chatted animatedly to Craig. "I think

I've always been a little bit fascinated by them. Probably because I had a koala when I was really little. A toy," she clarified quickly.

"Did it have a name?"

"Bear," she said with a shrug. "Just Bear. I know"—she rolled her eyes as Marcus smiled again—"it's a very creative name. I don't even remember when I got him, or who gave him to me. Probably one of my mother's friends or coworkers. Anyway, I used to take him everywhere with me. Slept with him every night, especially when I went away for summer intensives. He got so grimy and worn out after a while. His eyes popped off, and my mom had to sew one of his legs back on a bunch of times." She sighed. "I don't even know what happened to him, in the end."

That last part was a lie. Heather knew exactly what had happened to Bear. He had come with her to the dorms when she'd become a full-time student at NYB's school, then sat on her nightstand in the apartment she'd shared with Carly, slumping, floppy and stained, between her lamp and her body lotion. When Jack asked her to move in with him, she had shoved Bear into a storage box and hadn't dared to unpack him for fear that he'd think it was silly and childish. Somewhere in a storage unit on Avenue B, along with most of the belongings she'd taken from his apartment, Bear was still in that box.

"Well, now you've seen some real-life Bears." Marcus gestured up into the trees and looked hopefully at her face.

"And they're so cute I can bear-ly stand it," she quipped.

"Oh God," he groaned. Marcus hung his head and shook it in feigned dismay. "That was not a high koala-ty joke."

Heather chuckled and watched the real life Bears pull leaves into their mouths with methodical determination, munching slowly, rhythmically. At one point, one of the larger ones, which she suspected was a male, abandoned his breakfast and stretched back on his branch, revealing an off-white stomach that he proceeded to scratch with such evident pleasure that both Heather and Marcus burst out laughing.

Heather took Marcus's hand, and their fingers intertwined again. He took a tiny, almost imperceptible step toward her.

"Thank you," she murmured. "This is the best date I've ever been on."

"Me too," he said quietly. "But next time let's stay in a hotel."

Chapter 15

When Marcus woke up on Monday morning, his first thought was of how much he loved beds. *One of mankind's better inventions, the bed,* he mused as he luxuriated on the firm, supportive mattress under his back and the soft, plump pillow under his head. Two nights on a thin camping mattress had been enough to make him truly appreciate the wonders of memory foam.

He'd woken without an alarm, thanks to the lorikeets in the bottlebrush tree outside Heather's house, which screeched so loudly he could hear it through the window. Going by the weak shaft of cool winter sunlight that sliced into Heather's room, it was still barely dawn. Heather was asleep, her cheek on his chest and her feet wrapped around one of his calves.

Despite the warmth the sight of her brought him, Marcus's stomach swirled with the anxiety and dread he'd been ignoring while out in the bush. Today was the company's first day in the theatre. His first time setting foot in the Opera House since his injury. The company would take morning class on the very same stage he'd shredded his Achilles on, before moving their gear into the dressing rooms below and rehearsing the ballet, scene by scene, in the theatre. Now that Marcus was back in Sydney, now that the day was finally here, it was harder to shove those feelings down. After a year of barely allowing himself to look at the Opera House, he'd have to go back inside in just a few short hours.

Marcus peered across the bed at Heather's nightstand, craning his head to check the time without disturbing her. Heather stirred anyway.

"Good morning," he yawned. "At least, I think. I have no idea what time it is."

"Have you been awake long?" she asked, before giving herself over to her own yawn. "Sorry, I was just so tired after this weekend's adventure." She disentangled herself from him and lay back on the pillows.

"Yeah, I'm never camping again," Marcus said, rolling onto his side to face her, "or glamping, or sleeping on anything other than a real mattress. I'm too old and broken down for that shit."

"Same." She yawned again.

Marcus propped himself up on his elbow and looked at her, naked and relaxed. He didn't want this morning, or night, or whatever it was, to be over just yet. He wanted to stretch it out, put off the inevitable anxiety for as long as he could. Marcus ran his other hand along Heather's hip, caressing her smooth, warm skin with his fingertips.

"Maybe there's something we can do to wake you up a little?"

"Mmm," she said, letting her eyes fall closed. "You mean like coffee?"

He smiled and kissed her lightly on her temple. "I could get you a coffee," he murmured, letting his fingers trace wider circles now, brushing the sensitive skin over her rib cage and under her breasts. "But then I'd have to get out of bed, and I don't think you really want me to do that."

"I really don't," Heather sighed, eyes still shut. He kissed her cheekbone, then her jaw, letting his hand drift up over her ribs to cup her breast. She twisted to return his kiss, and as their mouths met, Marcus slid a thumb over her nipple. She whimpered into his mouth and his cock twitched eagerly as he kissed her deeply, taking his time tasting her mouth and swallowing her increasingly urgent moans.

Their pace was slower than before. Less frenzied, less frantic. Or at least, it started that way. Heather rolled on top of Marcus, pinning him between her knees as he held her close and kissed her steadily, insistently. Heather felt him grow hard against her, and harder still when she rolled her hips, eliciting a quiet, hungry growl from him that reduced her restraint to dust.

She slid off him and knelt between his legs, relishing the view of his taut, muscular thighs. *God bless every ballet teacher who ever made this man do pliés*, she thought, *and every ballet master who ever had him do grand allegro*. Heather slipped her fingers into the waistband of his boxer briefs and pulled them down. The last thing she wondered before she took his hard, waiting cock into her mouth was what kind of profane blasphemy she was about to get out of him this time.

She was not disappointed. "Oh, sweet holy Jesus *fuck*, Heather," he moaned.

She wrapped one hand around the base of him and slid in unison with her mouth, sucking and swirling her tongue as he swore. He put one hand lightly on her head and grasped at her hair, but after a moment, he shifted, and she heard a clunk and rustling. Heather sat up to find him tearing open a condom packet with his teeth, and a moment later, he had rolled the rubber down his shaft, grabbed her by the waist, and pulled her on top of him.

Heather braced herself on his firm chest and eased onto him as slowly as she could bear. She closed her eyes and sighed, wanting the sensation of being gradually filled by him to last as long as possible, and when he was fully inside her, she opened them. He watched her, his teeth clenched and his gaze hot and determined.

Heather met his eyes as she rocked her hips slowly, leaning forward and gasping at the sensation of his cock sliding so close to her clit. He moved one hand to her hip, guiding her movements as he thrust up to meet her. With his other hand, Marcus kneaded her breast gently and Heather squirmed against him, desperate for him to play with her sensitive, aching nipple. Finally, he obliged, and she cried out, grinding harder and faster against him as his hand tightened on her hip and she felt her climax build.

Marcus's breath was loud and hoarse in the silent, dimly lit room. He removed his hand from her breast and guided her own between her legs, pressing it against her.

"Touch yourself," he gasped, "I want you to come with me."

Heather didn't hesitate, didn't stop to think about how exposed she would be, naked and riding him and touching herself while he watched. She braced herself against his chest with her free hand and slipped a finger between her slick, hot folds, up to her clit. Heather let her head fall back as the pleasure spiraled through her body, threatening to overtake her. Raising her head, she saw Marcus was still watching her intently, jaw clenched. Waiting for her, holding back for her. At the sight of him, Heather tumbled over the edge and into her orgasm, releasing a sob of pleasure that sounded like his name. A second later, his fingers dug into her flesh, and he came as well, his hips pumping against her and his face twisted in pleasure.

Marcus pulled her to him, and she pressed her forehead against his, eyes closed, taking deep, steadying breaths. Once she felt his breathing slow, Heather lifted her hips to allow him exit. When she made to ease back onto the bed beside him, Marcus stopped her, wrapping one warm arm snugly around her waist and holding her on top of him.

"Stay?" he whispered, loosening his arm enough for her to roll off if she wanted to.

"Okay," she whispered back, and she closed her eyes again. She sensed, rather than saw, a small smile curve his mouth as his arm tightened around her again.

With his other hand, Marcus cupped her cheek, and when he kissed her, she kissed him back gently, too limp and tired to kiss him any other way. He didn't seem to mind, though, just like he didn't seem to mind when she kissed his forehead, or his dimple, which she did twice.

"Mmm," he said, his eyes closed as her lips roamed his face. "Now you can say it."

"Say what?" she murmured against his temple. His eyes popped open, and he looked at her mischievously.

"Thank you." He smirked.

Heather laughed and rolled off him, only to have him follow and pin her to the bed, chuckling.

"Such a shit stirrer." She grinned up at him.

"I think you like it," he replied.

"I think I do, too," she said.

Marcus's palms were clammy, and no matter how many times he wiped them on his tracksuit pants, they stayed damp and prickly with anxiety the entire bus ride to the Opera House. He and Heather had done their secret agent routine, taking different buses from different stops a few blocks apart, so Marcus was alone as he walked to the end of Bennelong Point, where the Opera House sat waiting. Unignorable in its hugeness, its strangeness. He wished Heather could have been with him, so he'd have something else to look at and think about instead of the building and all that lay inside. By the time he arrived at the stage door, his heart was racing.

Deep breaths, he told himself as he made his way along the concrete hallway below the stage. Around him, his colleagues were arriving, and theatre staff went about their work. Just ahead, a member of the stage crew pushed several large plywood crates along the hallway on dollies as Julie, the costume mistress, jogged alongside him, unwilling to let the company's expensive costumes out of her sight.

Marcus was still trying to marshal his breath when he arrived at the dressing room he used to share with the other half-dozen men soloists. He noticed the absence of his nameplate on the door and found a few dancers already inside, unpacking shoes and hoodies and plastic boxes full of makeup and Band-Aids. Marcus wasn't performing this season, so his usual spot at the mirror would either sit empty or become storage for everyone's stuff. Otherwise, the simple room looked just as he remembered: dressing mirrors and chairs along one wall, a slightly tired looking couch, and a clothes rack on the other. It smelled just as he remembered, too, a mix of hairspray, body spray, and sweat.

Marcus wiped his hands on his pants again, trying not to remember the nightmare that unfolded the last time he was surrounded by this scent.

But he could do this. He was ready. He'd spent the year preparing to come back here. Still, he lingered in the doorway, unwilling to step inside. He didn't feel ready. He glanced down the hallway at the dressing room for women principals. Heather had taken the earlier bus, and she'd already be inside. He wanted nothing more than to be back in bed with her, inhaling her scent instead. He'd settle for a smile or a brief squeeze of her hand, anything to reassure him that he could get through this and out to the other side. But they couldn't risk it here, not with every member of the company and half the artistic and administrative staff running around.

"You coming in, mate?" Ricky asked, and Marcus realised he'd been standing there a while. He was about to answer when the loudspeaker mounted over the door dinged, and Peter's voice crackled into the room.

"Dancers, welcome to the Opera House, and welcome to tech week. Please make your way to the stage. Company class will begin in ten minutes." There was another ding, and the room went quiet, but the hallway filled with dancers heading to the stage. Ricky gave himself a quick once-over in the mirror, seized his water bottle, and squeezed past Marcus with a nod. Marcus dropped his bag hastily on the couch, pulled out his ballet slippers and, little though he wanted to, joined the throng.

Alice was already there, helping to arrange the barres in neat lines across the stage. She then sat and began putting on her pointe shoes. When she saw Marcus hovering anxiously in the wings, she gestured for him to join her.

"You okay?" she asked as he sat next to her. "This is probably a lot."

Marcus nodded gratefully. "I'm fine, just . . . nervous."

"I know," Alice said quietly, adjusting her padded pouches before sliding one foot into a shoe. "But remember, it's just class. Same as you've been doing these last few weeks. Just in a different place."

"Yeah," Marcus sighed, pulling on his own shoes. He tried to muster the same excitement he'd felt when he'd come back to class, but it was futile. Whatever he told Alice, he wasn't fine. This place felt haunted, or cursed, even though he didn't believe in that kind of stuff. Alice then gestured someone else over, and a moment later, Heather dropped her pointe shoes next to her and sat down with a friendly smile.

"And how are you feeling, Miss America?"

"I'm nervous," Heather admitted, keeping her eyes on Alice. "The first run-through always makes me jumpy. And I didn't get to do my usual warm-up routine today."

"Well, you two make a fine pair," Alice said, and Marcus just managed to keep his face impassive. Heather looked at Alice with confusion on her face, then a flash of panic, before Alice added, "Marcus is nervous, too."

"*Oh*," Heather replied, her relief audible to him, though hopefully not to Alice. She met Marcus's gaze, and the side of her mouth lifted in a tiny, almost imperceptible smile. "She'll be right, mate. Isn't that what Australians say? She'll be right?"

He returned her smile, grateful for an excuse to look at her. "She'll be right," he repeated, hoping it was true. She lowered her head and busied herself with her ribbons.

"Are you going to stick around when class is over?" Alice asked him, rolling over onto her back and pulling one knee into her chest.

Heather lifted her head and gave him a brief, hopeful look.

He didn't want to stay. He wanted to get through company class and then get the hell out of here. But he couldn't refuse Heather. And if he took a seat in the audience, he'd be able to watch her dance the ballet in its entirety. As if he'd miss a chance to watch her closely, to take in her every movement without having to invent an excuse to look at her in public.

"Yeah," he said in Alice's direction, watching Heather's face relax into a smile from the corner of his eye. "I'll stick around."

When company class ended, Peter gave them an hour's break to eat and rest. In her dressing room, Heather pulled on a knee-length rehearsal skirt, the kind she'd wear in both acts of *Giselle*. The costume mistress had taken her measurements last week, and by the time she'd arrived at the theater today, her two costumes waited for her in the dressing room she shared with two other principal dancers. For act one, a brown and yellow peasant style dress, and a long white tutu for act two. Later this week, they'd do a full dress rehearsal with the orchestra in the pit.

Heather's heart fluttered with nerves as she checked her makeup and low bun in the mirror one last time. Something about performing an entire ballet in front of the company always seemed more nerve-racking to her than a performance for an audience of strangers, no matter how well-versed in ballet they were. It was one thing to perform in a theater packed with admiring ballet-goers, but it was another, much more vulnerable thing to run through a two-hour ballet in front of your eagle-eyed peers, who were close enough to see every tiny wobble and every finger out of place. Who knew exactly what the steps were meant to look like when done right and could tell instantly if you'd done them wrong.

Gathering up the pointe shoes she'd need for the run-through—a pair for each act, plus a spare pair just in case—Heather slipped from the dressing room and headed for the wings.

The stage was full of dancers, some stretching and chatting, some pulling on their shoes. She spotted Alice in the corner with her headphones in, running through snippets of act two choreography. She kept her eyes shut as her hands waved around her face in small, flittering approximations of the larger steps. Out in the audience, Peter sat a few rows from the orchestra pit. With him were two members of the artistic staff Heather recognized and two suits she didn't.

The whole place buzzed with excited chatter, anticipation heavy in the air as she nervously pulled a few pins from her bun, tightened them between her teeth, and pushed them back into place. She had to be careful not to stick them in too tight. Halfway through the first act, she would remove most of them, and then during the mad scene, she would throw herself on the floor and the dancer playing her mother would discreetly pull out the rest. When Heather stood, her hair would fall down, and there she would be: a mad, heartbroken woman.

Heather didn't feel heartbroken today. Anxious about the run-through in front of the full company, yes, but not heartbroken. On the contrary, when she'd woken up this morning to find Marcus awake and gazing at her, she'd felt her heart swell in her chest and give a pleasant, almost painful squeeze of longing.

She glanced around, checking the stage and the wings as casually as she could. Then she saw him standing on the edge of the stage, chatting with the rehearsal pianist. He had changed the tights and tank top he'd worn for company class for sweatpants and a snug white T-shirt. As he talked to the pianist, he ran a hand through his sweat-dampened hair, a gesture she now recognized as something he did when he was anxious. She watched from the wings as he gave the pianist a nod, then left the stage and headed into the audience, where he settled himself a few rows behind Peter and the staff. He couldn't see her, but knowing he was there made her feel less jumpy. Knowing he was there, when he would rather have left as soon as he could, made her heart swell and squeeze again.

Out in the theater, Peter stood, and the hum of conversation died swiftly. Justin, who'd been stretching near center stage, got to his feet and shook his legs out, then came over to her.

"Here we go," he said. "I'll make sure to hold on tight during those pirouettes, don't worry. Chookas!"

Heather looked at him blankly.

"It's Australian for *merde*," he said. "Chookas."

"Oh, uh, chookas," she repeated, and Justin wandered away toward stage right. On the day of the performance, there'd be a small hunting shack where Albrecht would hide his hunting horn and his sword, concealing proof of his true noble identity.

Peter cleared his throat, and Heather's pulse quickened as he looked around the theater expectantly and addressed the company.

"Ladies and gentlemen, are we ready to begin?" There was a murmur of assent, and a moment later, the pianist began. Even without the full force of the strings and woodwinds, Adolphe Adam's overture was a jolting, dramatic way to start a ballet, and the sound of it didn't help settle Heather's pulse. She stood in the wings at stage left, fiddling with the waistband of her skirt, eyes on the floor, too nervous to make eye contact with the other dancers assembled in the wings.

The first act pas de deux went off without a hitch. Despite their rocky start together, Justin was a gifted partner, and he'd learned to read her body and adjust to her musicality. At one point in the pas de deux, before they were to launch into a series of leaps in a wide circle around the whole stage, Heather waited a half a second longer than the choreography called for, to give the impression that Giselle couldn't tear her eyes away from her beloved's face. Justin didn't miss a beat: he held her gaze until she broke it, then made up the extra time getting into the jump so they could hit the height of the leap together and on the music.

As Heather returned to the wings, she could just make out Peter swiveling in his seat to speak to Marcus, who nodded and gave his boss what looked like a genuine smile. Heather wanted to catch his eye, seize that smile for herself, but she kept moving. She couldn't risk staring too long at Marcus with Peter sitting right there. But a few moments later, as she took her place in the center of the stage to begin her solo, she looked out into the audience and let her eyes adjust to the darkness until she found him in her peripheral vision.

He was a blur of white with a fuzzy brown splotch on top. She couldn't look directly at him, but she could see him there, and she knew that, like everyone else, he was watching her. The pianist played the high trill notes that signaled the start of the solo, then she began. The variation called for a series of double attitude turns that always felt like slow-motion flying when they went right.

Somewhere in the middle of the third attitude turn, Heather's nerves fizzled out, and with them gone, she felt nothing but the pleasure of dancing. Nothing but the firmness of the ground pushing back against the bottom of her pointe shoe and the lightness of her skirt catching the air and floating around her as she moved. The joy of it was crisp and sweet, like the warm Portuguese tarts Marcus had brought her the night they'd been to the hospital. Somewhere in the middle of the fourth turn, she realized she didn't much care what the other dancers saw when they looked at her. It didn't matter, actually, if they spotted minute technical errors in her jumps, or thought her arabesque was too low, or whispered about why she'd left New York. She was free and alive and exactly where she was supposed to be.

The thought fueled her muscles, buoyed her jumps and made her feet faster and more precise than usual, her body anticipating each note and clinging to every last balance as if it was unbearable to let go. *I am exactly where I'm supposed to be.* She had worked all her life to be on this stage, alone in the spotlight. Heather belonged here, and nothing—no man, no magazine, no ex-future-mother-in-law—could steal that from her. She had been broken and betrayed, but she'd found the courage to break free, and that's what she was now: free, whole, and more powerful than she'd ever known.

The knowledge rocketed through her, knocking the air from her lungs for a moment, but she took a deep breath and recovered, focused on the rest of the variation. The middle of the solo featured Giselle's famous hops on pointe, which she executed on her left foot, taking a long diagonal path from upstage all the way to the lip of the orchestra pit. When she'd first started learning the role in New York last year, she had struggled with this section of the choreography, but today it was easy. Today, she felt steady and controlled, even though her heart fluttered wildly from the exertion and the exhilaration of her realization.

When she came to the end of the variation, a series of sixteen piqué turns in a wide circle around the stage, it was easy to let loose, and Heather whipped her body around as fast as she dared, covering the entire stage in one swift, sweeping loop of turns. Her skirt swirled around her thighs, and the room blurred as she spun like a joyful tornado, half abandon, half precision. She moved so quickly she was ahead of the music, the pianist racing to catch her as she finished the turn combination with a quick double pirouette, then bent one knee to the ground so she landed the turn in a deep curtsy.

The music halted, and a split second later, the theater exploded into applause. Every single person in the theater, including the pianist, was clapping, and a boy in the corps, who she knew by sight but couldn't name, put two fingers into his mouth and let out a loud wolf whistle. Heather rose and tucked her back foot demurely behind her, even as she grinned in a very undemure way. She looked around the theater and permitted herself a small laugh, then let her eyes drift as discreetly as she could toward the audience.

Marcus was there, no longer blurry, but sharp and crisp and beautiful. She had been wrong: not every single person in the room was clapping. Marcus was beaming, his face lit up by a huge smile and the crinkles around his eyes deeper than she'd ever seen them. But he was stock still, as though he was too awestruck, too in the moment to break it by clapping for her. For a split second, she met his eyes and knew he'd seen it all. Not just the steps, but the truth behind them.

He'd seen it all along, and now she could, too.

Chapter 16

When Marcus stepped out of the shower that evening, there was a text waiting for him.

Alice, 5:23 PM: Are you home?

Marcus checked the time as he rubbed a towel over his hair. He was due at Heather's in an hour.

Marcus, 5:25 PM: Yeah, what's up?
Alice, 5:25 PM: Be there in 10.
Marcus, 5:26 PM: Are you ok?

She didn't respond. By the time he buzzed her into his building barely ten minutes later, Marcus was a little worried. The look on her face as she entered his apartment did nothing to assuage his concern. Alice had changed from her leotard and tights into a pair of baggy jeans, but her hair was still in a bun, as if she'd rushed from rehearsal without showering.

"Is everything okay?" Marcus asked.

"No. Everything is not okay. I've just come from seeing Ricky. He's been fired."

Marcus frowned at her. "Why? What happened?"

Alice fixed him with a steely look, and a sense of foreboding crept over him. When she spoke, she enunciated every word clearly and pointedly. "Ricky was seeing Kimiko. For a few months, apparently. Somehow Peter got wind of it, and . . ."

"Shit," Marcus breathed.

"Yes, exactly. Shit. Kimiko's probably going to have to go home to Japan unless she can find another job here, and I don't know what Ricky's going to do. He's absolutely gutted."

Of course he was. The guy had spent a decade in the corps and was just promoted to soloist last season. Marcus started to reply, but Alice kept talking.

"So I thought, 'Gee, I sure hope no one else in the company is sneaking around and violating Peter's policy, because that would be a really stupid, really easy way to get fired, too.'" She looked at Marcus, arms crossed over her chest.

He shifted uncomfortably under her gaze. "I . . . I agree. That would be stupid."

She glared at him. "Especially, if, for example, that person had spent a whole year in Shaz's office, trying to get back into shape."

When Marcus said nothing, Alice shook her head in disgust. "I don't believe you."

"How did you know?"

Alice's eyes widened. "That's your response? 'How did you know?' Not, 'I'm sorry for lying to your face, Alice?' Or for endangering your entire career—and Heather's, by the way? Or for jeopardizing everything you worked for in the last year, the *hell year* I just spent supporting you through? All so you could be her rebound from her dickhead fiancé? Fucking hell, Marcus, what were you thinking?"

Marcus had only ever seen Alice lose her temper few times, and only ever at people who truly deserved it. He hung his head, remorse gnawing at him. She was right, of course. He hated that she was right, but she was right.

"And as for how I found out, my girlfriend told me. She saw you come out of Heather's dressing room looking extremely flustered a few weeks ago. And I kept waiting for you to tell me, but you never said anything. You just cut me out and lied to me."

Marcus's head snapped up. Girlfriend?

"Oh yeah, by the way, I'm dating a woman, which I would have told you if I thought we were still being honest with each other." Alice glowered at him, and he felt as though she'd slapped him. Even worse, he felt he deserved it.

Marcus ran a hand through his hair. Alice had known about him and Heather the whole time, and worse, she had known he was lying to her from the start. She'd been the one to squeeze his hand right before he was rolled in for his first surgery, and the one who had waited until he came out from under the anaesthetic, because his mum was taking care of his dad. She'd helped him into his suit for the funeral and made sure he ate enough protein and drank enough water in those first miserable months. And this was how he'd repaid her. Shit, he'd really fucked up.

"I'm so sorry," he said. "I wanted to tell you, but it just seemed too risky. I mean, look at Ricky and Kimiko. But I should have trusted you. I'm really sorry."

Alice frowned and exhaled sharply through her nose but said nothing. He interpreted that to mean she accepted his explanation, even if she didn't accept his apology. He'd take what he could get.

"So, the girl you're dating works at Dancewear Central?" he asked, tentatively. "And she saw us?"

"The woman I'm dating is the manager at Dancewear Central," she corrected. "She texted me the moment you two left the shop a few weeks ago to say she had had Heather Hays and some ANB guy in the shop and she was pretty sure something happened in her fitting room. I mean, I assume she disinfected the cubicle and then texted me. Which brings me back to my original question: what the fuck are you thinking?"

"I know it's risky, but we've been trying to keep it quiet," he said desperately.

Alice snorted. "Well, you're doing a bang-up job. Izzy doesn't even work with us and she figured it out, and I've known for weeks. This is you trying to keep it quiet? I'm surprised Peter hasn't already found out, kicked you out of the company, and sent Heather packing."

She was right. For all their attempts at subterfuge, they'd been reckless, and he'd been a shitty friend. But even as his face flushed with embarrassment, he found himself wanting to defend their actions.

"Listen, I know I screwed up," Marcus argued. "And I know what we're doing is against policy, and that's bad, but . . . I don't know . . . it's *good*. It feels *good*. You said it yourself that I seem happier lately. She makes me feel like myself again."

And after the year he'd had, didn't he deserve to feel like himself again? He looked at Alice, who seemed to understand what he wasn't saying. Her face softened, and she sighed, leaning reluctantly against his kitchen counter. Marcus took a step towards her, unwilling to get too close in case she unloaded on him again.

"No one wants to see you happy more than me, okay?" Her was tone gentler now. "But Heather isn't a walking antidepressant, she's a person. And what you're doing could jeopardize her job and yours. Look what just happened to Ricky and Kimiko. And Adrian and Robbie last year? What if you get caught, too?"

Marcus said nothing. Again, she was right, and he couldn't deny it.

"I mean, you just got back on your feet," she went on. "All that work with Shaz so you can dance again . . . do you really want to risk it all—for what? For casual sex? For a short-term whatever? She's leaving after the run ends. What's your endgame here, exactly?"

Marcus frowned at her question and ran his hand through his hair, trying to think of an answer. Was this just casual sex?

On paper, he supposed that's exactly what it was. What they'd agreed to.

But it didn't feel casual. Waking up every morning to Heather curled in a gentle question mark against his torso, her long, glossy hair tangled on his spare pillow, that didn't feel casual. Feeling her rib cage inflate and contract under his arm as she slept didn't feel casual. Watching as, every so often, one of her feet twitched under the covers, like she was attempting tendus in her sleep, didn't feel casual. And it all felt like it was worth the risks he was taking.

"I don't know what the endgame is, okay?" Marcus said finally. "But I really like her, Alice. That's all I know right now."

Alice sighed and shook her head. "Well, *I* know this is a mistake. For about eighty-seven different reasons. But your secret is safe with me."

Fifteen minutes later, Marcus knocked on Heather's door, and she opened it beaming, her face shining with exhilaration from a successful run-through. She looked as beautiful as always, in jeans and a black sweater that revealed her collarbone and both shoulders, and those gold tassel earrings she'd worn at Café Luxor.

"Holy crap, that was the best first run-through I've—" she started, but the look on his face must have stopped her. "What's wrong? Did you hurt your Achilles? Oh God, did your mom have another fall?"

Marcus gestured down at his ankle. "I'm fine, and so is Mum."

Heather nodded, relieved, but studied his face. "Then what's going on? You'd better come in."

For a moment Marcus said nothing, he just looked at her, taking in the care and concern that wrinkled her forehead. Then he breathed a short, decisive breath and stepped into the house. Heather followed him to the living room, his sense of dread growing with every step.

"I need to tell you something," he said as she sat on the couch. Marcus ran a hand through his hair and told her about Ricky and

Kimiko and about his confrontation with Alice. As he spoke, he watched Heather's face sink until she looked just as grim as he felt. When he finished, she sat in silence, biting her lip.

"Is Alice angry with me?"

"I think she's mostly angry at me," he sighed. "She's my best friend. I know we said we wouldn't tell anyone, but I should have trusted her."

Heather was silent for a long moment, and he watched her think, his heart racing as though he'd just completed one of Alice's deadly petit allegro combinations.

"We have to stop this," she said finally. It was so quiet he could almost pretend he'd misheard her. Almost.

Heather sat with her elbows on her knees, that now-familiar determination on her heart-shaped face. He said nothing. Marcus had a feeling that if he spoke, anything he said would be drowned out by the sudden buzzing in his ears. He knew, when he decided to tell her about Ricky and Kimiko, that this might happen. He hated that he'd been right.

"I thought we were being so careful, but we've already slipped up without knowing it," she said. When he'd arrived, she'd looked exhilarated; now, she sounded exhausted. "And I know we can trust Alice and her girlfriend, but what if someone else finds out? Someone less trustworthy? Or what if someone already knows and hasn't said anything about it yet? It's only a matter of time, right?"

"Maybe," he admitted. "Or maybe we can just be more careful?"

Heather looked up at him, and he hated the hopelessness he saw in her face. "Marcus, we can't. We can't risk it. If we have to hide it from the people who know us best, it's a good sign we shouldn't be doing it. We worked so hard to be where we are. If we get caught, we'll lose it all."

"And if we stop, we'll lose each other," Marcus said, though he knew she was right. Heather looked away, then shook her head and sighed.

"I only see one way out of this. We can't keep pretending like it won't end in disaster otherwise. Let's just stay away from each other and get through the next two weeks. Then I'll go back to New York and . . . and we can both keep our jobs and our careers and our reputations. Which is what we should have done all along."

"Okay," he managed to say. After a long, miserable moment, Heather stood, her shoulders hunched protectively around her ears, and took a few steps away from him. Slowly, as if she wanted him to stop her. Marcus reached out and put his hand lightly on her arm, and she stilled.

Her shoulders slumped, and all the determination seemed to drain out of her. Heather pulled in a shuddering breath, then blinked, tears skittering down her cheeks. Marcus's heart ached at the sight of it, and he wanted to pull her close and stroke her hair and feel her rib cage rise and fall against him until her breath steadied and the tears dried. He took a step forward, arms open, tentative. She stepped into them, and he encircled her shoulders and squeezed tight. Heather sniffled against his shirt, and he kissed the top of her head.

"I don't want that," he said into her hair.

"I don't either," she replied, wrapping her arms around him. A stupid spark of hope lit up somewhere under his sternum, only to fizzle and die with her next words. "But it's what we have to do. You're risking everything, too. Everything you worked for this whole year. Your whole life. Is this really worth throwing the rest of your career away?"

Marcus thought about that moment at the lookout, the flash of perfect clarity that sliced through him as he watched Heather's ponytail flicker in the mountain breeze.

Yes, it's worth it, he wanted to say. *Because I'm falling in love with you, and I don't want to stop.* When he looked back on this night, when he was lying in bed alone and drunk and desperate for sleep, Marcus would wish he'd said it. Instead, he pulled back just far enough to gaze into her tearstained face, then leant forward to drop a light kiss onto her trembling lips. Heather kissed him back, tightening her arms around his waist as she did.

He broke away and whispered hopefully against her cheekbone. "Let me stay. One more night. And tomorrow we'll move on. Okay?"

For a moment she said nothing, and he prepared for her to pull out of his arms and walk him out the door. But then Heather turned and brushed her lips against his.

"Okay," she agreed.

Heather kissed him fiercely, sighing as his lips gave way to her tongue. If she only had tonight, if *they* only had tonight, she was going to make it count. Marcus's hands rested on her cheeks, cupping her face as he kissed her back with equal urgency and more than lust. She walked backward, toward the stair, and he clung to her, pulling her body hard against his even as they headed clumsily to the bedroom.

Heather willed herself to stay in this moment, to commit every detail of this night to memory so that tomorrow, when she woke and walked away from the man who'd brought her back to herself, she could say she hadn't wasted a second. She would remember the way he ran his mouth hungrily down her neck when he pushed her against the doorframe, the way his silky curls wrapped around her fingers when she slid her hands into his hair, and the way desire rocketed through her as he scooped her up and deposited her gently on the bed.

A now-familiar need gathered in Heather's muscles as she pulled him on top of her, want pulsing through her, her skin restless for his touch. She wanted to strip him down and press her body against his, wanted to wrap her entire self around him and hold him there. Imprint every inch of him onto her body, onto her memory, and keep it forever. But now that they were in bed, his breath seemed to change. His movements slowed, and he touched her carefully, as if he too were trying to stretch the minutes and seconds for as long as he could.

His hand slid under her sweater to caress her skin slowly, reverently, and Heather arched into his palm, urging him higher and moaning against his mouth when he cupped her breast and squeezed gently. Her body begged for more, but her heart ached with the need to make this last, to slow time and stay in this moment. Marcus sided with her heart, taking his time, brushing his fingers over her, caressing her through her bra, before he pulled her sweater over her head and lowered his mouth to her skin.

Feeling his cock harden against her, Heather slipped a hand into the waistband of his jeans and wrapped her fingers around it, stroking him with the same reverence and patience he showed her. Marcus groaned and stiffened further under her touch, and for a moment, his mouth stilled on her breast. His eyes dropped closed as she stroked him, his breath hot and thin. She watched him, taking in his clenched jaw and listening to his increasingly ragged breath as need throbbed, hot and insistent, between her legs.

She pulled his shirt from him as slowly and carefully as she could, matching his pace, trying to make this night last. A sharp pain twisted in her chest when Marcus stood and removed his jeans, the memory of their first meeting rushing in. Heather hadn't known then how precious he would be to her, and the kind of chances she would take to be close to him. How free and alive and willingly reckless he'd make her feel. Now she knew in every cell of her being—but it was too late and too risky to do anything about it.

By the time she'd found her box of condoms and fished one out with shaking fingers, Marcus had shimmied out of his clothes and kicked them to the floor. He lay on his back, one hand on his cock and the other reaching for her, his stomach rising and falling rapidly with his breath. The sight of him stretched out on the bed, his honed, muscular body naked and his cock hard for her, made Heather bite her lip so hard she nearly drew blood.

Impatient, she willed herself to stop and take him in, all the lines and shadows of him in the fading light. The undisguised need in his eyes as he watched her open the condom packet and roll it down his shaft. He reached for her again and pulled her close, nestling himself behind her, his chest firm against her back. She arched against him and felt his moan rumble through her own chest, wishing she could trap it there and keep it forever. Then Marcus positioned himself at her waiting, aching entrance, and pushed into her. Heather gasped, and he shuddered against her back, pulling her gently against him until he was fully inside.

They stayed that way for a moment, unmoving, unbreathing, his mouth hot against her neck and his heart pounding against her spine. When she moved against him, they both groaned. The relief of it made her want to sob, and the closeness and comfort of feeling him around her, inside her, made her eyes water.

Marcus said her name quietly, reverently, like speaking her name was a privilege he wasn't sure he deserved. He said it again and again as he moved inside her, one hand gripping hers tight so that they were connected in almost every possible way. After a moment, a whispered *oh fuck* interrupted his chant, and the curse wrung a watery, unseen smile from her mouth.

"Fuck, Heather, you feel so good. The best. The best I've ever, the best I'll ever—" His other hand, flat and firm against her stomach, moved down slowly, maddeningly slowly, and he ran one finger between her slick folds and up to circle her clit.

Heather closed her eyes and tried to feel it all, catalog it all so she'd never forget: His searing breath on her shoulder, his nimble finger dancing expertly on her clit, his feet tangled with hers, his cock deeper inside her than it had ever been. The heat swirling around them, holding them in the cool evening light of her bedroom. He thrust slowly, gently, murmuring in her ear how good she felt wrapped around him, and as his hips sped up, so did his finger. Heather felt her orgasm build, an ungovernable, inevitable wave rising, and she ground her hips back against him, her own breaths turning to whimpers as the crest took shape.

"That's it," he urged her, his hand moving still faster. "Fuck, Heather, that's it." The sound of her name from his mouth, so gentle and sweet pressed against the profanity, pushed her over the edge. The wave crashed over her, and she shuddered around him, gasping as she rode her orgasm and him. A moment later, his hand slipped from her clit and he held her hip tight, pulling her to him and groaning as he came.

Marcus held her, one hand pressing flat and firm against her sternum and the other holding tight to hers, and buried his face in her neck, breathing hard against her electrified skin. He said her name again, and this time the sound of it pulled a small, jagged sob from her throat.

Despite every wretched thing he had been through in the last year, Marcus had found the space in his heart to care about her. He had seen her panicked and frozen, and he hadn't written her off as childish, or damaged, or disappointingly human. He'd brushed against her prickles, her skeptical and untrusting spikes, and had only pulled her in closer. She'd spent months feeling foolish and humiliated, but he had decided she was brave. And so he had been brave for her, had sneaked around and kept secrets for her, because he thought she was worth it. He had decided the risk was worth whatever small pieces of her he could have, for however long he could have them. And despite everything *she* had been through in the last few months, she loved him for it.

She loved him. Heather loved Marcus. Loved the way he could never truly keep a straight face when he was poking fun at her, loved the way he tucked away little details of what she said or thought and committed them to memory. She loved how intensely he wanted her and how unabashedly impressed he was by her. Jack had wanted her with the cool assurance and languid ease of someone who'd been handed everything he'd ever asked for. Marcus wanted her like she was something precious few people ever got the chance to touch.

Tomorrow they'd be strangers again. But tonight they slept, still entangled, still together, still each other's best and most precious secret.

When she woke the next morning, Marcus was gone. A still-warm flat white stood on the bedside table, along with a handwritten note. *Chookas for Friday. I'll be watching. M.*

Marcus called in sick the next day. He gave himself a short barre at his kitchen counter after completing his physio exercises, trying not to think about what was happening on the Opera House stage as he did. Today the company would run through the ballet again with the lights and sets and tomorrow would perform a full dress rehearsal with the orchestra in the pit. And then it would be opening night. Heather would barely leave the theatre all day, and he tried not to think about all the chances he was missing to see her dance. To watch her smile and laugh with his colleagues. To catch her looking at him for a brief second and know she'd been thinking about him at the very moment he'd been thinking about her.

He'd be there for opening night, Marcus reminded himself, the dull ache in his chest turning sharp and bitter. He wouldn't miss that for anything.

Once showered, he went to visit his mum. Her stitches had been removed a few days earlier, her cut wasn't hurting anymore, and she seemed mostly back to her usual routine. Together, they visited a local homewares shop in search of a rug to replace the ruined one, but Marcus could hardly concentrate on the store's various offerings. His head was too full of Heather to focus on the differences between the three almost-identical rugs she was trying to choose between. If his mum noticed that he seemed out of sorts, she didn't say anything, though he suspected that wouldn't last long.

Marcus had just heaved the rug into the back seat of her car when his phone vibrated.

Alice, 12:04 PM: Peter announced the news about Kimiko and Ricky this morning, and the mood here is grim AF.

Marcus didn't know what to say to that. He was about to put his phone away when it buzzed again.

Alice, 12:05 PM: Heather looks off. Is she okay?

No, he wanted to reply. *She's not okay. I'm not okay. None of this is okay.*

Marcus, 12:06 PM: Took your advice. We ended it last night.
Alice, 12:06 PM: I'm sorry. I know it sucks but I think it's for the best. I'll keep an eye on her and make sure she's all right. Are you okay?

Marcus shoved his phone away without replying, and he and his mum drove home.

When he woke the next morning, the other side of the bed empty and cold, Marcus considered calling in sick again. But he had an appointment with Sharon, and he'd never missed those, not even in the depths of his fresh grief last spring. So he hauled himself out of bed and got on the bus, remembering all the days he and Heather had parted ways at his or her front door and walked to separate bus stops. All the lengths they'd taken to hide—and to fool themselves into thinking they could be together.

When he knocked on the physio room door, Shaz looked up from a clipboard and gave him a friendly smile he didn't manage to return.

"I've got some good news for you," she said, and Marcus raised his eyebrows weakly in reply. "We're gonna start grand pliés today. Just a few, but you're looking really strong, and I think you're ready to get back to full range of motion. Get excited, today's a big day!"

Shaz watched him expectantly, and Marcus hastily arranged his face into a joyless, mechanical smile.

"Sounds great," he lied. "Thanks for everything, Shaz."

Her smile didn't falter, but she tipped her head curiously, watching him closely, and for a moment he thought she was going to ask if something was wrong. He didn't know if he had the energy to lie if she did. But all she said was, "Of course, love. You should be proud of how far you've come. Now go get changed, and we'll get to work."

Opening night was cloudless and cold. The wind whipped off the harbor and buffeted Heather on her way to the stage door of the Opera House a few hours before curtain. She made her way through the winding concrete corridors to the dressing room, feeling a familiar nervous energy buzzing through the building, just like it did before a big show at NYB. Around her, dancers stretched and chatted in hushed whispers, and she spotted a costume assistant doing some last-minute adjustments on a tutu that, until yesterday, had been Kimiko's. It would now be worn by some other member of the corps.

The entire company had been distracted since Peter announced that two more dancers were fired for violating Pas de Don't. The corps had been out of sync in the first act peasant dances, and yesterday, they'd run one of the second act scenes so many times that one wili burst into tears on stage. The only upside to the pall that had fallen over the company was that no one had noticed that, when Heather wasn't dancing, she was distracted and listless—or if they had, they'd probably chalked it up to her dismay over Kimiko and Ricky's dismissal. Not to the fact that she'd woken up every morning for the last few days with a deep, empty ache between her ribs, one that only intensified when she arrived at the theater and found Marcus wasn't in company class.

Several times a day, she picked up her phone and considered texting him. But what would she say? They'd made their choices, the reckless ones and the responsible ones, and now they were living with the consequences. At least they'd ended it before anyone else found them out.

Heather took solace in the fact that every opening night—every performance, really—was guided by routine, no matter how nervous or heartbroken she was. She'd prepare for tonight the same way she'd prepared for *Giselle* two years ago, the night she'd been promoted and Jack had proposed. A company class on stage, then back to her dressing room to eat, shower, and do her hair and makeup. In the first act, her hair would be in a low bun with small flowers pinned into it, accentuating Giselle's youth and innocence. During intermission, once she'd taken her hair down and collapsed in the mad scene, she'd marshal it back into another sleek low bun, this time with her hair covering her ears. As she always did, she applied her stage makeup in a strict, fixed order, then put on her first act costume, followed by legwarmers, trash-bag pants, and whatever else she could to stay warm without rumpling her pale-yellow skirt. The familiarity was comforting, grounding. But she wasn't the person she had been that night at Lincoln Center anymore. She wasn't even the person she was when she'd arrived in Sydney a month ago.

Heather looked at her reflection in the brightly lit mirror, turning her face and blinking quickly to check her false lashes were even and firmly glued on. Her cheekbones were accentuated by contouring and heavy blush, and her lipstick made her chin look especially pointy. *Stage face,* she would have said a few weeks ago. *Heart shaped,* she thought now, looking approvingly in the mirror.

At least Marcus would be in the audience tonight. She'd woken up without him every morning for the last few days, but tonight he'd be out there in the dark, watching her from a safe distance. The thought comforted her as she sprayed her temples once more to be safe. She grabbed her first act pointe shoes, and a spare pair she'd set in the wings in case the first pair died unexpectedly, then noticed a missed call and a voicemail on her phone.

She frowned as she picked it up. It was the middle of the night in New York, and Carly had already called to wish her *merde* a few hours ago, as she'd been getting ready for bed. "You're Heather Fucking Hays, okay?" she'd said. "Kill it and text me when it's over."

Heather swiped and saw an alert that made her stomach lurch.

Missed call from: Jack

Heather hadn't heard a word from Jack since he'd shown up at Carly's apartment all those months ago. He'd ignored her in class, lavishing attention on Melissa and acting as if the last seven years of their lives had never happened.

Before she could stop herself, she hit play.

"You fucking slut." Jack's voice, drunk and belligerent, filled the dressing room, and her stomach lurched again. "I knew you'd fuck your way to the top down there. It's just what you do, isn't it?"

Heather hit stop and dropped the phone on the dressing table as if it had burned her. She stared down at the screen, heart pounding, trying to make sense of what she'd just heard. How had Jack found out about Marcus? She thought quickly of all the people who knew: Alice, Izzy, Marcus himself. That was it. The ballet world was small and gossipy, but none of those people would have told anyone who could have spread the news back to Jack this quickly. Surely if the word was out, she would have heard about it first?

As she racked her brain, fingers numb with panic, Heather saw a series of Instagram notifications on the screen, and dread churned her stomach. She swiped them open.

@balletfanatics: Check out this stunning impromptu out-back pas de deux featuring @NYB's @heatherhays and @ australianNB soloist @MRCampbell! So dreamy! Captured by @ElodieDupont in Sydney's Blue Mountains. #pasdedeux #balletinthewild

Above the caption was a slightly shaky but crystal-clear video of her and Marcus dancing at the campsite. Who the hell was Elodie Dupont? She clicked on the woman's profile and saw a huge follower count sitting above a grid full of koalas, tents, and views of the Blue Mountains. That French couple had filmed them from their tent, and they'd captured it all: the dance, the kiss, everything.

Heather's heart began to pound when she saw how many thousands of likes the post had already gotten in the hour since it was posted. Ballet Fanatics was a huge account, with followers all over the world. Horrified, she checked her other notifications, and saw that the video had been shared a dozen times to other ballet accounts.

"Damnit, damnit, damnit," Heather breathed. They were both going to be fired. Marcus's career was over. Peter was going to put her on the first plane back to New York tomorrow. There was less than an hour until curtain. . . . If Peter had already seen the video, would he fire her now? Understudies had gone on with less notice than this. Even if he let her dance tonight, her reputation would be destroyed by tomorrow.

Fuck your way to the top. It's just what you do, isn't it?

There was a knock at the door and Heather jumped, nearly dropping her phone again.

"Come in," she said shakily, fully expecting to see Peter when the door opened. But a second later, Alice slipped into the dressing room. She was in full ballet peasant gear, a pale green bodice and a matching knee-length skirt with a little white apron on top, and her hair was in two braids wrapped over the top of her head. Under her heavy stage makeup, she looked almost as horrified as Heather felt.

"You've seen it?" Heather asked, but she knew the answer. Alice nodded grimly. "Please don't say you told us so."

Alice's face softened with sympathy. "Hey, come on. I would never. I'm not here to gloat."

Heather nodded, fighting back tears. "Does Marcus know?"

"Yeah, I just talked to him. He's, uh . . . well he's not in a good way. And he wanted me to tell you he's not coming tonight."

"What?" Heather whispered, the last remnants of her hope draining out of her.

"He just . . . can't face it. You saw how hard it was for him to come here and take class this week. And now . . . after everything he's lost in the last year, he said he just can't. Peter'll probably call him into his office first thing tomorrow."

And fire him. All that work Marcus did, all for nothing. Heather wanted to scream. She wanted to find Peter and beg him not to, tell him they were over, that if it meant Marcus could keep his job she'd leave the theater now and never come back. She gripped her phone and tipped her head back so the tears wouldn't ruin her makeup.

"Alice, what do I do?"

"Do what you came here to do. Dance. If I've learned anything in the last year, it's that if you can dance, you should dance. Because you never know when it's your last time."

Chapter 17

AMERICAN BALLET STAR DAZZLES SYDNEY
Heather Hays's world class 'Giselle' stuns
at the Opera House
By Ivy Page, Senior Arts Reporter

Words like 'ethereal' and 'otherworldly' might suffice to describe some ballet dancers, but they don't quite do the trick for Heather Hays, the 29-year-old principal dancer at New York Ballet who joined Australian National Ballet as a guest artist this month.

When Hays dances, a strange illusion occurs: you know you're watching a human being, because you can see her muscles and her sweat, but her movements are so precise and delicate, so unlike anything you've ever seen a regular human do with her body, that you can't avoid the suspicion you're watching a member of a completely different species.

At last night's opening night performance of 'Giselle,' in which Hays danced the title role, this remarkable combination was on full display. Hays's commitment to the role of the tragic heroine was total, her acting eclipsing her considerable technical abilities at some moments as she performed before a rapt and dazzled audience. . . .

Marcus sat on the bench outside Peter's office and scanned the rest of the review—*exquisite artistry, standing ovation, seven curtain calls, sold-out run*—and for the first time since his phone blew up with notifications last night, he felt something other than panic and dread. Pride in Heather, the woman he loved. Then regret that he hadn't had the courage to be there to see her triumph.

He didn't have time to dwell on those feelings, though. Peter stuck his head out of his office door, his hair askew as though he'd run his hands through it many times today.

"Marcus," he said tersely. "Come in."

Marcus went, feeling disconnected from his body, watching himself walk to his inevitable fate.

He sat in one of the several chairs in front of Peter's desk as the artistic director took his seat on the other side, his mouth set in a firm, unsmiling line. Marcus glanced at the desk and saw this morning's *Morning Sun*, open to the review he'd just read, complete with a huge photo of Heather in her second act costume, suspended above the stage in a soaring grand jeté.

Peter followed his gaze and sighed.

"Marcus, I've done my best to build a company culture where dancers are treated like adults for a change, where you know you can come to work and be respected and safe," he said, sounding as if he'd delivered this speech several times lately. Which, of course, he had.

"Pas de Don't—yes, I know what you all call it behind my back—is part of that. I've been very clear with all of you about why it's in place, and how seriously I expect you all to take it. How seriously *I* take it."

"I know," Marcus managed.

"I'm sure you've seen the video that's circulating online, of you and Ms. Hays." It wasn't a question. He'd seen it. By now, everyone in the ballet world had seen it. Their moment of private, secret joy, on one of the best days of his life, captured without their knowledge and broadcast all over the world.

Marcus nodded, unable to form words. There was no use denying what was right there for Peter and everyone else to see. For a moment, he considered explaining that he and Heather were no longer together, that they'd broken the rules only briefly and had stopped before the video went viral. But he knew it wouldn't make a difference.

"Right. In that case, I'm sorry, but I can't let you stay on at ANB. Your contract is terminated, effective immediately. The administration will be in touch soon about your final paycheck."

Though Marcus had known it was coming, the blow was devastating. His eyes burned, but he said nothing. What was there to say? In the space of a few short days, he'd lost the only woman he'd ever loved and the only job he'd ever wanted. His identity as a dancer, gone. His Dad, gone. Everything he'd ever held dear, all of it, gone. His brain felt numb, overwhelmed by the sheer weight of it all. Peter gazed at him with a kind of paternal disappointment, and Marcus could barely stand to look at him. He swallowed and gave Peter another nod to let him know he'd understood.

Peter gave him a pained look. "I wish it didn't have to be this way. I know you've had an enormously difficult year, and I've been very pleased with your progress in the last month or so. I was looking forward to seeing you back on stage with us, we all were. I'm sorry I won't get to see that now."

The finality in Peter's voice was a gut punch. Marcus was unemployed. He wanted to ask about Heather, but he wasn't sure he could speak without crying. So he gave Peter a final nod, then rose from his chair and turned to leave.

"Good luck, Marcus," Peter said behind him. "I wish you every success."

Marcus pushed open the door and let it swing shut behind him with a soft whoosh, then turned, heading down the hallway as fast as he could to the men's locker room. There, he emptied the minimal contents of his locker into his backpack.

On his way out, he paused outside the physio room, where Sharon crouched on the floor, gathering up weights and resistance bands. She looked up and saw him standing there, then dropped the gear and scrambled to her feet.

"Love, I heard . . ." she said, hurrying to the door.

Marcus stared helplessly at her, the woman who'd quite literally gotten him back on his feet. Whose work and belief in him he'd thrown away because Heather Hays made him feel alive and happy for the first time in forever. He wanted to apologize to Shaz, tell her how grateful he was to her, but his throat was too thick for words, and she wasn't one for big speeches anyway. So when she held out her arms, he stepped into them, let her squeeze him into a tight hug, and wept into her shoulder.

Carly, 9:02 AM: This video is everywhere. Is that the tour guide guy?? What's going on????
Heather, 9:03 AM: I can't talk about it now. I'll tell you when I get home.

Heather watched the dots dance on her screen for a moment before disappearing. After a long pause, a reply appeared.

Carly, 9:05 AM: Please come home soon.

Heather replied with a hasty thumbs-up emoji, then dialed Marcus's number, pacing anxiously as she waited for him to pick up.

"What did Peter say to you?" he asked, without preamble, when he finally did. He sounded hoarse and congested, like he'd been crying.

"What did he say to you?" she asked, even more worried than she'd been before he answered.

"Exactly what he said to Adrian and Robbie and Ricky and Kimiko and you, I suspect. The policy is clear, and there are no exceptions. I'm out."

Heather hung her head and sank onto the couch. She'd known it was coming, but that didn't make it easier to hear.

"I'm so sorry, Marcus. If there's anything I can do . . ."

He gave a humorless laugh. "I think you've done enough."

"What is that supposed to mean? I didn't film that video, and it wasn't my idea to go up into the mountains with someone who turns out to be a French travel influencer."

Marcus sighed. "You're right. I'm sorry, that wasn't fair. And it's not like you can do anything to change Peter's mind anyway, since you're out of a job, too."

Heather paused, then willed herself to speak. "I . . . um . . . I'm not."

"Not what?"

"He didn't terminate my contract. I'm staying on and dancing the rest of the run, as planned."

There was a long silence. "I don't understand. You know how strongly Peter feels about Pas de Don't."

"I know, but when I talked to him today, he said because ticket sales are so strong, he had no choice but to let me stay on. He said the board would have his head if he made me leave." Peter had sounded furious but resigned. In the moment, Heather hadn't had time to feel anything but relief. Now, though, guilt stole over her, creeping hot and prickly up her shoulders.

"So the policy is ironclad unless ticket sales are good enough?"

"I . . . no, but—" Heather started, taken aback.

"Unless the person who broke it is a star?"

"No, it's not like that, it's just—"

"I guess rules can be bent when it's The Heather Hays and you don't want the board on your back, huh? But they're not worth bending for someone who's half washed up." Marcus's voice was heated and bitter, like she'd never heard it before. It made her stomach churn.

"Marcus, do you *want* me to lose my job?" she snapped.

"Of course not," he shot back. "All I'm asking for is a little consistency. Either sexual harassment matters, or it doesn't. Either you lose your job for breaking Peter's rule, or you don't. I didn't realize there was a carve-out for people who bring in enough money for the company. I thought you and I were taking the same risk, but I was wrong."

Heather sat frozen on the couch. How could he not understand the risks she'd taken? How much she'd gambled by leaving Jack and coming here in the first place, and how she'd nearly thrown it all away by getting involved with him? What was she supposed to do, insist Peter fire her?

"That's not fair," she said, hearing the tremble in her own voice and hating it. "This is why I came here. To work. I came here to show the world I exist without Jack, that I'm my own person who deserves to be here. I didn't come here to mess around and lose my job and go back to New York humiliated. I came here to dance. So I'm going to dance."

For a long moment, all Heather could hear was the steady pounding of her own heart, and the sound of Marcus's heavy, angry breathing on the other end. Silently, she begged him to say something. *Say you understand. Say you see why this matters to me. Say you love me and you want me to succeed.*

But when he finally spoke, his voice was cold and distant. The voice of a stranger.

"Good luck with the rest of the run, then."

Chapter 18

Heather had known all kinds of exhaustion in her decade as a professional dancer, and in her time as a ballet student before that. Once, when she was in the corps, she had danced forty-one of the company's forty-seven shows of *The Nutcracker*, showing up to the theater almost every day of the six weeks between Thanksgiving and New Year's Eve to climb into her snowflake and flower costumes and dance on that famed Lincoln Center stage. There had been a few nights when she'd had to sit down on the dusty third floor landing of the fifth-floor walkup she shared with Carly, because her quads and calves couldn't carry her all the way to the top without a rest in the middle. After the last show, she had slept for almost three days straight, waking up only to go to the bathroom, and when she finally got out of bed it was to find two of her toenails were about to fall off.

Still, Heather had never known the kind bone-deep fatigue she felt as she pushed her luggage cart into the arrivals hall at LaGuardia, her muscles tight and aching, her head throbbing. She'd slept through most of her flight from Sydney to Los Angeles, jerking awake only occasionally to remember how hard the last week had been. Five performances, eleven pairs of pointe shoes, dozens of curtain calls, and zero calls from Marcus.

The morning after closing night, she'd packed her suitcase and pushed the keys to the little Kirribilli house through the mail slot. Twenty-four hours later, a Taylor Swift song warbled over the airport's tinny PA system, the upbeat tune sounding ominous to Heather's exhausted ears. *Welcome to New York, it's been waiting for you.*

She spotted Carly immediately, leaning against the railing and holding a sign that read HEATHER FUCKING HAYS. Heather smiled despite herself, especially when she noticed the wide berth people made around her—people who were all holding signs without profanity on them. But then Heather got closer and got a better look at Carly's face. Her eyes were pink and puffy, and it looked like she hadn't brushed her orange-red curls in at least a day. Her usually glowing skin was ashen, and the smile she gave Heather when their eyes met was strained and unconvincing.

"Welcome home," she croaked when Heather wheeled her cart around the railing and pulled her into a hug.

"I missed you so much." Heather squeezed her friend tight. "You didn't have to come all the way out here on the bus to get me."

"Yes, I did. But we're splitting a cab back." Carly pulled away, and Heather studied her. She looked even worse up close, and for a moment Heather forgot her own troubles.

"Honey, did something happen?"

Carly shook her head, and her eyes watered. "I'll tell you later."

Heather crossed her arms stubbornly. "Tell me now. Or we're taking the bus home."

Carly sighed and closed her eyes. "Mr. K fired me last week."

"*What?* Why?"

"He said I'd been disruptive in rehearsals, which is code for 'Samuel and Brett disrupted rehearsals by talking shit about me.' But I know the real reason is Jack."

"What do you mean?"

"He figured out I was the one who told you about him and Melissa. I mean, he knows I've always hated him, so it probably wasn't hard to figure out. But the night the video went viral, he came over to my place at 2:00 AM, drunk and angry, yelling about 'how dare she leave me for that nobody,' and threatened to get me fired. I told him to fuck off or I'd call the police, and he punched the intercom box—which the building manager wants me to pay to fix, by the way. And I guess the next morning he went to Mr. K and gave him a choice: him or me."

Heather let out a shaky breath, remembering Jack's vile late-night voicemail. She'd had no idea he'd take his rage out on Carly, as well.

"Why didn't you tell me sooner?"

Carly gave her a sad smile. "You were down there conquering the world. And becoming a viral sensation. I thought you'd worry about me."

"Of course I'd worry about you! Carly, you're my best friend, it's my job to worry about you." When Carly's smile faltered and her lip trembled, Heather stopped. "I'm sorry. I feel like this is my fault."

"None of this is your fault. He cheated, got caught cheating, and then got angry about getting caught. For the hundredth time, you did nothing wrong."

Heather let out a grim laugh. "Except break company policy in front of the entire internet. I screwed everything up, Carly, but I didn't realize it would come back to hurt you, as well."

"You didn't screw everything up. That review was incredible. No wonder Jack was furious. You went over there and showed everyone you were always a brilliant dancer, and you never needed him at all."

Heather's eyes watered as Carly's words washed over her, and the tears she'd been suppressing since she left the Kirribilli house spilled down her cheeks. Carly hugged her and rubbed her back, sniffling, and they stood there, holding each other and crying as carts and suitcases rolled around them.

"What are we going to do?" Carly asked, pulling away and wiping her face.

Heather sighed and looked at the sign Carly had made for her. "You know what your parents always say."

"There's no problem money can't solve?"

"No, the other one. Everything looks better after a good night's sleep. Let's go home, order dumplings, and sleep. Tomorrow we'll make a plan. Okay?"

"Okay." Carly nodded, and together they pushed Heather's cart out of the terminal and toward the cab rank.

Marcus jolted awake from the pounding on his door, liquid splashing across his shirt as he started. He looked around his apartment, bleary-eyed and confused as the sharp smell of whisky met his nostrils. Outside the drawn blinds, it was morning. He must have fallen asleep mid-drink hours ago.

There were five more rapid, insistent pounds on the door.

"'Kay, 'kay, I'm coming, m'coming," he mumbled, wiping his wet hand on his already damp shirt and setting his glass on the coffee table. Marcus rose from the couch and the room spun around him. Carefully, head throbbing, he padded to the front door and leant his forehead against it.

"Who is it?"

"It's me," came Alice's voice. "And I brought backup."

"Let us in, please." His mum.

Marcus sighed against the door, then stood to walk back to the couch. He'd been ignoring Alice's calls and texts for days, and apparently, she'd run out of patience. And brought in reinforcements. Another few pounds and he jumped backwards, unsteady on his feet.

"Let us in," Alice called, "right now."

"Okay, okay," he muttered again. He fumbled for the lock and pulled open the door to reveal her standing in the hallway with her hands on her hips and her mouth pulled into a thin, worried line. Behind him stood his mum, looking just as concerned.

"You'll wake the neighbours knocking like that," Marcus grumbled.

Both women looked him up and down and wrinkled their noses. "And you'll wake the dead smelling like that," Alice replied. "Did you already get a new job at a distillery?"

Marcus shook his head and turned around, walking away to throw himself back on the couch. He'd been lying here for the last week, and he didn't see any reason to change that now.

Alice and his mum followed him into the living room, and he ignored the matching looks of shock and concern on their faces as they looked around.

The coffee table was cluttered with takeaway containers, each with a plastic fork or chopsticks sticking out of it. The almost-empty whisky bottle stood, cap off, next to a few empty beer cans, and the muted TV played sitcom reruns from the late 1990s.

"This is so much worse than I imagined," Alice said under her breath. "Leanne, can you turn the lights on?"

Light flooded the room, and Marcus groaned in protest, burying his face in the sofa cushions. He heard someone enter the kitchen, and the sound of the tap running. A moment later, he felt a pair of fingers pinch the ends of his socks and transfer his feet to the floor, then someone sat on the couch.

"Drink this, please," Alice said, and he turned to see she was holding a large glass of water in front of his face.

When he didn't respond, she sighed and said tartly, "We can go back outside and bang on the door again if you like." Marcus grunted and sat up, and his head pounded again. She thrust the water at him, and he took it. He sipped it, only realizing then that his mouth had felt like it was full of sawdust.

"Thanks," he muttered into the glass. Marcus looked up to find her surveying him closely with a concerned crease between her eyebrows. His mother had lowered herself carefully into the armchair across from him and was watching him too, her face unreadable. He took a few more mouthfuls of water, feeling his head unfog a little as he drank.

"I'm sorry I didn't come sooner, but you know how show weeks are. What did Peter say to you?"

"I don't want to talk about it. How did the run go?"

Alice looked at him for a moment, and he could tell she was wondering whether to insist on an answer to her question. "It went fine. The mood's pretty grim, seeing as we just lost three dancers in the space of a few weeks, but we put on a good show. Sold-out crowds, every night."

He nodded, wishing Alice hadn't mentioned ticket sales. They sat in silence as he finished his water, then he closed his eyes and lay back against the pillows.

"Have you eaten anything lately?" his mum asked.

Marcus closed his eyes, trying to remember. "Nah."

His mother tsked disapprovingly. "Right, then. I'm making cheese on toast. I assume you have cheese and bread?"

"Probably."

"Good. Alice, are you hungry?"

"Starving. Dancing men to their deaths is hard work."

While his mum busied herself in the kitchen, Alice went to the tap and poured him another glass of water.

"Have you heard from Heather?"

Marcus shook his head, and his temples didn't throb this time. He was still so furious at Heather he didn't know what he'd say if she contacted him. She hadn't given him the chance to find out.

"She looked pretty miserable any time she wasn't on stage," Alice said. "And no one will tell us the full story of what happened. Why didn't Peter send her back right away?"

Marcus sighed. "Sold-out crowds, every night."

Alice raised her eyebrows. "Are you serious? After he gave you and the others the sack?"

"It's not fucking fair. I'm out of a job, and she's just—"

"Probably halfway to New York already," Alice said quietly.

Good, Marcus wanted to reply, but he couldn't bring himself to say it. Alice seemed to understand from the look on his face, though. She studied him for a long moment.

"Marcus, what was she supposed to do? You know how much this gig meant to her, after the way she left NYB. It's bloody hard being a woman in this business, and while that's not an excuse, look at it from her point of view. She didn't have any good choices, and she chose the best bad option."

"At least she's still got options," he said bitterly.

"You have options, too," his mother replied from the kitchen. "For example, you could call the woman you love."

Marcus ran his hand over his face, feeling his own rough stubble against his palm, and said nothing.

"It is love, right?" Alice pressed. "That's why you look like eighteen kinds of shit right now?"

Marcus gave a humourless laugh. "There's also the small matter of having no job," he reminded her. He paused. "But . . . yeah. I loved her. But it's too late now."

Alice scooted closer and wrapped an arm around his shoulders. "I'm sorry, then. I'm sorry for everything. But you're going to be okay. I know it doesn't feel like it at the moment, but you're just going to have to believe me, because I was right then, and I'm right now."

"She is," Leanne said, placing two plates on the coffee table and pushing them towards Alice and Marcus. "Eat."

His stomach rumbled, and he reached for his plate and took a bite of toast. It was hot and crisp, and the melted cheese burnt the top of his mouth, just like it always had when his dad had made it for him and Davo. Alice picked up her own plate and moaned appreciatively as she chewed her toast.

"I know this is a blow, love," his mum said gently as he ate. "And I know it's been a terribly hard year. For all of us. But remember what your father used to say? You only fail if you don't try. So you have to try."

Marcus swallowed a mouthful of toast and looked into his mum's face, which was so like his own. "He really wanted me to dance again." And now Marcus probably never would.

"No, love. He wanted you to be happy again, and dancing made you happy. But life is long and strange and full of things that will make you happy. People, too. He believed that, and I need you to believe it as well."

Marcus hastily swiped away the tears that filled his eyes as she spoke. He had been happy these last few weeks, happier than he'd been in years. And now the person responsible for that was on the other side of the world, and probably just as furious at him as he was at her.

"Thanks, Mum. I'll try." Marcus stood and stepped around the coffee table to hug her, and she reached up to stroke his hair, rocking him gently side to side and sniffling into his shirt.

After a moment, she pulled away and wiped her eyes, then offered them both seconds of cheese on toast, which they accepted.

"Have you thought about what you'll do next?" Alice asked after their plates were clear. "You could teach, you know. Or go overseas and audition for some European companies. That video's not a great audition tape, but it's a start. Or I could ask Izzy if she's got any openings at the shop."

Marcus laughed, for real this time, imagining himself selling dance belts and ballet slippers as techno music throbbed overhead. "I haven't really thought about it, and I need a little more time, okay?"

The few times he'd tried to think about it, he hadn't come up with anything he wanted to do besides dance at ANB. That had always been the dream, even if it would've only lasted a few more years. He'd never imagined himself doing any other job. He hadn't been to university. He'd gone straight from high school to the company and stayed there ever since. And now, he was thirty-one and had to start all over again.

"Well, when you're ready to think about it, I'm ready to help. Listen." Alice paused for a moment, seemingly considering her next words very carefully. "I heard a rumour, about Heather's friend. Carly, I think?"

Marcus raised his eyebrows. "What about her?" He'd been ignoring the world, and especially the ballet rumour mill, for almost a week. He didn't want to know what it had to say about him.

"Well, it's just gossip, so it's probably only half true, but I heard after your video went viral, Jack Andersen had a fit and got Carly fired. He sounds like a real piece of work."

"Yeah, he is" was all Marcus managed. He remembered what Heather had said, that Carly was an acquired taste. But he also remembered the way she'd talked about her best friend, like a sister.

Alice seemed to realise she should leave it there. She gave him a pat on the back, picked up their plates, and rinsed them in the sink.

"We should go," she said to his mum, and they both hugged him once more. His mum still looked a little teary, and he gave her an extra squeeze and a kiss on the top of her head.

"I love you," she said, smiling tiredly up into his face.

"I love you, too. Thanks for feeding me."

"I'll be back tomorrow, but only if you promise to clean this place up," Alice said as she walked to the door. "It's starting to look like an audition video for *Hoarders*."

"Love you, too," Marcus called at her retreating back, then lay back down on the couch. He'd stay here one more day. And tomorrow he'd clean up and do laundry at last and wash the scent of Heather from his sheets.

Heather was the first to wake the next morning. After taking a quick shower and watering ZZ Pot, who was thriving, she ventured downstairs to the closest bodega and bought two bagels and two iced coffees. She walked slowly back to the apartment building, feeling every step of her closing night performance and every hour of travel in her hip flexors and lower back.

Had it really been just over a month since she'd left this place? She had forgotten how narrow the sidewalks were here, and the way the streets of New York smelled like hot trash by 9:00 AM in early September. The morning light seemed flatter and duller than she remembered it, or perhaps the light in Sydney had been sharper and brighter, and she'd simply become accustomed to it without realizing.

Unbidden, the image of Marcus's face swam into her mind, the way the morning light found every freckle, and every yellow-gold fleck in his eyes. Her heart twisted in her chest. She hadn't heard from him since that last, awful phone call, and she didn't expect to.

Heather gripped her coffee tight, exhausted by the conflicting emotions that had been swirling through her for days now. Pride at her success in Sydney, and anger that he hadn't understood how important it was to her. Mortification at how her time at ANB had ended, misery that she'd let him down. And an enraging sense of powerlessness when she thought about the choice she'd been forced to make.

"Honey, I'm home," she called as she stepped into the apartment, slightly breathless from five flights of stairs. "And I brought bag—"

The words died in her throat when her eyes fell on the woman sitting on the couch with Carly, her eyes swollen and a glass of water clutched in her hand.

Melissa.

Heather's stomach dropped as the young woman stared at her, trepidation in her pretty, round face. Heather looked at Carly, who sprang to her feet and physically put her body between her and Jack's new girlfriend.

"What is she doing here?" Heather's heart raced, and hot anger crawled up the insides of her ribs.

"I asked her to come," Carly said quickly. "I had an idea late last night, and I was going to tell you this morning, but she arrived a little early."

"Why didn't you tell me last night?" Heather hissed.

"Because I knew you'd say no," Carly said firmly. She glanced behind her at Melissa, whose eyes were now fixed on the water in her glass as they talked about her like she wasn't there.

"Why are you here?" Heather managed. She fixed the younger woman with the steeliest glare she could manage through her shock and jet lag.

"Because we need her help," Carly sighed. "And she needs ours."

"What the hell are you talking about? Why would we help the woman who slept with my fiancé and ruined my life? And what could she possibly do for us?"

"Fine, it's not for us," Carly shot back, "it's for me. So I can get my job back. I'm sorry I sprang this on you, but would you please just listen?"

"Carly, it's okay," Melissa said to the floor, so softly Heather barely heard her. "This was a bad idea. I should just go."

Heather opened her mouth to agree, but something about the flat, defeated tone of Melissa's voice stopped her.

"Fine," she said, making sure to direct her words at Carly, not Melissa. Heather set down the bagels and coffee before the shake in her hands could drop them, then took a step backward and pressed her shoulders against the living room wall, putting as much space as she could between herself and the younger woman. "I'll listen."

"Thank you," Carly said, sounding relieved. She lowered herself slowly onto the arm of the couch, as though moving too quickly would fracture the fragile peace.

Melissa took a deep breath and dragged her gaze up to meet Heather's eyes.

"First," she started, softly, "I'm sorry about what me and Jack did. About what I did. It was wrong, and we shouldn't have done it. I hate the idea that you hate me, because I've looked up to you for so long, ever since I was a kid in the NYB school. I really am sorry, but you have every right to hate me forever."

Heather scoffed. Like she needed Melissa's permission to hate her forever. Carly raised her eyebrows and shot her a look that plainly said, *Would you please just give her a chance?* Heather rolled her eyes in assent, and Melissa went on.

"Second"—and now Melissa was looking up at Carly—"I'm sorry for what he did the other night. And what he said to you. It was awful, and I tried to stop him from coming over here, and from going to Mr. K, but he didn't listen to me. He never listens to me."

Heather had forgotten how high Melissa's voice was, how girl-ish. She was so young, Heather thought, looking at her smooth, round face. Younger than Heather had been when she and Jack got together, by several years. When Heather'd found out about the affair, the thought of Melissa's youth had enraged her. Now it just made her feel a deep, heavy sadness for her, and a roiling, nauseated disgust at Jack, who had once again taken advantage of someone vulnerable and naive. Melissa's slim, hunched shoulders accentuated the sharp poke of her collarbone revealed by her tank top. Heather had the feeling that if she hadn't been gripping her glass with both hands, she would have been wringing them.

"That son of a bitch. That actual son of an actual bitch," Carly growled, but Melissa said nothing. She took another deep breath, this one shakier than the last.

"The things he called Carly," she said to Heather, "he's called me them too. A dumb bitch, a worthless slut." She swallowed hard but kept talking. "Sometimes to my face, when he's drunk and I've done something to make him angry. It feels like I'm always doing something to make him angry."

Despite herself, Heather nodded in recognition. She remembered that feeling.

"But sometimes," Melissa went on, "when we're apart, he'll text them to me, too." She glanced at Carly, and Heather saw a kind of understanding pass between them. Then Carly met Heather's eyes, grim satisfaction on her face, and after a moment Heather understood, too.

"She has the texts," Carly said. "And I have my broken intercom. And you have . . ." She paused for a second, then sighed. "You have whatever stories you want to tell about Jack."

"I have a voicemail," Heather said quietly. "From last week. When the video was everywhere."

Fucking slut. I knew you'd fuck your way to the top.

Disgust flickered over Carly's face, chased by relief. "He's fucking abusive, Heather. And as of a few nights ago, physically violent. Mr. K can fire one woman in a he-said-she-said situation. But three of us? He said, she said, she said, she said?"

Heather looked at Melissa, whose face was pinched and pale.

"I really do want to do the right thing," Melissa said. "It's not okay to treat women like this, and if we don't warn people, he's just going to keep doing it, right?" She didn't sound totally convinced, and her eyes darted to Carly as if she was looking for confirmation.

Carly inhaled to speak, but Heather cut in.

"Has he ever hit you?" The question hung heavily in the still, warm air, and the apartment was suddenly so silent Heather could hear the fridge humming.

"No," Melissa said softly but firmly, and Heather felt relief swoop through her chest. "But that's not the only way to hurt and control someone," Melissa went on, sounding like she was relaying information she'd only recently learned. "Just because abuse doesn't leave a physical mark doesn't mean it's not real."

"That's true," Heather agreed.

She thought of all the times Jack had cut her down in public, all his cruel drunken remarks and swift sober apologies. How many times had he made her feel less-than or complimented her only to pull his praise away when she got too comfortable? How many times had he let his friends and his mother insult her, sitting in silence and agreeing to their cruelty? The idea that he'd done that to Melissa—and much worse, it sounded like—made the back of her neck tingle with shame. *If we don't warn people, he's just going to keep doing it.* Should she have warned Melissa, all those months ago?

"What's your plan?" Heather asked the others. "Show the texts to Mr. K and show him who Jack really is?"

Carly gave a humorless laugh. "He knows who Jack is, he just doesn't care. But he might care if other people find out. That might be enough to save my job. Right?" She glanced at each of them. Melissa's nod was a little less certain than Heather's, but Carly looked relieved they'd both agreed.

"Okay then," Carly said, businesslike now. "I think it's time to set up a meeting with Mr. K."

Heather nodded. "I can call his assistant and ask to see him. Melissa, does Jack know you're here?"

"No, I told him I was meeting a friend for breakfast. But I should get home soon."

As Melissa finally took a sip of her water, Heather realized what she meant by "home." Jack's place on West Seventy-Fourth, the apartment that until a few months ago had been *her* home. Before Sydney, the realization might have made her feel sorrow or longing, but now it just made her worry for Melissa. Would she have a place to stay after she left Jack? Did she have a Carly of her own, to take her in and feed her dumplings?

Heather gestured at the coffee table, where her phone was charging. "Put your number in, and I'll text you when I know what time Mr. K can meet us."

"And make sure you take screenshots of those texts," Carly added.

"I already did," Melissa replied, sounding relieved and a little bolder now. "And I backed them up in two different places."

While Melissa busied herself with the phone, Carly threw Heather a knowing look, and Heather knew exactly what she was thinking. If she hadn't been so busy trying to forget Jack, she might have discovered how much she had in common with his new girlfriend.

Five minutes later, Carly walked Melissa out, then bolted the door with a sigh. Heather, realizing she was still pressed against the wall, walked to the coffee table and reached for the bagels and iced coffee.

Carly flopped onto the couch and took a grateful gulp of coffee, then slid over and made room for Heather. For a few moments, they sipped in silence. Heather had never been more grateful for the cold rush of coffee hitting her tongue. She swirled it in her mouth and swallowed slowly, letting her head loll back against the couch.

"How did you know?" Heather asked a while later. Carly's cup was almost empty.

"Unlucky guess."

"I'm serious." She sat up and looked into her friend's wan, freckled face. "How did you know there was something bad going on with her?"

Carly sighed. "Because she started showing up to class with the same look on her face that you used to get. Like she was getting the life crushed out of her so slowly that she barely noticed it happening. And I know I swore to hate her on your behalf, and fuck him forever and everything, but I just . . . couldn't watch it happen again."

Heather felt hot tears well in her eyes. "How did I let it happen to me? How did I let *him* happen to me?"

"Melissa told me something about him, before you got here. She said it was easy to explain away the little things he did to hurt her, at the beginning. By the time they got too big to ignore, and she realized she couldn't stop them, she was too ashamed to tell anyone about them."

Heather bit her lip, nodding in recognition. "That's how it was. You were right about him. At first, I didn't want to see it. After a while I just hid it from you. The truth was too scary. But you kept showing up, even when I was too ashamed to admit I wanted you there."

"I'll always show up for you," Carly promised.

"I love you," Heather said. She blinked her tears away and pulled Carly into a tight hug. Carly sniffed against her shoulder. "I didn't miss anything else about this place, but I missed you every day."

Chapter 19

The black leather couch outside Mr. K's office was firm, shiny, and extremely uncomfortable to sit on. As she and Melissa sat in tense, straight-backed silence, Heather couldn't help but wonder if the artistic director had chosen it for that very reason, as a way to ensure anyone who met with him was thrown off balance as soon as they arrived.

Posters promoting previous NYB seasons crowded the walls of the waiting room. Some dated back to performances in London and Paris in the 1950s, as if to remind people just how old, storied, and world-renowned this institution was. In a place of pride over Mr. K's personal assistant's desk was the poster from last season, featuring Jack in black tights and a drenched, clinging white shirt, standing thigh-deep in the fountain on the plaza ten stories below. *Like a sexy modern Prince Charming,* Heather had told him glowingly when the poster proofs had come in.

Now, she averted her eyes.

They'd left Carly downstairs in the baking hot plaza, looking more anxious than Heather had ever seen her. She'd chewed her nails down to jagged pink remnants, and splotchy purple circles were under her puffy, sleepless eyes.

In the waiting room, Melissa perched next to Heather on the edge of the couch, looking scarcely less nervous, and when the phone rang on the assistant's desk, she jumped. A moment later, Barbara set down the phone, turned to them, and informed them Mr. K was ready to see them.

"Breathe," Heather told Melissa softly as they stood, and Melissa exhaled on command. Heather turned to her and looked into her pretty round face, trying to project more confidence than she felt.

"We're doing the right thing," she said firmly, meeting Melissa's wide eyes and seeing her own doubt reflected in them. "We are going to go in there and tell him the truth, and that's it."

"What if he fires us, too? This company is all I've ever wanted."

"I know," Heather said. "But if this works, we'll all get what we want. You'll be free of Jack, Carly will get her job back, and we'll have made it safer here for everyone. Okay?"

"Okay," Melissa's voice wavered, but she managed a small, toothless smile.

As they walked in, Heather slipped her hand in her pocket and hit SEND on the text she'd prewritten.

Mr. K waited for them behind his large glass desk and gestured toward two low-backed chairs as they walked in. Behind him, the floor-to-ceiling windows looked down onto Lincoln Center plaza and the theater, an impressive backdrop that only served to remind Heather of the power he held over the institution—and over them all. Mr. K was dressed to lead company class later in the morning, in a pair of expensive-looking black sweats and a matching black zip-up jacket. Under his polished bald head, his gray eyes were shrewd and observant.

"I must admit I was surprised to see this meeting on my agenda," he said with a perfunctory smile as they took their seats. "I did not imagine the two of you were friendly with each other, for obvious reasons."

Heather returned his smile, hoping hers looked more genuine than his. There was no reason to let him make the situation hostile before it needed to be. Then she reached across and squeezed Melissa's hand. "We've discovered we have more in common than we realized."

"I see," he said coolly, but offered nothing else. He turned to Melissa, who still looked pale, and whose slender hands were clasped in her lap in what was either a ladylike habit or an effort to stop them trembling. "Well then, Miss Hall, what brings you two in today?"

Melissa seemed frozen, so after a moment, Heather spoke. "We're both concerned that you've let Carly go. And we both think you need to hear the rest of the story before your decision is final." Next to her, Melissa shot her a grateful glance.

"It's already final." Mr. K's voice chilled from cool to cold. Heather took a deep breath, trying not to let the frost faze her. She'd heard it plenty of times in rehearsal and class, after all.

"I'm not sure what Jack has told you about Carly," she said slowly, and though she saw him start to interject, she kept speaking, doing her best to keep her voice clear and steady. "Or what he said he'd do if she wasn't fired."

The poster over Barbara's desk had made it clear enough, though: subscribers and donors adored Jack, and they had no idea who Carly was. If Jack had asked Mr. K to choose between the company's biggest star and some nameless woman in the corps, the decision would've been easy.

"But the night before you fired Carly, Jack went to her apartment, intoxicated, and verbally abused her. Then he caused significant property damage." She pulled her phone from her bag, brought up a photo of Carly's intercom, and slid it across the smooth, cold glass. "Carly's property manager says it will cost almost five thousand dollars to replace."

Mr. K craned his long neck to look down at the screen, his face impassive.

"Anyone could have done that," he said dismissively. "There's no way to know Mr. Andersen was responsible."

"Yes, there is," came a voice behind Heather. She turned around to see Carly standing in the doorway, Mr. K's assistant hovering anxiously behind her. Heather suppressed a smile. Carly Montgomery always knew how to make an entrance.

"What is she doing here?" Mr. K snapped at Barbara, looking straight past Carly.

"She's here to confirm that it was Jack who broke her intercom," Carly said, striding into the room and standing behind Heather's chair, arms crossed and eyebrows raised. "And if you won't take her word for it, she'd be happy to show you the CCTV footage. Or the police report she filed."

Mr. K glared at Carly for a long moment, then waved his hand at Barbara, dismissing her. "These things happen," he said shortly. "Everyone loses their temper from time to time, as I'm sure *you* know all too well, Ms. Montgomery."

"That's true," Heather said, unsurprised by his response. "But this is part of a pattern. As I'm sure you know, both Melissa and I have dated Jack. And Melissa's experience has been quite similar to mine." Melissa pulled out her own phone and slid it forward, as Heather picked up her own phone, pulled up her voicemail, and hit play.

Jack's drunk, vicious voice echoed off the hard surfaces of Mr. K's office. When the message ended, Mr. K looked down again, taking in the messages on Melissa's phone, and Heather saw his mouth set into a firm, straight line.

"There's more like that," Melissa said grimly. "You can swipe through to see them."

"And as you'll see, Jack's name is on all of them," Heather added. "Melissa can email them to you, and I can send you the audio file, if you'd like."

Mr. K pushed the phone away. "That won't be necessary," he said tersely.

Heather glanced at Melissa with a knowing smile, then opened her email and hit send on the message she'd drafted the previous night.

"I've sent them to you anyway, just in case," she said and willed herself not to break eye contact as Mr. K's face turned thunderous. He knew as well as she did that once those messages were in his inbox, there'd be a paper trail, and no way for him to pretend he didn't know about them.

He paused, then spoke as he chose his words very carefully. "This is . . . unfortunate. Certainly not polite or gentlemanly behavior. But how Mr. Andersen conducts himself in his private life is a private matter."

"Even if the women he's mistreating are his colleagues? Your employees?" Heather asked.

Mr. K said nothing.

"This isn't simply impolite or ungentlemanly, it's violent and sexist," she went on. "Carly and Melissa and I are entitled to a safe work environment, aren't we? One where we aren't afraid of being abused by our coworkers, even if that abuse happens after hours, or in private, or from the other side of the world?"

More silence. Heather pressed on, determined to say what came next, and trying to make it sound as though she and Carly hadn't rehearsed it together last night.

"Carly was so pleased to be cast in a principal role in the new women's empowerment initiative," she said, amazed that her voice stayed steady as she dropped the hammer. "It would certainly be, uh, *unfortunate* if it became public she was fired in order to keep Jack happy."

"*Especially* if these screenshots somehow found their way onto social media or to a reporter," Carly added. "The company's spending so much money to finally look women-friendly, but people might start to wonder: does NYB really empower women, or does it silence them and protect the men who hurt them?"

Mr. K's eyes narrowed, and Heather felt a spark of triumph jump in her chest. It was a nightmare headline, one that would be all too easy for him to picture. And it wouldn't even need to be a headline to raise uncomfortable questions for the company. Heather knew better than anyone how small and gossipy the ballet world could be.

The silence stretched, tense and heavy, and Heather resisted the urge to fidget. Next to her, Melissa was frozen in her chair, and Heather could feel the nervous energy radiating from Carly. Finally, Mr. K spoke.

"What is it you propose I do, Miss Hays?" His tone was arctic now, but she could see a warm pink flush creeping up his neck.

"Give Carly her job back," Melissa said, before the others could reply. She nodded at her phone. "And decide whether this is the kind of person you want in your company. And whether you're prepared to defend that choice publicly." In her high, sweet voice, the implied threat somehow sounded even more menacing.

Mr. K looked across the table at Melissa, his gaze sharp. He had no doubt known her since she was a preteen ballet student at the company's school, just like Heather had, and surely he had been keeping a close eye on her since she joined the corps and started dating Jack. She was a gifted dancer, but now, Mr. K was looking at her as though he was realizing he had sorely underestimated her for reasons that had nothing to do with her dancing. Heather couldn't help but think she had, too.

"I'll consider it," he said in a flat, defeated tone. Then he got to his feet, pushing back his black leather chair with a loud scrape. Heather and Melissa stood and glanced at Carly, who had always enjoyed the last word.

"You do that," she said, with a triumphant smile. "You know how to reach me."

They didn't speak until the elevator carried them down to the lobby, where they'd strode out of the building and onto the wide expanse of Lincoln Center Plaza. The dark paving stones sparkled in the midmorning sun, and a breeze played unenthusiastically through the trees in the little park next to the NYB building.

"Oh my God, that was incredible!" Melissa said, words bursting from her at last. Her round face was jubilant, and her smile pure relief.

Heather chuckled, feeling a week's worth of tension melt from her shoulders. "That was pretty great," she admitted, linking her arm in Carly's. "Are you okay?"

Carly gave her a tight nod, then wiped her eyes. Heather and Melissa both gathered to her.

"What's the matter?" Melissa asked. "We won, didn't we?"

Carly took a deep breath, and a few more tears rolled down her cheeks. She looked exhausted. "Yeah. I just wish we didn't have to fight so hard."

Heather hugged her, ignoring the heat of the day. "At least we don't have to fight alone."

"That's true. And I fucking love a good fight."

The three of them laughed, then fell silent. For a moment, the awkward question of *what now?* hung in the air. Melissa wasn't their sworn enemy anymore, but she wasn't exactly their friend, either.

Melissa looked across the plaza at the theater, where some of their colleagues were likely warming up already in the largest studio. "I'm going to skip company class today. It might be a bit uncomfortable. I think I'll go uptown to Moves and take an open class." She hesitated, then added in a rush, "Do you guys wanna come with me?"

Heather smiled, surprised to find herself touched by the invitation. "Maybe some other time. I'm so jet-lagged."

"And I haven't slept properly in days," Carly added.

"Okay," Melissa said. She twisted her fingers together and took a shaky breath before she spoke again. "Heather, I truly am so sorry for everything. I hope one day you can forgive me. And I hope one day I can be as brave as you were up there."

Heather glanced at Carly, then pulled Melissa into a quick hug. "You're already brave. And you're already enough, okay? Don't let anyone tell you otherwise."

Melissa nodded into her shoulder, then pulled away, headed toward Broadway. Together, Heather and Carly walked to the 1 train and went home.

A few hours later, their stomachs full of dumplings from their favorite place around the corner, Heather and Carly sat on the couch. For the fifth time in as many minutes, Carly leaned toward the coffee table and checked her phone.

"He'll call," Heather said, reassuringly. "And remember, if this doesn't work, we have a backup plan. If Mr. K calls our bluff, he'll regret it. For once, the ballet gossip machine might actually do some good in the world. But hopefully it won't come to that."

Carly flipped her phone over, then leaned back and swung her legs over Heather's lap.

"Thank you for doing this for me."

"You'd do the same for me. You saved me from marrying Jack; it's only fair that I save you right back."

Carly sighed. "I missed you. But I'm glad you went down there and showed the world what you could do."

"I wish I hadn't shown the *entire* world, but thanks."

"I wish I'd been there. And I wish I'd met Campsite Guy."

Heather bit her lip. "Marcus," she said softly. She'd missed the shape of his name in her mouth.

"Marcus. Are you going to tell me what happened with him?"

Heather didn't know where to start. She knew where it ended, though, so she told Carly the whole story: from walking in on Marcus to their wrenching, ultimately pointless decision to end it, to their awful fight, to Marcus's headshot vanishing from the company's "Meet Our Dancers" page.

"How was the sex?" Carly interrupted at one point.

Heather grinned despite herself.

"The sex was good." She thought about that final night with Marcus in her bed. About the sound of her name in his broad accent, and his fingers digging gently into her hips as he pulled her against him and pushed her inevitably over the edge into orgasm. "Really, really good."

"Better than with Jack?" Carly's own smile was eager and vaguely evil.

"Well, yeah, because he wasn't having it with anyone else." For the first time since Heather arrived home, Carly laughed, and the sound of it flooded Heather with relief.

"It must have been good for you to break the company's cardinal rule," Carly said when her cackle subsided. "For you to do something that naughty? I didn't think sex of that caliber existed."

"Yeah, well, it didn't work out. I'm not very good at breaking the rules, apparently."

"I've been telling you for years, it takes practice," Carly said. "So . . . that's it?"

"That's it. I haven't heard from him, and I don't think I will. At least the video isn't everywhere anymore. Everyone's moved on to the next piece of ballet gossip."

Carly shook her head and smiled at Heather with a mix of pity and awe. "That must have been some damn good sex." Heather managed a weak smile, her mind still on what she and Marcus said to each other the day he was fired and she wasn't. Carly's smile drooped.

"Hey, I know you," she said in a suddenly solemn voice. "You didn't just sneak around for the sex. Right?"

Heather's throat tightened, and she shook her head, rolling her eyes up to the ceiling as she felt them fill with tears.

"No," she admitted. "I thought I was in love with him. He was so kind and so sweet, and he took me to see koalas . . ." She blinked the tears away and tried to pull herself together. "It's for the best. I have a job to get back to here, and it was too soon after Jack to be anything real. It was just a rebound."

Carly eyed her skeptically. "I don't believe that. What if you're just scared?" When Heather didn't reply, Carly pressed. "You stayed with the wrong person for so long because you were scared to leave. Don't let fear keep you from being with the right person."

"You don't understand. They kicked him out. His career is over because I was stupid and reckless, and I broke Peter's rule. And I was lying to everyone again. I hid it from you, just like I did when things were bad with Jack."

"My best friend is not stupid, so stop it," Carly said firmly, rising from the couch to pour Heather a glass of water. "Were you being reckless," she asked, after Heather had swallowed a few mouthfuls, "or were you doing something you really wanted for a change?"

"I—" Heather started, eyes wide. She was ready to argue, but her friend interrupted again.

"For real. Think about it. Because I don't think you were being stupid. I don't think you've ever been stupid. And okay, so you broke a rule, but it was a *bad rule*. And you don't always have to follow the bad rules. They're, like, bad."

Heather gave her a watery smile despite herself.

"I know, I should have been a lawyer, right?" Carly smirked. She looked at Heather intently. "It wasn't really like being with Jack. Was it?"

Heather chewed her lip for a moment and thought. About Marcus's bark of a laugh, about his apology the night he'd shown up with food from Café Luxor. About how many different ways he'd asked her what she wanted, and then given it to her. Unbegrudgingly. Enthusiastically. Because he wanted to give it to her, not because he wanted something from her.

"No, it was different," she finally sighed. "He was different, and I was different with him." Her eyes swam again, and she let the tears fall, too exhausted to hold them back.

"Hey, hey, it's going to be okay," Carly said, putting her arms around her and pulling her into a tight hug. Heather sniffed hard and let her friend hold her. "You are Heather Fucking Hays: world-class dancer, world-class friend, not quite world-class rule breaker—yet, but we can work on it."

When Carly pulled away, Heather gave her a grateful smile. She liked the sound of all of that, just as she'd liked it when Marcus called her brave and stubborn and heart shaped. And she was different now. She was not the twenty-two-year-old corps de ballet dancer who'd been willing to wave away Jack's unkindnesses because he made her feel special. Heather knew who she was now, and she knew the real Jack Andersen. Let her colleagues gossip all they wanted, let his mother think she was a charity case who screwed her way to the top. She knew the truth. Carly had always known it.

"I'm Heather Fucking Hays," she said, wiping her cheeks with the backs of her hands.

"Damn right," Carly agreed. For a moment they sat in silence, broken only by Heather's occasional sniffles. "Maybe you can go back to ANB. And hey, maybe if Mr. K doesn't change his mind, ANB would hire *me*." Under the bravado, Heather heard the uncertainty in her friend's voice.

"He'll change his mind," Heather reassured her. "And Peter won't take me back, although he'd probably love to have you." Smiling, she imagined Carly teaching a Thursday company class, jumping up and down and fist-pumping at the front of the room just like Alice did. Carly would fit in wonderfully at ANB.

Heather, on the other hand, had burned her bridges there, personal and professional. She'd let Peter and the whole company down. And Marcus. With a sigh, she climbed to her feet.

"I think it would suit me," Carly mused. "But tell me the truth: is 'taking someone to see the koalas' Australian slang for something super dirty?"

Heather guffawed and headed for the tiny kitchen. She had just finished shoving their empty takeout containers in the trash when Carly's phone rang, blaring the chorus of "Good as Hell" into the cramped living room. She froze and stared at Carly, who was gazing down at the screen.

"It's him." Carly sounded panicky, not a trace of bravado left.

"Answer it!" Heather urged. When Carly didn't move, she waved the dishcloth at her. "Answer it! Whatever happens, remember, we've got a plan."

Carly nodded, licked her lips nervously, and then reached for the phone.

When Marcus turned onto his mum's street Sunday evening, he was unsurprised to see Davo's ute already parked outside. He was surprised, however, to find his brother waiting for him on the front steps, Banjo sitting obediently at his feet. Davo stood as Marcus came up the front path and greeted him with a nod.

"Hi," Marcus said warily. The last time he'd seen his brother, they'd spent a surly, silent hour cleaning up the house together and then parted without speaking.

Davo looked him up and down. "Mum told me about your job. Sucks, I'm sorry."

"Um, thanks," Marcus said.

"Shouldn't be too hard to find another one, though, right?" Davo said as Banjo got to his feet and stretched. "It's not that big a deal."

Marcus stared at his brother. *Actually, it will be hard to find another one*, he wanted to say. *How many national ballet companies do you think a nation has? Plus, I'm thirty-one and barely in shape and everyone knows why I was fired.* If his brother had bothered to learn the first thing about Marcus's career, about the art form he'd devoted his life to at the age of eight, he would know that this was, in fact, that big a deal.

He said none of this. He wasn't going to let Davo get under his skin tonight. He'd done that last time, and it had blown up in his face, so tonight he'd just take deep breaths and ignore the little shards of irritation jabbing him in the gut. He gave Davo a noncommittal shrug, then made his way inside.

They found their mum in the kitchen, carefully ladling steaming pumpkin soup into bowls. She stopped when she saw them enter and hugged Davo, then Marcus.

"How are you, love?" She looked into his face, scrutinizing him with concern etched into every line of her forehead.

"I'm okay," Marcus said, though she didn't look convinced. "Eating three square a day and laying off the whisky for a bit."

"I'm glad to hear it," she said, turning back to the counter.

She spooned dollops of sour cream into the middle of each bowl, then held them out one at a time using both hands. Once they were seated, she took her time stirring the cream into her soup and adding salt and pepper.

"You're probably wondering why I asked you both here," she said eventually, and Marcus looked at her expectantly. Davo merely grunted around his spoon. "I went to the doctor today," she said, and Marcus's stomach dropped.

"Is something the matter?" he asked. "Is it your leg?"

"My leg's fine." She smiled before eating a spoonful of soup.

Davo looked at her sceptically. "Are you sure?"

"Yes," she said, stirring again.

"Are you positive?" Marcus asked.

She arched her eyebrows and levelled a look at him across the table. "I was only a nurse for twenty-three years, so I might be wrong about a minor cut that required half a dozen simple sutures, but yes, I'm quite sure."

"So, what is it?"

"When I went to get the wound checked today," she said, "I had a conversation with Dr. Greenleaf. And I've come to a decision about this house."

Davo's eyes snapped up from his soup, and Marcus put down his spoon with a clatter.

"And?" Davo asked.

She sat up straighter in her chair and looked at each of them in turn, then she glanced around the room. "I've decided I can't live here anymore. I need to be in a smaller space, without stairs and without a garden to take care of. My joints aren't going to get any better, and if I keep trying to move around this place, it will only make them worse faster. I need to move out."

Davo opened his mouth to speak, and Marcus knew he was about to say "I told you so." He gave his brother a warning look.

"So, um," Davo said instead, "are you going to sell? Where are you going to go?"

"I don't want to sell," she said firmly. "It's too soon. It's one thing to get rid of your father's belongings, but this house is different. It's our family home, and though he might be gone, our family is very much here." Her voice wavered slightly as she finished, and Marcus reached over and rubbed her shoulder gently. Across the table, Davo looked confused.

"So if you're not going to sell, what are you going to do?"

"I'm going to swap," she said. Davo didn't look any less perplexed, and Marcus couldn't blame him.

"Swap?"

"With one of you. I'll go live in one of your flats, and you'll come live here," she declared. When he and Davo said nothing, she continued, looking extremely pleased with herself. "It would mean I'd live in a place without stairs, and I'd be close enough to my doctors, and to you, that I wouldn't be totally lost. You'd keep paying rent at your place, but you'd get to live in the house. And you'd get to stop worrying about me living here on my own."

And they wouldn't have to say goodbye to this place, Marcus thought, which would feel like saying goodbye to his dad all over again. He looked at his mum, stunned, then glanced over at Davo. Why hadn't they thought of this?

"It's only a temporary fix," she continued. "I imagine we'll have to sell up eventually, unless one of you decides you want to have a family."

At this, Davo snorted. As far as Marcus knew, his brother wasn't dating anyone seriously, and hadn't for a few years—although who really knew what Davo got up to in his limited free time? As for Marcus, well, a wife and kids seemed highly unlikely for him right now, too.

For one miserable, mesmerizing moment, he allowed himself to imagine waking up with Heather in this house, pictured pouring her coffee in the sun-drenched kitchen before they headed down the street to walk along the beach. He gave his head a tiny shake and pulled himself back to the kitchen table.

"Er, whose apartment would you move into?" Davo asked cautiously.

"Well, if you're up for it, and it seems like you are, I thought I'd let you two decide. David, I know how much you love that loft." She wrinkled her nose slightly. She'd never cared for the concrete floors and high ceilings at Davo's rental in the Inner West—it didn't feel enough like a home, she'd once said. But now, she was apparently willing to move in. Or perhaps not, because she went on to say, "I wouldn't mind a view of the Bridge, to tell you the truth. And Marcus, since you don't have to commute to ANB anymore . . ."

Marcus's stomach sank as she trailed off, looking apologetic. He looked at his brother and saw relief flash across his face. Davo gave him a little shrug, his eyebrows raised.

"What do you reckon?"

Marcus thought about it. It was a tidy temporary solution, and certainly easier than trying to find her an affordable place close by. Since he'd moved out of home, he'd missed being close to the beach—and if he wasn't dancing anymore, he could surf every day, instead of staying out of the waves for fear of getting hurt and missing a whole season.

"I'll give you my flat, Mum," he said, and she beamed with satisfaction. "As long as it's okay with my landlord." It would be a huge effort to pack up both places and swap their contents. They'd probably have to have a garage sale or donate a bunch of the clutter in the house.

"Of course," she nodded, dipping her spoon back into her soup like she hadn't just fixed a problem they'd been trying to solve for months. "I'm sure David will be more than happy to help us with the moves, especially since you've saved him from having to give up his cold, grey flat." She said it like it was a suggestion, with her eyebrows raised and deep creases in her sun-aged forehead, but it was a clear instruction.

When they finished eating, she excused herself for the bathroom. Marcus heard her slowly head up the stairs and breathed a sigh of relief when he remembered she wouldn't have to contend with them much longer.

He stood and cleared the table—after the soup, Leanne served a large salad, followed by apple crumble, which had been his dad's favourite dessert—and Davo ran hot water into the sink to wash up.

"Well, that's that," his brother said tersely, staring into the soapy water.

"Yep," Marcus replied as he took out some plastic containers for leftovers.

"Problem solved. You saved the day."

"Um, I guess." Marcus shrugged, picking up the ladle from the soup pot.

"And hey, even if you don't have a job anymore, you can still dance around on the back verandah like when we were kids."

Marcus took a deep breath. He tried to focus on spooning the soup into the Tupperware, instead of on the audible eye roll in his brother's voice, but he couldn't do it. He'd barely slept in days, his heart was shredded, and despite putting his sheets through the wash twice, he still woke up every morning haunted by the scent of lavender. Marcus whirled to face his brother.

"What the fuck is your problem?" he growled.

Davo looked up from the suds-covered salad bowl. "What do you mean?"

"What the fuck is your problem with me, and with ballet, and with . . . me?"

"I'm just joking, jeez, calm down." Davo gave his head a little *come on, mate* shake, then turned back to the sink.

"You're not joking, so don't give me that shit," Marcus pressed, unwilling, or perhaps unable, to let this go. "You're always doing this, talking about me like I'm silly, talking about ballet like it's stupid, and I've fucking had it." He tossed the ladle back into the pot with a clatter, orange-yellow droplets spraying onto the counter.

"Oh, you've fucking had it, have you?" Davo snapped, turning off the tap to look at him. His pale face, so like their father's, was blotchy and red, and his chest rose and fell rapidly under his hoodie. "Well, I'm sorry not everyone in this family is as impressed by you as Dad was, okay, but I'm sure you'll get over it. The rest of us had to."

Marcus gaped at him. It was the most words he'd heard Davo say about their father in one go since he'd died. Marcus just didn't understand any of them.

"What are you talking about?"

"The fuck you think I'm talking about? Dad never shut up about you and ballet, did he? Never stopped talking about how great *Marcus* was at this concert, or how well *Marcus* did at that competition. All the fucking time, like he didn't have a whole other son who was good at school, and good at footy, and really fucking good at building houses. Nothing I ever did was enough to make him notice me or give a shit. It was all Marcus this, Marcus that." Davo was shouting now, his whole body rigid with rage, and Marcus took a step away and felt his lower back hit the counter.

"Why do you think he was like that?" Marcus shot back. "Because you and Uncle Gaz were so embarrassed having a ballet boy in the family, and he had to make up for it!"

"He didn't have to ignore me! He didn't have to miss all my footy games or act like my career didn't matter. I'm one of the youngest and most successful residential contractors in the entire city, and he never gave a shit because I wasn't dancing the lead in *Swan fucking Lake*. He was so bloody proud of you, and I was just . . . there." Davo's voice cracked, and he looked to the floor with a quiet sniff.

"Oh," Marcus said quietly, realization half dawning. He gave his brother a moment to compose himself, and after a few more sniffs, Davo lifted his head. His eyes were rimmed red, but he looked at Marcus defiantly, as though he was ready for round two.

"I had no idea," Marcus said. "I guess I never noticed. I was just grateful he was there for me, and it never occurred to me he wasn't doing the same for you."

Davo gave a little snort of disbelief.

"It's true," Marcus said. "But I'm sorry. That wasn't fair to you. And I do think he was proud of you. How could he not be?" Davo swallowed hard and nodded. There was a long silence, and Marcus wondered when their mum was coming back. It occurred to him that she might have heard them arguing and was deliberately taking her time upstairs.

"I'm sorry I was such a shit back then," Davo mumbled, after staring at his shoes for a full minute. "But I was just a kid, I mean . . ."

Marcus raised his eyebrows and fixed him with a look.

"Okay, okay. I'm sorry, full stop. Really."

"Thank you," Marcus said. "Did you say any of this to him before he . . . before he died?"

Davo looked back at his shoes. "Didn't really see the point."

Marcus shook his head. "*This* is the point. Not walking around being a stroppy shit all the time is the point." He gestured to the hallway in the direction of the stairs. "Being there for each other when they're not around anymore is the point."

"Okay, okay, I get it," Davo said. "Are we done with our big emotional moment now?"

"Sure, if you want to be." Still a stroppy shit, then. That wasn't going to get fixed with one conversation. All the same, when Davo turned back to the sink and busied himself with the dishes, Marcus resumed packing the leftovers, feeling a bit unsteady—but with his mind clearer than it had been in days.

Leanne came downstairs a few minutes later, acting impressively and unconvincingly normal. She thanked them for cleaning up, then handed each of them a container of leftover apple crumble and walked them to the door, Banjo at Davo's heels. Then she kissed them both goodnight—Davo first, then Marcus—and closed the door behind them.

Marcus hovered awkwardly on the front steps, wondering what to say to his brother. *Fuck it,* he thought, then held his arms out and offered Davo a hug. To his surprise, Davo accepted, and they gave each other a brief squeeze. Relief seeped into his muscles, and he could feel tears threatening behind his eyes. Against his shoulder, he felt Davo clear his throat and released him.

"I am proud of you, you know," Davo said, meeting his eyes with what looked like a lot of effort. "I don't really understand your job, but I know you love it and you're good at it."

"Was good at it," Marcus corrected, but he nodded his thanks all the same. "I'm proud of you too."

Davo gave him a clap on the shoulder, then turned down the front steps towards his ute, Banjo trotting beside him. Marcus headed for the bus stop, but he'd only walked a block or so when his phone buzzed in his pocket.

Alice, 8:14 PM: Big NYB news 👀 👀
Marcus, 8:14 PM: ???

Alice's reply was a link, and when Marcus hastily clicked it, his phone pulled up an article from the *New York Times*. The first thing he saw was a photo of a man—a dancer—wearing white tights beneath a white singlet, which had one shoulder strap and a knot tied at the hips. He recognized that costume instantly. It was Apollo, and the dancer was Jack Andersen. He scrolled down, his stomach suddenly fluttering with anxiety, and read.

Shock Departure at New York Ballet
The city's premiere dance company
loses its brightest star

New York Ballet announced Saturday the departure of prin-
cipal dancer Jack Andersen, a beloved second-generation star
of the company whose presence on the program has for years
guaranteed a sold-out crowd.

In a brief statement, the company's board of directors said
Mr. Andersen, who has danced with NYB for a decade and
is a graduate of the company's highly selective feeder school,
had resigned earlier that day and would not be appearing
with the company in the upcoming fall season. The board
did not give a reason for Mr. Andersen's departure, and
Andersen did not return requests for comment.

Andersen, the son of two former NYB principal dancers
and a fan favorite since he joined the company at eighteen,
rocketed to principal status . . .

"Holy shit," Marcus murmured. He scanned the rest of the article, but it was mostly a recitation of Jack's professional biography—
the many principal parts he'd danced, and quotes from the sparkling
reviews the *Times*'s dance critic had given him over the years—with
no real news beyond the headline. Jack Andersen, Prince of American ballet, abdicating out of nowhere, just days after threatening
Heather's best friend? Had Heather had anything to do with this?

Marcus read the article again, more closely this time. Looking for
any hint of Heather, any clue about what really happened behind
the bland statement the company released to the press. The ballet gossip machine would circulate the truth sooner or later—and
probably sooner—but he needed to know now.

His phone vibrated again; Alice had sent him another link.

Alice, 8:16 PM: Looks like someone got unfired.

When he clicked the link, his phone pulled up an Instagram post, and his heart cramped painfully at Heather's smiling face. She was sitting on a sagging burnt-orange couch, holding a dumpling between disposable chopsticks in one hand and a glass of what looked like sparkling wine in the other. She looked tired and washed out, but her smile was sheer sunshine.

"Celebrating a few things, including the return of my fave person and partner in crime," the caption on @carlymontgomery's photo said. "Can't wait to light up the stage with her very soon."

Marcus stared at Heather's frozen smile, wishing it was for him. But it wasn't. Heather had made her priorities clear: She'd come to Sydney to dance, and everything else had been a distraction. And everyone else. And now she was back in New York where she belonged. He stared for one more second before closing the app and shoving his phone back in his pocket. She looked happy, he thought as he headed for the bus stop. She was probably happy. He hoped she was happy.

Chapter 20

Carly, 12:29 PM: How is apartment #876169?
Heather, 12:37 PM: Can't I just buy you a new couch and live on that?
Carly, 12:37 PM: 😱 😱 😱

"So what was wrong with this place, exactly?" Carly asked later that night, as they sat cross-legged on her existing couch.

"Nothing's wrong with it," Heather explained. "It's just not a good fit."

Heather had been looking at apartments for the last month, and she had run out of optimism about six crappy one-beds ago. She'd seen another today, and she needed it to be the one. She couldn't stay on Carly's couch forever, and finding a place now would mean she would have some time to get settled in before the winter season and the *Nutcracker* marathon began.

She stifled a yawn. Heather wasn't sleeping well, and it wasn't just the lack of lumbar support in Carly's couch. The atmosphere at work was tense, to say the least. Mr. K was even frostier than usual, Jack's coterie of principal dancer friends was devastated he'd resigned, and the gossip mill was churning. There were whispers Mr. K was under review from the board, which was not at all pleased he'd allowed the company's star dancer to suddenly and inexplicably quit.

"He should be under review for being willing to overlook Jack's behavior," Carly had said, rolling her eyes over dinner last night, and Heather, her mouth full of noodles, had nodded in agreement. But they'd take what they could get.

"What do you mean it's not a good fit?" Carly asked now, sounding exasperated. "You said it's a good size, it's got good light, good closets, good bathroom, it's in a good location, and it's a good price. Sounds to me like it's . . . good."

Heather shrugged. "I'm just having trouble picturing myself living there." It had been true of all the other apartments, too, even the less crappy ones. Every time she tried to imagine arriving home there after a long day at the theater or waking up there in the morning to prepare for a new day of rehearsals, her brain produced nothing.

"You said that about the last four apartments," Carly objected. "Even the one with the dishwasher."

"I know, I know." Heather fiddled glumly with the hem of her dress.

"Please don't make me kick you out," Carly said. "I love you, and I want to hang out with you all the time, but I also want my couch back. Please. I love you. But just sign the lease."

"I . . . I don't want to," Heather said flatly.

"Well, what do you want?"

What do you want? Heather looked down at her bare feet and thought about the last time someone had asked her that. She sighed as the memory of that first morning with Marcus swept over her, making her insides ache with longing. She wanted the same thing she'd wanted when she'd woken up the final morning and found him gone. She wanted to talk to Marcus. She wanted not to have hurt him or lost him his job. She wanted him to admire and want her again, so much he'd do stupid, risky things to be with her.

She wanted Marcus. She wanted him, and no amount of good light or closet space could make her forget that.

"I want to fix things," she said, getting slowly to her feet. "With ANB."

Carly eyed her closely. "With ANB? Or with Marcus?"

"I don't know. Maybe both? All I know is I don't think he deserved to be fired over what we did. I don't think any of those dancers did." Maybe she could fix that for him, even if it meant telling the world about the mistakes she'd made. She wanted to try.

"Okay, then." Carly's tone was all business, but she was smiling. "Sounds like we need another plan."

Moving day dawned bright and cool, and Marcus awoke in a room bare and full of boxes. The only things unpacked were his bedding and the clothes he'd left out to wear today.

He yawned widely, screwing up his eyes against the light flooding through the curtainless windows, and stretched his body beneath the covers. It had been weeks since he'd done any exercise beyond walking and packing, and his body felt like it belonged to someone else entirely. Several times he'd considered going to a drop-in ballet class, just to take barre and feel like himself for a few minutes, but he couldn't seem to follow through with it. The pain of being booted from ANB was too fresh, too raw.

He certainly wasn't going to a ballet class today, he thought as he leant over and plucked his phone from the two stacked moving boxes that served as a makeshift nightstand. He unplugged it from the charger and settled back onto the pillows.

He had several texts from Alice, which were probably questions about the plan for today. She'd agreed to help him, Davo, and his mum as they swapped living spaces and even agreed to help unpack them both. *Thank God,* Marcus thought. It was a huge job, and they needed all the help they could get.

But he also had several notifications that he'd been tagged in people's Instagram posts, which struck him as strange. He barely used Instagram, especially since the video from the mountains had gone viral.

Alice, 7:43 AM: Have you seen the story in the Morning Sun?
Alice, 7:45 AM: ???
Alice, 7:57 AM: OMG wake up!

The last message contained a link to an article in the paper. Marcus tapped on it, wondering sleepily what had Alice in such a tizzy. As soon as the story loaded, Heather's face looked back at him, and his stomach gave a miserable jolt. Her features were sharper in this photo than they were in his dreams. Sharper, more beautiful, and harder to look at. He was about to close the story when the headline caught his eye, and his curiosity got the better of him.

'THE BALLET WORLD IS SLOWLY CHANGING':
BALLERINA HEATHER HAYS GETS REAL
By Ivy Page, Senior Arts Reporter

Sydney's ballet enthusiasts were dazzled last month by New York Ballet principal dancer Heather Hays's performances as a guest artist at Australian National Ballet. Hays, now widely acknowledged as one of the world's foremost interpreters of the titular role in 'Giselle,' performed to sold-out crowds, at the same time as a video of her canoodling with an ANB dancer went viral online. This week, in an exclusive, no-holds-barred one-on-one, Hays opened up to senior arts reporter Ivy Page about backstage ballet drama and what really went down during her stay in Sydney. Hays spoke to the Morning Sun *from New York City.*

Ivy Page: When we last spoke, in August, you were in your final week of rehearsals for 'Giselle,' a ballet that's played a significant role in your career. Why do you think this ballet remains so popular in this day and age?

Heather Hays: I think a lot of people can relate to Giselle. It's a timeless story, I think: A woman thinks she knows the person she loves, and they turn out to be something else entirely. Lots of us know what it's like to be lied to, and to lie to ourselves rather than face the heartbreaking truth. I also think a lot of people see Giselle as a story about the power of love and forgiveness. But I see it differently: I think it's a story about a man who hurts a woman and gets away with it. And a lot of people can relate to that, too.

IP: Can you personally relate to that part of the story?

HH: I can, and I think a lot of women in ballet can, too. But I think the ballet world is slowly changing, and men are learning there are consequences for mistreating women.

IP: Are you referring to your ex-fiancé, the former NYB principal, Jack Andersen?

HH: I don't want to go into specifics about my relationship with Jack, because I'm entitled to my privacy, and so are the other women he's been involved with. Besides, this problem is so much bigger than one person, or even one ballet company. I respect the ballet companies that are trying to solve it, even if some of their solutions are a bit misguided.

IP: What do you mean by 'misguided'?

HH: Well, for example, Australian National Ballet has a very strict no-dating policy between dancers. It's part of a reform effort by the new artistic director, who I really respect and admire, and who has been very kind to me. But I think banning dancers from dating each other to prevent sexual misconduct misses the point. It sends the message that men can't control themselves and can't choose to be respectful and decent, which of course they can. And if a dancer were to break that rule and then be abused by their partner, they'd have no choice but to stay silent about it, because they'd be fired if they came forward. So it's easy to see how a well-intentioned policy could backfire and actually make the problem worse.

IP: It sounds like you're speaking from experience here.

HH: You could say that. Anyone who follows a ballet account on Instagram knows by now I violated that policy. I was allowed to stay on, but it cost the man in question his job. That's a real loss for the company, because he is a beautiful dancer who treated me with nothing but kindness and respect. But I can't say I regret what we did. Some rules are just wrong, and it's okay to break them, especially if you also do the work to change them and make them more fair. And as I said, I don't think the policy is fair, especially if it's not applied consistently. Either it applies to everyone, or it shouldn't apply to anyone. Sexual harassment is serious, and it should be taken seriously all the time, not just when it's convenient or profitable.

Marcus's mouth had gone very dry. She'd told the paper what he'd told her in their final, ugly conversation, almost verbatim. He read her answer again, pausing to take in the words that made remorse and longing simmer in his stomach—*I can't say I regret what we did*—then kept reading.

> IP: *You're preparing for the winter season in New York now, but Sydney audiences are clearly big Heather Hays fans. Do you think you'll come back to Sydney one day?*
>
> HH: *I would understand if ANB isn't in a hurry to invite me back, but I hope I get a chance to visit again anyway. Sydney's a wonderful city, and, well, let's say I have some unfinished business there. And I hope I get to finish it one day.*

Marcus swallowed hard as he reread Heather's final words, his eyes hot and stinging. His heart did strange, fluttering petit battements against his ribs, and he was suddenly aware of his shallow, shaky breathing. Thumb trembling, he pulled up Instagram.

Justin had posted a photo of the article in print, the paper open on what looked like a café table. "Bravo to you Heather for speaking up about what real change looks like in ballet," his caption read. "I hope ANB offers @MRCampbell his job back, and all the others they let go."

Katarina, who danced Giselle on the nights Heather hadn't, had posted about the story, too: "Talk about brave. I was already a big Heather Hays fan but now I'm even more impressed by her. Too often ballet dancers are treated like children, but we're adults and we can make our own good choices (and face the consequences if we make bad ones). Miss you, @MRCampbell and @kimikoforever."

Several more of his former colleagues had posted similar captions or commented approvingly under Justin's and Kat's photos. Marcus scrolled through the comments in disbelief, admiration swelling in his chest. Shit, she was brave. And she'd made everyone else brave, too.

His phone vibrated and rang in his hand, and Marcus jumped.

"Hey," Marcus said, his hand shaking slightly.

"Did you read it?" Alice asked without preamble.

"Y-yeah, I read it. And I saw the posts. Pretty gutsy."

"Yeah, she is. And apparently, she's a trendsetter. A bunch of other dancers have started posting about shitty policies at their own companies. Weigh-ins, low pay, racism, all of it. A bunch of American dancers are calling out their companies for not having proper health insurance. Like, finally the ballet gossip mill is being used for good instead of evil. Kind of feels like the start of something."

She was breathless and sounded like she could talk about this for another hour. But she stopped, and he heard her take a deep breath. "Are you okay?"

"I'm fine," he said, sitting up. "I mean, no, I'm not fine, but I will be, you know?" *At some point,* he thought. Marcus cleared his throat. "Are you still right to come pick up the first load of stuff and take it over to Mum's?"

"I'm on my way now. I'll be there in a few minutes, and I'm bringing coffee, okay?"

"You're a legend, thanks," he said gratefully.

By the time Alice arrived, Marcus had stripped the bed, dressed, and somewhat distractedly washed his face. He'd just finished shoving his sheets and pillows into an almost-full box when she knocked.

"It's open," Marcus yelled as he taped the lid shut. He lifted the box onto the kitchen counter with a grunt, but when he turned around, it wasn't Alice standing in the doorway with a coffee in each hand.

It was Heather.

Marcus stared at her, his mouth open in surprise, and the adrenaline that had been buzzing in her body since her plane touched down a few hours ago suddenly surged through her limbs, making her legs feel shaky.

"Hi," Heather breathed. "I, um, I brought coffee."

He blinked slowly, as if he wasn't sure his eyes were working properly. "You're not Alice," he said, and she couldn't stop her nervous smile.

"No, I'm not. She's downstairs. She picked me up from the airport."

"What are you—I, uh, what's—why are you here?"

"Oh, Alice said you needed help with your move, so I thought I'd come on over," she said lightly, stepping into the apartment and looking around at the dozens of boxes. When he raised his eyebrows, uncomprehending, Heather bit her lip and tried again, her tone more somber this time. "I came to apologize. I know you read the interview, but I wanted to do it in person."

"You don't have to—"

"Yes, I do. I should have fought harder for you. For us. I should have told Peter he wasn't being fair, and that he couldn't keep me if he was going to fire you. I'm sorry."

Marcus stared at her, eyes glowing green in the morning sun, his face more beautiful than she'd allowed herself to remember. She stepped farther inside and set the coffees on the counter, buying herself a few seconds until she was ready to say what she'd rehearsed with Carly—and all the way from New York to Sydney.

"I was so scared of what people would think of me, and what they'd say about me. It's easy to get caught up in that in this job, you know? Everyone's always looking, always finding faults. But I don't care what they think anymore. I care what you think, and what Carly thinks, and what Alice thinks. And what I think. None of the other stuff means anything if I let down the people I love. The person I love."

Marcus had gone very still. But for his chest rising and falling, he hadn't moved since she started. She watched him, waiting for him to speak, hope fluttering in her stomach like a desperate bird in a cage.

"I was so angry."

"I know," Heather said softly, her heart sinking. "And I understand if you still are, but I had to try to make this right for you.

And I remembered what Peter said, about the board having his head if he let me go early, so I called the chair and offered ANB another year of my time . . . if Peter changed the policy and offered everyone their jobs back. And just to be sure they knew I wasn't bluffing, I did the interview. It worked." She couldn't keep a small, triumphant smile from her face. "The chair emailed me overnight to say Pas de Don't is over, and you're all getting your jobs back. And I'm here for the next year. Turns out Jack isn't the only star who can throw his weight around."

Marcus's eyebrows rose with every new piece of information, and the look of awed disbelief on his face erased any lingering doubt that she'd done the right thing. "I messed up, and I know you're angry with me, but I—"

"I'm not." He took a step towards her. "I wasn't. I was angry at Peter for being unfair. And at myself for getting caught. And at . . . the world, for the hand it dealt me this year. But I shouldn't have taken it out on you, because you're the best thing that's happened to me this year. Maybe ever."

Heather let out a shaky breath, relief threading slowly through her body. "I'm sorry I let you down. Action is the best apology, but still, I'm sorry."

"I know. The entire city of Sydney knows. That was a hell of an apology you got the *Sun* to print," he said, taking another step forward. They were a foot apart now, and Heather could see the gold flecks in his eyes and the faint freckles on his forehead. He shook his head in what looked like awe. "What you just did is so fucking brave, I almost can't believe you're scared of anything, Heather."

She swallowed hard, and stepped in close, reaching for his hand. He let her take it, and she held it loosely, tentatively, as if it would evaporate if she held it too tight.

"I am, though. I'm scared of lots of things. I'm scared of hurting you again. I'm scared of losing you again. I'm scared of not being the person you helped me become. Because I really like her. Stage face and all."

Marcus lifted his other hand and cupped her jaw, stroking his thumb gently over her chin.

"I like her, too. She's incredible. With a face shaped like a heart."

Heather let her eyes fall closed and leaned into his hand, sighing at the rightness of his touch. She hadn't allowed herself to imagine this. But even if she had, she wouldn't have been able to conjure the wave of longing and love that swelled in her chest as he laced his fingers with hers and held on tight. When she opened her eyes, he was looking at her, his gaze traveling over her face as if he were relearning every curve and line.

"I love you, Marcus Campbell. You're kind, and patient, and you make me want to do things that are hard and scary and right."

A smile broke over his face, radiant and boyish and just for her. "I love you, too, Heather Hays, so much. And what you've done is amazing. If you're not careful, you're going to end up starting a movement."

"Oh no, not that," she said, grinning, "anything but that."

Marcus laughed his big bark of a laugh, and Heather thought her heart might never recover from the sound. She smiled, almost dizzy with joy, and felt behind her for the counter, hopping up onto it as gracefully as she could. Then she looped her arms around his neck and pulled him close. Marcus kissed her—a deep, determined kiss full of promises—and Heather pulled him closer, wondering where she'd ever find the strength to let him go.

When they broke apart minutes later, Marcus dropped a kiss on her forehead, then stepped back.

"Hang on a second, do you even have a place to stay?"

She laughed. "I haven't worked that part out yet. But I don't think Peter is going to let me have company housing this time. He's not that forgiving."

"I've got a place," he said, kissing her temple, then her cheek. "I can finally show you Freshwater Beach."

"Well, if there's one thing I've found you need in Sydney, it's a good tour guide."

Epilogue

One year later

Heather padded down the hallway, careful to step over the two creakiest floorboards. The floor was cold, and she wished she'd stopped to put on her slippers before coming downstairs. Too late now, she thought, wincing as she entered the kitchen and the chilled tiles pressed against the soles of her feet.

The kitchen was already flooded with sunlight, and as she stood at the sink waiting for the kettle to fill, she looked out into the back garden, where the grass was glossy with dew and the trees were still in the breezeless morning air. Last night's dishes still clustered around the sink where she and Marcus had left them, too tired from cooking and serving and the solemn celebration to wash them right away.

The dinner had been Davo's idea, Marcus had told her—though later, when she'd pressed him, he'd revealed it had been Davo's therapist's idea. The first anniversary of their father's death had apparently passed without much comment from Davo, but this year, he'd suggested they mark the date by getting together and having a family meal, perhaps with some of Richard's favorite foods.

So Davo and Marcus had manned the barbecue together while Heather baked an apple crumble, supervised by Leanne. They'd sat around the table in Marcus and Heather's living room, which once had been Richard and Leanne's, and she listened while the three of them told stories about him. Some of them she'd heard before, some of them were new. Some of them had to be told twice because Marcus and Davo each remembered different versions of events.

Eventually, Marcus had turned in—since he'd enrolled in his physical therapy degree and started surfing every morning, he'd become dedicated to getting a full-night's sleep, and Heather often came home from the Opera House to find him passed out and unwakeable. When ANB had offered him his job back last year, Marcus had taken a full week to make up his mind, and eventually decided he was ready to retire from dancing.

"I just needed to do it on my own terms, you know?" he'd said, the night he announced his decision. "Not because of injury or because someone else made me." He'd decided he wanted to do what Shaz did—help injured dancers get back on their feet—and she'd been more than willing to help him apply to university programs for mature-age students.

The kettle started steaming, and Heather hurried to stop it before it whistled. She quickly heaped some coffee grounds into the French press, then seized two travel mugs from the cupboard. There were days when she missed the finger-numbing plastic cups of bodega iced coffee, milky and sweet and sweating in her hand, but she'd come to love their Sunday walks along the beach with their reusable mugs.

Once the coffee was ready, Heather padded back down the hallway and put the cups on the hall table before creeping back upstairs. Marcus was still asleep. On her nightstand, next to the clock reading 8:31 AM, sat Bear, sagging and a little discolored but propped lovingly against the wall, a reminder of what she'd been through to get here.

Heather crawled onto the bed and lay down behind Marcus, her head on his pillow, and breathed in the scent of him. He murmured contentedly and reached to pull her arm over him. His body radiated heat, and she resisted the urge to tuck her cold feet between his to warm them. For a while they lay there, Marcus somewhere between sleeping and waking, as Heather listened to his breath and the birds outside, wondering if she'd ever get used to the strange melody of Australian birdsong.

"I made coffee," she whispered eventually.

"Mmm," he hummed groggily. "I love you."

"But you have to get out of bed to get it," she added. This time, his *mmm* was more of a groan. He rolled over to face her and opened his eyes, his face puffy and adorable in his sleepiness. "Let's stay in bed."

"We can't, it's Sunday morning. And you've got studying to do."

"And I take that studying very seriously," Marcus said, a little more alert now. He put an arm around her waist and lowered his head to kiss her shoulder as his hand traced down her lower back to gently fondle her ass. "I can study your piriformis, and your psoas, and your *ischial tuberosity*," he said in a husky, would-be sexy whisper.

Heather laughed. "You can't show up to your first PT final and write about all the ways you've groped your girlfriend."

Marcus traced his hand down the back of her thigh, then up the inside, and she shivered.

"What about your adductor longus?" he asked, his fingers teasing the sensitive skin. He moved his hand even higher, and she whimpered. "Or your adductor magnus?"

"Please stop talking about ligaments," she gasped, arching her back slightly.

"You're right," he said, slipping his hand inside her underwear. "There are much better things I could be doing with my mouth."

When they finally got out of bed and reheated their coffee, they found Freshwater Beach almost empty, as it had been for most of their winter morning walks. Once the weather warmed up, the parking lot would be full by the time they arrived, the surfers unloading boards from their vans and families unpacking sun shelters and coolers from their SUVs. The kids' surf lifesaving league would start in October, and on Sundays half the beach would be overrun by children in matching swimsuits—or cozzies, as she'd learned to call them—racing each other along on the sand and paddling frantically in the water.

But today, they had the beach mostly to themselves, except for the seagulls scuttling across their path, dipping their orange feet in the foamy shallows as the waves rolled and crashed. For a few minutes Heather and Marcus walked in silence, letting the coffee and the brisk morning breeze wipe away the last of their morning lethargy.

"I have a proposition for you," Heather said, once her coffee was mostly gone.

Marcus raised his eyebrows inquiringly. "Proposition me."

"My contract will be up next month, and Peter says he wants to have 'a conversation about my future with the company.'"

"Right, and he's going to offer you another year," Marcus said, kicking a pile of dried seaweed out of their path. "He'd be an idiot not to."

It had been a relief to them both to realize, halfway through the sold-out spring season, with Heather's photo printed all over the banners that flew from the lampposts around the Opera House, that Peter would have no choice but to forgive her for publicly pressuring the company to eliminate Pas de Don't and offer all the fired dancers their jobs back.

They'd already asked Leanne if they could stay in the Sand Castle house for another year, and she hadn't objected. Since she'd found a physical therapist she loved around the corner and become a regular at Café Luxor, she wasn't in any hurry to leave Marcus's apartment.

"He will probably offer me another year," Heather agreed, feeling her pulse quicken. But it wasn't enough for her. She'd had the realization in company class a few weeks ago, as she stood at the barre with Alice and Justin and Katarina, listening to Alice tell some long, hilarious story about one of her brother's ill-fated baking attempts: She belonged here now. She belonged on this beach, and in Marcus's bed, and in a company full of dancers who liked and respected her, and who she liked and respected right back.

"But I don't want to stay another year," she said, and Marcus pulled up short, looking vaguely alarmed. She turned to face him. "I want to ask for a longer contract."

"Oh, yeah? How long were you thinking?"

Heather smiled. "I was thinking . . . forever. Until I have to retire, I mean."

Marcus looked down into her face, eyes alight. "Forever, huh?"

"Forever. I'd still want to go back to New York sometimes and dance with NYB, especially now that Mr. K's gone and Carly might finally get promoted. But I want to stay here. With ANB and with you. What do you think about that?"

Heather saw a grin flash across Marcus's face, but he quickly suppressed it and brought his hand to his chin in a gesture of faux thoughtfulness.

"Well, I don't know," he mused. "I'd have to think about it. Do I want the woman I love to stay here, where I get to live with her and watch her dance all the time, and do I want to occasionally let her drag me to New York City to watch world-class ballet? Or do I want . . . not that? I don't know, Heather, it's a tough call. . . ."

She grabbed his hand and pulled him close. "You're such a shit stirrer," she said, smiling up at him.

"I think you like it," he said, looping his arms around her waist and kissing her cheek.

"I do," she conceded.

"In fact," he added, and he brushed his lips gently against her mouth, "I think you love it."

"I do," Heather sighed.

Marcus pressed his forehead to hers, and they closed their eyes, sharing their warmth as the chill morning air played with their hair and the water nipped at their feet.

"And *actually*," he murmured, "I think you want to marry it one day."

"I do."

Acknowledgements

A book is like a ballet performance: it takes dozens of people to make it happen, but most readers or ticket holders only ever see the name on the stage or on the title page. This book exists because of two particular women who believed in me, the story I wanted to tell, and the way I wanted to tell it.

My agent JL Stermer didn't even blink when I told her that after a dense and deeply serious nonfiction book, I wanted my next project to be . . . something very different. If not for her encouragement, I never would have finished the first draft of *Pas de Don't*, and I will be grateful to her forever.

I am indebted to my editor Alicia Sparrow, who saw right away what I was trying to do with this book and found a hundred ways large and small to help me do it better than I could ever do alone. I pledged eternal allegiance to Alicia on the day she corrected my description in a sex scene, noting that when a person is aroused, their vagina expands, and thus, I should avoid using the word "tight." For this and so many other reasons, I would follow her into battle. She is a gifted gift of an editor.

So many people read this book before it reached its final form, making useful suggestions and preparing me for the terrifying day when it would be out in the world for anyone to read. Thank you to Alexa Martin, Andie J. Christopher, Emma Barry, Hannah Orenstein, and Laura Hankin for their early encouragement. Thank you to Amanda Litman, Elizabeth Cruikshank, Ellen O'Connell Whittet, Jess Morales Rocketto, Jessica Luther, Jordan Kisner, Nina Elkadi, Remy Cawley, and Sarah Chabolla for reading some very undercooked drafts, and to Veronica Grijalva, who helped me find love in a tropeless place.

Thank you to Jami Attenberg, whose #1000WordsOfSummer has helped this and so many other books take shape. Thank you to Cat Sebastian, Olivia Dade, and Stacy Finz, who gave me useful advice about marketing and publicity. Thank you to Allie Parker, who helped with the cover reveal. Thank you to Christine Hayes, Erica Duke Forsyth, Julie Anna Block, Molly Borowitz, and Whitney Williams Skowronski for their support and friendship. Thank you to Dada Masilo, who gave *Giselle* a different ending and a whole new meaning.

At Chicago Review Press, thank you to Sarah Gavagan, who created an absolute stunner of a cover, and to Jon Hahn, who worked with Sarah on the practical parts of the cover design. Thanks to Jon for his work on the internals, and to Devon Freeny for the same. Benjamin Krapohl is a thorough and enthusiastic wizard of a copyeditor who had to deal with ballet terminology and Aussie slang and made the manuscript sparkle like Sydney Harbo(u)r.

I'm grateful to Michelle Williams for her enthusiasm for this project and her spot-on insights about the third act. Thank you to Alayna Parsons-Valles, Candysse Miller, and Chelsea Balesh for their work to ensure that this book finds people who will love it, and to Karen Krumpak for proofing it to within an inch of its life.

All my gratitude to Andie J. Christopher, Laura Henkin, Alexa Martin, and Denise Williams, authors whose work I have read and loved, for agreeing to blurb my debut novel. I'm so honored.

Cécile Dehesdin was the first person to show me what an unapologetic love of romance novels looked like, and I hope this book has earned me a spot in her giant romance library. Vanessa Zoltan taught me how to think critically about romances and helped me understand their political and spiritual power. Brittney Mmutle helped me out of many a plot hole and was an enthusiastic and profane cheerleader from meet-cute to HEA.

My parents are not allowed to read this book, but they've left their marks on it anyway. My mother's essential work on senior housing affordability, especially for women, made its way into these pages. On a memorable trip to the bush, my father listened to me vent about a major problem with the first draft and helped me find the motivation to write a second one.

While I was deep in drafting mode, Zach Wahls cheered every time I hit my daily word goal and made sure there was a notepad by my bed so I wouldn't forget half-asleep dialogue ideas. When I was deep in revision mode, he walked the dog, cooked our meals, and delivered exceptional pep talks. He is the kind of partner every woman writer deserves and that too few get. Zach, I could spend my life trying to invent a meet-cute as good as ours, but I'd never succeed. I love you so.

ABOUT THE AUTHOR

CHLOE ANGYAL is the author of *Turning Pointe: How a New Generation of Dancers Is Saving Ballet from Itself*, which was the result of years of reporting on gender and power in American ballet. Her writing about ballet has appeared in *Jezebel* and the *Washington Post* and has been quoted in the *New York Times*. *Pas de Don't* is her first novel. She holds a BA from Princeton and a PhD in arts and media from the University of New South Wales. She lives in Iowa.